"Krista Davis h̲a̲s̲ ̲c̲r̲e̲a̲t̲e̲d̲ ̲a̲ unique setting, an engaging heroine in Holly Miller and her furry sidekick, Trixie, and a wonderfully quirky supporting cast of characters—two- and four-legged. I'm looking forward to my next visit to The Sugar Maple Inn."

—S̲ author of
̲ ̲ ̲ ̲ ̲ ̲ ̲ ̲ ̲ ̲ ̲ ̲ ̲ ̲ Mysteries

"Krista Davis ha̲ ̲ ̲ ̲ ̲ ̲ ̲ ̲ ̲ ̲ ̲ ̲ ̲ ̲ ̲ ̲ ̲ ̲ ̲ ̲ry series featuring witty, ̲ ̲ ̲ ̲ ̲ ̲ ̲ ̲ ̲ ̲ ̲ ̲ ̲ng canine sidekick, Trixie. ̲ ̲ ̲ ̲ ̲ ̲ ̲ ̲ ̲ ̲ ̲ ̲ ̲ f Wagtail Mountain will appeal to animal lovers and mystery lovers alike and the intriguing plot twists will keep you guessing to the very last page."

—Kate Carlisle, *New York Times* bestselling author of
the Bibliophile Mysteries

"Krista Davis has created a town that any pet would love—as much as their owners do. And they won't let a little thing like murder spoil their enjoyment."

—Sheila Connolly, *New York Times* bestselling author

Praise for the Agatha Award–nominated
Domestic Diva Mysteries

The Diva Digs up the Dirt

"Perfectly enjoyable." —*RT Book Reviews*

"A satisfying, complex story . . . [An] enjoyable mystery . . . Poignant, but also funny at times." —*Vibrant Nation*

continued . . .

"A fun mystery and a great way to spend a few hours by the pool or at the beach."   —*Booking Mama*

The Diva Haunts the House

"The quirky characters are well developed, the story line is as crisp as a fall apple, and the twists and turns are as tight as a corkscrew."   —AnnArbor.com

"Davis finely blends mystery and comedy, keeping *The Diva Haunts the House* entertaining and alluring."   —SeattlePI.com

The Diva Cooks a Goose

"For fans of Donna Andrews and Diane Mott Davidson . . . [A] real winner."   —*The Season*

"A great whodunit."   —*Once Upon a Romance*

"This is not your run-of-the-mill cozy; the characters are real to life, interesting, and keep you wondering what will happen next. Krista Davis writes one enjoyable read."   —*The Romance Readers Connection*

The Diva Paints the Town

"[Davis] handles this tricky tale with aplomb and fills it with a cast of eccentrics . . . And the three animals are endlessly amusing."   —*Richmond Times-Dispatch*

"Another delectable whodunit, complete with recipes. Indeed, [Davis's] novels are every bit as good as Diane Mott Davidson's Goldy Schulz mysteries."   —*Shine*

"[An] enjoyable mystery that includes decorating tips, a few pets, an unusual bequest, and recipes . . . Once again, Krista Davis brings us interesting, fun characters." —*Lesa's Book Critiques*

"Ms. Davis immerses the reader into the world of interior design." —*TwoLips Reviews*

The Diva Takes the Cake

"*The Diva Takes the Cake* does just that—takes the cake." —*The Romance Readers Connection*

"Mistaken identities, half truths, buried secrets, missing jewelry, wedding jitters, and family squabbles are whipped into a sweet froth in this second of the Domestic Diva Mysteries . . . A fun little bonbon of a book to enjoy on the beach or as a break from any wedding plans." —ReviewingTheEvidence.com

"Sure to thrill cozy fans." —*Fresh Fiction*

"[A] delightful romp, with engaging characters and a nicely crafted setting in which to place them . . . Just the right tone to match her diva's perfect centerpieces, tablescapes, and lighting effects." —*Shine*

The Diva Runs Out of Thyme

"[A] tricky whodunit laced with delectable food . . . [A] fine mystery that's stuffed with suspects—and a reminder that nobody's Thanksgiving is perfect." —*Richmond Times-Dispatch*

"A mouthwatering mix of murder, mirth, and mayhem, nicely spiced by new author Krista Davis." —Mary Jane Maffini, author of *The Busy Woman's Guide to Murder*

Murder, She Barked

Krista Davis

BERKLEY PRIME CRIME, NEW YORK

THE BERKLEY PUBLISHING GROUP
Published by the Penguin Group
Penguin Group (USA) LLC
375 Hudson Street, New York, New York 10014

USA • Canada • UK • Ireland • Australia • New Zealand • India • South Africa • China

penguin.com

A Penguin Random House Company

MURDER, SHE BARKED

A Berkley Prime Crime Book / published by arrangement with the author

Berkley Prime Crime Books are published by The Berkley Publishing Group.
BERKLEY® PRIME CRIME and the PRIME CRIME logo are trademarks of
Penguin Group (USA) LLC.

For information, address: The Berkley Publishing Group,
a division of Penguin Group (USA) LLC,
375 Hudson Street, New York, New York 10014.

ISBN: 978-0-425-26255-9

PUBLISHING HISTORY
Berkley Prime Crime mass-market edition / December 2013

PRINTED IN THE UNITED STATES OF AMERICA

10 9 8 7 6 5 4 3 2 1

Cover illustration by Mary Ann Lasher.
Cover design by Diane Kolsky.
Interior text design by Kelly Lipovich.

For my own beloved Oma, Elizabeth Jäger Pflüger,
who loved nothing more than a good book

Acknowledgments

Many thanks to my new cover artist, Mary Ann Lasher, who captured the Sugar Maple Inn so beautifully. As always, thanks to my fabulous editor, Sandra Harding, and terrific agent, Jessica Faust. I count myself lucky every day to be able to write mysteries. Sandy and Jessica bring joy and humor to the process, making it all the more wonderful. Fletcher Cochran was kind enough to brainstorm plot ideas with me, for which I am most grateful. I hope you're pleased with the result, Fletcher.

Thanks also to my friends in crime, Janet Bolin, Daryl Wood Gerber, Peg Cochran, Janet Koch, Kaye George, and Marilyn Levinson for always being only an email away. Also to Susan Erba, Amy Wheeler, and Betsy Strickland, for their friendship and for sticking with me through thick and thin. I would be remiss if I did not thank my mother, who remains my biggest fan. She's not as mischievous as Holly's Oma, but there's a little bit of mom in that character.

Trixie and Twinkletoes are based on my own dog and cat whose antics keep me in stitches and provide fodder for their animal characters in Wagtail.

Last, but most certainly not least, I have to thank my readers for their continuing encouragement and support. Without you, I wouldn't have the best job in the world!

If you pick up a starving dog and make him prosperous he will not bite you. This is the principal difference between a dog and man.

—Mark Twain

Holly's List

SUGAR MAPLE INN EMPLOYEES

Oma (Liesel Miller)—owner
Sven Berg—front-desk night shift
Casey Collins—front-desk night shift
Shelley Dixon—waitress
Zelda York—front-desk daytime
Chloe Kane—front-desk daytime
Tiny Goodwin—handyman, grounds

RELEVANT GUESTS

Mr. Luciano

WAGTAIL RESIDENTS

Jerry Pierce—mayor
Ellie Pierce—Jerry's mom, co-owns Dolce with Oma
Rose Richardson—Oma's best friend
Holmes Richardson—Rose's grandson, my childhood
   friend
Dave Quinlan—Wagtail police officer
Thomas Hertzog—chef-owner of the Blue Boar
Prissy Clodfelter—co-owns dog accessory store,
   part-time police dispatcher

Peaches Clodfelter Wiggins—Prissy's mom, co-owns dog accessory store

Mr. Wiggins—Peaches' husband, Oma's friend

Brewster Byrne—Hair of the Dog pub owner

Eric Dombrowski—pharmacist at HEAL! Drugs and Sundry

Mortie Foster—Ben's boss, Kim's dad, has fishing cabin (married to Jacqui)

Kim Foster—Mortie's daughter

Hazel Mae and Del Izard—live near Mortie's cabin

Philip Featherstone—1864 Inn bed-and-breakfast owner

Ben Hathaway—my boyfriend

One

It hadn't been the best day. And now rain fell so hard on the windshield that the wipers whisked back and forth in overtime. If the needle on my gas gauge dipped any closer to *E*, it would turn into one of my top-ten worst days, and that was saying a lot, considering that I'd recently left my job without any prospects. I should have filled up on gas an hour or two ago, but I'd been in such a hurry that I pressed on. I squinted through the windshield in search of a gas station. I'd forgotten how far apart they were out in the country.

Relief surged through me at the sight of a combination convenience store and gas station. I turned off the road and pulled next to a gas tank, thanking my lucky stars I hadn't been stuck in the rain miles from nowhere.

A spotlight cut through the downpour to reveal a bedraggled dog watching me. She stood up and offered a tentative wag of her tail.

The little dog huddled near the wall of the gas station, her eyes never wavering from their lock on me. The poor wet baby. Rain hammered sideways, plastering my hair to my head and soaking through my jacket while I filled my tank with gas. I could only imagine how drenched the dog must have been.

Laws probably prevented the owners from allowing their dog inside the gas station store, but they could at least provide a doghouse or some kind of shelter.

I dashed into the shop, biting back my desire to scold them for being so cruel to their dog. A lone hotdog turned in a roller grill on the counter, and I thought about buying it for the dog.

The woman behind the counter glanced my way for a second. "Been in there two months. Trust me, you don't want it."

Her hair billowed in an uncontrolled frizz as though she'd been as wet as I was. In her mid-forties, she had a good ten years on me. She returned to the magazine in her lap.

Self-consciously pushing my own hair back, I twisted it into a makeshift knot that I knew wouldn't hold. There wasn't much of a selection for dinner. I picked up a bag of nacho cheese Doritos. I'd given them up to lose weight but it was a well-known rule that all diets were off during road trips. Besides, I was about to explode from stress. If they'd had decent doughnuts, I would have bought one—or two or three.

"Coffee's fresh," she said. "I just put it on."

I thanked her and poured half a cup full. "Any point in buying milk?"

"The stuff on that shelf is okay."

I found little cartons, the kind kids take to school in their lunchboxes, dumped the entire contents of a box into the coffee and added sugar. It hardly resembled the lattes I liked so much, but it was the best I could do. I took my items to the cash register.

She looked up from her magazine and stared at me briefly before hopping off her stool. While she rang up my purchases, she glanced out the window into the night. "Where you headed?"

"Wagtail."

"Be careful. The fog on the mountain will be so thick you won't be able to see your own hands."

I didn't bother running through the rain to the car. The way things were going, I would surely spill my coffee or fall and land face-first in a puddle. Besides, at this point, I didn't think I could be any wetter.

I opened the driver-side door, and the dirty little dog vaulted inside. She sat on the leather passenger seat, eyeing me.

Oh no. Not in Ben's precious car. My boyfriend couldn't tolerate a wisp of lint on a seat. He would have a fit when I brought his car back wet and muddy.

I leaned toward the dog. "I'm sorry, honey. I know you're soaked through, but you can't go with me." I reached toward her, and she jumped into the backseat. *Oh good. Let's just spread the mud and dirt around a little bit more.* Would a good car detailer be able to get mud stains out of the carpet?

Rain pelted me when I opened the rear door. No wonder she wanted to stay in the dry car. "I'm so sorry." I reached for her, and she scrambled to the front, her slick fur allowing her to slip right through my fingers.

I trudged back to the convenience store. "Excuse me, but your dog is in my car. Maybe you could call her?"

The frazzle-haired woman narrowed her eyes. "So you're the one she's been waiting for."

"What?"

"She picked you, darlin'. Some idiot dumped her out here two weeks ago. Three people have tried to catch her but nothin' doin'. She's smart as a whip. The animal control guy even set up a trap out there for her. She's half starved, but she never went for the meat in the trap. She's been waiting for you."

Homeless, starving, and wet. I could relate—in a way. A mere week ago, I had walked away from the security of my fund-raising position over a breach of ethics. Theirs, not mine. It had been stupid to leave a job without another one lined up, but who expected that kind of development in life? I had done the right thing, and I knew it. I still had a home, but without a paycheck coming in, things would start getting tight pretty fast.

The dog's situation was certainly more dire than mine. In a couple of hours, I would be in my grandmother's inn, wearing a fluffy white bathrobe and sneaking something delicious from the kitchen.

I wiped water off my cheek. My own precious yellow lab had succumbed to old age about the time I met Ben. Every day I drove by the animal shelter on my way to work and thought about adopting a dog. When I'd mentioned it to Ben, he'd nixed the idea, insisting we didn't have time for a dog in our lives. Maybe we didn't . . .

I sighed. Except for my grandmother's dog, they weren't allowed in the inn. "I . . . I can't take her with me." My words faded at the end of the sentence. *I wanted to take her.* I *wanted* to rescue her from her miserable life.

"If you don't, she'll get hit by a car or shot."

"Shot? Who would shoot a harmless little dog?"

"Sooner or later she's gonna go for somebody's chickens. Darlin', just take her with you. It's karma, you know. That little girl knows something we don't. Lots of cars come by here every day. There's a reason she picked you."

I suspected the unceasing rain was probably the driving force behind her choice, but I just nodded my head and hurried back to the car. If nothing else, I would find a home for her.

When I opened the car door and lights illuminated the interior, I looked closely at the muddy yellowish dog with black ears, a black spot on her rump, an orange muzzle, and a Dorito clenched between her teeth. A Jack Russell terrier, I guessed. Her lively, intelligent eyes and body shape certainly suggested that.

The bag of Doritos had been ripped open, and orangey chips lay on the seats, carpet, and middle console. If that wasn't bad enough, she'd managed to chew the lid off my coffee and spill the entire contents on the carpet.

Her eyes reminded me of a baby seal's. Rimmed in black, with sweet white lashes, they studied me, waiting for my reaction. I burst out laughing. This day couldn't get any worse. It was either laugh or cry, and I always preferred laughter.

I bought more Doritos, another cup of makeshift café au lait, and a roll of paper towels.

The dog promptly retreated to the backseat when I opened the passenger door and cleaned the mess she had made. Like the suede shoes I wore, the carpet would never recuperate. "Ben is not going to be happy about this," I told her.

Water squished out of my wool skirt when I settled into the driver's seat for the last two-hour leg of the trip. Trying to ignore the discomfort of sitting on waterlogged wool, I put the car into gear and headed out on the nearly deserted road.

Ben would never loan me his car again. He hadn't had much choice when my phone rang during the tour of his boss's vineyard. During the drive there, he'd asked me not to mention my employment issues. *Issues*, he'd called them! I got the message, though. The vineyard invitation was about him and his future with Mortie Foster's law firm. He needed to put his best foot forward. I wasn't offended. I understood the importance to him, and he deserved my support. But then he'd said something that blew my hopes to smithereens.

"They will all find out soon enough that you're persona non grata in the fund-raising community."

It wasn't as though I hadn't realized it somewhere deep in my subconscious. But when he said it out loud like that, I had visions of whispers about Holly Miller spreading like the threads of a spider web. No matter that I had been in the right—no one wanted a troublemaker. Finding a new job might not be as easy as I had hoped.

I'd put on a happy face, though, for Ben's sake. Not the easiest thing to do considering the way his boss's daughter, Kim, had latched onto him. Easily ten or twelve years younger than Ben and me, probably still in her twenties, her bottle blonde hair curled like she'd just romped in bed. Her upper lip curled, too, suggesting a doctor had plumped it up.

Jacqui Foster, his boss's wife, had clutched Ben's arm and snuggled up to him. "I always thought our Kim would marry Ben," she'd said. "They made such a cute couple when they were dating."

A fine time to learn he had dated Kim. Didn't Ben know he was supposed to tell a person when she was going into enemy territory?

Jacqui had lifted my left hand to examine my ring. For a moment, I'd thought she might pull out a jeweler's loupe to study it more precisely. "What, no engagement ring yet?"

Translation: Kim, there's still hope!

No one could confuse the little band of five square-cut emeralds I wore on my middle finger with an engagement ring. Could she have been more obvious?

We had just finished dinner when my phone rang. Ben had shot me a look that could have fried an egg. "I thought we agreed no phones tonight," he'd hissed. Under his disapproving glare, I excused myself to take the phone call.

"Holly, honey? Is that you?"

I hadn't recognized the voice.

"It's Rose, sweetheart. I think you ought to come to Wagtail as soon as you can."

Rose had been my grandmother's best friend for as long as I had been alive, maybe longer. "What's wrong? Is it Oma?"

"Now don't be alarmed. But you best come right away."

Two

I hung up, feeling lower than I'd thought humanly possible. My grandmother, whom I called Oma, German for *grandma*, was the Miller matriarch. Our family had scattered to the four corners of the earth. Geographically, I lived the closest. Even so, Wagtail Mountain was a good six-hour drive southwest of Washington, D.C.

Jacqui pointed out that the vineyard lay two hours south of Washington and if I went home to pack, I would lose four hours just in driving time.

There'd been no mistaking Ben's discomfort, though whether it stemmed from Jacqui's offer for him to stay overnight or the thought of leaving the vineyard at that moment wasn't quite clear to me. The coveted invitation to the vineyard for dinner with other partners was a feather in his cap and a major step in his quest to make senior partner at his law firm. But in my mind, Oma came first. Ben would make partner whether I left or not.

Jacqui pressured Ben into staying the night, promising Kim would drive him back to D.C. the next day. That way, I could take his car to Wagtail without wasting time by going home first.

"Don't tell Mortie, though," she'd said. "We have a horrid

little fishing cabin on Wagtail Mountain. It's his favorite place in the world. I loathe it. I can't imagine why your grandmother would want to live in Wagtail. There's just nothing to do. There's not even a decent shopping mall! And, quite honestly, the only ducks I want to see are the ones on a platter in a Chinese restaurant."

Mortie, on the other hand, had viewed me with new interest. "Why didn't you say you were from Wagtail? Miller?" He peered at me. "Is Liesel your grandmother? You look a lot like her."

When I said yes, he wrapped his arm around my shoulders as though I was suddenly part of their crowd.

"I had no idea you were a Miller from Wagtail! You must see to Liesel right away. Ben! We should take a few days and drive up together."

Although I resented the cozy situation with Kim, I would never forgive myself if Oma was ill and needed me and I didn't go. I had left immediately, but not without noting Jacqui's whole-hearted encouragement to depart. "We'll take care of Ben," she'd promised.

I just bet they would.

Given the situation, I didn't have much choice. Besides, Ben and I had been dating for more than a year. One of the nice things about nerdy guys was that they could be trusted. Not that Ben was without charm. The dimples on either side of his mouth fairly melted me whenever he smiled. He wore his hair short on the sides and just a touch longer on top. It reminded me of the color of coffee beans, a rich dark brown that didn't quite make it to black. The frames of his glasses were the same color on top but faded to nothing at the bottom.

I grinned at the thought of his discomfort at having to stay overnight at the vineyard. Ben was a city guy more comfortable in a library than among trees. How many times had I tried to talk him into a long weekend at Wagtail? The dimples always appeared. He would gaze at me briefly, shake his head, and go back to whatever history book he was reading. Nerdy guys weren't usually the most exciting fellows in the room, but they were as smart and trustworthy as Boy Scouts. If Ben and I didn't trust each other, we had nothing.

Panic welled up inside me as my thoughts shifted to Oma.

Why hadn't I been to Wagtail in five years? I could have gone without Ben. Had I really been that busy? Too busy for the grandmother who meant the world to me? Ben and I had seen her on vacation in Florida with my dad and his wife only a few months ago. Her eyes had sparkled when she told me she had a surprise for me. I'd pressed her for a hint but she had reveled in her little secret. Dad cringed with embarrassment when Oma said something about us meeting her handsome young Scandinavian stud.

It never occurred to me that she might be ill. It would be just like her to be sick, or even dying, and not tell anyone.

The dog startled me by jumping forward into the passenger seat. She eyed me warily.

"We're on our way to the Sugar Maple Inn." I explained. "Here's the deal. They don't allow dogs, undoubtedly because you make messes."

She listened, but didn't seem particularly ashamed of herself for what she'd done to Ben's car.

"Oma had a German Shepherd when I was a kid and spent my summers at the inn. She used to go everywhere with me. The summer my parents divorced, I told her all my secrets and troubles. Staying with Oma during school vacations was always the highlight of my year."

I peered at the dog. "Are you housebroken?"

I had a feeling I would find out soon. "I can try to talk Oma into adopting you, but don't get your hopes up. I don't even know if Oma is well enough to care for a dog."

She curled into a little ball for the final hour of the trip, but every time I looked over at her, she jumped into a sitting position as though prepared to flee to the backseat. "I won't toss you out into the cold night, sweetie. I promise."

Thanks to the drizzle and heavy fog, the last leg of the drive, winding up Wagtail Mountain, was treacherous at best. I flicked my lights between the high beam and the low beam, but nothing cut through the white soup more than a few yards. My eyelids were growing heavy in spite of the coffee. I rolled down the window in hopes that the cool night air might refresh me, gripped the steering wheel tighter, and leaned forward in the vain notion that it might help me see better.

The dog sat up and barked at a pitch that sliced through my daze like a knife through butter. She barked wildly, pausing only to paw at my arm.

"Why are you barking? Hush! Someone needs to learn about using an indoor voice."

She persisted, and I had to hold her back with my right arm, not at all what I wanted to do on the winding mountain road.

I glanced over at her for a split second, wondering how to make her stop barking, and when I looked back at the road, a man stood in the middle of it.

Three

· *·* *·*

My scream nearly drowned out the dog's high-pitched barks.

I hit the brakes. The car swerved.

I feared we would careen off the mountain. Jerking the steering wheel, I prayed there wasn't any oncoming traffic. We screeched to a halt on the wrong side of the road.

I threw open the door and jumped out, leaving the engine running, the door open, and the lights on so I could see. My heart hammered in my chest as I dashed to the back of the car, fearing the worst. I didn't think I had hit him. At least I hadn't felt a bump or a jolt.

"Are you okay? Hello? Hello?"

But no one was there. Raindrops pattered on leaves, and the engine still purred, but an ominous stillness made me painfully aware of being alone. A shiver shuttled through me, and it wasn't because of the cold wet night. Something wasn't right about this. I backed to the side of the car and bent over to look, heaven forbid, *underneath* it.

In the dark of night, I couldn't see well, but I didn't make out any odd shapes.

Renewed barking alarmed me, and I jerked upright. The dog had run out of my range of sight.

I swallowed hard. I'd read about pranks like this. People pretended to be in distress, then attacked the driver or stole the car.

"Here, doggie! Come on girl!"

She continued barking. Very briefly, I weighed my options. I could find her and put her back in the car, or I could take off. Who was I kidding? Leaving her there wasn't an option.

As relieved as I was that I hadn't hit the man, I hated that I didn't know where he went. He could jump out of the pea soup any second. I whistled for the dog, longing to leap into the safety of the car and lock the doors, but I couldn't bear to strand her there.

Thank goodness she ran back to me. She stood in the glow of the headlights, barking incessantly.

"Come on, sweetie."

Did she know any commands? "Come!"

I tried not to convey my nervousness to her. With a furtive glance around, I edged toward her, ready to bend and snatch her up.

But the little devil backed up, ever so slowly, until we were in the shroud of dark mist. I could barely make her out. At the edge of the road, she turned and barked like crazy. Even though I couldn't see the vista, I knew she was yelping out over the valley. There, on the murky roadside, she allowed me to pick her up. She didn't even squirm.

The man had to be around somewhere. Had he gone over the side? Shivers engulfed me again as I considered how vulnerable we were.

An explosion shattered through the air not too far beneath us. I screamed and staggered backward. Flames roared upward, cutting through the drizzle. Waves of heat pummeled us. I ducked and jerked away, holding the little dog tighter. She pressed against me, her body rigid with tension.

Flames licked skyward. The blaze lit the night. It was bigger than anything I'd ever seen.

Clutching the dog to me, I ran for the car, slid in, checked the backseat to be sure no one was hiding, and locked the doors. The dog hopped into the passenger seat and watched me. My fingers trembled as I dialed 911.

"Hello?" The woman's voice was sleepy.

Had I misdialed? "I'm sorry. I'm trying to call the police."

"Yeah, you got 'em. What's up?"

What kind of police dispatcher spoke like that? "Something just exploded off the side of Wagtail Mountain. It's burning."

"Uh-huh." She sounded bored. "Where are you exactly?"

I hadn't paid any attention to mile markers. In the mist it wasn't as though I could make out landmarks, either. "I'm just guessing. Maybe two or three miles outside of town?"

"Near Forrest Road?"

Didn't ring any bells. "I can't see much in the fog." I drew on childhood memories. "Maybe a little down mountain from Buzzard's Roost."

A long silence followed. "Who is this?"

For pity's sake. "Don't you have caller ID?"

"There's no need to be snippy. You're calling from a cell phone, dufus. All it says is Virginia."

"Sorry. It's Holly Miller, Liesel's granddaughter."

Another silence.

"Hello? Are you still there?" I asked.

"I'll let him know." She hung up.

The haze near the edge of the road glowed a faint yellow. In early September, the trees hadn't turned color yet. I hoped that meant they would be strong against a spreading fire. The rain would surely help, too.

The dog raised her paw and stroked the air in my direction. I reached over and ran my hand down her back. In addition to being wet, her fur felt coarse and unpleasant to the touch.

I decided it would be prudent to move the car to the correct lane. On the steep mountain, there probably wasn't a good spot to pull over. In fact, if it hadn't been for the mysterious man I'd seen for a second, I would have thought it safer to wait outside of the car in case someone came along too fast and plowed into it.

I eased the car up mountain, far enough away from the blaze that it wouldn't be in danger. The emergency lights flashing, I parked and waited with the engine running, wishing I didn't feel so helpless. There wasn't anything I could do to control the flames or prevent them from spreading into a wildfire.

A scant ten minutes later, the glow of headlights broke

through the night on the opposite side of the road. I breathed easier when I saw the police emblem on the door.

It stopped next to me and the window rolled down. A dark-haired man with a long oval face peered at me. "Did you call about an explosion?"

He'd barely gotten the words out of his mouth when a second blast shook us so hard I felt the tremor in the car.

He leaped out of his vehicle and ran to the edge of the road. I shut the dog in Ben's car in case she got ideas about running down to the fire. I ran along the edge of the road to the police officer.

He pulled out a radio and spoke into it. When he hung up, he said, "The firefighters are on their way. Did you see a car go over the edge?"

"No. I saw a man in the road. I hit the brakes because he appeared out of nowhere, and I thought I was going to hit him, but he disappeared."

He frowned at me. "Show me where this happened."

I gestured to the road. "Right about there. Shouldn't there be skid marks?"

"Not with the roads this wet. What did he look like?" He flicked a strong beam up and down the road.

"I only saw him for a second. He was wearing a jacket or hoodie—something with a hood. Navy blue or black, maybe."

"Mustache?"

"I don't think so, but I couldn't swear."

"Could it have been a woman?"

That was an odd question. "I guess. It was a split second, and then he was gone."

"You sure you didn't hit him?"

It was fairly obvious that he wasn't lying in the road. Did he think I'd pitched him over the edge? "I honestly didn't feel a bump or any impact." I waved at the pavement. "He's not here. He must have been able to leave."

"It's pretty late. You been drinking?"

"No!" My voice sounded high and testy. "Don't you believe me? I'll take a sobriety test. I'm tired but I haven't had a drink."

"You're lucky I know you, Holly Miller." His stern expression softened a little bit. "Do you remember me? Dave Quinlan?"

"Dave! You were headed for the navy the last I heard."

He stood a little straighter. "Seems a long time ago now."

A Jeep pulled up behind Dave's police car. The glimmer of headlights grew as a fire truck arrived and several more cars lined up on the road.

"Excuse me," Dave said. "That'll be the volunteer firefighters."

He spoke with the driver in the lead car. In less than a minute, six firefighters peered over the edge of the mountain at the blaze. Two of them scrambled down the mountainside to assess the situation.

Dave's radio crackled. He didn't seem to have trouble understanding it. All I could make out was "car."

"You staying at your grandmother's?" asked Dave.

I nodded.

"Go on then. I know where to find you."

I headed for Ben's car.

"Hey, Holly."

I turned around.

"I'm sorry about your grandmother."

"What?" But he'd already disappeared into the fog. My heart heavy with worry, I slid into the car and locked the doors.

It was nearing three in the morning when I passed the line of firefighters' cars and drove toward Wagtail. In an odd way, I felt guilty for leaving. But there wasn't a thing I could do to help. I could only hope no one was in the car that was burning. Besides, I had to see Oma. A tiny part of me wanted to drive slower, to make the trip last longer. As long as I didn't know anything for certain, she was still okay.

The rain had finally stopped, but the road no longer seemed familiar. In the past, the road had led directly to the inn, but now a huge parking lot with a guardhouse blocked my way. "What in the world?" I muttered.

This wasn't right. Could I have taken a wrong turn in the mist?

A new sign for the Sugar Maple Inn pointed to the right. I had to turn left or right, so I went with right and hoped the sign was correct. The road later turned left and led me along the edge of town, with houses to one side and forest on the other. It ended abruptly at the inn, but not where I had expected.

Golden lights burned through the fog as we drove up. I pulled into a small, new porte cochere, with stone pillars supporting the roof. A warm glow shone through large windows, a welcome haven in the night.

I rolled the windows down a crack. "Stay here while I figure out how to smuggle you inside, where it's warm."

Disoriented, as though I'd driven into some kind of time portal, I ventured inside unfamiliar doors, which slid open on their own. Oma had built an addition that moved the registration desk from the lobby to the side of the inn. The new addition must be the surprise Oma had mentioned. A large antler chandelier hung in the middle of an intimate and charming reception area. Overhead, a European-style wrought iron railing on a balcony smacked of my grandmother's taste. I spied a small store, the windows dark.

A young man, not much more than a boy, snoozed fitfully on a loveseat. His legs stuck up in the air over the armrest. One of his arms had fallen off the sofa. A shock of straight chestnut hair hid his forehead, touching the tops of wire-rimmed glasses that had gone askew.

"Hello?" I spoke gently.

He jerked into a sitting position, sending his glasses flying to the floor. He raised his hands, palms outward. "Don't hurt me!"

"I promise not to." What a skittish fellow. I picked up his glasses and handed them to him. "That must have been some dream."

"Oh, gosh. I'm sorry." He jumped to his feet. "Welcome to the Sugar Maple Inn." He slid the glasses on, pushing them onto the bridge of his nose with his middle finger.

"Thank you. I'm here to see Liesel Miller."

His eyebrows lifted. "*You're* Holly?"

"Yes."

He appraised me, his mouth twisting. "We've . . . been . . . expecting you." He extended his hand. "Casey. Your grandmother talks about you all the time." He gripped my hand and pumped it earnestly.

"Is she"—I paused, afraid of the answer—"okay?"

Four

❧ ❧ ❧ ❧ ❧

"I think so," said Casey. "She's a strong woman, but it shook all of us. Everyone is nervous."

My knees nearly buckled with relief. "I'll just peek in on her." I headed toward the store.

"Um, that's the wrong way." Handing me a key, he pointed upward at the elegant rounded balcony. "The last door. I'll get your luggage."

He would see the dog! I held up my hand like I was stopping traffic. "No need. I don't have any."

He raised an eyebrow, and muttered, "Okay, that's weird."

Paying him no heed, I trotted up a short flight of stairs, turned right and walked up more stairs to the balcony, eager to see my grandmother. I knocked on her door and unlocked it. "Oma?" I called.

Her apartment wasn't like I remembered it, but that made sense since it was clearly part of a new addition. Undoubtedly part of the surprise she had mentioned.

I felt more at home when I recognized an inlaid table and her collection of Hummel figurines in a lighted curio. The drapes hung closed at the far end of the living room. I tiptoed toward what I hoped might be the bedroom. A golden retriever greeted me at the door, wagging her tail. I scratched behind her ears. "Oma?"

"Holly! You came."

I looked for a light switch.

"No light, please. It's too hard on my old eyes."

She sounded terrible. I rushed to the side of her bed and kissed her forehead.

She clasped me with cold hands. "Ach! You're damp. And in this chilly weather, too. You must take a hot shower or you will catch cold."

It was just like her to be worried about me when she was the one with a problem. I held her hands, gently rubbing them between mine to warm them. "How do you feel?"

"Much better now that you are here."

"Are you in pain?"

"Not so much. I took an aspirin."

"Your hands are getting warmer. Do you need another blanket? Maybe I should turn up the heat."

"No, no. Don't trouble yourself. I prefer to sleep in a cold room—you know that."

"But not when you're ill."

"The mountain air is good for my lungs."

Did she have a respiratory problem? "What's wrong with you, Oma?"

"We will talk about that in the morning. You need to get out of those clothes. Have Casey warm some goulash. It was always your favorite."

I didn't want to press her about her illness if she was tired. "Okay, you get some rest. After I park the car, I'll come back up and sleep on your sofa. Just call out if you need anything."

"No, no! I have a special room waiting for you. I'll see you in the morning." She patted my hand. "Don't worry. Now that you are here, I will be fine."

I resisted. After all, what was the point of coming if I couldn't help her? "You're so thoughtful. But I would feel better if I slept nearby."

A dog yipped outside. I hoped it wasn't the one in Ben's car. Oma didn't seem to notice.

"No! I won't sleep if I know you're suffering on the sofa. You go to the room we prepared."

She might be sick, but she was clearly still as stubborn as ever. I took that as a good sign.

"Okay. Good night." I kissed her soft cheek. "Call my room if you need me."

I was already in her living room when she called, "Holly?"

"Yes?"

"Be sure you lock my door, liebling." ·

When I tiptoed out, the golden retriever stayed with Oma. As I locked the door behind me, a calico kitten wound around my legs.

Large green eyes assessed me from a mostly white face. The markings on top of her head reminded me of sunglasses with one lens butterscotch and the other dark chocolate. I bent to stroke her.

"Hello, Kitten." The sweet girl rubbed her little head under my hand, wanting attention. Oma had always kept a cat or two in the inn.

I returned to the registration area.

Casey waved a hand at me. "Ms. Miller! I have your key."

How could I sneak the dog past this guy? He didn't seem to miss much. Would I have to linger outside until he fell asleep again? I took a deep breath and walked to the registration desk. What kind of excuse could I make? He must leave the desk sometime. "I'll sign in first. I suppose it's too late to grab a bite to eat in town?"

"Mrs. Miller's granddaughter doesn't need to sign in, and she asked me to bring a meal up to your room on the third floor."

I heard the doors behind me slide open, but I didn't think anything of it until I saw the horror on Casey's face.

When I turned around, a stocky man staggered in. A rivulet of blood marred his broad forehead. He hunched slightly to his right, rubbing the knuckles on his right hand.

"Mr. Luciano!" Casey scurried to him and helped him to the loveseat.

Mr. Luciano pressed his fingers against his head and saw the blood when he pulled them away. "Could I trouble you for a tissue?" His deep rumbling voice and accent came straight from *The Godfather*.

I grabbed a box of tissues from the desk and handed them to him. "Casey, bring Mr. Luciano a wet washcloth. Do you need a doctor, Mr. Luciano?"

He eyed me briefly. "No. I'll be okay. You must be Liesel's granddaughter. I see her confidence in you is not misplaced."

His comment surprised me. Did Oma talk about me with everyone? "Thank you."

"Should I wake Mrs. Miller?" asked Casey.

"I don't think that's necessary. Where is Oma's office? She always had rubbing alcohol and a first-aid kit."

"She keeps them behind the desk." Casey disappeared to look for them. "They're here somewhere," he said. "I see them all the time. Where did they go?"

I excused myself and took a deep breath as I walked toward the desk. One glance and I had everything in my hands. Casey was clearly distraught.

"The washcloth?" I reminded him.

Casey hurried to a restroom, nearly tripping over his own feet in the process.

Pouring a bit of rubbing alcohol on a piece of gauze, I said, "Hold your breath. This will sting."

Mr. Luciano smiled. "I can take it."

I dabbed the wound on his head. He wore his hair slicked straight back. The laceration wasn't large. More of a significant gouge on the left side of his head, where his hairline had receded.

"How about your hand?" I asked.

He held it out to me. A ginormous nasty bruise had begun to take shape. His knuckles appeared bruised and swollen.

I wiped them with the alcohol anyway, just in case the skin was broken.

"You have your grandmother's delicate touch."

Oh? Just how well did Mr. Luciano know Oma? "What happened?"

Casey returned with a hot washcloth and handed it to Mr. Luciano.

"I was restless and couldn't sleep, so I went for a walk in

town. The front door was locked when I returned. I came around to this entrance—and some guy jumped me! In Wagtail! I never expected that."

"Whoooooa!" Casey turned as pale as a ghost.

"We'd better call Dave." If I dialed 911, I would get the sassy woman again. "Casey, would you make the call?"

He nodded. "First I'm locking the doors."

But just as he reached under the desk for the switch, the doors whooshed open.

Five

Yelping all the way, a yellowish-white tornado of fur bounded through the registration area and halfway up the steps.

The calico kitten sat at the midway landing of the stairs and regarded the dog regally, twitching her tail to demonstrate mild annoyance. She didn't budge, though. The kitten stared down the impish dog, who scrambled to a stop and wisely retreated a few steps.

How did she get out of the car? What to do now? I took my room key from Casey, who acted as though the confrontation between the dog and the cat was perfectly normal. He picked up the phone and dialed.

After a couple of irritated barks, the dog trotted over and stood by me.

"You didn't dock her tail," observed Mr. Luciano.

I studied him. Could he be the person I'd seen on the road? Was that where he'd gotten his injuries? Medium height with a large head and expansive forehead, bushy eyebrows, and a stocky build. Probably about fifty. Could he have injured his hand pushing the car over the cliff?

"Officer Dave is on his way," announced Casey.

Officer Dave? That was so cute. Only in a small town! The sweet dog eyes fixated on me.

"How did you get in here?" I hissed at the dog.

I bent over to pick her up but she backed away. If I kept coming toward her, she might run, and then she'd be on the loose in the inn. She didn't have a collar, and I didn't have a leash. What a nightmare. Would she follow me if I simply walked toward the door? I wasn't eager to go out in the fog, especially after hearing Mr. Luciano's tale. But I was a tad skeptical about his story. Why would anyone be hanging around at the inn waiting to clobber a guest? Unless that person had been waiting just for Mr. Luciano . . .

"She's a Jack Russell, isn't she?" asked Mr. Luciano. "I thought it was traditional to dock their tails." He tilted his head at me like a dog trying to understand. "You know, cut them so they're short."

Casey stretched up and peered over the desk, trying to see her. The cat was out of the bag, so to speak.

The dog wagged her tail tentatively, unsure of herself. The tail wasn't long, about ten inches or so. It curved upward. A black spot covered part of her rump and extended one-third of the way down her tail. The other half was yellowed white, like her body.

I smiled at Mr. Luciano and said the obvious. "Her tail is intact." Clutching my room key, I walked toward the exit door, my heart pounding. Would she follow me?

"What's on her nose?" asked Mr. Luciano.

I couldn't be rude. This was my grandmother's inn, and if there was one thing she had pounded into my head it was that I represented the Sugar Maple Inn, and I could never *ever* be rude to a guest. But I thought I'd gone about as far as I could with evasive responses. "Doritos."

He chuckled. "You fed her Doritos?"

"She helped herself."

"What's her name?" he asked.

"My apologies, Holly," said Casey. "I had no idea that you brought your dog. She's not wearing a collar. Did she lose it?"

I trudged back toward them. Might as well be honest about

it. I couldn't sneak her in now anyway. I told them the whole sad story. "I'm very sorry. I'll try to coax her outside."

Casey ducked down for a second. When he reappeared, he rounded the front desk and walked toward me slowly, a collar and leash in his hand. "This is a Sugar Maple Inn collar. There's no leash ring on it, because it's only for locating dogs, but you could sling this leash under it. Do you think she'll come to you if you offer a treat?" He handed me a couple of teeny bone-shaped cookies and a sunflower-yellow collar bearing the words *Sugar Maple Inn*. A plastic box hung on it.

"A Sugar Maple Inn collar?" Since when did inns have collars?

I knelt on the floor and held out the dog cookie. "Treat!"

She studied me.

I broke the cookie in half and pretended to eat part of it. She promptly bolted toward me, snatched the cookie, and retreated before I could grab her. I handed the collar back to Casey. "Maybe you can latch it on her if I catch her?"

I held out the second piece of the cookie, but this time I was ready. When she darted at me, I tackled her, flinging my arms around her.

Casey snapped the collar on and looped the leash through it in spite of her wriggling attempts to be free. He handed me the leash when I stood up. "Well, at least she won't get away from you again. All Sugar Maple Inn collars have GPS in them. Um, nothing personal, but she reeks. The groomers in town are closed at this hour. I can recommend You Dirty Dog. They'll be open in the morning."

I'd been away too long. Since when did Wagtail have enough business to support a dog groomer? When I was growing up, a dog bath in the mountains involved a swim in the lake or a splash through a garden hose in the backyard. "So she can stay?"

"Your grandmother said you hadn't been here in a while. Didn't she tell you that the Sugar Maple Inn is now a premier pet resort destination?"

I couldn't have felt more stupid. "What does that mean? There are boarding facilities for guests' pets?"

"No, nothing like that." As though it was a slogan, he proudly stated, "We never board, we pamper. People come here to vacation with their pets. Dogs are our specialty, but we have a building just for cat lovers, too. The Cat's Pajamas, a wing where no dogs are allowed."

No wonder Mr. Luciano had been so inquisitive about the dog. He was probably a dog lover. I hadn't given any thought to her tail. "Thanks, Casey. I'd better park the car."

The little dog seemed unsure of herself when I walked toward the entrance, pulling gently on the leash. She bolted and stopped. She tested the leash in various directions, clearly confused.

"Looks like she's never been on a leash before," said Mr. Luciano.

I was beginning to suspect the same thing. Walking slowly, we headed outside. Just in case Mr. Luciano had told the truth about someone attacking him, I listened carefully. All I heard was crickets. The rain had finally stopped.

I opened the passenger side door and found the glove compartment hung open.

"Did you do that?"

She readily jumped into the car. I slammed the door shut and hurried to the driver's side. The thick fog prevented me from seeing more than a few feet ahead, but I found a parking space and began to have inviting visions of a cozy bed.

Cold mountain air pierced my damp clothes when I stepped out. The mist swirled around us, thick as a London fog.

The dog strained at the leash. I followed along behind her. Much as she had when we saw the man on the mountain, she barked with crazy excitement. Goose bumps raised on my arms.

Straining to see through the mist, I gazed around but saw nothing. I tugged at her and headed for the inn. She quit barking and stopped to do her business, while I waited impatiently.

Mr. Luciano had planted notions in my head, I told myself. After all, this was Wagtail, not some big city where people were attacked at night. Nevertheless, the second she finished, I ran for the inn. Happily, the dog bounded along ahead of me—blindly into the misty night. High heels were never meant for running. Stumbling, I tried to pick up speed when the lights of the inn became visible. The dog and I raced through the door.

"Now you can lock the doors, Casey."

I paused to catch my breath.

Casey scrambled to hit a button under the desk. Mr. Luciano rested on the couch clutching a bottle of water in his hand.

"I'll wait with you for Officer Dave."

Casey gazed at me with worried puppy dog eyes. I could see the relief in his expression. He shoved his hand up his forehead, lifting the shock of hair that grazed his eyes.

The inn wasn't very big, but I wondered if he might be too young for so much responsibility. Oma had me pull the night auditor shift when I was a teen, but no one had ever been clobbered right outside the inn. Maybe I should cut him some slack.

I smiled encouragingly. "How long have you been working here, Casey?"

"Since June. I work Mondays and Tuesdays, but this is the first time I've worked a weekend. Mrs. Miller asked me to come in, since, well, you know," he choked up, "since Sven died."

Six

❀ ❀ ❀ ❀ ❀

"Sven?" I had no idea who he meant. "Sven was Oma's regular night auditor and he died?"

Casey nodded, holding back tears. "He was such a great guy. He taught me to ski." Casey rubbed his eyes with the heels of his hands. "He was hit by a car several hours ago."

"That's awful. I'm so sorry." I couldn't help wondering if there was a connection with the burning car. After all, Wagtail wasn't very big. Two car accidents in one day?

But the name, Sven, also made me wonder about something else. Could it be that Oma hadn't been joking about the *young Scandinavian stud* she mentioned when she was on vacation with my parents and me?

"How long did Sven work here?"

"I don't know." Casey sniffled. "A few years? I skied with him for about seven years."

Headlights outside heralded Officer Dave's arrival. Casey unlocked the door, and Dave strode in. He wasn't the biggest guy, but his presence brought a reassuring air in spite of the overwhelming odor of smoke that clung to his blue uniform.

Comfortable that Mr. Luciano was in good hands, I dared

to leave them alone. If nothing else, I could wash my face and freshen up a little.

I glanced at the key Casey had given me. The word *Aerie* was etched on it. "Aerie?"

Casey smiled. "It means a nest on a mountaintop. Third floor."

Not counting the basement, the inn was only two stories high. *Not the attic. Ugh.* I'd spent hours up there as a child, playing among the dusty furniture and creepy pieces of out-of-season decor. They must have carved out some rooms when they renovated.

The dog sniffed happily along the corridor as we ventured into a more familiar part of the inn. I located the elevator and pressed the up button. When the doors opened, my new friend backed away as far as the leash would allow. The collar threatened to pull off over her head.

I had no choice but to pick her up. She wriggled and fought like I was taking her to her death. I held her close and hit the third floor button with my elbow.

The door shut quietly, causing the dog to fight me even harder. Oy. Wasn't my day of misery over yet?

The elevator opened to a quaint landing. A simple bench upholstered in a provincial-style fabric of purple thistles on a yellow background stood against the wall. The calico kitten sat in the center of it, alert, as though she had been waiting for us. To my left, an *Employees Only* sign hung on a door. On the right, a staircase offered an alternative route down, and a single door bore a plate that read *Aerie*.

Daring to place the dog on the floor, I unlocked the door and swung it open. She stretched her neck and sniffed the air but didn't budge. She pinned her ears back and watched me with frightened eyes.

The kitten sauntered past us into the room.

Soft lights beckoned me inside. I lifted the scared dog, walked inside, and closed the door behind me with my shoulder.

Yellow and burnt orange chrysanthemums spiked with cattails filled a vase on a half round table. A mirror behind them doubled the impressiveness of the arrangement. I caught a glimpse of my face and set the dog down in a hurry.

Another look in the mirror and my hands flew up over my mouth in shock. The rain had smeared my mascara and eyeliner into frightening black circles around my eyes. It looked like horror movie makeup. A zombie would have been proud. My hair was plastered to my head, except for little wisps that kinked in odd directions. No wonder Casey had reacted so peculiarly toward me. I looked over at the dog. "Thanks for telling me."

She wagged her tail and ran to the right, into a comfortable sitting room. A stone fireplace dominated one wall. If I hadn't known I was on the third floor of an inn, I would have thought I was in a cozy mountain cabin. A plush red sofa and deep chairs clad in red and white toile with red ottomans begged me to put up my feet and read a mystery by the fire. Apparently, they also appealed to the dog, because she already sat in one, looking quite at home.

Long red, yellow, and green plaid curtains hung open, revealing two sets of French doors topped by a semicircular window. I opened a door and breathed in the frigid night air. A spacious deck offered a table and chairs as well as two chaise longues.

Soft lights shimmered beneath the fog in a wing to my left, probably the new Cat's Pajamas wing Casey had mentioned. Although I couldn't see it, I was certain the view from the deck would be of Dogwood Lake and the mountains beyond. The dog trotted out, raised her nose, and scrutinized the air.

"Anything interesting?"

She wagged her tail again. Did that mean she liked it when I spoke with her? She followed me inside.

A small but complete kitchen adjoined the sitting room, divided by a counter. To my complete surprise, a cozy dining room opened off the kitchen. Or was it a library? Red roses swelled over the edges of a bowl in the middle of a round table. Sunlight would surely spill in through the windows on both sides of the little room. The far wall featured bookshelves, and a plump country French buffet sat under a window to the left.

As I wandered through the suite, I realized that it spanned the depth of the inn. Oma had decorated it in what she liked to call European-American country. A master bedroom, also with a fireplace, featured identical French doors with a semicircular window over top of them. They opened to a balcony but fog blocked the view.

After checking out a second bedroom with its own private bath, I returned to the kitchen feeling guilty for using what was no doubt the swankiest digs in the entire inn. I'd have been happy to collapse on a bed in one of the standard rooms.

The dog's ears perked, and she barked excitedly.

She might not be much protection, but she could wake anyone with those high-pitched yaps. "Shh. People are sleeping!"

Someone knocked on the door, prompting her to bark more.

I looked out the peephole. Casey waited in the hallway.

When I opened the door, he scooted past me with a room service cart. I closed the door and trailed after him.

He made his way into the kitchen and unloaded several covered dishes on the counter. He handed me a T-shirt. "My sisters like large T-shirts to sleep in, so I brought you one from the store."

I held it up. Artistic logos said *Sugar Maple Inn* on one side and *Wagtail* on the other. "That's so thoughtful of you. Thanks!"

He spotted the kitten curled up on an ottoman. "Your grandmother calls her Twinkletoes. She's the nosiest cat I ever saw. I hope you don't mind her in here. She took up residence in this suite on her own—like she chose it." He shook his head. "I think that's very peculiar, but your grandmother accepted it as though it was perfectly normal."

"I don't mind. Is there a litter box?"

"It's in the bathroom. You'll see. It looks like a little cabinet with a cutout door in it. This salmon is for her, and there's more cat food in the fridge if she gets hungry."

"Are you sure I'm supposed to be in this suite? It's huge!"

He nodded and smiled at me. "No luggage? Really?"

"I left in a hurry when Rose called me. I didn't take the time to go home and pack anything because I was so worried about Oma." I gasped. I'd been so enamored of the suite that I forgot to wash off the dreadful smeared makeup. Using my fingertips, I wiped underneath my eyes.

Relief swept over his face. "Ah, that makes sense. I should have realized. Everything happened very fast. We're all a little spooked. Things like that don't happen in Wagtail. I can't believe someone jumped Mr. Luciano. Perhaps you'd like the fireplace on while you eat." He picked up a remote control, pressed a button, and flames flickered.

I debated asking him about Oma's health, but as worried as I was, I knew it would be wrong to discuss anything so personal with one of her employees. Her staff might not know what ailed her, and asking him could fuel rumors.

No one at the inn had ever served me in a room before. I wondered if I should tip him. "Just a minute, please." I retrieved my purse from the console in the foyer.

Casey balked. "No, no! I'm just doing what your grandmother asked of me. I should get back to the desk, especially since the doors are locked. Enjoy your dinner."

"Casey, would you like for me to come down and," I chose my words carefully so he wouldn't think I meant to babysit him, "work with you tonight?"

Casey swallowed but raised his chin. "No. I'll lock the doors when Officer Dave leaves. It'll be dawn soon anyway. My mom says everything looks better in sunshine."

"Call me if you want company."

"Thank you, Miss Miller. I appreciate that."

I hung out the *Do Not Disturb* sign and headed for the shower. I'd never been so glad to remove clothes. I didn't have anything else to wear, though, so I dutifully washed out my blouse and unmentionables and hung them to air dry. My wool suit might be rescued by dry cleaning, but I didn't dare wash it. I hoped it would just air out and dry.

Wrapped in a towel, I picked up the dog and carried her into the bathroom. She fought me again, her eyes desperate, but I spoke to her in a soothing voice, trying to assure her that everything would be fine. I wished that were true. "We'll know more about Oma in the morning," I said, even though I knew that wasn't why *she* was scared.

She trembled when I set her in the bathtub. I loosened my grip for one second to turn on the water, and she made a mad scramble to exit. I nabbed her and managed to rub a tiny dab of shampoo into her fur. She stood as still as stone, undoubtedly certain that this was the end of her life.

Unfortunately, that gave me a false sense of security, and

I must have loosened my grip a tiny bit. Nicely lathered and full of suds, she sprang from the bathtub and shot out the door. I chased her around the suite. She proved to have an uncanny ability to duck and run, while I lumbered behind her like an elephant. She finally made a poor choice and found herself cornered in the guest bedroom. I carried her back to the bathroom, shut the door this time, and she freaked out. I had never seen an animal quiver so violently.

"Look, I have to rinse that shampoo out of your fur. It won't hurt—I promise." I made quick work of rinsing her fur. She shook off the excess water, and once again, I was thoroughly wet. How could one little dog hold so much water in her fur?

I opened the door, and she flew past me. I noticed, though, that she didn't go far. She returned almost immediately, settling in the hallway where she could watch me.

A hot shower did wonders to relax me. I pulled on the T-shirt and wrapped myself in the inn's signature fluffy white bathrobe. Oma had had my name embroidered on it in a script with rich forest green thread.

I ventured into the kitchen, my new companion by my side every step of the way. "Are you hungry?"

A tiny bone shape was embossed on the lid covering a small dish. "This must be for you." It looked like beef and rice with flecks of something green. Spinach? I set it on the floor along with a bowl of water.

Twinkletoes stretched leisurely and strolled to the kitchen. She vaulted onto the counter with ease and promptly sniffed the dishes. The kitten weighed next to nothing when I lifted her. I placed her on the floor with the bowl of salmon.

When the Jack Russell finished her meal, she danced in place, focused on Twinkletoes's dinner. She hovered impatiently, sneaking closer and backing up again, intent on the salmon, her little forehead wrinkled.

"She'll smack you if you go for it," I cautioned the dog.

For no apparent reason, Twinkletoes pawed at the hardwood floor. She scraped it with her paw in a furious rhythm.

I watched for a moment before picking her up. "Are you okay?"

She purred.

I took that as a yes. When I set her on the floor again, she sauntered into the sitting room, lounged by the fire, and washed her face.

In the meantime, the dog polished off the salmon, washing the bowl clean of every last morsel.

A snack of goulash, fruit salad, and a basket of assorted breads and cheeses awaited me on the counter. The refrigerator had been stocked with a selection of waters, beverages, and even a bottle of wine.

I opened a cranberry spritzer and carried it and my bowl of goulash to one of the cozy chairs by the fire. The dog followed me, sat on the ottoman, and watched my every move, no doubt hoping I might abandon the bowl for a split section so she could wolf down the contents.

When I finished, I turned off the fire and found an inn toothbrush in the bathroom.

In minutes, I tumbled into bed, ecstatic to see that Oma still used the luxurious down comforters and featherbeds that I remembered. They fluffed up around me like a comforting cocoon.

When I finally rested my head on the down pillow, the dog crept up onto my chest. I ran my hand along the rough fur on her back, wondering if I would be able to sleep with a dog on top of me.

Seven

❀   ❀   ❀   ❀

Apparently not. As exhausted as I was, I couldn't sleep. My thoughts kept returning to Oma. I should have pressed her to tell me what was wrong with her. Not knowing might be worse than the truth because I imagined all sorts of terrible things.

And I couldn't stop thinking about the man I'd seen on the road and the fire. I'd managed to wash the smell out of my hair, but the image of the flames came back to me every time I closed my eyes.

When the first rays of sunshine announced a new day, I stretched and gently moved my doggy friend to the side, even though I'd barely slept. I wrapped the robe around me, and ventured to the balcony.

A wrought iron railing arced around my little vantage point above Wagtail. The area below was just waking up. The mist from the rain had cleared, leaving a blissfully crisp fall morning. I inhaled the clean mountain air.

They say you can never go home again. Except for the first few years of my life, Wagtail hadn't really been my home, yet I found myself smiling and curiously happy to be back. In the distance, graceful mountain ridges seemed to undulate in green waves. Farther away, the waves turned to blue with wisps of white clouds rising into the sky.

Maybe my contentment sprang from temporarily leaving my job troubles behind.

No, it was more than that. I didn't hear any traffic. No trash trucks chugged through the streets. No horns blared. Birds twittered in the trees, and even though the town stretched out in front of me, it was blissfully quiet and serene.

The stores were still closed, but a few joggers and brisk walkers exercised, every single one of them accompanied by a dog, or two, or three.

Originally a resort built around crystal clear natural springs, Wagtail's waters had drawn guests for their healing powers. Stores and hotels had catered to wealthy visitors. Even today, the center of town remained a pedestrian zone, free of cars and exhaust.

Adorable stores and restaurants lined the sides of the walking area. Wide sidewalks provided ample space for pedestrians, benches for the weary, and outdoor tables at restaurants. In the center, a green grassy section stretched away from me. Trees lined the sides, and a charming gazebo graced the center.

Beyond the pedestrian zone, the roofs of quaint houses made for a picturesque scene, with chimneys rising above the rooflines.

Eager to see Oma, I ironed my silk blouse in a hurry. It would never be the same. I doubted that even a talented dry cleaner could remove the stains, and there I was, ironing them so they'd be set in the fabric. Unfortunately, I now knew why my suit was dry-clean only. The wool had shrunk, but the lining hadn't. The jacket wasn't fully dry, so I canned that immediately. The lining now draped below the skirt, and caused the material to tug and pucker. I had no makeup except for the lipstick in my purse. My suede shoes had stiffened but I jammed my feet into them because they were all I had. After I checked on Oma, I would have to take a stroll through town and buy a few things to tide me over.

My hair kinked from sleeping on it wet. I brushed it into a ponytail, one of the benefits of long hair on bad hair days. How good could a person look in a stained blouse, no makeup, and a dry-clean-only skirt that had air-dried and shrunk? I looped the leash on the dog's collar and hurried out to the elevator.

The kitten pranced to the elevator with us and readily boarded it as though she'd been riding elevators her whole life.

The dog hesitated. She didn't want to enter the elevator again. Silly girl. I picked her up, and she squirmed when the elevator doors shut. At least she hadn't soiled in the inn. I set her down. Terrified, she froze.

When the doors opened, she shot out.

The kitten danced past her, headed toward the registration desk.

We followed Twinkletoes and proceeded outdoors, where I found a very thoughtfully placed doggie restroom. The dog still seemed a bit confused by the constraint of the leash, but she did what she needed to, and we headed back inside to more familiar territory in the main part of the inn. The dog readily trotted along with me. She paused now and then for a sniff, but who could blame her for that?

Oma had knocked down some walls, opening the Dogwood Room, the main gathering room, into the old lobby area. The huge stone fireplace remained, along with the rustic pine mantel that I remembered. I paused in front of the grand staircase. Opposite it, the original entrance of the inn fronted on Wagtail's pedestrian zone. The Dogwood Room lay to my left and a corridor led away to the new reception area.

I hoped Oma hadn't updated the wonderful old kitchen that she maintained for her personal use. I had spent countless hours in its warmth and hated to imagine it gone. But before I reached it, my grandmother called to me from a table overlooking the lake in the dining area on the other side of the grand staircase. She had removed the narrow old windows in favor of a breathtaking window wall where guests could enjoy the panorama of the lake and the mountains. A few brave guests sat outside at tables on the stone terrace.

The relief I felt at seeing Oma reminded me how much I loved her. I didn't like the looks of her elevated leg, though.

I rushed over to her and planted a kiss on her cheek.

Officer Dave sat at the table with her. Heavy bags sagged under his eyes. He probably hadn't gotten any sleep at all. He clutched a mug of coffee in his hands.

A crisp white square topper covered a rose tablecloth. Dave's breakfast—a waffle covered with blackberries—made my mouth water. The delicious scent of sage wafted from sausages on a side dish. A basket of croissants and hearty breakfast breads looked so incredible that I wanted to select one, slather butter on it, and sink my teeth into it.

A vase of sunflowers graced each of the dozen round tables. I reveled in my surroundings. Oma seemed fine, the sun glittered on the lake below, and it felt great to be back at the inn.

Oma grasped my hand and didn't let go until she noticed the dog. "Ja, who is this? Casey mentioned that you brought a dog."

Oma hated that she still had a German accent after fifty years in America, but it sounded charming to most people, including me.

"She doesn't have a name yet. I found her yesterday when I drove up here."

Dave murmured, "Morning," before digging into his breakfast.

The dog placed her front paws against the seat of Oma's chair and wagged her tail with delight. Oma reached down to pet her. There was a little spark between them. Maybe Oma would keep the dog after all.

"When I was a child, this kind of dog often performed in the circus." Oma reached for a little glass canister on the table and pulled out a tiny cookie in the shape of a bone. She held it over the dog's head and asked, "Do you know any tricks?"

The dog's ears perked up, and she pranced on her hind legs briefly, her nose uplifted for the treat. Oma chuckled and fed her the bone.

"What happened to your leg?" If it hadn't been for the elevated foot, Oma would have looked perfectly normal. She wore her silvery hair in a short, sassy cut. For a woman just over seventy, her skin showed remarkably few wrinkles. She'd never been fond of makeup and didn't really need it. She wore a white turtleneck, brown trousers, and a hand-knitted red vest embroidered with tiny white hearts. I assumed she had knitted the vest herself.

"You didn't tell her?" asked Oma of Dave.

"There was a fire, Liesel."

"Yesterday evening," said Oma, "someone murdered Sven, one of my employees."

Eight

❀ ❀ ❀ ❀

"Murdered? Are you sure?" In my astonishment, I spoke much louder than I'd have liked. A couple of guests who were eating breakfast looked in our direction.

"He was a ski instructor at Snowball Mountain in the winter but worked as night auditor for me in the summer months." Oma heaved a sad sigh and dabbed a tissue at her eyes.

An attractive waitress arrived at our table, unintentionally interrupting the conversation. A few streaks of blond in her wavy, light brown tresses suggested she might have been blond as a child. She had pulled her hair back into a loose bun but had skipped makeup altogether. Not that she needed any, with those startling blue eyes. I guessed she was in her thirties, close to my age. There was a calmness about her. I couldn't tell whether she was simply a serene person or exhausted. She wore a white Sugar Maple Inn golf shirt with a khaki skirt. "You must be Holly. Your grandmother never stops stalking about you."

"I'm so sorry! That must be boring." I sent a little glare of disapproval to Oma. "A pot of hot tea, please." I paused, finding it hard to shift my thoughts to food. Should I stay on my diet or dive into a waffle? The mere thought of blackberry syrup almost had me drooling. How could I pass it up? I sighed. "Two soft-boiled eggs, please. No sausage or bacon." I would have to resist the breads and pastries.

"That's all?" asked Oma. "You should eat something you wouldn't make for yourself. A little indulgence while you're here. Wouldn't you rather have the blackberry French toast? And perhaps a small Liver It Up breakfast for the little one?"

I'd have been thoroughly upset if my mother changed my order, especially when I was younger. But grandmothers fell into an entirely different category. I smiled and accepted it. Oma merely wanted to spoil me a bit. Besides, she was right. I could return to eating my two bare eggs when I was home again. "And sausages, please?" No point in doing it halfway.

After the waitress left, I said in a hushed voice, "Casey said something about a car accident."

"A hit-and-run," said Oma. "Right in front of me. I was crossing the street just a few feet behind Sven when a big car flew at us and hit him. Right before my eyes. We didn't hear a thing. Suddenly it was upon us."

"The fog was terribly thick," I said. "Was it raining? Maybe the driver didn't see him."

"Liesel, she needs to know the truth." Dave wiped his mouth with a napkin. "The car had no lights on. Wagtail has become a golf cart community. There's limited access for cars. That car had no business being there whatsoever. And Liesel is lucky she got off with a twisted ankle. The car hit them both, but only sideswiped Liesel. She could just as easily have suffered Sven's fate."

My fingers felt cold against my cheeks. "Did you see the driver, Oma?"

"I wasn't looking, though I doubt I would have seen much in the dark. It all happened very fast." She gestured with her hands as she spoke. "One minute, all I heard was the peaceful pitter-patter of rain. The next thing I knew—" she snapped her fingers "—a car came at us, and suddenly I was laying on the road, and Sven was dead. It was horrible. He was such a lovely young man with everything to live for." She reached out and curled her fingers around my hand for a moment.

The waitress delivered steaming tea in a tall rounded porcelain mug with a touch of gold on the delicate handle. I stirred in sugar and a splash of milk. "Driving with the lights off is certainly suspicious, especially last night because I could barely see anything with my lights on. But why do you think it was murder? How would anyone know that Sven would happen along? Did he run there regularly or something?"

"The phone call." said Oma. "Someone called the inn about Ellie needing help because Dolce was running loose. Sven was hanging out at the inn," she smiled wistfully, "because he has—had—a crush on Chloe, who works for me. He went over to help Ellie find Dolce."

"Dolce is a dog?" I asked.

"An amazingly beautiful show dog. Ellie and I own him together. Our Scandanavian stud!" A breath escaped Oma's lips. "Thank goodness he was found."

"Then it was someone who knew Sven well." I sipped my tea.

Dave frowned at me. "Why would you say that?"

"The caller knew Sven would be at the inn and that news of a loose dog would bring him running to the rescue."

A stubby man wearing a preppy argyle V-neck vest over a light blue, button-down shirt marched in with a basset hound, who stuck to his side, doing his level best to match the man's stride. The basset hound extended his nose toward my Jack Russell. When the man sat down with us, the basset edged toward my dog and polite sniffing ensued.

I put the man somewhere in his fifties, although his grim expression aged him. He exuded restless energy that made me wary.

Ignoring my presence, he lifted his hand, one finger raised. "Shelley, I'll have coffee, one of these waffles and an order of bacon." He leaned toward Dave, but turned his head to me and demanded, "Who are *you*?"

Oma projected an oasis of calm in his presence. "Holly, Jerry Pierce is the mayor of Wagtail. Jerry, this is my granddaughter, Holly."

"Uh-huh." Jerry's mouth puckered in annoyance.

Oma found a treat in her pocket and split it in half. She fed one part to my dog, and the other to Jerry's. "And this handsome basset hound is Chief."

The waitress delivered our breakfasts. My gorgeous round waffle was dusted with powdered sugar and topped with a mound of fresh blackberries and a dollop of whipped cream. She left a carafe of maple syrup and another of blackberry syrup next to my plate. It would have been a wonderful decadent breakfast, had Sven's death not cast a pall over us.

The waitress placed a little dish in a short stand on the floor for my dog. I peered over. Chopped liver mixed with rice rested on a bed of green beans. The dog snarfed her breakfast like it was the best food she had ever eaten. It probably was.

"Holly, wouldn't you and your little dog rather eat outside on the terrace so I can have a word with Dave and Liesel?" asked Jerry.

This time Oma bristled. Someone who didn't know her might have missed it, but I knew what it meant when her jaw tightened like that. "It's fine, Jerry. There is nothing you can't say in front of Holly."

He didn't bother hiding his irritation. "Very well." Lowering his voice, he aimed his ire at Dave. "What the devil is going on? People are saying that Sven was murdered. Do you know what that will do to tourist business in this town? It will shut us down, that's what. People will be afraid to come to Wagtail!"

My eyes met Oma's. He seemed a bombastic type. Surely he was exaggerating.

"It's bad enough that I have to field phone calls every single morning about the noise from Hair of the Dog when it closes at midnight. I swear I have to dodge Birdie when I see her coming. If it's not the noise from the bar, then it's that ridiculous tree house Tiny built. If she mentions it again, I will scream. Do you know she dragged me out there to measure the distance from her lot in the air? *In the air!* I've given Tiny notice about it but he won't move it. I half think he's refusing just to irritate Birdie. Not that I'd blame him."

I cringed. I would have to pay my grouchy Aunt Birdie a visit while I was in town or I would never hear the end of it.

"That woman complains endlessly. And last night, some idiot

reported trees down on power lines clear up near Hazel Mae and Del's place. I went up there but couldn't find nary a downed tree and the electricity was working just fine," Jerry continued. "I will not have Wagtail turn into a lawless mire like Snowball Mountain, with a burglary every weekend." He paused for a moment. "Any word on the trouble over there yet? I heard they set up a sting that bombed. Think it's an inside job?"

Dave looked up at the ceiling briefly. I got the impression Jerry wasn't supposed to leak that information.

Dave kept his cool though. "No leads that I know of."

Jerry pulled a white athletic sock out of his pocket and, after a swift glance around, poured out the contents. Two gold coins rested in his hand. "I fear their problems have come to Wagtail. I found these this morning."

Dave grimaced. "And now they have your fingerprints all over them." He produced a plastic zip top bag and held it open so they could fall into it. "I'll check the reports to see if they match anything that has gone missing."

"What's going on at Snowball?" I asked.

"Big trouble," said Oma. "Someone is stealing jewelry and small gold valuables. Entering hotel rooms and houses when no one is home. They will have a very poor ski season if they don't find the culprits and put a stop to it."

"Gold coins? Who brings gold coins to go skiing?"

"They're popular investments," said Dave. "Some of the people with vacation homes around here think it's safer to stash them here than back in the city. It all started shortly after Sven won a gold coin in a poker game with some well-heeled guys over on Snowball Mountain last winter. Sven was so excited. It was the talk of Wagtail and Snowball."

"I'm not exactly in that investment category, but if I had gold coins, I believe I'd keep them in a safe."

Dave grinned. "You'd think so. The thieves bust into safes. But some people take pride in sewing them into mattresses and hiding them in fishing tackle boxes. One woman stashed her jewelry in a fake soup can and stuck it in her pantry."

Jerry sat back, his arms folded over his chest. "Are you quite through? I knew you would gab."

I was taken aback by his attitude. Excuse us for breathing.

"Where did you find these?" Dave asked as he examined the coins.

"Next to my front door, under a bush, like someone tossed them on my stoop and they slid off."

I glanced at Dave. Was that some kind of warning to the mayor? Or a payoff to keep him quiet? It hadn't worked if that was the case. It seemed to me that Sven's death could have been connected to the gold coin he won but I didn't dare say anything in front of Jerry.

Dave didn't appear to be perturbed about it. "Holly's the one who called in the explosion from the car last night."

Oh, very nice. Switch the subject by bringing up my name.

The mayor glared at me as though he thought I had caused his problems. I followed Oma's lead and didn't let him suck me into his vortex of aggravation. I wondered if Oma knew what had happened to Mr. Luciano yet, but I decided this might not be the best time to bring it up. Besides, the blackberry syrup on my waffle tasted like summertime. I was far too engrossed in my delicious breakfast to be concerned about what Jerry thought of me. I did notice that he ate a little bit like the Jack Russell, fast—as if he hadn't seen food in a while.

"I expected to receive a phone call last night about someone else who didn't make it home, but it never happened. Whose car is it?" He might not have been happy about my presence, but genuine concern etched wrinkles into Jerry's face.

Dave swallowed the last of his sausages. "I don't know."

"Well, what model of car was it?"

"Some kind of SUV. It's nothing but a burned out hulk."

"If you don't mind my asking, why aren't you down there right now figuring out who was in it?" Jerry fed Chief a piece of bacon.

I thought Dave might pop. "Good grief, Jerry. I was out there all night. Went home for a shower and a change of clothes because I was drenched and reeked of smoke. Then I thought I'd better check on Liesel. I'm headed back there as soon as I finish my breakfast. Since you're so worried about it, why don't you come along and see for yourself?"

He'd curiously omitted mentioning the attack on Mr. Luciano. I caught Dave's trick, though. That wasn't an invitation, it was a taunt. Apparently it went right over Jerry's head.

Jerry huffed. "Now there's a good idea. Maybe I can recognize it or read the license plates so we'll know who died in that car. I swear I have to do everything myself in this town. I'll change clothes and meet you . . . No. I have a meeting . . . Then I have a luncheon."

Was that a smirk Dave was hiding behind his coffee mug? "Take it easy, Jerry. No one was in the car."

Jerry scowled, looking disappointed. "You mean some idiot just threw a perfectly good car over the mountain?"

"Pretty much."

Jerry shot a disbelieving look at Dave. "You sure about that? I do not want to have egg on my face when it turns out somebody is missing and died in that car."

Dave kept his cool. "I'm positive."

Unlike his crabby owner, easy-going Chief had made friends with the Jack Russell. They lay together peacefully, as though they'd been pals for a long time.

I minded my own business, but it didn't prevent Jerry from sputtering at me. "And I'd appreciate it if you wouldn't tell folks that you saw a ghost out on the road last night. People around here are ghost crazy. They'll latch onto that in a heartbeat."

Ghost? Where did he get that idea? "I never—"

He went on without listening to me. "As if I don't have enough problems with my own mother. How does she seem to you, Liesel?"

"Fine. Why? Are you worried?" asked Oma.

Jerry shook his head. "I wonder if she's thinking straight anymore. For pity's sake, she left the gate open last night, and Dolce got out. I hope this isn't the first sign of memory lapses."

"Anyone can make a mistake. Don't be so hard on Ellie." Oma tsked at him.

Jerry wiped his mouth as he rose from the table. "I have to get going." He pointed his forefinger, jabbing the air repeatedly. "Dave, keep me informed. I want to know everything immediately. I hate to be the last one to hear about something. And you—" he pointed the pudgy forefinger at me "—stay out of trouble."

He left in the same breathless rush with which he had entered, his basset hound struggling to keep pace.

A look passed between Oma and Dave. They laughed, like it was a private joke.

"Did I miss something?" I asked.

"It's just Jerry," said Dave. "He's such a wuss. Did you see how fast he backpedaled on having to climb down the mountain?"

"It's not nice of us to make fun of Jerry," said Oma. "But he's full of hot air. Always talking big. In actuality, he is a very good mayor."

"I never said anything about a ghost. What's he talking about?"

Dave seemed a little bit embarrassed. "I don't know how these things get started. I heard it from two people this morning. I guess something got back to the mayor."

"You never believed in ghosts." Oma smiled at me. "Even as a little girl. The summer someone told you about the ghost of Obadiah Bagley, you brushed it off like it was nothing. Your cousin Josh wouldn't sleep alone for three weeks."

"It wasn't a ghost that I saw on the road," I insisted. *What nonsense!* "It was a man wearing a hood." Eager to change the subject, I said, "I noticed that you didn't mention Mr. Luciano."

Oma kept her head bowed, but I could see that tension in her jaw again.

Dave, on the other hand, looked directly at her. I sensed they were in disagreement.

"We're keeping that under our caps at the moment. Well, as long as we can in such a small town." Dave rested his elbows on the table and intertwined his fingers so tightly he cut off his own circulation. His hands faded white and his fingers turned crimson. He spoke in a hushed voice. "Given Sven's untimely death and the attack on Mr. Luciano last night, it's not—" he glanced at Oma "—unreasonable to believe that the two incidents are somehow related to the Sugar Maple Inn."

Oma shook her head vigorously. "No, no, no. I refuse to believe this. There is nothing," she hissed, "nothing that could have provoked such vicious behavior."

Dave's mouth twisted with skepticism. He locked his eyes on mine as though he was trying to send me an unspoken message.

Maybe Oma's troubles ran deeper than just her twisted ankle. What if the events were connected to the Sugar Maple Inn? I understood Dave's logic, much as I didn't want to think that the inn was involved in any way. An employee and a guest had been targets, though. Oma would have to come to grips with that.

I moved on, hoping to break the tension between them. "What did the doctor say about your leg?" I looked around for crutches but didn't see any. "Are you allowed to walk on it?"

Dave snorted. "Doctor? There are a couple of bone experts over at Snowball Mountain's ski area, but would she go to the doctor? Of course not."

"I'll be fine. I don't need a doctor to tell me I twisted my ankle."

At least Oma wasn't dying from some horrible illness. Or was she? Rose had spoken with such urgency. "You're not sick, then?"

Oma avoided my eyes and sipped her tea. When she set the cup down, she patted my hand. "I'm sorry if I worried you."

It didn't escape my notice that she deftly skipped over any mention of the state of her health. Maybe she didn't want to talk about it in front of Dave. She certainly looked hale and hearty.

A couple with two chocolate labs strolled in and sat down at a table. Their dogs cast a couple of inquisitive sniffs in the Jack Russell's direction, but she ignored them. Surprisingly calm, she watched Oma and me, as though she did this every day.

"Is that the latest fashion in the city?" asked Oma.

It never took long for passive-aggressive mothering to come out in my family. I laughed out loud. "I was sopping wet by the time I got here last night. When Rose called, she led me to believe it was a dire emergency, so I didn't bother going home for clothes." Hah. I'd been trained by the best. I'd just shifted the guilt to Oma's corner.

"You'd better buy a few things. I can loan you jackets and sweaters, but you'll need trousers. My waistline is a bit larger than yours. I'm sure you'll want something more modern, anyway. There are a few cute boutiques in town. How long can you stay?"

Oof. I had to tell her sometime. "I, um, left my job. There's no big rush to get back if you don't mind me borrowing your computer. I can follow up on job applications from here." How long would it take for a twisted ankle to be better? A week, maybe? I still had to get to the bottom of Oma's health problems, if there were any. She might need me more than she was letting on. And if she insisted on closing her eyes to the things that were happening in Wagtail, it might fall to me to make sure the inn wasn't in the middle of it all.

"Ohhh! This is wonderful." Oma held her arms wide for a hug. I stood up and embraced her.

"I'm so glad to have you around for a while. Your Ben—he won't mind?"

I sat down again and thanked Shelley for refreshing my tea. "I doubt it." I had his car, though. That might upset him. He would have to use my car for the time being. "Did my eyes deceive me this morning or has the pedestrian zone been spruced up?" I finished the last bite of waffle, nicely coated with sweet blackberry syrup.

"It is charming, no? Wagtail obtained a few grants and made major changes to attract tourists. We didn't want to bring industry here. This way we can preserve the natural state of Wagtail Mountain so everyone can continue to enjoy it. It was a perfect solution. We already had the pedestrian area. They call the grassy part in the center *the green* now."

"Making Wagtail into a pet vacation destination was the boost we needed. The town is flourishing. Way beyond anything we anticipated. Wagtail is going through a development spurt." Dave raised his open palm and gestured around him.

"The whole town? Not just the inn? Why didn't you tell me?" I asked.

"I told you I had a surprise." Oma appeared pleased with herself. "Can you believe I was able to keep it a secret? Of course, in the beginning, we didn't know if it would work out.

But dogs and cats are part of the family today. So much so that we've had a remarkable influx of residents. Land prices have soared. We're having a little building boom. It's all about lifestyle and living where pets are appreciated."

"I wondered how you managed to get around the health code. Is it legal to have dogs in the eating area?"

Dave coughed. "Technically, the law doesn't prohibit dogs or cats. There are rules and regulations, but they're about food preparation areas. You'll find that every eating establishment—"

Oma interrupted him, "And there are quite a few!"

"—has made special arrangements to provide for companion animals within the bounds of state law. In addition, we have passed an exception here in Wagtail which we're trying to get through the state legislature so we'll have more leeway."

"Looks like a beautiful day after all that rain. If only Sven . . ." Oma's voice trailed.

"Uh, Holly, where did you drive from yesterday?" asked Dave.

"A vineyard near Charlottesville."

"Sounds nice."

"It was."

"Were you there with anybody?"

I looked at Oma, who shrugged.

"My boyfriend."

"Anybody else?"

"Is this an inquisition? What are you getting at, Dave?"

He sucked in air. "I just feel like I ought to verify your whereabouts and the time you left there."

I stared at him, momentarily speechless. "You can't be serious! You think I was involved in Sven's death? I didn't even know him."

Nine

❀ ❀ ❀ ❀

"I'm not accusing you of anything. Still, it would be helpful if I knew you were elsewhere at the time it happened."

It was my turn to look down at my plate—mostly so he wouldn't see me trying not to smile. I'd bet anything this was his first murder investigation. "Got a pen?"

He handed me one, as well as his little spiral notebook. I jotted down Ben's name and phone numbers.

"Thank you, Holly. I'd better get down the mountain to that car. Thanks for the breakfast, Liesel."

"Anytime." Oma lowered her leg and tried to put some weight on her foot.

I jumped to my feet, scaring the dog, and assisted Oma in standing.

"Such a nuisance. You're a dear to come and help an old woman."

"You're not that old." Since I was the result of a high school tryst between my parents, they were younger than the parents of my friends, some of whom had parents who were seventy-two, like Oma.

"This ankle is reminding me that I'm not as young as I usually feel."

Together we hobbled to the front door of the inn, the little dog staying just ahead of us.

"Now go buy something pretty. I'll be fine."

I watched as she shuffled away. She turned around. "And don't forget to buy your cute dog a proper collar with a name tag."

I caught my reflection in a mirror. Oma was right. I looked terrible. The stores probably wouldn't be open yet, but I could have a walk around town. Prepared to give my credit card a little exercise, I stepped out onto the stone porch that fronted Wagtail's pedestrian zone. Stone pillars supported the porch roof and a wrought iron railing ran between them.

The crisp, cool air of fall invigorated me. A man in a beret sat in one of the rocking chairs far to my left. He cupped a steaming mug in both of his hands, the picture of contentment. His bulldog peered through the railing at the goings-on in town.

"Holly!"

My grandmother's best friend, Rose, trotted up the front steps and threw her arms around me. "Oh my goodness. It's been far too long. Let me look at you." She stepped back. Rose's warm hazel eyes took me in. Wrinkles of wisdom had moved in around them, and laugh lines etched her face under cheeks as round as lady apples. She still wore her hair short and yellow blonde, but gray streaks had lightened it a bit. I suspected she still drew admirers, even in her seventies. She wore a long-sleeved red boatneck T-shirt and navy trousers. Had I ever seen her when she wasn't smiling?

"Is this how they're dressing these days? You're a mess, child!"

I laughed. "Did Oma tell you to say that? I was drenched yesterday and need to buy something to wear."

She hugged me again. "I'm so glad you're here." Holding my hands, she tugged me over to a set of rocking chairs and sat down.

She faced me, reaching down to stroke the Jack Russell. "I hear you have a serious boyfriend. Tell me about your sweetheart. Is he handsome?" Her shoulders lifted in excitement.

"He's nice looking." Ben was cute in a bookish way.

Medium height, he had never been much of an athlete, but that didn't matter to me.

"Nice looking?" Her mouth puckered like she had bitten into a lemon. She recovered quickly and swiped her hand through the air. "Aw, we girls are always more interested in what's inside a man. Does he make you laugh?"

"He's fairly serious. Not much of a joker."

Rose blinked at me. "But he makes your toes tingle, right?"

She was so cute, believing all those silly tales about love. "Rose, he's a good man. You'll like him."

"Good man?" Her chin pulled back, and she drew the words out as though they were repulsive. "What kind of phrase is that to describe your boyfriend? Honey bunch, if you're not feeling fireworks and tingling toes . . ."

Panic raised its ugly head for a moment. I hadn't given Ben more than a passing thought since I left him in Kim's clutches. Could Rose be right? Nonsense! I was being silly. Oma had been my overwhelming concern. Who could think of anything else with all that had happened?

"Rose, is Oma ill? She won't say."

Rose's upper lip pulled inward and her eyes darted to the side. Sucking in a deep breath of air, she said, "I'd better let her tell you that."

My heart sank. It must be bad. If it weren't bad news, they'd have told me by now. I melted against the back of the chair, glum, and the dog leaped into my lap.

Rose clutched the arm of my rocking chair. "Now honey, don't be upset. To be honest, I'm more worried about you than I am about Liesel. You brought your dog with you, but not your boyfriend."

"She's not mine." As soon as I spoke, I knew that wasn't true. I would be keeping this rascal with the bright eyes, no matter what Ben said about it. I told Rose the sad story about how she came into my possession. "I don't suppose there's a car detailer in Wagtail? I hate to take Ben's car back to him in such a sad state."

"I'll ask around."

"Thanks, Rose."

She disappeared into the inn, and I strolled down the steps into a little plaza.

I turned to gaze up at the inn. Much smaller than a hotel, but larger than a bed-and-breakfast, the inn fell somewhere in between. Wagtail had been a popular destination in the late 1700s, thanks to the mineral springs. Old documents proved that Thomas Jefferson and his family had visited regularly to partake of the waters. It had been a booming resort for decades.

The inn had been built in the 1800s by a wealthy man whose ailing wife frequented the waters for their curative powers. His son later expanded the huge six-bedroom house to eight bedrooms with an addition. Local stone covered the walls in a variety of colors that we had delighted in as children. They ran from white to deep red, and gold to brown, with plenty of pink and salmon and the occasional black stone. We used to hunt for green and blue rocks, but there weren't any.

The building featured two main levels with a dormered third floor attic—where I was now staying. The roof had been raised in the center of the attic level to accommodate my suite. The addition of the circular balcony with a wrought iron railing on the suite added a stunning architectural element. A somewhat smaller addition had been built on the left side, presumably the cat wing.

Family lore had it that my grandfather had won the inn in a heated poker game. His family had already owned one-thousand acres of mountain property, but nothing as chic or elegant as the mansion. I'd never quite believed the story about the poker game, but that was the tale I'd always been told.

As I studied the inn, Mr. Luciano bolted out the front door and down the steps. He certainly wasn't dressed for jogging in those laced-up leather shoes, but he sprinted away from the inn, his expression decidedly more distressed than it was last night.

Ten

He ran along the other side of the walking zone. I didn't think he saw me. I watched him until he disappeared around a corner.

In the heavenly fall air with the sun beaming down on us, and the mountains crisply defined in the distance, the problems of the previous day evaporated. It was impossible to imagine that Sven's death had been anything but an accident.

The joy of Wagtail was contagious. Dogs romped with puppyish exuberance. Their people smiled and laughed. With the sole exception of Mr. Luciano, no one hurried anywhere like they did in the city. People relaxed at outdoor tables, enjoying breakfast. The scent of bacon wafted to me, and to my dog, too, if her twitching nose was any indication.

Could it be because everyone had come here on vacation? Were they unwinding and letting the stress go? I strolled along, taking in the fenced dog play areas in the grassy median. The Jack Russell tugged toward them. "You can run and play with them once we get you a collar with a tag."

An old-fashioned drugstore on the corner of a side street was already open for business. The sign above the door read

HEAL! Drugs and Sundry. I held the door ajar and called out, "Hello? Is my dog allowed inside?"

"By all means." A pharmacist in a white coat beckoned to me. In his mid-thirties, he teased an older woman who flirted with him. Either his tan hid his blush, or he was used to that sort of attention. She had the audacity to reach up and touch his neatly cropped hair, almost the same shade as my own milk chocolate brown tresses.

I wandered through the store, passing an old-fashioned penny candy display. Rows of large glass jars showed off hard candies, toffees, and gumballs as well as assorted dog treats in the shapes of bones, mailmen, and drumsticks, and dried fish treats for cats.

Next to it was a soda fountain. I had vague memories of a shabby old lunch counter in Wagtail, but this modern version was adorable. A polished wood countertop shone under the store lights. No one sat on the chrome stools with seats of bright red Naugahyde yet, but a coffeepot rested on the counter next to paper cups, sugar, cream, and a *Help Yourself* sign. On the wall, a chalkboard listed ice cream flavors, along with floats, banana splits, and sundaes, and an additional list of frosty treats and drinks just for dogs and cats. I looked down at the dog. "You'd like a doggy ice cream cone, wouldn't you?"

Fascinated by a scent on the floor, she ignored me until I opened the treat jar with the drumsticks and took one.

She twirled around and pranced on her hind legs. I couldn't resist that cute tail and those hopeful eyes. "We have to pay for this before you can eat it. Okay?"

As though she feared I might eat it myself, she kept her nose aimed at the cookie in my hand as we wandered on and found the makeup section. I didn't need too much. I'd had a brush in my purse. Shampoo and conditioner had been provided in my bathroom at the inn. Mostly I needed eyeliner, mascara, and blush.

When I brought my purchases to the checkout counter, the pharmacist said, "Welcome to Wagtail. Are you on vacation?"

Painfully aware of my messy outfit, I explained that I was visiting my grandmother.

"Liesel! She's crazy for our pecan praline ice cream. Not

that I can blame her—I can barely control myself around pecan praline turtles made with a little bourbon and covered with chocolate. My idea of heaven!"

"Are you from Wagtail?" I asked.

"No. My parents came up here on vacation and fell in love with the place. Dad had this crazy idea to open an old-timey pharmacy, and Mom had always wanted to breed ocicats, so instead of planning for retirement, they moved to Wagtail to do what they love." He placed my purchases in a bag. Like Ben, he was medium height, but he seemed happier, more relaxed than Ben. He smiled as he spoke, drawing me in with his warmth. "I didn't have any intention of moving here, but when I came to visit last Christmas, I didn't want to leave. And here I am! There's something addictive about Wagtail."

The man behind me seemed a little pressured. After I paid, I paused to feed the dog her treat.

The pharmacist greeted the man like an old friend. "I've got your son's asthma inhaler right here, Del."

Del dumped a jar of loose change on the counter. "I don't know that I've got quite enough."

"Close enough for me." The pharmacist didn't bother to count the money. He handed him the bag with a smile. "Give Hazel Mae my best."

I left the store, impressed by the pharmacist's generosity.

Across the way, a woman rolled a rack of dog coats out of a store called Putting On the Dog. I headed for the store, hoping she carried more mundane items like collars and leashes. As we approached it, my dog came to a complete halt. She refused to walk one more step.

Thinking she might need a doggy bathroom, I looked for one along the grassy strip, and sure enough, there were areas marked for that purpose. I led her over to one. She sniffed but showed no signs of needing to relieve herself.

"We're going back to that store because you deserve a real collar with your name on it." The inn collar was fine, although it clearly wasn't meant to replace a regular collar. But she didn't have a name yet. "What was your old name? Spot? Snowflake? Spunky? Maggie? Lulu? Zola?" She listened to me very politely but didn't react to any of them. "We'll get you a collar, and add your name later on. For now, we'll just make sure my name and number are on the tag, in case you get lost. Okay?"

I took her wagging tail to mean she was in agreement. But when we neared the store, she balked and planted her feet firmly.

I tugged gently, "Come on, sweetie."

Nothing doing. I picked her up and carried her into the store. Collars and leashes in every imaginable color lined a wall. Perfect. "A white dog can wear any color. What do you think?" I shifted her so I could reach the collars with my right hand. "Something pink and girlie? A bold red? Or would you prefer sky blue with daisies on it?"

She didn't wriggle or move. In fact, she seemed scared, like she had in the bathtub the night before. I set her on the floor and stroked her head. "It's all right, sweetie pie."

A pair of truly large feet clad in silver sequined sneakers came to a halt at the dog's nose. I stood up, but still had to look up to the woman's face. She towered over me. I was used to everyone being taller than me, but this woman had to be well over six feet tall.

She'd pulled her light brown hair into a ponytail and wore no makeup at all. Large eyes and a voluptuous mouth filled her broad face. She was stunning.

My dog didn't seem to like her, though. She backed away.

"You need a collar?" She plucked a hideously ugly gray and black one off the wall. "Let's try this on for size."

Scooping the dog up in her arms, she walked over to the open door, set the dog down, removed the inn collar and pinched the dog's behind!

The dog and I yelped simultaneously. My dog took off running as fast as she could.

"Whoops!" The woman turned to me with a smile that put dimples into her cheeks. "Sorry." She shrugged.

I dashed out of the store after the dog. *Ack*! She didn't have a name. "Doggie! Little one. Here, sweetie!"

The man who had bought medicine for his child spied me. "Looking for a Jack Russell?"

"Yes!"

"She went thataway." He pointed down the side street.

My heels weren't made for running. I would never catch up to her. Taking a chance with rocks and heaven knows what, I removed my shoes and ran down the street, calling, "Sweetie! Puppy!" Six blocks later, I was forced to acknowledge that she could be anywhere—behind a fence, in a garden, under a bush, or still running like the wind to get away.

I'd spent less than twenty-four hours with her, yet I felt her loss like a death. The last couple of weeks had been nothing but a slew of problems—first the nightmare at work, then Kim chasing Ben, now Oma and her mysterious illness, and the attack on Mr. Luciano—but this was the catalyst that made me want to melt down and cry. My poor little dog, lost and alone again.

Across the road, in a farm field, a young rabbit watched me without moving. She folded her ears flat against her back. Did that mean a wild little dog had zoomed by her recently or that she was afraid of me? Beyond the farmhouse in the distance, the woods held dark secrets. If my dog had run that way, she could be lost forever.

Sucking it up and trying hard to hold myself together, I trudged back to the pedestrian area of town reminding myself that I had to be upbeat for Oma. She had enough problems without me moping around. But it wouldn't be the same without that sweet little girl.

I blamed myself. She hadn't wanted to go into that particular store but I didn't pay attention. Why had I forced her? Why didn't I see that something bad would happen? The rational part of me knew I couldn't have predicted that from her behavior. There had probably been a scent she didn't like. Maybe there was a big dog in the back that scared her or . . . or maybe she was just being ornery.

Anger welled in me, fighting my heartbreak. What was wrong with that woman? You'd think a person who owned a store that sold dog gear would like dogs.

I returned to the scary store, fuming. Oma's lessons did battle within me. *Never burn bridges. The way you call into the woods is the way it will come back to you.* I knew I shouldn't confront the evil woman, but . . . *but I wanted to!*

The tall woman leered at me. "What now?"

She had her nerve. She ought to be contrite. Apologetic, at least. "The Sugar Maple Inn collar, please."

"I threw it out."

"What?" Why would anyone do that? I tried to keep my irritation out of my tone. "I feel I'm safe in guessing that no one picked up your trash in the few minutes I've been gone."

The dimples made an appearance even though the corners of her mouth turned down. She held out a trash can to me, and I plucked the collar out of it. "Thank you."

I walked toward the door, doing my level best to get out of there before I said something I would regret.

"You have your nerve coming in here."

Clearly I had missed something. I turned around. "Excuse me?"

"Oh, puleeze! Don't pretend like you don't know who I am."

Eleven

❦ ❦ ❦ ❦

I didn't have to pretend. I truly didn't have the first clue who she was. The woman obviously didn't like me for some reason. If I said I didn't know her she would surely perceive it as an insult, and her ire would escalate. She'd already wounded me in the worst possible way, though, by causing me to lose my darling dog.

And who would have a reason to be angry with me?

Not a single wrinkle or errant gray hair marred her appearance. Late twenties? Large rings encrusted with stones sparkled on her fingers but I didn't see a wedding band. I sighed. I was at a complete loss. Of course, if I had known her when I was fifteen and she was eight or ten, I probably wouldn't have paid much attention to her. Even one or two years made such a big difference at that age.

"Don't you have *caller ID*?" She said it in a prissy, flippant way.

Aha. She had to be the woman who'd answered my call about the explosion and fire the night before. Perhaps I had offended her when she asked for my phone number and I impatiently asked if she had caller ID.

"I didn't mean anything by that. The situation put me on edge." But as soon as I said it, I wondered why I was apologizing to this horrible woman who intentionally caused my cute dog to run away and hadn't been in the least bit remorseful other than an amused *sorry*. "You did that on purpose! You took her to the door and pinched her so she would run out. What is wrong with you?"

She leveled a torturous gaze at me. "They run away when they don't love you."

The nerve! This woman had some serious issues. I didn't need that kind of nonsense. I left the store in a huff. My adorable dog was lost because of her. I couldn't even put the dog's picture on a flier because I didn't have any photos of her.

Still barefoot, I hobbled over to a shoe store.

A painfully thin woman about my age admired a pair of pink ballet slippers. Her clothes hung on her, a couple of sizes too large.

I browsed in the sale section of the store and found a pair of black leather thong sandals on sale.

When I bent over to try one on, I saw the thin woman deftly slip a ballet slipper into a deep pocket on each side of her voluminous skirt.

I looked around for the sales clerk. A portly woman pushed back graying hair. She caught my glance, frowned, and shook her head horizontally ever so slightly. The thief paused on her way out of the store and gazed longingly at a pair of four-inch heels with a leopard pattern before moseying out.

The much more sedate and boring sandals I had found fit me perfectly. It was too late in the season for them, which was undoubtedly the reason they'd been marked down so much, but I wanted to go back to the road where my dog had last been seen before more time passed. They were practical and inexpensive.

I took them to the cash register. "What was that with the ballet slippers?"

"Hazel Mae? She and her husband, Del, have a passel of kids. I'd have given them to her for free but she's too proud to ask."

Somehow I didn't think allowing her to steal was sending

the right message. There must be a better way. Leaving the ballet slippers on their doorstep during the night? But what did I know?

When I left the store, I watched Hazel Mae amble along, window-shopping. Carrying my bag from the drugstore, I ventured back to Oak Street, hoping against all reason or logic that the dog might show up. She didn't. The rabbit had left, too.

I whistled and called until every dog in the neighborhood barked. Did I hear high-pitched yapping? Somewhere, one howled, long and sad.

I listened, not daring to breathe. Dogs barked all around me. It was probably wishful thinking to imagine I had heard my dog. I had to pull myself together. Okay, so I didn't have a photo of her. I could still put up *lost* fliers. Maybe Wagtail had a community website or a little newspaper where I could place an ad.

My teeth clenched, I tried to focus. Buy clothes, work up fliers, find out about newspapers and web communications, and, in between all that, trick Oma into revealing what was wrong with her.

Relieved to have a plan, I returned to the walking zone and found a store called Houndstooth. My temporarily unemployed budget weighed on me, but I found some summer items that had been marked way down. Three cotton tops, a pair of jeans, khakis, and two summery dresses that I couldn't pass up at the drastically reduced prices. Remembering my mom's travel advice, *one to wash, one to wear, and one to spare*, I added two lacy bras and a couple pair of panties and was set.

I'd just stepped out of the store, bags in hand, when I heard my name. My heart thudded like a drum in my chest at that voice—deep and masculine, yet as soft and comforting as a cuddle.

Holmes Richardson loped in my direction. All I could think was why hadn't I worn one of the new outfits out of the store?

I hadn't seen Holmes in ages. Not since he went to college. Summers at Wagtail hadn't been the same after Holmes and my cousin, Josh, graduated from high school and pursued other interests. Although I was a couple of years younger, the three of us had spent countless hours together working at the Sugar Maple Inn.

Oma had always hired Holmes, Rose's grandson, to work with Josh and me. She hadn't differentiated between sexes, either. We all did the same tasks, whether it was carrying luggage to rooms, washing dishes, weeding, clearing trails, or doing laundry and making up the beds. We'd had a lot of fun, though. Taller than Josh, sandy-haired Holmes had always pulled the role of Han Solo to espresso-haired Josh's Luke Skywalker. As Princess Leia, I had wielded my share of fallen branches as light sabers.

At the end of each summer, Josh and I had been shipped back to our parents, while Holmes remained in Wagtail and rode the bus down the mountain to school. But I never forgot about the first boy I had ever kissed. I'd written *Mrs. Holmes Richardson* in my grade-school notebooks over and over again.

I straightened my blouse, painfully self-conscious.

An ever-so-slightly-crooked smile spread across his face. "Holly?"

A good foot taller than me, he had no problem literally sweeping me off my feet in a bear hug.

He set me down, beaming at me. "What are you doing here? I can't believe it's really you."

"I came to check on Oma." He looked great. A little bit older and more polished, but the smiling blue eyes and genuinely happy grin were as inviting as ever.

"I heard what happened to her. How's she doing?"

"Stubbornly pretends nothing is wrong."

Holmes laughed. "That's probably a good sign. I'd like to stop by to see her while I'm here." He glanced around. "Is Josh here, too?"

That sucked the wind out of my sails. For a few seconds, romantic notions had danced in my head. With a huge sigh, my lofty visions crashed back down to earth. Holmes lived in Chicago, and he was engaged to be married. We weren't in grade school anymore. I consoled myself with the fact that my cousin Josh had been Holmes's best friend growing up, so it was only natural that Holmes would ask about him. "No. Just me."

Holmes glanced at a gold watch on his wrist that exposed the works underneath the crystal. "I'm on my way to a meeting. Walk with me so we can catch up?"

"Pretty snazzy watch, sir," I teased.

"A gift from my fiancé. My folks warned me that some chump is stealing gold over at Snowball and thought I should leave it at their place. But I feel naked without a watch and this is Wagtail, you know? That incident with Oma last night has to be a fluke."

He held his hands out for my bags. "They don't have stores in Washington?"

I explained my haste to come to Wagtail while we walked. "And now I don't know if Oma is sick or not. I asked your grandmother this morning, but she wouldn't tell me."

"That's strange. If she called because of the accident, then it seems like she would have said so." Two worry wrinkles appeared between his eyebrows. "I don't like the sound of that. Will you let me know what you find out?"

I nodded. We strolled along Pine Street, where elegant white Victorian-style houses nestled under towering trees. Whitewashed fences surrounded cute bungalows. It seemed each house had a front porch.

"You have a meeting in Wagtail?" That was odd for someone who lived in Chicago. "Are you planning to move here?"

Holmes stopped dead in his tracks. He winced. "Not really." He scuffed the toe of his elegant brown loafer against the sidewalk. "My fiancé would never move here. I . . . I can't."

It was totally inappropriate, and I never would have asked if I hadn't known him and his family so well. "Then why the meeting?"

"My family owns a piece of property that they want to develop as rental cabins, but Jerry Pierce, the mayor, is blocking them."

"And they brought you in to find out why?"

"We think we *know* why. Jerry is a real estate agent who rents out his own properties in and around Wagtail. He doesn't want the competition."

"So you're supposed to be big, bad Holmes and beat him up a little bit?" I suppressed the urge to giggle. Holmes might have the physical size to appear imposing, but he didn't have a mean or vicious bone in his body.

"Something like that. He doesn't have a leg to stand on. He's just being a bully and throwing his weight around by refusing to give them the permit. You know my family—they don't want to make a fuss or go to court over it."

I did know. My family was much the same way. And from what I'd seen of Jerry that morning, he could be obnoxious. We walked on, and Holmes stopped in front of an old white house with a turret. I couldn't determine the style. A cross between Victorian and Italianate? Most likely the original architecture was hidden under layers of modifications, but the turret certainly made it stand out among the other more modest homes.

"Your meeting is in his house?"

"I'm told he has an office on the first floor where he entertains his subjects. Rose calls him King Jerry, but he sounds more like a dictator to me." Holmes grinned at me when he handed over my purchases. "Wish me luck with the curmudgeon."

With a light, agile gait, he jogged up the stairs and onto the front porch. I watched him, still engulfed in the warmth of a Holmes-induced euphoria.

I turned away. What was wrong with me? I had a perfectly nice boyfriend. Just yesterday I had been worried about Kim making moves on him. Yet it had taken me only seconds to fall back into a childish crush. I wasn't usually so . . . fickle. That's what I was! *Fickle*. And silly.

I hadn't taken two steps when I heard a stifled yelp and the screen door slam shut. Had Jerry already thrown him out? I looked over my shoulder. Holmes stood on the porch, his back to the door, his face ashen.

"Holmes? Are you all right?"

Twelve

✤ ❋ ✤ ❋ ✤

Holmes stepped forward, grabbed the porch railing, and gasped for breath.

I hurried up the steps. "What is it?"

He held out a long arm meant to prevent me from going inside. "Holly, don't . . ."

I dropped my shopping bags and threw open the screen door. Jerry Pierce sprawled on his stomach near the bottom of the stairs as though he had fallen but hadn't slid all the way down. His right arm stretched out toward me in a horrifyingly sad effort to crawl or grasp something. Blood matted his hair and stained his argyle vest. Around his neck hung the silver chain of a dog choke collar.

In spite of myself, I screamed and slapped my hand over my mouth. I trembled when I asked, "Have you checked for a pulse?"

"Not yet. See if you can find a phone to call 911."

Holmes knelt on the floor in front of Jerry.

Gulping air through my mouth as though I couldn't get enough oxygen, I raced into a dark room that appeared to be Jerry's office. A dense white curtain hung over the front window, blocking light. Jerry's massive desk with gargoyle legs dominated the room. Thankfully, a phone rested on it.

I picked it up and dialed 911, hoping the big, evil woman wouldn't answer. This time the call was handled professionally. Assured an ambulance was on the way, I hung up and returned to what I feared was a corpse.

Holmes moved his fingers under Jerry's jawline. "I think it's too late for an ambulance. He's cold."

"Cold? You mean cold because he's dead or that he needs a blanket?"

"Dead. I can't feel anything but skin that's way colder than it should be."

"It looks like somebody bashed him over the head. I don't think you would bleed like that from a fall." I whispered when I asked, "Do you think someone choked him to death with the collar?"

"Gross. I hope not. It left marks on his neck, though. There's not much blood on the stairs," said Holmes, rising. "But there's a lot on his hair."

I shuddered. "Oh, Holmes! It appears as if he was running away from someone and was pushed or tripped. Look at that outstretched hand."

Holmes wrapped a comforting arm around my shoulders. "It's a nightmare. If you weren't here, I'd be pinching myself, hoping I'd wake up."

It wasn't long before Dave dashed through the front door. "Good grief! What happened?"

"This is how I found him," said Holmes.

"You didn't give him CPR?" Dave knelt and checked for a pulse. "Oh." It was a small simple word that said everything. He ran the heel of his hand up his forehead. "Jerry could be a jerk, but I never saw this coming. He must have ticked off someone big time." He stood, pulled out his radio, and stepped out on the porch for a moment.

He returned and asked, "Did either of you touch anything?"

"Just the screen door," said Holmes, "and I checked for a pulse on his neck. Holly called 911 from the phone in there." Holmes pointed to the office.

"Is anyone else here?" asked Dave.

Whoa! It hadn't even occurred to me that someone might be lurking upstairs. Chills ran through me, and I shivered.

"I haven't heard anyone." Holmes looked to me. "Have you?"

A mournful yowl startled us. Loud and shrill, it sank to a guttural wail. At the top of the stairs, a Siamese cat stared down at us and cried.

"She knows," said Dave. "She might have seen his killer." He glanced around. "Where's Jerry's dog?"

"Chief!" I said. "I haven't seen or heard him. I'll check the backyard."

"Stop!" Dave held up one palm like he was directing traffic. "I can't have you contaminating the crime scene." He frowned at me. "Where's your dog?"

I wasn't following his train of thought. What did my dog have to do with anything? "She's lost. The horrible woman at the dog store in town pinched her and scared her away."

Dave and Holmes froze. I'd clearly said something wrong.

"Exactly what time did that happen?" asked Dave.

Before I could answer, Holmes blurted, "Oh, come on! Surely you don't suspect Holly of whacking Jerry over the head or choking him."

The corner of Dave's mouth twitched. "I'm the cop, Holmes. You might not be aware of the fact that Holly appears to be involved in almost every crime in this town over the last twenty-four hours."

Holmes tilted his head like an adorable puppy. "Is that true?"

I bristled. "Involved is a totally incorrect word. I wasn't *involved* in any of them. Besides, I had nothing to do with the attack on Mr. Luciano, and I wasn't even here when Sven was killed."

Dave pulled out his notebook and jotted something in it. "How long are you going to be in town, Holmes?"

"Now you suspect Holmes?" I asked.

"Look, Holly. Up to now, the most serious crime in Wagtail has been public intoxication, and then most of the time, I just walk the person home. I might have a cushy job here in Wagtail, but I'm still part of the county police force based over on Snowball, and I'm not messing this up. *Capisce?*"

I understood all right, but some little part of me couldn't resist the desire to point out his folly. "What about you? Jerry was pretty hard on you this morning at breakfast."

His pen stopped moving.

It would have been smart to let it go, but I didn't. "I'm just saying that you should do what you have to, but of all the people in Wagtail, the three of us are about the least likely suspects. I didn't even know of Jerry's existence until I met him at breakfast this morning. And Holmes doesn't live here anymore."

"I have a flight out tomorrow morning," said Holmes in irritatingly diplomatic fashion.

"Better make other arrangements," said Dave. "I'd appreciate it if you would stick around for a few days."

"Look, Dave, you know where to find me." Holmes sounded reasonable, not at all agitated. "I have a job I have to get back to. It's not like I'm a suspect."

Dave stared him down without blinking. "I'm in charge here, Holmes. Don't make me prove it."

The thunder of heavy boots on the stairs announced the arrival of backup police.

"You two get out of here." Dave cocked his head toward the door.

We hurried out and picked up my shopping bags before the other cops piled in.

Dave flapped the screen door open so hard I thought it might have cracked. "Hold it!"

What now? I had thought Dave was a decent guy, but he was turning into a domineering terror.

"Leave those here." He gestured toward my shopping bags.

"Excuse me? I won't have anything to wear."

Holmes opened one and pawed through it. "Come on, Dave. It's just undies and dresses."

My face burned, and I knew it must have gone bright red.

Dave relented. I could see it in his face.

But at that exact moment, one of the cops inside said, "Secure the premises."

Panic invaded Dave's eyes. He grabbed the bags, and looked through them, turning redder than me when he lifted a lacy bra. Handing the bags back, he said, "Hurry."

We hustled down the sidewalk. A parade of golf carts full of people and dogs drove slowly along the sleepy street.

"What on earth?" I asked.

"You haven't been here in a while, have you? They probably arrived by bus for a day of sightseeing. The buses park about two miles out and everyone is brought in by golf cart. They call them Wagtail Taxis."

"That explains the big parking lot I encountered when I drove up. It's a little different, but I like it! There's something very calming about no traffic."

"Life moves at a slower pace here. Locals take their golf carts everywhere—grocery shopping, to restaurants, to cabins up the road. Jerry's murder is going to freak everyone out."

"The golf carts are so quiet. They barely hum. It's eerie! I had no idea they could be nearly soundless."

Holmes brightened briefly. "When the town became a car-free zone, they decided to use electric golf carts to keep noise pollution to a minimum. Isn't it incredible how quickly city noises become part of our norm, and we barely hear them? I love coming back to Wagtail. I wake to birdsong every morning. And at night, sitting on the porch and listening to the crickets is better than any medicine for calming raw nerves."

We had reached the pedestrian zone and watched people pile out of the golf carts.

"Are you okay?" Holmes placed a gentle hand on my shoulder.

"What's going on, Holmes? I like the new Wagtail. It's so charming and peaceful, but something scary is happening. A car exploded just outside Wagtail last night. There was the strange hit-and-run that killed Sven, and now this? Poor Jerry, lying there, with his hand outstretched . . ."

"I don't think I'll ever forget that grisly scene. I'd better get back to the house to tell my folks what's going on. They'll worry about me if they hear it from someone else since I left for his place. Guess we'll be around for a few days, huh? Maybe we can catch a drink at the bar one night."

"Sounds good." I trudged back to the inn feeling guilty for being glad that maybe the Sugar Maple Inn wasn't at the core of the crimes being committed after all. Two murders and the attack on Mr. Luciano in such a short period of time—they had to be related. I didn't know any of the people involved. I hoped that Dave knew what *or who* linked them together.

The front porch that ran the length of the inn's main building had filled with chatty visitors. The smell of coffee wafted to me, and I spied croissants. All the guests had dogs with them, except for one couple that doted on a longhaired white cat that sat between them on a swing in the corner. A Persian, perhaps?

They all seemed so happy, so content, completely unaware that the mayor of Wagtail had been brutally murdered.

I raced past them and took the elevator up to my suite. Setting my bags down, I opened the door, and Twinkletoes ran to me, mewing.

"How did you get in here?"

She rubbed against my ankles, turning in tight circles. I picked her up and cuddled her. "Our dog is gone," I whispered. "And Jerry is dead."

She head-butted my chin, no doubt in sympathetic solidarity.

I carried the bags into the bedroom and set them on the floor. Twinkletoes wasted no time jumping into each of them in succession. While I hung up the clothes, she investigated every corner of the walk-in closet. When I closed the door, she returned to the bags, jumping in and out of them and sniffing carefully. I changed into a deep pink sleeveless top with a V-neck and the khakis. As usual, the pants needed to be shortened, but I had no time for that and rolled the bottoms up.

Twinkletoes followed me when I left the room, but she didn't wait for the elevator. She scampered down the main staircase. I probably should have too, just for the exercise, but the elevator doors opened, and I took the easy route.

Suspecting that Oma's office must be somewhere in the vicinity of the reception area, I headed that way. No one manned the desk, but I heard voices, so I peered into the room behind it.

Oma and Rose relaxed in cushy chairs covered in a bright floral fabric. The desk and office equipment gave it away as Oma's office. Floor to ceiling bookshelves lined the wall behind her desk.

The two of them were enjoying lunch at a coffee table in front of French doors, which had been thrown open to enjoy the sunshine glittering on the lake. Twinkletoes had beaten me there and was already stretched out on a semiprivate terrace.

Oma was on the phone when I entered. Rose signaled me to keep quiet by placing a finger over her lips. Oma continued the conversation but waved me in and pointed to the food on the coffee table.

After Jerry's horrible death, I would have thought food would be the last thing on my mind, but the glistening slices of pineapple and kiwi on the fruit platter with a selection of ripe cantaloupe and juicy watermelon enticed me. The loaf of crusty artisan bread, and the curious cheese with something red rolled into it in a swirl, simply had to be sampled. Unless I missed my guess, that was creamy chicken salad full of green grapes, crunchy celery, and almonds. I had to try it all. Just a taste, I promised myself.

I pulled up a chair and realized that a third, unused mug rested on the table along with a napkin, silverware, and a plate. They had expected me.

"Of course I believe you!" Oma spoke sympathetically. "Never mind him. Children can be so bossy. Mine treat me like I've gone daft. I'm not a doddering fool yet. Don't give it another thought." Oma hung up the phone. "That was Ellie Pierce, Jerry's mother."

I nearly choked on my chicken salad. His poor mother!

Oma sipped her tea. "She's beside herself about losing Dolce last night. Jerry was quite hard on her."

Rose poured tea for me and passed me the mug. "Eat slowly, dear, so you won't choke. I'm telling you, Liesel, Jerry has gotten out of hand. He thinks someone made him the King of Wagtail. He had the nerve to tell me I had too many roses along my fence and that the blooms are not—" Rose changed to a whiny tone meant to mimic Jerry "—allowed to cross the fence line." She leaned forward. "My prize roses!"

I swallowed and washed the chicken salad down with tea. Clearly they didn't know about Jerry's death yet.

Oma roared. "The next thing you know, he'll be out there with pruning shears, clipping off the roses that dare to peek over the fence. He sent Ellie a notice that she had put out decorative pumpkins too soon—his own mother!"

"He's dead," I hacked.

Thirteen

❖ ❖ ❖ ❖

"He may be pompous and imperial, but that's no reason to kill him." Oma dabbed her lips with a napkin.

"You don't understand. Someone did kill him. Holmes found him."

Now I had their attention.

"This is not funny, Holly." Oma scolded me like I was a child.

"I'm not being funny. Somebody bashed in the back of his head and strangled him with a dog's choke collar. It was . . . horrific."

"No, liebchen. It's Sven who died. Ellie would never have complained about Jerry the way she did if he was dead. Besides, she would have told me immediately." Oma leaned toward us. "Ellie thinks someone opened her gate on purpose to steal Dolce."

I put down my fork. "Ellie probably doesn't know yet. I just came from there."

Rose and Oma stared at me. Oma reached for her phone.

"I don't know how well you know Ellie, but I'd let the police tell her if I were you." I drained my tea and poured more into the mug.

Oma set her phone down. "No. This is a joke?"

"It's not a joke. Who jokes about something like that? He was . . ." I debated whether I should tell them the gory details or spare them. Wagtail was tiny, they would hear eventually. "He was sprawled on the stairs, like he was running away from something."

Rose gasped. "A ghost! I knew that old house was haunted. He laughed it off every time I mentioned it." She let out a little shriek. "It's cursed. Now there have been two deaths there."

I knew Oma and Rose took a different view of the supernatural than I did. More specifically, I just didn't believe in ghosts. It was all nonsense and hogwash. I knew better than to criticize them for their stand, though. I looked up at the ceiling and took a deep breath, which I hope conveyed skepticism at the very least. "Would he have bled if a ghost attacked him?"

"Of course. The ghosts might not bleed, but we would." Rose spoke with conviction.

"What is happening here? This is not like my beloved Wagtail. Not at all. Rose," said Oma, "I don't think we're dealing with a ghost this time. Someone killed Sven, and now Jerry. This cannot be a coincidence."

"Our meeting! I forgot all about it," exclaimed Rose, looking at the clock on the wall.

"Rose, we'll call Ellie after the meeting, yes? Holly, would you mind keeping an eye on the desk?" Oma stood up.

"Not at all. Do you mind if I borrow your computer?"

"It's a deal." She hobbled toward me and glanced around. "Where's your dog?"

I told them my tale of woe in abbreviated form.

Oma couldn't have looked sadder. "Perhaps someone will find her. We will spread the word," Patting my shoulder, she said, "I'll be back soon."

"Where are you going?"

"Just to the terrace." She scowled at me. "We will be fine, Holly. Don't look so worried. You can leave as soon as Zelda returns from her lunch break."

They left through the French doors. Oma hobbled slowly, with Rose by her side. Their heads were bowed, but their agitated murmurs drifted to me as they made their way toward the terrace, where guests enjoyed the beautiful day and views of the lake and the mountains.

It didn't take long to whip up a flier. When the printer started, Twinkletoes ambled indoors and sprang onto the desk. Fascinated by the paper that churned out of it, she reached a tentative paw toward it every time a new sheet appeared.

"I'm back from my lunch break, Mrs. Mil—" An attractive, ever-so-slightly-plump woman in her thirties with kind eyes and corn yellow hair that flowed down her back stepped into the doorway. "Oh! You must be Holly. I recognize you from your picture." She pointed at a framed photo behind me.

I peered at it. My cousin Josh, Holmes, and I were posing on the dock. "I must have been about eight years old."

"You still have that lovely long hair, but I bet you don't wear it in pigtails anymore. I'd have known you anywhere." She gasped and stared at Twinkletoes. "Oh my word! Did you know that Twinkletoes has adopted you? She says you're the one."

Huh? I shifted my focus from the kitten to the woman in the doorway. She'd spoken as though she thought she had said something very normal.

"I had such a hard time getting a reading on her. She was very protective. Perhaps now I can find out why. She's a real sweetheart. You're very lucky." The woman turned around and helped someone at the front desk.

I gathered the stack of fliers and ran my hand over Twinkletoes's silken fur. Whispering, I said, "I think someone might have a screw loose."

The woman popped back into the doorway. "I should have introduced myself. I'm Zelda. Well, really Jane, but Zelda sounds so much more exotic, don't you think? I'm the seven-to-three shift, except on Fridays and Saturdays because I'm really a pet psychic and those are my busiest days. Well, not really a psychic because that would mean communicating with the dead, which I don't do. More like an animal whisperer, really, but that confuses people, and they think I'm going to train their animals, so I just say I'm a psychic."

She didn't stop talking to take a breath but I felt like *I* needed one.

"I have some whopping bills to pay off thanks to marrying a boozer who laid around on my sofa and ran up my credit cards, so I'm working here to get back on my feet."

She stopped her rapid-fire chattiness and gazed upward rotating her hand just below her chin. "I'm getting something . . . A white dog is looking for you. Do you have a white dog?"

Teeny hairs on the back of my neck pricked up. For a moment, I gaped at her in shock. How was that possible? How could she have known? Then I realized that Oma or Casey had probably told her about the dog. Or Shelley or Rose. A dozen people had seen me with her. "She's lost." I handed Zelda a flier. "If you see her, please let me know."

"Of course." She drew her hand in a circle again. "She's trying to find you."

I didn't believe that Zelda could really read animals' minds, but I had to ask, even if I felt stupid doing it. "Can you see where she is?"

"Stairs. She's sniffing around stairs. That's all I'm getting. Not very helpful, is it? Maybe if you had something that belonged to her? A ball or a stuffed toy?"

"I didn't have her long enough to give her any toys."

"Oh!" She tucked in her chin, as though that was the oddest thing she'd ever heard.

I got the feeling she disapproved. "If she comes back, she can have all the toys she wants."

"I'll let her know! And when she comes home, we'll schedule her for a massage. All the dogs love massages. And maybe a nice hike? We have some openings over the next few days. Or you could take her swimming. Does she like to swim?"

"I have no idea. Dog massages?"

She nodded eagerly. "We don't do everything in-house, but I can book anything you like from right here. The masseuse usually comes to the inn, and the acupuncturist will, too."

I thanked her politely. The whole town had turned into a resort for pampered pets! I collected supplies to post fliers, picked up Twinkletoes, and hustled for the main part of the inn.

Twinkletoes purred, soft yet steady. She didn't squirm or try to jump from my arms. Soft as cashmere, her fur brushed my chin. "You'd better adopt Oma if you want to live in the inn. Not that I would blame you. What cat or dog wouldn't want to live in a town that caters to your every whim? My place in Washington is small, and there's no masseuse or acupuncturist or pet psychic, but there's a greenhouse window over the kitchen sink." Why did that window sound so insignificant in comparison? "Assuming I get another job and can pay the mortgage, that is."

If she had a response, unlike Zelda, I couldn't detect it. I scurried into the Dogwood Room, the grand sitting room where guests gathered, and tried not to be too obvious as I looked out the glass wall onto the terrace. Mugs on the table in front of them, Oma and Rose conferred with Mr. Luciano, who tugged at the short sleeve of his casual golf shirt as though he wasn't used to it. He wore his dark hair swept straight back off his broad face. A white bandage covered his injury.

At least a dozen guests relaxed in the gentle fall sunshine at other tables, and Shelley, the waitress at breakfast, still worked, serving everyone. It all seemed peaceful enough for me to dash through the walking area to post fliers.

I set Twinkletoes down. Without a care in the world, she jumped onto a sofa, strolled to a sunbeam, and curled up in a ball for a nap.

Armed with two rolls of tape, thumbtacks, and a sheath of fliers, I walked the quaint streets of Wagtail tacking fliers to telephone poles. The town bustled with tourists and their dogs. An occasional person carried a cat or walked one on a leash. If word of Jerry's demise had swept through Wagtail, the tourists didn't know about it yet.

I returned to the last place I had seen my dog, but it was a long shot that she might be there.

Avoiding the store where the evil woman had pinched her, I strolled the walking area, asking shop owners if I could tape my flier to their windows. Every single one of them promised to spread the word and be on the lookout. Except for the evil one, Wagtail had a remarkably friendly population.

For such a small town, Wagtail offered an amazing array of stores, and most appeared to carry higher-end merchandise.

If it had a cat on it, The Cat's Meow sold it. Everything for feline lovers from cat jewelry, both for cats and their people, to cat lamps, presumably to be used by both cats and their people, and cat handbags far too big for cats to carry but large enough for a cat to ride in.

The residents of Wagtail had embraced their dog and cat friendly theme with gaiety and cleverness. Some of the shop names were a little confusing though. Did Au Bone Pain sell bread for people, bread for dogs, or bones? Bread in the shape of bones?

Dogs played in the grassy middle of the walking zone, catching Frisbees and romping together. Some strolled with their people, tossing only a curious sniff in the direction of other dogs.

Seeing them just deepened my sense of loss. I already thought of her as *my* dog. I'd spent less than twelve hours with her, and she'd become part of my life. I forged ahead with my fliers, hoping against hope that she might be found. The thought of her, lost and alone, maybe injured, hit by a car, or attacked by a coyote was simply unbearable. I had to push those images out of my mind and do everything I could to find her.

After hanging my last flier, I hurried back to the inn to check on Oma. She was at work in her office and looked up when I peeked in on her.

"Liebling, we have a group arriving at four o'clock. Yappy Hour begins at five, and I've arranged dinner with Rose tonight at The Blue Boar. It's a little bit dressy. If you want to borrow something from my closet, feel free."

"Maybe I could help you?"

"Ja? You would do that?" Oma lowered her reading glasses to look at me. "Wonderful! That would be such a big help. I'm slow like a turtle with this ankle injury."

She handed me a ring of keys and a printout on a clipboard. "Please check the rooms on the list to be sure they are ready.

Each room should have a special welcome basket for a cat or a dog, as the case may be. It's all marked on the list. Then double-check with the kitchen to be sure we have their preferred dog or cat food on hand. It should already be there, but I like to be certain nothing slipped though the cracks. And inspect all the bathrooms carefully, please. I'm trying out a new housekeeper."

Truth be told, I was glad to have something to do. It would take my mind off my missing dog and the murders, at least for a while. Besides, poor Oma couldn't hobble through the entire inn doing this. It would take her forever. Clutching the list, I headed past the sitting room. Just as I reached the front door, Dave barreled through it, grabbed me by the elbow, and propelled me past the small dining area through a wide curved archway into the new addition on the other side.

Fourteen

✿ ✿ ✿ ✿

A single guest lounged in a cushy chair before an enormous window wall like the one in the great room.

Dave shot a look of daggers at the poor guest, and tugged me past the fireplace. Bookshelves lined the walls from floor to ceiling, with a few comfortable nooks carved out among them that were full of inviting cushions. A built-in seat in a bay window overlooked the plaza in front of the inn.

"Shouldn't you be dealing with Jerry?" I asked.

His jaw tightened, and pain etched creases in his face. He breathed heavily as though he'd run all the way to the inn. "Yeah, I have to get right back. Tell me exactly where and when you ran into Holmes."

"This is ridiculous," I whispered. "You know Holmes didn't kill him."

Dave's nostrils flared. "Jerry's neighbor saw Holmes running away from Jerry's house this morning. The neighbor didn't think much of it at the time, but then he found Chief wandering around in his backyard. The neighbor took the dog home and left him on Jerry's back porch."

"If Holmes was there at all, I'm sure he had good reason."

Dave glared at me.

"Okay, okay. I ran into Holmes outside of Houndstooth, and we walked over to Jerry's. Simple as that. I don't know exactly what time it was, maybe twenty or thirty minutes before we discovered Jerry's body, and I called the cops."

"Was there anything unusual about him?"

"Like what?"

"Nervous? Sweating? Talking too fast? Not talking at all?"

"Completely normal, I assure you. Look, I know about the conflict between Holmes's family and Jerry. But they're not the kind of people who resolve their problems with violence. Surely you realize that."

Dave locked his eyes on mine. "I would have said that about everyone in this town. But somebody killed Jerry, and very possibly Sven, too." Dave rubbed his face with both of his hands. "I don't know what's going on. I thought I had a handle on it. Seemed logical that the person who killed Sven threw the car he used over the cliff to get rid of the evidence."

That did make sense. A chill shook through me. "You mean I saw Sven's killer out on the road?"

"Hmm? Yeah, maybe." He seemed distracted. "But the attack on Mr. Luciano and now Jerry's death don't fit into that equation at all. If you pick up on anything, you'll let me know, won't you?"

"Dave, I was wondering if Sven's death could be connected to the gold coin he won."

Dave's lips pulled tight. "I thought about that, too. But it hasn't led anywhere. The men involved in that poker game weren't here, and they all appear to have alibis. Besides, he won it fair and square. There wasn't any animosity about it."

"I'll let you know if I hear anything. Right away. I promise."

"Thanks, Holly." Dave took off in a hurry. From the bay window, I watched him race along Wagtail's pedestrian zone. I understood where he was coming from. In a small town, you think you know everyone. But he couldn't afford to make assumptions about any of us. Still, I *knew* he was wrong about Holmes.

The guest across the room looked up from his book. I smiled at him in what I hoped was a reassuring manner, tapped the clipboard, and ventured into a short corridor that led to The Cat's Pajamas wing. I inserted a master key in a door labeled *Purr.*

It opened to a cat paradise. A foot-wide catwalk circled the walls near the ceiling. Stairs and landings offered ease in springing up to it. A tunnel and assorted wider areas provided spaces for lounging.

Sliding doors led to a screened porch. A cat door in the wall allowed access that could be closed to keep the cat inside the room.

I stepped out on the porch and ran my hand over a tree to see if it was real. It was! Very clever. It was installed at a slant, and I couldn't imagine any cat not wanting to climb it. Their inner tigers could come out.

A bird and squirrel feeding station had been erected in a private clearing just outside the porches. The feeders buzzed with activity, providing live theater for cats. I wondered if Twinkletoes knew what she was missing.

I returned to the room. People comforts hadn't been over-looked. Two cozy chairs nestled by the fireplace. The bed had been made with a fluffy feather comforter, and over the head-board, written in a beautiful golden script and framed, *What greater gift than the love of a cat? ~Charles Dickens.*

That reminded me to check the gift basket. Locally crafted cat toys and treats filled a cat bed, which bore the name *Sugar Maple Inn.* A catnip mouse, three cute, trial-sized containers of different cat snacks, and a ball that crackled accompanied the treats—a bottle of Cat's Meow cabernet sauvignon and a chocolate mouse—were undoubtedly meant for the person footing the bill. I peered at the name on the list, Mr. Gary Parson, who would be arriving with Tabushkin.

I tore myself away from the amazing cat room to peer at the bathroom. Spotless. The new housekeeper was doing a great job. A disposable eco-friendly litter box was ready for the lucky feline guest, Tabushkin.

The remaining rooms on the list were located in the main section of the inn. I took the grand staircase up to the second floor.

Oma had renamed all the rooms after dog activities. The

shabby chic white room with a tall four-poster bed, sparkling chandelier, and whitewashed floors had become *Play*. Next door, *Sniff* reflected Oma's European roots, with painted furniture that looked like it belonged in an Alpine bedroom. The adjoining room, *Wag*, featured two beds painted blue and nestled in a cozy nook under a semicircular wood ceiling. I recalled sleeping there one summer and pretending I was a princess.

Like the cat baskets, the dog baskets featured toys and treats made in Wagtail. But the cobalt blue bottle of white wine bore the Our Dog Blue label from a Virginia winery. I sniffed the air. Very subtle lavender. No musty dog odors, but my inferior nose couldn't begin to pick up what a dog could smell. The gleaming hardwood floors left little chance for scents to linger. Not that people would notice anyway, only their dogs, whose powerful olfactory capabilities would make a person a superhero.

I checked off rooms on the clipboard as I visited them. Everything was in order. Only a double-check of the cat and dog food on hand was left to be done.

Heavenly aromas wafted to me when I opened the door to the official kitchen.

A guy wearing a white chef's coat pulled a roast turkey from the oven. I introduced myself to him. "Are we serving dinners at the inn now?"

He laughed. "Only small fare. Goulash, chili, sandwiches, cheese and fruit platters, that sort of thing."

"Then what's all this?"

"Dog and cat food. We use only the best people-grade ingredients." He pointed to pots as he spoke. "Barley, lentils, brown rice, green beans, carrots. We have a whole menu, and we make custom meals for dogs with special needs."

I looked at the chart in my hand. "But I'm supposed to be checking for commercial food."

He gestured toward a large pantry. "A lot of people like to keep their dogs and cats on the food they eat at home. We stock it on request so they don't have to worry about packing it or finding it locally."

I admit that I was a little bit blown away. "Everything is geared toward the pets."

He laughed. "Not everything. We want to indulge our human guests, too."

He took the green beans off the stove, poured off the hot water and blanched them with ice water to prevent them from overcooking.

I ambled into the pantry. Checking my list, I confirmed that every cat and dog food that had been specially requested was indeed on hand.

I waved to the chef and made my way back to the registration desk, pleased to assure Oma that everything was ready.

At four o'clock a line of golf carts trundled up to the registration area. People piled out of them, some with pet carriers, and others with cats and dogs on leashes.

I showed Mr. Gary Parson and his Russian Blue cat, Tabushkin, to their room. From his perch on Mr. Parson's shoulder, Tabushkin took in his surroundings with great interest.

An amiable guy with a head of curly almost-black hair, Mr. Parson had come for a week of rest and relaxation. "I hear they have a cat aviary where Tabushkin can play."

I apologized for my lack of knowledge. "Let me know, okay? That sounds like fun for cats." On my way back to the registration desk, I wondered how much fun it was for the birds that lived there.

Time flew by as we settled the new visitors in their rooms. Each dog guest was issued a Sugar Maple Inn collar with GPS for the duration of the stay.

Oma vanished for a few minutes and returned dressed in an equestrian-motif silk blouse, pearls and a gold chain, and a mid-calf length camel skirt that buttoned down the side.

"You're so chic," I said.

She tapped her watch. "Better hurry. It's almost time for Yappy Hour."

I couldn't match Oma's elegance, but I did twist my hair up with a clip that I found in my purse, and I changed into one of the new dresses. It was pink cotton and very 1960s, with a dipping round neckline, tight bodice, and big skirt. It would have to do.

I trotted down the grand staircase into a cluster of guests and dogs. Oma spied me and waved me out to the porch, where

Rose and Holmes waited for us. It seemed the whole town had turned out for Yappy Hour.

The tables outside of restaurants had filled up, as had our porch, a wonderful vantage point from which to watch the parade of proud people and well-heeled dogs. The smaller dogs and many of those with shorter fur wore coats. And what coats! Embellished with their names, glittering with sequins, elegant with pearls, sparkling with crystals. The dogs didn't seem to care. Hunting breeds happily mingled with uptown dogs. No one was a snob in Wagtail.

"We've started serving drinks, too?" I asked Oma.

"Not at Yappy Hour. That's to get everyone out and mingling at the restaurants. But some people take their drinks and rock on our porch." She winked at me. "No one notices or minds. Kids," I assumed that meant Holmes and me, "there's been a slight change in plans." She draped a deep ruby-red shawl over her shoulders.

Rose patted Gingersnap, Oma's golden retriever. "Would you mind if we skipped Yappy Hour today? We'd like to visit Ellie. She must be reeling from Jerry's death."

"We'll be back to join you for dinner," said Oma, handing me Gingersnap's leash. "Maybe we can talk Ellie into coming."

I glanced at Holmes.

"We'll go with you." He said it fast, as though it was all decided.

"Terrific," said Rose. "You can carry my pimento-cheese tea sandwiches and Liesel's German potato salad."

Did Holmes know that a neighbor had reported seeing him at Jerry's house that morning? How could I ask him about it? Holmes carried the food and I set out with Gingersnap. Her tail wagged like crazy, and she tugged me in all directions as she tried to greet each dog and person who walked by. She kissed everyone within reach. Gingersnap took her job as the Sugar Maple Inn's canine ambassador very seriously. There wasn't a soul she didn't like.

We walked slowly, to accommodate Oma's injury.

As we strolled by the shops, I realized that my fliers about my Jack Russell were missing from many of them. "Where did my fliers go?"

We came to a halt.

"If I didn't know he was dead, I'd be blaming it on Jerry," said Rose. "He never liked fliers around town."

"This is so disappointing. Is there a local newsfeed or website where I can post about my dog?" I asked.

"That's not a bad idea," said Oma. "We have a website about the town, but nothing that shares news or alerts."

We turned and walked along a thoroughly charming tree-lined street.

"Is this where Sven was killed?" asked Holmes.

Fifteen

Oma winced. Holding her head high, she sucked in a deep breath. "The car came from that direction. We were crossing the road right here when it hit him."

"There's something I don't understand," I said. "When I arrived, I had no trouble driving straight to the inn but it sounds as though no cars are allowed."

Holmes nodded. "There are two roads that run parallel to the pedestrian zone, six blocks over on each side. The speed limit is twenty-five miles per hour. Most vehicles, like tour buses, stop at the parking lot outside of town. The person who hit Sven must have turned down this road in the dark, parked, and waited."

"Then it really couldn't have been an accident. No wonder Dave thought it was intentional."

We stood there for a moment in silence. "Well," I said brightly, "I can't wait to see this beauty—Dolce."

Holmes clapped me on the shoulder, and the four of us crossed the street.

"Why aren't there barriers so cars can't drive down these side streets?" I asked.

Rose sighed. "Residents have an exemption to park in their garages, but there's almost no traffic anymore. Besides, no one anticipated anything like this. We thought we could save the cost because they wouldn't be necessary. Most visitors park at the far end and take a Wagtail taxi into town."

Holmes opened the gate and held it for us. The front door of the white bungalow hung open. Inside, people milled about, murmuring respectfully. Holmes opened the screen door without ringing the bell. Chief and a Great Dane greeted us. He had a fawn coat, golden in color, with a dark muzzle. Triangular ears hung down on the sides of his enormous head.

Gingersnap kissed him, while Oma and Rose made a big fuss over all the dogs.

A tall man, whose reddish-blond hair billowed in waves so high above his head that he seemed even larger, nodded at us and said, "Holmes."

Holmes introduced us. "Brewster owns Hair of the Dog, the local watering hole."

I shook his fleshy hand. Freckles dotted ruddy skin on his face and hands. Prominent cheekbones bore a rosy glow that reminded me vaguely of Santa Claus. Flushed and round, they perched over a nicely trimmed mustache and beard that were morphing from strawberry blond to white. His rectangular wire-rimmed glasses only served to enhance the Santa image.

"I'm surprised you could take time off during Yappy Hour," said Holmes.

"Can't stay long, but I felt I had to come over and, you know, pay my respects. It's awful." Brewster licked his upper lip. "Just awful."

"Do they have any leads yet?" asked Holmes.

Brewster snorted. "There's not a person in Wagtail who didn't have a beef with Jerry."

"You did, too?" I hoped I didn't sound too nosy.

He grimaced. "Hair of the Dog has been a bone of contention since it opened. You might say it was a thorn in Jerry's paw. Half the residents call him daily to complain about noisy drunks walking home."

"The other half, the people who frequent the place," said Holmes, "don't want it to move outside of town because there would be car accidents. They love being able to walk home at night."

"I guess that's the kind of thing that happens in every community. There's no good solution." I spied Oma waving at me. "Excuse me. I believe I'm being summoned."

Brewster nodded. "You two come on by for a drink when you ditch the old ladies."

I suspected they wouldn't appreciate being called old ladies, but maybe it wasn't as bad as some things he might have called them. Rose and Oma spoke with a woman whom I would have recognized anywhere as Jerry's mother. They shared the same body structure, the same eyes, though I thought hers were kinder, and while her face was a softer, more feminine version, he had been the spitting image of his mother.

Ellie clasped her hands to her cheeks. "My goodness, Holly! I remember your mother pushing you in a stroller. You favor your father, though. A Miller through and through."

She hugged me, and I said, "I'm so very sorry about Jerry."

She closed her eyes and turned her head away. "If only I hadn't been so awful to him today. I . . . I told him that I had *not* lost my mind and that if he persisted in that nonsense then he needn't bother coming over anymore. And now he won't!"

Oma turned Ellie toward her, and Ellie wept into Oma's shoulder.

How perfectly awful. Losing her son was bad enough, but now she had to live with the knowledge that she hadn't been loving and warm during their last conversation. No one could ever possibly anticipate that. If we tried, there would never be any angry words. And from the sound of it, he *had* been obnoxious about her carelessness leaving the gate open. That was little consolation to her now that he was gone.

I backed away to give her some privacy. She needed the comfort of her friends, Oma and Rose.

Across the room, a woman scrutinized me. She had an angular body and a face with sharp eyes that didn't observe me kindly. She made her way over. Golden bangles jangled on her wrists. She wore giant pearl earrings that stood out against hair set so tightly that it didn't move. She was about the age of my mother, so I guessed that the brassy orange hair wasn't her original color.

"If it isn't Holly Miller." She didn't extend her arms for a hug or a hand to shake. "I'd heard you were in town."

Her voice jogged memories. I had a vague notion of running away from her and not being as fast as Josh and Holmes.

I forced a smile and said, "How nice to see you." Why didn't I have a better memory for names and people? It was too embarrassing. Hoping she might mention her own name, I said nothing more. The ball was in her court.

She tsked at me. "I spent the better part of the afternoon removing your fliers." She lifted her chin as though she thought she was superior. "We don't litter in Wagtail."

"That wasn't littering. Some idiot woman at Putting On the Dog removed my dog's collar and pinched her behind. Who does something like that? Now she's lost. I need those fliers to let people know to be on the lookout for her."

"Well, I never! You're as rude and horrible as your grandmother. I see your mother didn't bother teaching you any social graces."

She turned abruptly and stalked away, holding her head so high that it tilted backward.

Holmes ambled toward me. "What did you do to upset Peaches?"

Now there was a name I recognized. "That's Peaches Clodfelter?" She had certainly changed in appearance, though she had always possessed that haughty demeanor. "Wow. She's aged!"

"Technically, I guess she's Peaches Clodfelter Wiggins now."

"She married Old Man Wiggins?"

"That she did. Her fourth husband. Makes a person wonder what kind of magic she wields over men."

"How do you know all this stuff? I don't remember most of these people."

"I went to school here. Plus, I come back more often because my whole family lives in Wagtail." He paused for a moment, his eyes on the floor. "I've spent quite some time here over the last couple of years because my dad was sick. I flew back and forth from Wagtail to Chicago for a while, then finally took a leave of absence and stuck around here until things settled down. He's fine now, though." Holmes's face brightened, and he smirked. "You need to catch up so you won't keep offending people when you talk about Prissy."

It came to me in a flash. My face burned, and I slapped a hand over my mouth. "The tall woman who pinched my dog—that was Prissy Clodfelter!"

He bobbed his head. "And she's dating Dave."

I wanted to shrink into a little ball, roll across the floor, and fall into a hole. I had been ugly about her to Dave and to her mother.

"It's not surprising that you didn't recognize Prissy. Who'd have thought a kid would change so much? But she's just like her mother—thinks she's Wagtail royalty."

"Now that they're officially Wigginses, it's no wonder that they think that. They could buy and sell just about everyone in this town."

"They complain a lot about being kept on a tight budget, but he set them up in that store, and it couldn't have been cheap."

"But Prissy answered my 911 call."

"Dave got her that job at the headquarters over on Snowball. She only works there on weekends."

Rose edged up to us. "We're shooing everyone out for a bit. Ellie needs some rest."

Oma and Rose managed to empty the house in minutes.

Holmes and I stepped outside with Gingersnap and waited for them. Across the street, a sturdy fellow raked grass clippings.

Holmes waved at him. "Remember Tiny Goodwin?"

He might have been Tiny once, but he'd caught up. "He played football, right?"

"Star of the team. He was a celebrated guy around here in those days."

We crossed the street. "I guess you heard about Jerry," said Holmes.

Tiny gripped his rake with both hands. "Aw, man, it's terrible. I'll go 'round and pay my respects to his mom tomorrow."

His eyes squeezed to slits. "Holly Miller? I heard you were in town."

"Hi, Tiny. Just visiting my grandmother. I hear you've got a tree house that's upsetting Aunt Birdie."

He snorted. "I built it for my kids. My wife has custody so I don't see 'em much. I knew they'd get a kick out of it."

"The fancy one with blue doors and the balcony with cutout pickets that look like cat silhouettes?" asked Holmes.

"That's the one. I think it came out right pretty. But you know Birdie. She says it's too close to her property because we're not s'posed to build anything within fifteen feet of the neighbor's lot. The base of the tree is seventeen feet from her line, but up high, she says the tree house encroaches in the fifteen-foot zone. Now, you tell me–how'd she get up there to measure it in the air? It's not on her property no matter what she says."

He glanced at the house behind him. "I better get busy before Miss Foyle catches me taking a breather. You two stop in at Hair of the Dog while you're here, and we'll catch up." He pointed at Holmes. "You owe me a basketball rematch. I'll get you this time."

Oma and Rose joined us, and after a polite exchange of greetings, we finally walked to The Blue Boar.

Oma walked up the stairs slowly, with Holmes's help. I hung back with Gingersnap so she wouldn't trip Oma. My phone played the jingling notes that always made me think of a fairy waving her wand so that magical sparkles appear. A text! It had to be about my dog.

Sixteen

❊ ❊ ❊ ❊ ❊

Oma turned with alarming speed. "Get rid of that thing," she hissed.

Rose pointed at a sign mounted near the top of the stairs. *Cell Free Zone.*

From their horrified expressions, I gathered that didn't mean it was a free Wi-Fi zone. The Blue Boar appeared to be an upscale restaurant. I didn't blame them for banning cell phones. It would be nice to dine without ringtones pealing, people talking on their phones, or texting. It was sort of old-fashioned, but it appealed to me.

"I'll just check to be sure it's not about my dog." Calling to Gingersnap, I hurried away with her so I wouldn't offend anyone.

I swept the phone open. The little message bubble contained the cryptic words, *marE me?*

It took a second for me to sound it out and realize it meant *marry me?* I looked up at the restaurant seeking out Holmes. They had already been seated on the deck. He laughed at something Oma said.

Ohhh, that was a very bad sign. I'd looked for Holmes

before I gave Ben a single thought. I checked the message again. Of course it was from Ben.

Had he lost his mind? Who would say yes to a proposal like that? We weren't übercool kids. This was . . . well, positively offensive. He didn't have to get down on one knee, but it would be nice if he had given it a little bit of consideration. He'd shown more enthusiasm about picking a movie to watch.

It wasn't as though I had never considered marrying Ben. He was a solid, steady man. Great job, great prospects. We would have a good life together.

Rose's silly questions from the morning floated back to me. Did he make me laugh? Did he make my toes tingle? Honestly! What was wrong with me? Real life wasn't like those fairy tales. Fireworks didn't shoot off. Real people didn't quiver when their one and only soul mates drew near.

But even if I was being completely sensible—a texted proposal? With a *humph* loud enough to worry Gingersnap, I turned off my phone and marched up the stairs to join Oma, Rose, and Holmes for dinner.

A dashing gentleman with a broad smile and a heavy dose of salt in his hair held out his arms to Oma and kissed her on both cheeks. "Liesel, I have only just heard about your terrible accident. You should have called me. Should I bring a footrest for you?" He snapped his fingers in the air, and like magic, a footrest appeared.

"I'm fine, Thomas." She pronounced his name *Tow-mas*, with emphasis on the first syllable.

He clasped her hand in both of his. "I make you a special dinner tonight."

Oma introduced me.

I also received the hug and double cheek kisses. "I imagine Liesel looking just like you when she was young. I am so happy you have returned to Wagtail—"

Unless I was mistaken, either Rose or Oma kicked him under the table at that point.

He clapped his hands together. "Special dessert to celebrate? You like chocolate? Of course you do. Everyone does."

He scooted off, and a waiter descended upon us for drink orders. I stayed with plain old iced tea, not the kind with alcohol. After the long drive last night and my early morning, liquor would surely put me to sleep. Besides, that little kick had served as notice that something was definitely afoot. Tomorrow I would have to confront Oma. She had brought me here for a reason. It was time she told me what.

"I believe Thomas might be sweet on you, Oma." I watched her carefully. Her cheeks had flushed, she'd taken care with her appearance, and except for the twisted ankle, she didn't appear to be in any pain. Whatever was going on, I hoped it wasn't her health.

"Don't be silly."

But the twinkle in Rose's eye and the slight nod of her head told me otherwise.

The waiter arrived and set a small white plate before each of us. Thomas had a flare for presentation. Two scallops gently seared until they bore light caramel-colored tops had been drizzled with a golden sauce and accented with a tiny basil leaf. The robust scent of garlic wafted up to me.

"Thomas is so thoughtful," said Oma. "He knows this is my favorite appetizer."

For a moment, we ate in silence, savoring the rich flavors. I thought I detected a hint of lemon.

"Poor Ellie," said Rose. "I can't imagine losing a child." Her hand slid over to rest on top of Holmes's hand. "Or a grandchild. It would be unbearable."

"Our Dave has a big problem on his hands. There wasn't anyone in town who didn't run up against Jerry sometime," said Oma.

"Why didn't you kick him out of office and elect someone else?" I asked.

The waiter removed our empty scallop dishes and replaced them with a salad. Apples and walnuts rested on a bed of red cabbage. I dug in right away. The vinaigrette had been sweetened with honey.

Oma sipped her wine. "It's complicated. Wagtail would never have been such a success if it weren't for Jerry. He worked hard at obtaining the grants that enabled us to spruce up the town and improve the pedestrian zone. You have to be tough when everyone in town wants something that will be solely to his or her own benefit."

"He might be responsible for our economic success but the man was a menace. He treated us all with pompous disdain, like we were servants." Rose broke a piece off a crusty artisanal roll and slathered it with creamy butter.

"Oma, did *you* have a conflict with Jerry?" I asked.

Rose nearly choked on her bread. "Do you know anyone more outspoken than Liesel? She stood up for everyone in the community."

"Come now, Rose. Jerry and I agreed on many things, too. It won't be easy to find a replacement for him. You have to have a thick skin to be in that sort of position."

Thomas reappeared with a waiter in tow who set plates before us.

"This is rosemary and Parmesan-encrusted lamb with my special harvest mushrooms in wine sauce, and mashed potatoes." He patted Oma's upper arm. "Enjoy, my friends."

The waiter set a small dish in front of Gingersnap, who didn't wait for the rest of us to start eating. It appeared that she had also been served lamb and mashed potatoes, but instead of mushrooms in wine, she scarfed cubed sweet potatoes.

"Do I detect an accent when Thomas speaks?" I asked.

"He grew up in Austria and moved to the States as a young man," said Oma. "But he returned to Switzerland for culinary training."

Rose murmured with delight. "Mmm. Fantastic, as always." She whispered, "I think the accent is a bit of an affectation, but he's an incredible chef. He could work at any five-star restaurant. We're lucky to have him here in Wagtail."

"Holly, did you get news about your dog?" asked Holmes.

"No, I wish I had. It was a marriage proposal."

Oma choked.

Rose dropped her fork.

Holmes raised his eyebrows. "In a text?"

I nodded in the affirmative. "Oma, are you okay?"

She waved a hand in the air and drank water, hacking. "From the Ben?"

She could not have asked with more distaste. I hated it when she called him *the Ben*, like he was an object.

"Why, why . . . Holmes! Don't you ever propose that way!" Rose shook her finger at him.

"Don't think that's likely, Grandma. I'm already engaged." Holmes suppressed an amused smile. "Is Ben a techie type?"

"Not techie enough for me to think it was cute or clever. He didn't even spell it out."

Oma fixed me in her gaze. "Have you been talking about marriage?"

"Not really. I suppose there's been an undercurrent of thought there. Sometimes we mention things in the future, and the assumption is that we'll be together."

After a moment of rather painful silence, everyone began to eat again, except for Gingersnap, who had finished her dinner and decided that I was the most likely to part with some of my lamb. She focused those big brown eyes on me, and I didn't need pet psychic Zelda to interpret what Gingersnap was thinking.

The conversation veered to my missing dog and the notion of a community website for local announcements and news. The existing Wagtail website only offered information of interest to visitors and those planning vacations.

Holmes and Rose were enthralled with the idea, and before I knew it, we had polished off heavenly, creamy, decadent chocolate mousse. Gingersnap didn't have to feel left out. The waiter brought her a special doggy dessert made with pumpkin.

The grandmothers began to eye empty rocking chairs on the inn porch.

"Hair of the Dog?" asked Holmes.

"Sure, but I'm pretty beat. I might not stay long."

With our grandmothers comfortably ensconced on the porch, and Gingersnap back to kissing all the Sugar Maple Inn guests, Holmes and I strolled down to Hair of the Dog. We passed Jerry's house on the way. A yellow police tape hung across the front door.

"Is it just me, or does it seem like it was a long time ago that we found Jerry's body?" asked Holmes.

"So much has happened since I arrived that it feels like time is flying by."

The pub turned out to be on the same street, but at the very end, next to the road that cars could use. The front yard had been turned into a sprawling patio with tables and umbrellas. It was packed with people and their dogs.

"Where did all these people come from?"

"You'd be surprised how many houses are tucked away in the woods around here. There's a lot of new construction going on. Plus—" he pointed across the street "—there are new developments. Everyone calls that one Hobbitville."

Someone had built cute cottages reminiscent of hobbit houses with eyebrow arches over doors, round windows, and little peaked roofs. They were set back off the road a good distance. But not too far to comfortably walk to Hair of the Dog or the pedestrian mall.

Hair of the Dog was located in a bungalow-style house that had been painted cream. Brown beams had been added to give it a quaint and inviting Tudor look reminiscent of English and Irish pubs. Huge windows fronted the street. Lights glowed with warmth inside, reminding me that the days had already grown shorter.

Men greeted Holmes heartily when we entered. The shadows of flames from a large fireplace flickered across the burnished red fur of an Irish setter, who raised his head to observe us. We snagged a table not too far from the bar. The setter strolled over to check us out, carrying a sock in his mouth.

Holmes strode up to the bar to place our order while I played tug with the Irish setter and took in my surroundings. Brewster leaned against the bar listening to a group of animated guys who clustered before him. Tiny sat on a bar stool and engaged Holmes.

And everywhere, under barstools and next to tables, dogs lounged near their people.

"You must be new to Wagtail."

I changed my focus to a man who had approached our table. He wore snug-fitting jeans with a navy turtleneck and a blue plaid flannel shirt. All very tidy and tucked in. His mustache reminded me of Tom Selleck's, lush and full but neatly trimmed.

His hair had receded just enough to give him a prominent forehead, but he made a very good impression. This was a man who was in control. I bet his house and car sparkled.

"May I?" He gestured to a chair.

"Sure." What else could I say? Besides Holmes would be back any minute.

He sat down, and crossed an ankle over his knee, evidently comfortable with himself. "Are you staying at the inn?"

"As a matter of fact, I am."

"Mmm." He handed me a business card. "Philip."

"Holly." I shook his hand.

"What do you think of Wagtail?" He glanced around the table. "No dog?"

"She's lost," I said.

"Oh. Those must be your fliers around town. I'll be on the lookout for her."

"Thanks."

"You came in with Holmes, but I don't think I'm going out on a limb here—you're not his fiancé?"

"Right again. We're just friends."

"You're from Chicago?"

"Washington, D.C. You sound like you're from—North Carolina?"

"Good ear!" His hand rested on the table and it curled into a ball, squeezing his thumb. "It was my wife's dream to have a bed-and-breakfast. It was all she talked about. She pored over photos, planned breakfast menus . . ." He bowed his head. "It was an obsession. We went skiing over at Snowball, and the B and B owner told us about Wagtail. We bought a B and B here, and all was well until my wife realized that she liked *staying* at B and Bs better than she liked having to work at them. Now I'm single again, with two B and Bs."

"That's terrible. What's your ex-wife doing now?"

"She's a travel writer." He glanced at the ceiling, sighed, and shook his head. "You should stay at my place on your next visit."

"You didn't go with her." I observed.

"I made that mistake once. How could I know if she would be any happier with the next thing? I didn't want to tear up roots and start over again. I've done pretty well for myself, and I'm not done yet. Being a hotelier suits me. One of these days, I'll own a big place like Old Lady Miller." He flashed a coy look at me. "Would you like to have dinner with me tomorrow night?"

I hadn't seen that coming. "That sounds really nice, but I'm afraid I'm seeing someone."

He reached for my left hand. "No ring. Maybe there's still hope for me?"

I disengaged my hand as politely as I knew how. "If the situation changes, I'll let you know."

Holmes brought over an Irish coffee for me. Fluffy cream filled the top of the slender glass mug. He plunked down an amber draft beer for himself.

Tiny ambled over with a bottle of beer in hand.

Perfunctory greetings flew around the table.

Holmes pointed a thumb over his shoulder. "All anybody can talk about is Jerry and Sven. Did you know Sven, Philip?"

Philip ran a hand down his mustache. "Great guy. I took some skiing lessons from him. He used to hang here at Hair of the Dog in the summertime on his days off. Tragic, just tragic. Did you meet him?" He looked at me when he asked.

"No. I didn't get to town until after his death."

"Holly saw his killer when she drove up the mountain," said Holmes.

Philip and Tiny stared at me like I had grown an extra nose.

"It wasn't like—"

"You? You're the one who saw the ghost?" asked Tiny.

"No! It wasn't a ghost. Why does everyone think it was a ghost?"

Philip made a funny face that I couldn't quite read. "That's what everyone is saying, but a person must have pushed the car off the cliff."

Tiny leaned toward me. "You don't have to be embarrassed. I've seen that ghost out on the highway myself."

Seventeen

❁ ❁ ❁ ❁ ❁

"It wasn't a ghost!" For heaven's sake, what was wrong with these people? It was one thing to tell a fun ghost story, but they were adults. "I'm the one who was there. Come on, you guys don't believe in ghosts, do you?"

Silence. Once again I'd put my foot in my mouth and chomped down hard.

Philip flicked a finger on the table. "I didn't believe in them until I moved to Wagtail." He leaned in toward us and whispered, "There's one in Brewster's house. I've seen her at night in the tiny window upstairs."

Tiny nodded vigorously. "Wagtail is loaded with them. You should know that, Holly."

"Come on! You're all big boys. You can't be serious. I never believed in ghosts." I looked to Holmes for help.

"Haven't you ever experienced something that couldn't be explained?" he asked.

He was on their side! *Oh no. Not Holmes!* "Everything has a rational explanation," I said calmly.

The three of them smiled like Mona Lisa. Like they thought

they knew something I didn't. I sipped my Irish coffee, tasted the cream, and felt the warmth as it went down.

Philip looked at Tiny and asked, "So what's the scuttlebutt on Jerry's killer? Do the cops have any leads?"

Tiny slugged back his beer and wiped his mouth with his wrist. "Not that I know about."

"Really? You're usually on top of local gossip," said Philip.

"I get around and keep an ear to the ground." Tiny grinned, evidently pleased to be acknowledged as an expert on local matters. "Ole Jerry liked to act above his raisin' and pretend he was better'n the rest of us. There's more'n one person had an axe to grind with him."

"How about Sven?" I asked.

Tiny clutched his beer bottle between his fleshy hands. "They're sayin' it was somebody from Snowball. Probably kids that got drunk."

That didn't seem right. Kids who got drunk, killed someone, and then threw the car off the mountain? Now that I considered it, maybe it did make sense. They probably panicked. Was it a kid that I saw that night? I thought better of mentioning it again, given their belief that it had been a ghost.

Philip raised an eyebrow. "I heard from a very reliable source that Old Lady Miller knows who the killer is. They're keeping it quiet so the killer won't find out."

I nearly blurted out that Oma most certainly did not know the identity of the killer but stopped myself and drank my Irish coffee. Was that why she had been acting so odd? Did she know who killed Sven?

"Gentlemen, I hate to break up this party, but I rolled into town pretty late last night." I dug some bills out of my purse and shoved them toward Holmes. "If any of you see my little white dog, you'll call me at the inn?"

They assured me they would. I rose to leave, and Holmes stood up as well.

"I'll walk you back."

I debated briefly. I was in the pedestrian zone, and it wasn't terribly late, so there should be plenty of people milling around. "You stay and have a good time. I'll be fine."

He tilted his head. "With everything that has happened—"

Tiny looked up at us. "She'll be okay. Ain't nobody got a beef with her."

I didn't think anyone had issues with Sven, either. Nevertheless, I pulled out my cell phone and said, "No problem. I can call for help in a snap."

That set the three of them into hysterics.

"What did I miss?" I asked.

Philip grinned. "Cell phones get very spotty reception up here in the mountains. There's only one carrier that works with any regularity. It drives my guests crazy. Their cell phones never receive a signal inside my B and Bs. But my cell phone is like a beacon in the tower room of my house. I get five bars every time."

"I guess I have the right carrier then. I called 911 last night out on the road," I said smugly.

"A lucky break. Sometimes when I can't get a signal, I walk twenty feet away, and suddenly my cell phone works fine. You'll do best close to some of the cafés that offer free Wi-Fi."

"With that reassuring news, I bid you all a good night." I slid the phone into my purse and left.

The outdoor tables still teemed with people having a great time. The walk became darker as I headed toward the main part of the car-free zone, but I didn't feel in the least bit afraid. Lights shone in the windows of lovely homes, and I encountered several people out walking their dogs.

I turned onto the shopping area, surprised to find that it still buzzed with business. Stores were open and chatter came from restaurants.

The night had grown too chilly for my sleeveless dress, though. I hurried back to the inn, gorgeous and romantic at the end of the plaza, its lights glowing a warm welcome.

Twinkletoes sat on the front stairs of the porch. She mewed and mewed like she was crying and ran to me.

I swept her up and nuzzled her. But instead of purring, she fidgeted and mewed complaints.

When I set her on the ground, she circled my ankles, winding in and out, making it nearly impossible to walk.

"What is with you?" I lifted her again and trotted up the steps.

When I opened the front door, she leaped from my arms and hissed at the man sitting on the grand staircase. She danced backward like a Halloween cat, then turned and ran so fast she was gone in the blink of an eye.

"Crazy cat," said Dave.

He looked worse than ever. He blinked at me wearily as though he could barely keep his eyes open.

"You need some sleep."

"I'd like some sleep. If you'd come clean and give me some answers, maybe I could go home to bed."

"Aha. So whatever brought you here is my fault?"

"Who is Ben Hathaway?"

Ben? He couldn't have startled me more. "My boyfriend."

"Uh-huh." He consulted his notebook. "And he just happens to work for Mortie Foster's law firm. Is that right?"

"Yes." I wasn't following him at all.

Dave rested his elbows on his knees, letting his hands hang down between his legs. He stared at me as though he was annoyed.

"Am I supposed to think it's only coincidence that the car you pushed over the cliff belonged to one Mortie Foster?"

"Mortie? Are you kidding?" I leaned against the banister and tried to piece together any likely scenario but had no success. How could it have been Mortie's car?

His tricky little mention of me pushing the car over the mountainside hadn't escaped me though.

"In the first place, I didn't push anything over the cliff. And in the second place, how would I know anything about that car at all? I never saw it. All I saw were flames."

I glared at him, irritated by the very notion that I might have staged the car situation myself. "And what does Ben have to do with any of this?"

"Good question. Thank you. That's what I'd like to know." Dave snorted a derisive little laugh. "Most people drive their own cars to Wagtail, yet you are in possession of Ben Hathaway's car. I presume you know Mortie Foster?"

"We've met. And you know perfectly well that I left so fast that I didn't even bring a change of clothes with me." I whispered so Oma wouldn't overhear if she happened to be somewhere close by. "I thought Oma was dying."

Dave hung on like a dog on a meaty bone. "That car was stolen a few weeks ago. So I've got a stolen hybrid SUV that belonged to your boyfriend's boss and mysteriously turned up in a blaze on the very night that you arrived in *your boyfriend's* car."

I shrugged. "So?"

"So? Are you kidding me? There has to be a connection to you."

"Oh, gosh, you're right. You figured it out. I stole the car and hid it, then returned to push it over the cliff."

Dave shot a look of daggers at me.

"How do you know all about Ben, anyway?"

"I'm a cop. Not that many people around here respect that. I go where leads take me, Holly. I don't much like that they keep bringing me back to you."

Our conversation came to an abrupt halt. Upstairs, something knocked lightly. *Thud-dump. Thud-dump.* It grew closer. *Thud-dump. Thud-dump. Thud-dump.*

Dave sprang to a standing position and rushed next to me. "What the devil is that?"

Eighteen

❖ ❖ ❖ ❖ ❖

Thud-dump. Thud-dump.

"It's coming from up there," Dave said.

We craned our necks to look upward but nothing seemed amiss.

We backed away from the stairs, and Dave actually moved a shoulder in front of me as though he meant to protect me. I couldn't help feeling a teensy bit satisfied. If he really thought I was guilty of something, he wouldn't have tried to be protective.

And suddenly it appeared.

Twinkletoes jumped down one stair as a time. She carried a puffy cat toy in her mouth that was attached to a stick that dragged behind her. She made the *thud* noise on each step and the stick followed with *dump* as it hit the step.

"What's she doing?" asked Dave.

"I have no idea." She reached the main floor and walked off, her head held very high to drag the stick between her legs.

We both laughed, breaking the somber mood.

"Look, Dave, I'd be happy to help you in any way that I can. But I didn't have anything to do with the weird stuff that's going on. Not that it's my place, but wouldn't it be more important to figure out who killed Jerry and Sven anyway? Is it true that you think Sven was killed by some kids from Snowball?"

"Where'd you hear that?"

"Hair of the Dog."

"Figures. Don't believe everything you hear." He rubbed his head with both hands and yawned. "Mortie's car has to be the car that killed Sven. It defies logic that it would have gone over the cliff the same night as Sven's death by coincidence. If I can figure out who stole the car, I'll have Sven's killer. We're not going to get much evidence off that car. It's a burned-out hulk. You sure you don't remember anything about the guy you saw?"

He believed me now? "On TV they get all kinds of evidence from burned vehicles."

"You're kidding me, right?"

"What do you call those people—crime scene investigators? Haven't they been here?"

"I call that fiction. We don't have CSIs. That's only in big cities."

"So who investigates?"

"I do."

"Who takes the pictures?"

"Me."

"Who secures the crime scene?"

"Again—me. I call the guys over on Snowball for help when I need it, but it all boils down to me. I'm responsible for Wagtail."

"You collected evidence, right?"

"Not that there was much to collect. More at the scene of Jerry's murder."

"He was fleeing someone, wasn't he?" The image of his outstretched hand had burned itself onto my brain.

Dave's mouth bunched up. "I really can't talk about it."

"Your first murder investigation, I guess?"

"I hope these two are my last." He yawned again.

"Maybe you should head on home and get some sleep. You look exhausted."

The thought of my comfy bed upstairs lured me, and I hadn't been under the stress of solving two murders.

We said good night, and he departed through the front door. To my right, guests still lounged and chatted in the sitting room. Even though I was exhausted, I churned up the two flights of stairs in the hope that Twinkletoes would notice and come with me.

She didn't.

I unlocked my room, thinking sadly of the dog I had lost. I might never see her again. Was she cold? Afraid? Was she huddling next to another gas station, hoping someone would come along with food? Had—I could hardly bear to think it—had someone shot her?

Voices murmured inside my suite. "Hello? Is someone here?"

Canned laughter cued me in. A TV was on in the sitting room. Twinkletoes lounged comfortably in the middle of a comfy chair watching TV, her odd toy next to her.

"How did you get in here?" I asked. How did you turn on the TV? I gazed around for the remote control. It lay on the coffee table. She must have jumped up and landed on it.

I changed into the Sugar Maple Inn T-shirt, which fell to mid-thigh, and located a pen and a pad of paper. Taking a cue from Twinkletoes, I settled in the other chair. I jotted down the names of the people of Wagtail and their connections to each other. Although I studied it with weary eyes, I couldn't see a connection. I was an outsider, who didn't know the currents that existed beneath the obvious.

Pondering the locals and their motives, I headed for bed. The covers had been turned back, and a chocolate rested on the pillow. Twinkletoes must have slipped in when the bed was turned down.

I picked up the chocolate and discovered that it wasn't chocolate at all. It was a cookie that could be shared with a dog. I set it on the nightstand. Maybe if my dog came back . . . "Did you snarf a kitty treat that was left on the pillow?"

Green-gold eyes observed me, round and innocent. But then she licked the corner of her mouth, which told the whole story.

I slid under the comforter. Twinkletoes walked around me

a few times, jumping over my legs as though she wasn't quite sure what to do. She finally settled about a foot from my head, and I fell asleep to the soothing sound of purring.

At six-thirty in the morning, I woke to the phone ringing. A man's voice apologized for calling so early. "This is Eric Dombrowski, the pharmacist. I think I saw your dog this morning on my way to work."

I sat bolt upright. "Was she okay? Where was she?"

"Out near the zip line. She was carrying a dead animal in her mouth."

Eww. Poor baby. "Thanks, Eric. I'll get right out there."

I hung up and jumped out of bed. I swapped my T-shirt for a fresh cotton top and pulled on jeans. Moving as fast as possible, I jammed my feet into the sandals, grabbed my purse, and glanced to be sure Twinkletoes had dry food in her bowl. She did. My haste must have irritated her. She strolled into the kitchen and stretched. This time, we hurried down the grand staircase together.

Casey still manned the reception area.

I scooted behind the desk to grab a collar and a leash. Helping myself to a handful of dog treats, I asked, "Where's the zip line?"

He pulled a little map of Wagtail from under the desk and drew a circle on it. "That's where Eric saw your dog? Why don't you take one of the inn's golf carts? That will be faster."

"Thanks!"

He rushed outside with me and pointed to a cute red cart. "I like that one."

He showed me how to operate it.

"It's so quiet. I can barely hear the engine."

Casey grinned. "Cool, huh? They're electric. One of these days I'm gonna sneak up on some of my friends and spook them."

I consulted the map and tore down the road at a whopping ten miles per hour. Minutes later I spotted Bird Dog Zip Adventures.

They were closed up tight.

I cruised by slowly, on the lookout for a flash of white. If the pharmacist had seen her on his way to work, it must have been from the street. I turned around, puttered back, and parked.

I whistled and called out words I hoped she might know, like *cookie* and *treat*. Birds twittered in the trees.

Although I knew I was technically trespassing, I climbed over the gate at the ticket booth and trotted up the stairs to the launching area, panting by the time I reached the top.

The morning sun kissed the treetops, and the view down the mountain was nothing short of amazing. A light smattering of yellows and oranges heralded the coming of autumn. In spite of the peaceful quiet and stunning views, my heart sank. A dog, even a white one, would be lost under the canopy of the trees.

And then, like a miracle, she appeared below me, in a trail beneath the zip line. She carried something in her mouth.

"Cookie! Cookie!" I called, hoping she remembered what that meant.

A gunshot rang out. I heard myself scream, "No!"

Nineteen

❀ ❀ ❀

Like an apparition, my dog vanished.

I shouted, "Don't shoot, don't shoot! Cookie! Cookie!" As I scrambled down the tower praying she hadn't been hit, I yelled the words over and over.

At the bottom, I bounded down the slope to the spot where I'd seen her.

Crouching, I spoke softly, hoping she would be brave enough to come to me.

A couple of yards away, the base of a large green fern wavered. I held my breath. Was she inching toward me?

"She's gone."

I looked up. A tall man with a weather-beaten face gazed at me. Wrinkles etched deep into his bronzed skin. Round glasses rested on the bridge of his nose.

I rose to my feet and staggered back a step. "What do you mean *gone*?" Not dead. She couldn't be! I didn't see her anywhere.

"I assume she's your dog, or you wouldn't be tromping around and shouting like a bonehead so early in the morning. You should know she can run like the wind." He smiled and gazed away as though remembering it. "I don't think her feet touch the ground. I never saw a dog move like that."

"Are you the one doing the shooting?"

He raised his hand to show me that he carried a gnarled walking stick. "I don't kill God's creatures." His eyebrow twitched up. "Not anymore."

"Is hunting allowed here? So close to the zip line?"

"No. It's not. Somebody has been tracking her. I don't know what she did, but you better find her and take her home before she's shot."

I gazed around. "Tracking her? Like hunting her? Why would anyone do that?" The blood in my temples pounded. "Do you know which direction—" he had disappeared as fast as she had "—she went?"

No wonder everybody around here believed in ghosts. What was wrong with people? Shooting dogs and disappearing in the woods? What was that old guy doing out here anyway?

I scanned the base of the trees again. If she ran from the sound of gunfire, she was probably headed back toward town. With that thought in mind, I began the ascent to the tower.

And stopped within two feet. It had been simple enough to clamber down. Viewed from the other direction, the mountain posed a vertical challenge that might as well have been Kilimanjaro. I found myself leaning forward and climbing. Bracing myself with my hands, occasionally grasping briars, tree limbs, and even weeds for support.

At the top, I had to stop to catch my breath. I might not be superstitious like my grandmother, but this day wasn't starting well at all.

Relieved to be back in the golf cart, I dusted off my jeans. My hands bled from grabbing rough plants. I puttered slowly in the direction of Wagtail's pedestrian zone, watching the underbelly of the dense forest for any sign of the dog.

Would she return to the heart of Wagtail? I turned left into the residential area of Wagtail on the lookout for her as the town came to life. Bird feeders were being filled. An occasional whiff of coffee brewing or frying bacon floated my way. Bathrobe-clad residents stepped out to collect their newspapers from their stoops. Dogs were being walked everywhere I looked.

I recognized the Great Dane, Dolce, and Jerry's basset hound, Chief, sitting together on the porch of Ellie's house. Her curtains remained drawn, though. Unlike other homes, the dogs were the only sign of normalcy.

At the end of the street, where it joined the shopping area, I turned the golf cart around, and finally understood why Dave thought Sven's death couldn't have been an accident.

There really wasn't a good reason to drive down this road unless you had business there. I stopped the cart and surveyed my surroundings. To my left, a large white Italianate home with fancy windows and an ornate cupola dominated the street. An equally ornate sign in the front yard identified it as the *1864 Inn*. I fumbled in my purse for the business card Philip had given me the night before. Indeed, the 1864 Inn was one of his bed-and-breakfasts. Considerably smaller, a beige cape cod next door bore a plaque with the name *Cheshire Cottage*. Light-blue shutters and dormer windows on the second floor added to the cozy appearance.

On the opposite side of the street, I recognized Rose's house. It hadn't changed much. Colorful blooms spilled over a white picket fence. I had played in the rose-covered archway with seats on either side at the gate. Worn slate shingles on the steep roof of the two-story house reminded me of quaint homes in English villages.

Anyone who lived on this end of the street could have parked and waited for Sven without being noticed. I rubbed my forehead. Who would do such a thing? Certainly not Rose! Never!

I barely knew Philip, but it seemed like someone that tidy would have chosen a different method if he intended to murder someone. Hitting a person with a car was bound to be a messy proposition.

Besides, wouldn't it make sense to murder someone as far away from your own home as possible? More likely it had been someone from the other side of town. Or an outsider.

Ellie's house, up the street, was hardly visible because of the angle. Old-fashioned streetlights added to Wagtail's charm, but in the thick fog, I doubted that they had cast a broad beam. Whoever sat here, exactly where I was now, had expected Sven and gunned the car at him when he stepped into the street. Even easier to do in a hybrid SUV with almost no engine noise. In the dark, with the lights off, he wouldn't have seen it advance on him.

Oma had already deduced that the killer had called the inn about Dolce running loose. He knew that would bring Sven to the street.

Or would it? Dolce wasn't Sven's dog. She belonged to Oma and Ellie. Shivers shuttled down my arms. Wouldn't that phone call have been directed to Oma, as Dolce's co-owner? Or had the person asked for Sven?

I had to talk to Oma right away and find out more about the phone call. My heart pounded at the thought that she might have been the intended victim.

I rubbed my face with both hands. Maybe I was wrong. I hoped my reasoning missed the mark. For all I knew, Sven might have made a pass at the wrong woman, and an irate boyfriend with a snootful had done him in.

But that didn't prevent me from heading back to the inn as fast as the golf cart would take me. I pulled into the parking spot and ran into the reception area.

Zelda's eyes widened when she saw me. "She's here."

The dog? Had she found her way back to the inn? "Where?"

"They're all having breakfast."

"Thanks."

"Holly? Don't hit her. Keep your cool."

"Hit her? I would never do that."

"Really? I'd be awfully tempted."

I ran up the stairs with Zelda at my heels.

But when I reached the dining area, I stopped cold.

Twenty

❀ ❀ ❀ ❀

Ben and Kim sat at a table with Oma. What were they doing here? *The text*. He'd come to propose in person! But why did he bring Kim?

Ben motioned me over to the table.

I scanned the floor. No sign of the dog. Turning to Zelda, I asked, "Where's the dog? You said she was here."

"Oh, honey! I'm so sorry. I meant," she lowered her tone, "*her*." Kim. She'd meant Kim.

Ben rose to greet me. "You look like you've been crawling through the woods." He grazed my cheek with a kiss, reached up, and tugged a twig out of my hair.

I had to admit that Kim couldn't have looked more beautiful. Beaming, you might say. Had I been too quick to trust Ben with her?

I said good morning to everyone, painfully aware of my appearance. "If you'll excuse me for a moment, I'll run upstairs and wash up."

"Is that blood on your face?" asked Kim.

I'd forgotten about the blood on my hands. I must have touched my face. "Probably."

Zelda fell in step with me as I hurried toward the main staircase. "I'm so sorry. But there's someone better out there for you. I'm sure of it."

I paused. "What are you talking about?"

Her eyes opened wide. "Oh, honey, they've been . . . together."

It wasn't as though the thought hadn't crossed my mind. Nevertheless, I wasn't sure I was ready to concede that anything had happened between them. "You read people's minds, too?"

She fidgeted with a button on her blouse. "Not usually. But I'm sensitive enough to pick up on some things."

She seemed so sad that I blurted, "They used to date."

"Oh! I'm not usually that far off. Still, I'd watch out for her."

I trudged up the stairs. Zelda had to be wrong. He would never have texted a proposal, awful as that was, if he had gotten involved with Kim again. When I reached my suite, the door stood open, a cleaning cart parked outside the doorway. I stepped around it, and a petite woman with a jet-black ponytail and intelligent dark eyes jerked upright from dusting the coffee table.

She held up a finger over her lips in a sign to be quiet and pointed toward the terrace.

I tiptoed over. Had she brought her baby to work?

And there, on a chaise longue, upside down, all four feet in the air, twitching as though she was running, was my dog. I didn't care if I woke her. Laughing, I swept her up in my arms.

"Don't ever do that again! Do you know how worried I've been?"

She licked the tip of my nose and proceeded to wash my chin. When I lowered her to the ground, she stood on her hind legs and placed her paws on my thighs. I bent over, and she buried her head into me, her tail wagging like crazy.

I pulled the inn collar out of my pocket and fastened it onto her. "No one takes this off except for me. Okay?"

The cleaning woman had left when we went inside.

The dog trotted alongside me to the bedroom and never let me out of her sight. Not even while I took the world's quickest shower. She positioned herself outside the bathroom door, which I left open for her benefit. I blew my hair halfway dry, leaving it straight and simple.

My meager selection of clothes couldn't match Kim's designer outfit. I decided on the khaki trousers with a sleeveless white turtleneck. It wouldn't win any fashion awards, but it was quintessential daytime attire for Wagtail.

Filled with joy at having my little friend back, I looped the leash under her collar, and the two of us went to breakfast.

Oma cried out and clapped her hands together when she saw the dog. "Where did you find her?"

As if she understood, the Jack Russell tugged me to Oma and reached up to her to be petted.

Kim fussed over her, too.

Even Shelley raced to us. "I'm so glad she's back!" She bent to the dog. "You must be starved. How about a nice bracing bowl of oatmeal with chicken and apples?" Looking my way, she added, "Our special today is two eggs over easy, with home fries, buttered toast, and bacon. We also serve a dog version of that."

The dog would probably be happy with anything. "We'll both have that. And a pot of tea for me, please."

Ben seemed surprised. "That's a hearty breakfast."

"You weren't out climbing a mountain this morning." Maybe that was too defensive. "I can't believe you drove all the way up here!" It blew me away. Ben didn't even miss work if he had a cold, but he'd taken time off to be with me. That meant a lot. Zelda had to be wrong.

"Daddy insisted." Kim nibbled at a blueberry muffin.

"There's an issue with a car that belonged to Mortie," explained Ben. "I need to speak to an Officer Dave Quinlan."

"This is work?" So much for thinking he'd come because of me. On the other hand, maybe he'd used the car as an excuse to talk Mortie into sending him up here. "You must be beat after driving all night."

"It wasn't so bad. We arrived around midnight." Kim chugged black coffee.

"Midnight?" Where had they slept?

Ben speared a piece of kiwi on his plate. "A fine young fellow named Casey put me in a room called *Chew*."

"I thought he should come with me. I hate being in the cabin all alone." Kim wrinkled her nose. "It's not too far from here by golf cart, though."

Shelley brought me a pot of water and English Breakfast tea bags.

I poured the steaming water into a mug, dunked a tea bag into it, and added milk and sugar. "I'll call Dave to let him know that you're here."

"Your grandmother has been telling us about these horrible crimes. I don't know if he'll have much time for us with two murders on his hands." Kim pushed a lock of expertly curled hair off her face.

I couldn't help myself. I had to say it. "I think Dave will have time for you since it was your father's car that killed Sven."

Guilt swelled through me as soon as I spoke.

Kim turned green and sputtered coffee onto her plate. "It was stolen! He reported it stolen weeks ago."

Ben turned to her and spoke with steely determination. "What did we talk about on the way up here? You don't say anything to anyone about this."

"But we're among friends."

Ben remained calm, but I heard the exasperation in his tone. "*Everyone* includes friends, too. How hard is that to understand?"

Kim tucked her chin in, like a scolded child. An appropriate response, I thought. Ben didn't need to be so harsh with her. Unless . . . unless she was involved in some way.

She couldn't have been the driver. She'd been with us when the call came from Rose. How would I react if I knew my father's car had been used to kill someone? I'd probably turn green, too.

That reminded me of Ben's car and the mess inside it. I had to get it cleaned—pronto! And I had to talk to Oma, or perhaps to Zelda or Shelley. Maybe they knew more about the phone call regarding Dolce the night Sven was killed.

Shelley delivered my breakfast and a cute tiny version for the dog—one egg surrounded by a few home fries, sprinkled with bits of bacon. A teensy wedge of toast stood at an angle as a garnish.

The dog ate like she was starved, but I left my meal for a moment, made an excuse, and followed Shelley to the kitchen.

Her wavy hair, the color of light brown sugar, was pulled back into a loose bun again. Small tendrils around her face had worked their way loose. Her skin was like porcelain. Whispering, I asked if she was working the night Sven was killed.

"I worked that day, but I left in the afternoon. Is something up?"

"I'm just trying to get some things straight in my head, that's all. I thought you might know more about the phone call regarding Dolce."

"Chloe would know. She was working that night. Would you like me to call her?"

"Chloe? Sven's girlfriend?"

"I don't know that it had gone that far, but they were working toward it. She's a friend of mine. I'm sure she wouldn't mind."

"That would be great. Thanks, Shelley."

She placed a comforting hand on my arm. "We're all rooting for you, by the way. Would you like me to spill a pot of coffee on her?"

It took me a second to realize she meant Kim. I giggled. "Thanks for the offer, but I have a feeling she has much bigger troubles. It's nice to know you've got my back, though."

Ben accosted me as soon as I returned to the table. "This *isn't* your grandmother's dog?"

I swear she lifted her lip at him, showing him tiny front teeth. "She's mine. She still needs a name, though."

"Trouble," muttered Ben.

Kim laughed, but I dug into my breakfast. Now that she was back, I had every intention of keeping her. The subject was not open to discussion or negotiation.

Happily, the conversation moved to the subject of Kim's father, Mortie. Oma knew him fairly well and gave the impression of liking him.

"So, Kim, what do you do that you're able to take time off to come up here?" I asked in between bites of salted, slightly spicy potatoes, crispy on the outside but soft and warm inside.

She held her coffee mug in both hands and rested her elbows on the table. "I work for myself. I'm a day trader."

"Apparently, a pretty good one," said Ben. "She's given Mortie some great tips."

She waved him off, like she was embarrassed, but she moistened her lip with her tongue and tossed her hair back.

Shelley brought me a fresh pot of hot water, leaned over, and whispered, "Chloe will meet you at Café Shot at eleven."

I could hardly wait. For some reason that I didn't understand, I felt the need to be rid of Ben and Kim for that event. It didn't make sense to me that I should feel that way. I chalked it up to instinct.

After breakfast, I rushed Kim and Ben out to the front porch, where Gingersnap made a beeline for them. Kim rubbed her head and told her what a pretty girl she was.

Ben grabbed my hand. "Holl, we need to talk."

People never had anything good or happy to say when they broke it to you like that. He would undoubtedly pressure me to give away the adorable dog. *No way.*

"Maybe later. Excuse me." I hurried to the reception desk to call Dave.

"So this is your scamp!" Zelda rubbed the dog behind her ears while I left a message for Dave. "What about naming her Scamp? She's certainly been up to tricks."

Her ears perked up.

"Or Scampi? She's a little shrimp," said Zelda.

I hung up the phone and tried it out. "Scampi? Is that your name?"

"Scampi!" called Oma, bending and holding her hand out to her.

But the scamp didn't budge. She just stood there, wagging her tail. Not that I blamed her. I'd been called a shrimp plenty of times and had never particularly liked it.

Zelda circled her hand under her chin again. "She's thrilled to be home."

You didn't have to be a psychic to figure *that* out. Zelda struck me as a lovely person, but I found it hard to believe that people paid her for that kind of insight.

"She says her name is Bad Dog."

Oma turned away quickly to hide a smile.

"I'm not naming a dog *Bad Dog*!" Talk about a self-fulfilling prophecy. "What else did you say a minute ago?" I asked. "She liked something."

"Hmm. I said she'd been up to tricks."

And just like that, she ran to Zelda.

"Trixie. That's her name." I knelt and called out, "Trixie, come!"

Clearly thrilled by the attention, she dashed to me, her tail wagging so hard that I didn't need Zelda to interpret her thoughts.

I reached down to pat her. "No more Bad Dog. You're Trixie now." She cocked her head to the side and held up her right paw. I shook it. We had a deal.

Oma laughed and retreated to her office.

I whispered to Zelda. "Keep an eye on Oma for me? I have an appointment."

"Eleven at Café Shot."

"How could you possibly have known that?"

She shrugged and said, "I'm psychic."

I narrowed an eye and gave her a skeptical look.

She bounced up on her toes and then down again. "Okay. Chloe called me. She wanted to know about you."

Of course. The people who worked at the inn were hard-wired into each other's lives. "What did you tell her?"

"That you are exactly like your grandmother."

People had said worse things about me. "Can I take Trixie into Café Shot?"

"Honey, there isn't anywhere in Wagtail that you can't take Trixie. That's what we're all about."

I waved and left through the reception door to avoid walking by Kim and Ben on the front porch. They'd see me strolling up the shopping area if they were paying attention. There wasn't much I could do about that.

A lovely, wide brick walkway lined on both sides by manicured shrubs led us to The Blue Boar. We dodged around the front of the restaurant and walked as fast as I could go. There wasn't much doubt in my mind that Trixie would have dashed ahead if she weren't on a leash. How would she ever get enough exercise if I couldn't take her off the leash? This baby needed to run. Dog school was definitely in order.

I passed cafés and restaurants with outdoor tables. Why hadn't I asked Zelda for the exact location of Café Shot?

A woman browsed at books on rolling shelves outside of Tall Tails Bookstore.

I asked if she knew the location of Café Shot.

She pointed across the walking zone. "Outsiders never get it. It's cute, but not obvious."

Across the way, tables clustered before an arched double door with large windows on both sides. Over the top of the entrance were the words *Café Chat*. Sleek, stylized cats curved to create the capital *C*s. I stared at it for a minute, thinking the woman had misunderstood me. And then it dawned on me. *Chat* was pronounced something like "shot" and meant "cat" in French—a bilingual double entendre.

I thanked the woman and hastened over. As I approached, I scanned people at the tables for a young woman sitting alone and spotted her right away. Chloe had curly strawberry blonde hair that bushed out around her shoulders. Pale and so thin she seemed fragile, she fidgeted, twisting a ring on her middle finger and glancing about nervously. When I introduced myself, I realized that carefully applied makeup had hidden dark circles under her eyes, but nothing could conceal the red rims, no doubt from crying.

A handsome waiter scurried over to our table. He could hardly take his eyes off her. We ordered café au laits and croissants. I was going to have to embark on a major diet when I went home. Much to my surprise, Trixie sat quietly next to my chair, taking everything in.

"I'm so sorry for your loss."

She nodded and dabbed at her eyes with a crumpled tissue. "Am I fired? Please don't fire me. I love working at the Sugar Maple Inn."

Twenty-one

❧ ❧ ❧ ❧ ❧

Fired? Chloe's question threw me for a loop. I reached out to her and placed my hand over hers. "Good grief. Of course you're not fired." No sooner had the words left my mouth than I realized I didn't have the power to promise anything of the sort. But I wondered why she thought that. I sat back and hoped she might say more about it.

The cute waiter arrived with our café au laits and croissants. He set a small bowl of water on the concrete floor for Trixie. I assumed the croissant-shaped biscuit on a plate near mine was meant for Trixie, too.

I placed it near her water. At the inn, I had noticed hand wipes in a rectangular container on each table, just like sugar packets. I tore one open and wiped my hands.

Chloe drank half her coffee before I touched mine. "I haven't eaten much since it happened. I don't even have the energy to make a cup of coffee."

She wasn't going where I wanted. I should have waited, but I asked, "Why would you be fired?"

"I love Mrs. Miller like my own grandmother. I don't want to offend you, but you've probably noticed that she's pretty precise about things. She's more punctual than anyone I've ever known. I thought if she found out that I left the inn during my shift, well, that would be the end of my job. Is she mad?"

I debated what to say. I shouldn't have said she wouldn't be fired. I had no power over that decision. "Honestly, she hasn't said a thing to me. Where did you go?"

She slumped in her seat and closed her eyes briefly. "To break off my relationship with Philip." She said it in a dull, lifeless voice.

"Philip? The guy who owns the bed-and-breakfasts?"

"Same one."

"Isn't he a lot older than you?" If I had to guess, I'd put Chloe in her mid-twenties. Philip must be closer to my age, late thirties or maybe forty.

"Fifteen years older. It was a mistake."

"The relationship or the breakup?"

"The relationship. He's a controlling sort of guy. You know the type? Everything has to be just so. He even irons his jeans. He's very ambitious. Being so precise and planning everything has made him pretty successful. One of these days, I'm sure he'll be like your grandmother and own the fanciest place in town. He has the drive to do it. I think he liked me because I was younger, and he thought he could manipulate me and shape me into what he wanted me to be. It wasn't healthy, but I didn't realize it until I met Sven. He was incredibly intuitive."

"So you broke off your relationship with Philip to start a relationship with Sven?"

"It had already started." She pushed her hair back, out of her face, and turned guilty eyes up at me. "Sven and I had a full-blown romance. We hid it from everyone because of Philip. I've never been with anyone as gentle and caring as Sven. People talk about romance all the time, but I thought they were exaggerating—that love wasn't really like that, except in books and movies. But it is . . . and now I've gone and killed the only man I'll ever love!"

Fortunately, she didn't sob out loud. She cupped a hand over her mouth and bowed her head. Her slender fingers trembled.

I gave her a moment, saddened by her deep grief yet alarmed by what she'd said. "What do you mean *you killed him*?"

She blinked back tears. "If I hadn't told Philip about Sven, he would still be alive."

I lowered my voice and bent toward her. "You know for a fact that Philip murdered Sven?"

She glanced around. "You can't tell anyone. Promise? He'll kill me, too, if he finds out I blabbed."

"Have you told Dave Quinlan about this?"

She nodded vigorously. "Immediately. As soon as I heard about Sven's death."

Yet Philip hadn't been arrested. "Tell me exactly what happened." I tore off a piece of croissant and chewed on it.

"I was working the evening shift, and Sven was scheduled to work midnight. He came by the inn early to cover for me while I met with Philip."

"How did that go?"

"I . . . I tried to keep Sven's name out of it, but Philip wore me down. He was ugly. He called me a tramp and said he never should have wasted his time on someone uneducated, which isn't true, and . . . and *insignificant*. And then he said that I should know beauty really is only skin deep. It doesn't last long and neither would my relationship with Sven."

That sounded like it could be incriminating to me. "And you told Dave all of this?"

"I think so. I was in such a state when it happened, you know?"

"And then you returned to the inn?"

"Right. I was helping Mr. Luciano with directions when the phone rang. Sven answered it for me. He said someone had called to let Mrs. Miller know that Dolce was running loose, and Ellie Pierce needed help finding her."

I interrupted. "Who? Who called?"

Her head turned to the left. I had the feeling she was replaying events in her mind.

"I don't know," she wailed. "Sven went to look for Mrs. Miller. She was up in Aerie—where you're staying. Anyway, when they came downstairs, they left for Mrs. Pierce's house to help find Dolce."

Her voice quavered at the end. More tears were on the way.

I sat back, nibbling at the end of my croissant. Trixie fixed me with liquid eyes. Who could resist? I pulled a tiny piece off and fed it to her. After all, she was being surprisingly well behaved.

The phone call could have been a coincidence, but it didn't seem like it to me. The killer must have made that call expecting his victim to come to Dolce's rescue. Ellie had insisted that she hadn't left the gate open. What were the odds that someone would be parked in that very spot at that very moment and tear along the short road with no lights? I gulped cold water from the glass on the table. If I was right, then the target could have been either Sven or Oma.

"Did you tell Philip that Sven was filling in for you at the inn?"

Chloe's eyes opened wide. Both of her hands rested on the table. Her delicate fingers rotated up and down in a busy wave. "No! I'm sure of it."

It was the answer I didn't want to hear. It meant Sven had been in the wrong place at the wrong time. The caller had meant to lure someone else. And I feared that person was Oma. It would be a lot easier to hit an old lady crossing the street than to hit a young, athletic ski instructor. Then again, if the phone call *was* a setup, the killer had taken a big chance. Oma could have sent someone else to look for Dolce. I suspected everyone in town knew Oma would rush to the rescue of her show dog, though.

Chloe grasped the situation immediately. "It wasn't Philip! He couldn't have known Sven would be there." She took a huge bite out of her croissant. And another, and another like a ravenous vulture. Her mouth full, she said, "Aren't there phone records? Can't they trace the call to find out who made it?"

"I think so." Dave had probably already set that request in motion.

Her cheeks stuffed with food like a chipmunk, she stopped her hungry chewing. "Mrs. Miller." She swallowed hard. "He intended to kill Mrs. Miller!"

Chloe had verbalized my fear. She was a sharp cookie to have realized what it meant. I spoke softly. "Let's keep this between us for now, okay? I'd like to talk to Dave about those phone records."

She nodded vigorously, her mouth full of croissant again.

Mindful of the fact that she might blab to other inn employees, I asked casually, "Is there anyone who is angry with my grandmother?"

She dabbed her mouth daintily with a napkin. "Most people admire her." She gasped. "That Mr. Luciano gives me the creeps, though. He's too *Godfather*, if you know what I mean."

"Are you aware that someone attacked him outside of the inn?"

"The Mafia has arrived in Wagtail! That's what he wants with Mrs. Miller. I bet he's shaking her down!"

Chloe had watched too many movies. "Let me know if you think of anything else that could be important." I paid the check. "When will you be coming back to work?"

"Tomorrow, after the memorial service. I can help you keep an eye on Mrs. Miller then. Are you sure I shouldn't spread the word among the other employees?"

"What if it was one of them?"

Her eyes widened. "I see what you mean. Mum's the word."

Poor kid. I felt terrible for her. Though if the longing glances from our waiter were any indication, Chloe wouldn't be alone for long.

Trixie and I took a roundabout route back to the inn, taking care to walk by Ellie Pierce's house. I caught a lucky break. Ellie sat on a bale of hay in her yard, listlessly staring at the grass. She wore gardening gloves and held clippers in her hand.

Trixie yelped and pulled at the leash.

Dolce stayed close to Ellie, but Jerry's dog, Chief, perked up and trotted to the fence to see his pal, Trixie. They sniffed each other through the pickets, their tails wagging.

"Good morning, Mrs. Pierce." I called out to her softly.

"Holly!" The glimmer of a smile crossed her lips. "It's so nice to see you around town. I bet Liesel loves having you here."

"I wish it were under better circumstances. How are you holding up?"

She stood and crossed to the fence. "Chief's having a tough time adjusting to life without a doggy door. And I . . . I still can't believe Jerry's gone. I think of all the times I was blazing mad with him, and I wish I could have those precious minutes back. But life doesn't give you a do-over. Once they're gone, you can't go back and spend more time with them or be kind or patient. I . . ." She plucked at a rough fence picket. "I think the worst will be Saturday nights when he always came to dinner. It wasn't much, nothing exciting really, but I'll miss that." She gazed at me and waggled her forefinger in my direction. "Enjoy the company of your grandmother while you can!"

Did she know something about Oma's health? "How is Oma?"

"She's been such a dear friend. I was concerned about going into business together to buy and show Dolce." At the sound of his name, the tall dog came over to us and reached his head out to me to stroke. "But it has worked out just fine. Liesel wasn't upset with me about the gate, only Jerry." Her mouth twitched into a scowl.

"Is this the gate in question?" I asked.

"Yes." She demonstrated the latch as she spoke.

I peered at it. "There's a hole for a padlock."

"I've never used a padlock. Never had to. You have to pull up this part and scoot it back to release the gate. I chose this lock because it's simple but unlikely to be opened by dog paws." She scratched the back of her left hand. "In thirty years of living in this house, no dog has ever opened it. It's not impossible, I guess, but it seems unlikely. Even if a dog pawed at it, that locking mechanism would move downward, latching it closed."

I chose my words carefully so I wouldn't put ideas in her head. "What do you think happened?"

"Oh, I can tell you what happened!" she said angrily. "Someone opened the gate!"

Twenty-two

❀ ❀ ❀

It was anger that put color back into Ellie's cheeks but I was glad to see she still had spunk. "Did someone visit you that night?"

"It should all be so clear to me, shouldn't it? I haven't gone daft yet, no matter what my darling son said, but part of me died with him. If it weren't for the dogs forcing me to get up and out, I'd be hiding in my bed. Let's see . . ." She closed her eyes and took a deep breath. "It was rainy and foggy that night. Jerry was supposed to come for dinner but an emergency arose. Such is the life of the mayor. I had made chicken and dumplings because it was such a rotten, cold day and," she smiled wryly, "I was worried about how to keep it warm for him. Funny the things that were so important to me only a day or two ago. Shelley stopped by on her way home from the inn. Liesel likes to send leftover dog food, which is such a help with dogs this size. Shelley knows better than to leave the gate ajar. Other than that, I don't remember anyone coming by. Actually, Dolce wouldn't have been outside in the rain, but he got the zoomies after Shelley visited."

"The zoomies?"

"He runs around like a crazed animal. Our trainer told us to always make him go outside when he gets the zoomies because—" she gestured toward him "—you can imagine the chaos and broken furniture if a big dog like this runs wild in the house. I shooed him outside so he could work off that energy. A little while later, I heard a scream, and when I ran outside, Sven and Liesel were laying in the road."

It all sounded very plausible to me, except for one thing that set me on edge by its glaring omission. I pussyfooted around it. "Was the gate open when you ran outside?"

"Now let me think on that a minute." She pulled off her garden gloves. "It was so misty but I could hear Liesel calling for help. There's no mistaking that accent . . ." She concentrated. "Yes, of course the gate was open. At the time I was so focused on Liesel that I didn't give it much thought."

I held onto the picket fence to steady myself. The situation grew worse by the moment. "When did you realize that Dolce was missing?" The words escaped my mouth as a whisper.

Ellie Pierce's eyes met mine. "Not until the ambulance left with Sven in it, and Liesel asked about him."

I tried to rationalize. Maybe someone had seen Dolce running loose and had called the inn. It didn't mean someone had tried to lure Oma down here. Only I wasn't able to convince myself of that. "Who found Dolce?"

"He showed up at Hair of the Dog. Brewster walked him home."

He probably had an alibi for the time of the accident. If he was working at his bar, dozens of people would have seen him. "Thank you, Mrs. Pierce. Is there anything I can do to help you?"

"Not unless you find the heathen who took my Jerry's life."

"I'm sure Dave is working on that."

"Dave." She spoke his name like an exasperated schoolteacher. "He's a very nice boy. Always was. He's a big help when someone is hurt on a trail or loses a purse. But he doesn't know anything about murder. Right now, as we speak, Jerry's killer lurks somewhere among us, probably enjoying a hearty lunch and laughing to himself about Dave's inexperience."

I should have felt for Ellie, for her loss. But at that very moment, I sympathized with Dave. He *was* a nice guy. That didn't mean he was incompetent.

"Maybe Wagtail is lucky to have him. I can't imagine anyone who would try harder to find Jerry's killer."

A familiar voice accosted us. "As I live and breathe, Holly Miller! My second-closest living blood relative arrives in town, and I have to find out about it from strangers."

That voice grated on my nerves like fingernails on a chalkboard. I shivered. There was no point in defending myself. Aunt Birdie would only twist whatever I said. My mother's older half sister never let me forget that I had brought great shame upon the family name by having the nerve to be conceived while my parents were still in their senior year of high school, thus necessitating their hasty marriage.

I pasted on a big smile and held my arms out for a hug.

High cheekbones jutted out of her bony face. The streak of silver in the part of her mahogany hair was new to me. Did she not realize that it was frighteningly reminiscent of Cruella De Vil?

She bent to embrace me. "Still short like your father's side of the family, I see."

Really? Did she really expect me to keep growing taller in my thirties? "It's good to see you."

"Obviously not good enough," she said crisply, "or you would have had the decency to call on me."

I faked distress. "You know I would have dropped by but these murders have just thrown everyone for a loop."

"They don't concern you." She directed her attention to Ellie. "I'm very sorry for your loss." She didn't sound sorry. If her words had been any icier, they would have frozen in midair as they left her mouth.

"Thank you, Birdie."

Birdie's hawk-like gaze drifted down to Trixie, who backed away from her as far as her leash could go. "I certainly hope that's one of Liesel's beasts. She's made quite a pigsty of this town with that ridiculous pet friendly business. I've a mind to move."

Wagtail residents would probably take up a hefty collection to assist with moving expenses if she were serious. "This is my dog, Trixie."

"Does your mother know about this? I swear Liesel is a bad influence on you. I've always thought so. I told your mother that no good would come of shipping you out here to Liesel every summer. You should have stayed with me, where you would have learned proper manners and decorum."

Ellie made a production of looking at her watch. "My goodness, Holly! Didn't you say that you promised Liesel you would be back at the inn by one? You'd better get going, honey."

I fell in step with her game, flashing her a grateful smile. I owed her a big favor for this. "Oh dear! Must go. I'll see you both later." I turned quickly and hustled away before Aunt Birdie could demand I stay.

"Your mother is going to hear about this, young lady!" Birdie shouted.

The woman could not give up. I had never heard her utter a kind word. Everything that came out of her mouth dripped with dissatisfaction. Truth be told, she was an attractive woman. But bitterness pinched her face, and that wicked tongue of hers lashed out constantly. My mom insisted that Birdie hadn't always been so caustic. Their parents had moved to California around the time my parents divorced. My mom packed us up and moved to be near them, but Birdie staunchly remained in Wagtail. Behind her back, my dad called her the wicked witch of Wagtail.

I should have called her yesterday, but with everything that had happened, I'd honestly forgotten all about her. Once I had everything with Oma straightened out, I'd go by with a basket of muffins or a box of chocolates.

Oma's situation weighed heavily on me. My instinct to sleep on her sofa the night I arrived had been on the mark, only for a different reason. My worst suspicions had been confirmed. If Ellie hadn't realized that Dolce was running loose, then the person who called the inn to say she needed help had very likely done so to lure Oma to Ellie's house. Otherwise, wouldn't he or she have called Ellie? That person must have waited in the cover of darkness and the heavy fog and then unwittingly killed Sven.

We picked up speed and dodged visitors as we returned to the inn. Ben spotted me in the foyer and called out my name.

Rather rudely, I shouted, "Later!" and whipped along the corridor and down to the reception area. The door to Oma's office was closed.

Zelda looked up at me. "Sorry, you can't go in right now. She's with Mr. Luciano."

Twenty-three

❀ ❀ ❀ ❀ ❀

I drifted over to the loveseat to wait. Was there a romance between Oma and Mr. Luciano? He was far too young for her! Why was she having so many meetings with him?

Trixie whined at me.

"I'll take off the leash inside the inn, but you have to promise you won't run away again." I unlatched it, secure in the knowledge that she wore the inn collar with GPS. Trixie jumped up beside me and wedged her nose under my elbow so that my arm hugged her.

"That's very cute. You're a sweet girl."

Ben barreled down the steps. "Holly! Where have you been? You keep running away from me."

I motioned him over. "I have a problem." I glanced up at Oma's office door. I needed to speak to her about what was going on. But it might not hurt to hash it out with someone I could trust, like Ben.

"Take a little walk with me." I debated whether to hook Trixie up to her leash. She probably needed some exercise. "Can I trust you?" I asked.

She wagged her tail, her ears perked, and her eyes looked hopeful.

We headed for the lake, Ben taking my hand as we walked down broad stone steps lined with giant pots of orange and gold chrysanthemums. I immediately second-guessed myself about removing Trixie's leash. She ran just like the man in the woods had described—without her feet touching the ground. She zigged, she zagged, she flew across the lawn, chased a squirrel up a tree, and finally slowed to circle around the base of the tree with her nose to the ground.

We strolled down to the lake in silence. Sunlight caught the water in tiny stars, and a glimmer of orange kissed the sugar maples around the inn. A couple of fishing boats bobbed gently on the water, but we had the dock to ourselves. Lanterns with pine trees etched into the panels decorated posts around the dock. I rolled up my pant legs, took off my shoes, and sat down, dangling my feet in the cold water.

I patted the dock next to me, meaning that Ben should join me, but it was Trixie who arrived at my side and sniffed the water.

Ill at ease, Ben fetched a chair from the lawn. He sat down and crossed his legs. "Sorry that Casey wouldn't put me through to you last night. I tried calling you, but my phone wouldn't work."

"Something about the mountains. Apparently there are a lot of dead spots and only one carrier."

"Casey was amusing. I wanted to go up to your room, but he said, 'You're not planning to sleep with her in front of her grandmother, are you?' He's a funny guy."

Ben uncrossed his legs, rubbed his hands together, and leaned forward, his elbows on his knees. "Look, I know you're worried about your job. I realize that I upset you when I said you wouldn't find work in your field. Everyone wants players, you know? Nobody wants to hire a troublemaker."

"But I'm right!"

"You're so stubborn. But that's not the point." He studied his hands. "You could move in with me. We'll sell your house, and your car, too, since I'm on the metro line. That way you won't have a mortgage or car payments, and you won't have to worry about finding a job. If things go like I hope they will, I'll be moving up at the law firm, and we won't need a second income."

I splashed my hands in the water and rubbed my burning forehead. In a way, it was a generous gesture. But the thought of giving up everything that was *me* and becoming an appendage to Ben was too depressing to contemplate. Not to mention that there wasn't enough room at his place for my shoes, let alone anything else.

Trixie lay down beside me and rested her head on my thigh.

Besides, I was pretty sure that dogs were not permitted in his building. I fought overwhelming sadness. Normally, I considered myself a fairly reasonable person with both feet planted firmly on the ground, not prone to flights of imagination or nonsense. I'd blown off Rose's questions about Ben as silly. Yet here I was, totally crushed by Ben's offer. I wasn't even sure if it was meant to be a proposal of marriage. No declaration of love, undying or otherwise. No passionate kiss, no rose, no ring. I'd been through business deals that involved more romance. He didn't need to get down on his knee or make a big production out of it, but he left me wondering if marriage to him would be . . . empty. Could Rose have been right? Or was I just being silly?

Maybe I wasn't seeing things clearly because of the chaos with Oma. I'd give Ben and our relationship more thought when I went home and my life resembled normalcy.

I tried to make light of it. "Where would my shoes live?"

"We'll rig up a pulley system for boxes on the ceiling."

His joke broke the tension.

"Thanks for offering, Ben, but I'm not that desperate yet."

"You have to be desperate before you'll marry me?"

"That's not what I meant. I'm not so desperate that I have to sell everything I own and give up on my life."

"Oh." He frowned at me. "I hadn't thought about it like that. Well, um, the offer stands if things get rough."

There was a marriage proposal no girl could turn down!

"Although my state of unemployment will have to be remedied, I have a bigger problem at the moment. I think someone is trying to kill Oma."

Ben listened in horror while I explained my reasoning.

"You're saying whoever was driving the car that was stolen from Mortie intended to kill your grandmother?"

"Whoever killed Sven probably meant to kill Oma."

"Do you have any idea why? Is there something about your grandmother that I don't know?"

"Probably plenty. She can be pretty hardheaded. She's run this inn by herself for long time. She's sure to have clashed with some people. I need to sit down and have a heart-to-heart with her."

"So this Sven guy died because he was just being a nice guy, trying to help out a couple of old ladies and a dog?"

"Looks like that might be the case. I can't bear to think that. Maybe I'm wrong about all of it. What did Dave say this morning?"

"Not much. He asked questions about the car. Where it was located when it was stolen, that kind of thing."

I peered at him. Something was up. Those questions should have been answered by Mortie. "Why did you really come to Wagtail?"

"Mortie sent me to straighten out this business about his car."

"What's to straighten out? It was stolen. Mortie and his family were with us when Sven was killed. If it was his car that hit Sven, then it's pretty clear that someone else was driving it."

Something flickered in his expression. "I can't talk to you about the details. Mortie needed somebody to watch over her."

"Her? You're babysitting Kim?"

"It's not like that. He's just a concerned father."

Really? Concerned about what? Kim was a grown woman. Were her parents so determined to hitch their daughter to Ben's wagon that they threw them together? Or was Kim somehow involved in this mess? "Where's your ward now?"

"She's not a ward, Holly. She went back to her cabin to do her nails."

I burst out laughing. "She gave you the slip!"

"Did not."

"Honey, a woman like Kim doesn't do her own nails, and

she sure wouldn't go back to the cabin, where she doesn't like to be alone."

His eyes widened in alarm. "Why would she ditch me?"

"I don't know. Why do you have to babysit her?"

Ben picked up the chair and returned it to the lawn. "Well, come on. Where's my car?"

Eek! "A golf cart will get you there faster." I had to get his car cleaned immediately!

We raced up to the inn. Trixie beat us to the door and waited impatiently, dancing in circles.

Zelda fixed up Ben with a golf cart.

The minute he left, I said, "You've got to help me. Who can detail a car around here?"

"Tiny does a lot of odd jobs like that." She picked up a walkie-talkie. "Tiny, could you come to reception, please?"

"He's here?"

"He keeps the grounds in shape and does handyman work for your grandmother."

"You're wonderful." Relief and hope that the car could be cleaned surged through me.

Ten minutes later, Tiny was shampooing the carpets, and I breathed easier. Now to deal with Oma.

I braced myself and marched into her office. She worked at her desk. Trixie ran around the desk to Oma and placed her forepaws on Oma's chair.

Oma smiled at Trixie and fussed over her, telling her what a smart dog she was to come home. "Your expression tells me that you are unhappy about something, Holly."

"I want you to tell me what's going on."

She rose from her chair and focused on something outside the French doors. "What do you mean?"

I closed the door in case Zelda was listening. "I think that the person who killed Sven meant to kill you."

She turned toward me and smiled briefly. *Smiled!*

Her expression became serious. "I am aware of this. It troubles me greatly, of course. Imagine anyone being so angry with me that he should wish me dead."

"How long have you known?"

"Since the moment Ellie told me that she didn't realize Dolce had gotten out. Someone orchestrated that horror, and it wasn't Sven he was after."

"I have a proposition." I held up my hand, ready for her automatic refusal. "Please think about this. What if you and Rose went to my house to stay for a week or two? I could probably manage the inn without burning it down."

"You would do that for me?" She seemed interested.

"Of course!" Maybe she *would* take me up on it. "The two of you could have a little vacation, take in the sites, visit the Smithsonian, maybe go to a play at the Kennedy Center."

She cupped my face in her hands. "I love you, too, my little Holly."

"Wonderful!" I gave her a big hug. I would feel better the minute she left town. "Let's call Rose so she can start packing. Then you can show me what's going on over the next week or two."

She returned to her desk and slid on reading glasses. "I am not running away from this . . . this villainous individual. This is my home. We will find Sven's killer and bring him to justice."

"We?"

Twenty-four

❀ ❀ ❀ ❀

"You, Dave, and me," said Oma. "You will tell Dave, and we will assist him in uncovering the killer."

"Whoa. This isn't *Murder, She Wrote*." Sometimes I thought Oma fancied herself a Mrs. Fletcher. "This is a flesh and blood, real live killer who put a lot of thought into murdering you. And he came—" I raised my hand with my thumb and fore-finger an inch apart "—this close to doing it, too."

Her mouth twitched to the side. At least she was taking it seriously.

"Please reconsider my offer for you to stay at my place for a while." I picked up a stack of papers on her desk and tapped them into a neat pile. The color brochure advertised *Mystery Weekends at the Sugar Maple Inn*.

I waved one at her. "You can't be serious?"

"People love those weekends. We are always sold out, and when they leave, some people book ahead for the next year. You would enjoy them! Or don't you like mysteries anymore now that you're all grown up?"

"I love mysteries, but that doesn't make me Nancy Drew."

She shook her head sadly. "You were so much more fun

when you were younger. When did you turn into such a dry person? You're like a piece of zwieback."

"Excuse me for being concerned about the fact that someone is trying to murder you. It's not a game! You, yourself, said that he planned it very carefully. You don't think this person is going to try again? He or she could be on his way at this very moment. Or worse, he or she could already be here, staying in the inn." I sighed, loudly.

"What do you want from me, Holly? I refuse to run away in fear. Let's say I take a vacation and go to your house—what happens if the killer isn't found in a week or two weeks? I never come home to Wagtail? No, this is not a solution."

"Okay, then tell me who you suspect." Dave needed leads. People with motives.

Now Oma fidgeted with papers, shuffling them and rearranging them. "I don't know. I have always been very outspoken, as I'm sure you realize. There were hot tempers about turning Wagtail into a pet friendly town. Many residents were against it, vehemently so. Including your Aunt Birdie."

"You think Aunt Birdie gunned that car at you?"

"No! I'm simply saying that she was opposed to the plan. And she has never liked me."

"I suppose the list includes Peaches Clodfelter and her dreadful daughter, Prissy."

"Nonsense. Peaches and I coexist. She holds a grudge but that goes back many years. I hardly think she would have waited until now to take such dire action. At least we know Jerry can't be a suspect. We certainly had our differences, but now he has been killed."

I let her keep talking, but it dawned on me that just because Jerry was dead didn't mean he hadn't tried to knock her off. In fact—now that I thought about it—maybe Jerry had tried to kill Oma, and someone had murdered him in revenge.

"I get along with most of the people in Wagtail and consider them dear friends."

"What about employees?" I whispered.

She slapped a hand against her chest, appalled. "No! I am very good to my employees. No, no, no. It is not possible."

I took the opportunity to ask the other question that had

been weighing on me. "Oma, I want you to be honest with me. Are you ill?"

Her eyes darted to the side.

Rats! She was evading me again. "This shouldn't be so difficult to answer."

"Liebling, you worry too much. I want to see you be happy again. Your little Trixie is a good start."

Trixie! I'd forgotten all about her. I needn't have worried. She had jumped onto the back of a loveseat and watched us like a ping-pong match, her attention moving back and forth between us as we spoke.

"I blame the Ben for this. He has no zest."

"Oma, it's offensive when you call him 'the Ben.'"

"Yes? It's my poor English, I'm sure."

Poor English, my foot. She didn't like "the Ben" and this was her coy little way of showing it.

Oma limped around her desk to me and grasped my upper arms. "Liebling, don't worry about my health. As you can see, I am quite fine. This silly ankle will heal soon. Now, you have wasted enough of my time with this useless speculation."

"It's not useless. Oma, you really don't have any clue who might be this angry with you?" I baited her. "That doesn't seem like you."

She laughed. "There's hope for you yet! I will think about this. I promise. In one hour, Betsy Wheeler and her parents will arrive to look at the inn for her wedding. Would you mind showing them around? Then I will meet with them here in my office to discuss details. Yes?"

"Of course. I would be happy to."

"Then scoot and get a bite of lunch while I prepare for them."

Zelda's back was to me when I emerged from Oma's office. She looked over her shoulder and smiled casually, like she was pretending to be disinterested. Crooking her finger to follow her, she skittered toward the stairs. She held out her hand, full of teeny tiny dog treats. "Here, let Trixie see you putting these in your pocket. She tells me she love treats, so give her one every now and then to reward her for staying close by you."

"Thanks. That's a great idea." I took the treats and made a production of slipping them into the pocket of my trousers.

Trixie observed carefully. She stood on her hind legs to sniff the contents of my pocket.

"I don't want your grandmother to hear this," whispered Zelda. "We're all very worried about her. We're making a point of watching her. All the employees are taking turns."

"You're all looking out for her?" I wondered if Oma knew how highly they thought of her. Did the whole town realize that Oma had been the intended victim?

Zelda craned her head toward me and continued to whisper. "Chloe told us what's going on. Rest assured that we all love Mrs. Miller, and we won't let harm come to her."

So much for Chloe keeping it quiet. "Thank you, Zelda. I appreciate that."

"Casey says he has trouble with her at night, that sometimes she manages to slip by him."

"It wouldn't be hard. I walked up to him dead asleep right there on the loveseat. Maybe I'll set up camp outside her door after she turns in."

"Great! Casey's kind of young and easily spooked." She glanced around. "For what it's worth, I think it was Prissy Clodfelter."

Trixie whined and pressed against my legs.

"See?" said Zelda. "Trixie knows. Prissy is just plain mean. And she would think she could get away with something like this. Dave will never consider her a suspect because he has the hots for her."

Oma called to Zelda, who patted my shoulder and nodded in a gesture of solidarity before hurrying back to the office.

"Come on, Trixie. Let's see if we can rustle up some lunch."

I had every intention of snooping around for leftovers in Oma's private kitchen, but Shelley snagged me as soon as we reached the dining area.

"We need to talk." She led me to a table wedged in a private corner. Perched on a chair, she twisted toward me. "I don't have much time. We always get a good lunch crowd."

I believed her. Not a single table on the terrace was available.

"Waitresses see a lot and overhear things, you know? Mr. Wiggins, do you know him? The wealthiest man in town?

Well, he comes by here every week to see your grandmother. Now, I'm not saying that they're having an affair or anything, but Peaches used to spy on them. It was kind of funny, because she'd sit out on the porch, or amble through the inn, pretending to be casual. Well, this one day, Mr. Wiggins and your grandmother were eating lunch out on the terrace when Peaches flew in on her broomstick and made a scene that you would not believe. I don't have to tell you how much Mrs. Miller despises big scenes. From that day forward, they took their lunches down in Mrs. Miller's private office."

She excused herself, picked up a coffee pot, and made quick work of visiting all the outdoor tables with a smile and a refill.

Behind me, the chef rolled open a window and set plates on a ledge. "Hi, Holly. Buffalo burgers with caramelized onions are the lunch special today. Can I make you one?"

Could he? My mouth watered at the thought. "Absolutely, if it's not too much trouble."

"No trouble at all. Hot tea?"

"Sounds perfect."

Shelley whipped by me, loaded the plates on her arms like a pro, and hustled them out to the terrace. I would have dropped them all.

When she returned, she placed the tea and a platter in front of me. Trixie stood on her hind legs and pranced, fixated on the second dish Shelley carried. Laughing, she set it on the floor for Trixie. I barely managed a glimpse of her lunch—crumbled buffalo burger mixed with raw shredded carrot and garnished with two home fries—before she gobbled it up.

"Don't worry," said Shelley. "No onions in the dog servings."

I bit into the juicy burger and grabbed for a napkin. The slightly sweet onions blended perfectly with the meat. Crispy, golden brown home fries and a tangy shredded carrot salad accompanied the burger.

Shelley sat down again. "There's something else I have to get off my chest. I was the last one through Ellie Pierce's gate, but I know I closed it. I've gone over that night again and again in my mind. Someone had to have unlatched that gate and opened it for Dolce—but it wasn't me, I swear!" She took a deep breath. "What I want to know is, where was Jerry when Sven was killed?"

Twenty-five

❧ ❧ ❧ ❧

I nearly choked. Coughing, I set my burger down.

The kitchen window opened, and a glass of water appeared like magic. I stood up to get it, flapping my hand as though it would help me breathe. I gulped the cold water, certain my face had flushed red.

The chef leaned forward. "Shelley's right. Listen to her."

I sat down and drank more water.

"I was there," said Shelley, "when Jerry called his mom to tell her he would be late for dinner at her house. But nobody knows where he went. I've been asking around town, kind of private-like, you know, and nobody saw him."

"He said something about downed electrical wires up near Del's place. But that could have been a fabrication. You think Jerry drove the car that killed Sven?"

"Don't you find it suspicious that he conveniently disappeared at that exact time?"

"Then who killed Jerry?"

"Lord, now there's a question. Could have been just about anybody. I know Rose and Holmes are friends of yours, but all the Richardsons were just madder than wet cats at Jerry about that land development that he blocked. There are others, too. Brewster was upset with him for trying to move Hair of the Dog out on the highway even though there are other restaurants in town that don't shut down until late. Jerry's own mother complained about him!"

She glanced out the window. "I gotta get back to my tables, but just one more quick thing—you know that girl, Kim, that came in for breakfast? Her dad, Mortie, comes by the inn to see Mrs. Miller every time he's in town. He always brings her flowers."

She jumped up and returned to the terrace, all smiles and southern graciousness.

My head reeled from all the information she had spewed at me. Especially the part about Oma and Mortie. He was a good bit younger than Oma. I couldn't imagine it was anything romantic. But flowers? That was hard to interpret in a different way.

I finished my burger and tea, told Trixie to stay, which I didn't imagine she understood, took my dirty dishes into the kitchen, and stacked them to be washed.

Happily, Trixie had waited by the door. I patted her and rewarded her with a mini treat for being so good.

She readily went with me to meet the bride and her parents, who had brought along a short-haired red dachshund and a black lab who would be the ring bearer at the wedding.

Trixie chased and played with the Wheeler dogs as we strolled the lawn. I had seen enough weddings at the inn to be able to describe where the tent would go and where the bands usually set up. The lake cooperated by sparkling in the sunlight, the perfect opportunity for me to tell them how romantic it was when a full moon shone its beams on the water.

"It must be wonderful to live here," said Mrs. Wheeler. "I'd love to take my little Schatzi everywhere with me."

Mr. Wheeler nodded in agreement. "Not to mention the lack of traffic and noise. It's so peaceful."

If they only knew about the troubling undercurrents! But once the murderers had been arrested, Wagtail would be a charming place to live again. No wonder Holmes kept coming back. No sitting in rush-hour traffic. Clean air. Birds singing in the trees. Dogs and cats everywhere. It wasn't surprising that the Wheelers liked it. They had left their lives, their problems, and headaches behind.

As Betsy and her parents discussed their plans, I couldn't help wondering about my own wedding. What was it about weddings that made them so contagious? I pushed thoughts of Ben out of my head. Oma was far more important. I had to get her squared away first.

I led the Wheelers up to the terrace, inside to the dining area, showed off the new library, explained about the special cat rooms, and finally returned them to Oma's office. They settled on the cushy chairs and the loveseat. Even though I'd recently eaten lunch, I longed to stay because a gorgeous platter of cake slices had magically appeared next to a silver coffee and tea service. Oma's antique Empress Dresden Flowers china took me back to my childhood.

When I stayed with her, once a week Oma had sent the boys to do something rough-and-tumble, while Oma, my stuffed Steiff dog, Lassie, and I had a little tea party with her exquisite floral china. Colorful flowers rambled around the edges, interrupted by scrolls of gold. It hadn't been in vogue for a very long time, yet there was something about afternoon tea that called for ornate, girly china.

As I closed the door behind me, I overheard Mr. Wheeler say he would like to book the entire inn for the weekend of the wedding. *Whoa.* "That'll be a crazy weekend," I said to Zelda.

She laughed. "It's always like that around here. Sometimes I wonder if it's not too much for Mrs. Miller. She rarely gets a day off. I think the last time she left was when she went to see your dad in Florida."

Zelda introduced me to her replacement, who gave me a thumbs-up and promised to watch out for Oma. He handed me a pink message slip.

Zelda said apologetically, "He's called here six times in the last hour."

"I'm so sorry. I left my cell phone in my room." I glanced at the message. *Ben called. He can't find Kim.* That wasn't terribly surprising. Something was up with her and that stolen car. I knew she had ditched him.

I used the inn's phone to call Ben. His cell phone rang and rang, and finally rolled over to voice mail. I left a message.

I reached under the desk and borrowed a leash. "Is there a store in town that doesn't belong to the Clodfelters where I could buy a collar and tag for Trixie?"

"Loads of them," said Zelda, "though Prissy's store is by far the largest and has the biggest selection. Not surprising, since it was funded by Mr. Wiggins. Personally, I like Puppy Love."

Tiny trudged through the door. Handing me the keys to Ben's car, he said, "I am really sorry I didn't have more luck with the carpet. It's still drying, but I don't think those stains will ever come out. I tried three different stain removers. I'm afraid it's as good as it's ever gonna get."

"Thanks, Tiny. What do I owe you?"

"Nothin'. I was happy to do it for you."

"Oh no! You tell me what you charge for that kind of work."

He stated a fair price, and I hurried upstairs with Trixie for my checkbook and wallet. He still chatted with Zelda on our return. I handed Tiny a check.

"I sure appreciate this." He rubbed the back of his ear. "Both my kids need braces. Man, but they're expensive. I need all the odd jobs I can get. You need anything else at all, you just call me."

I slipped the leash around Trixie's GPS collar. "Thanks for taking care of that for me, Tiny. Guess I'd better have a look."

Zelda followed me outside. I opened the car door and stared at coffee-colored and orangey-red blotches that marred the carpet.

I winced. "Do you think it's expensive to install new carpet in a car?"

"At least the leather seats cleaned up nicely."

I couldn't help liking Zelda. She might think she was an animal psychic, but she always seemed to look at the brighter side of life. "You're absolutely right. How much could new carpet cost? It's not like a whole room. Right?"

Her eyes big, Zelda lifted her shoulders in a shrug, and the two of us burst into nervous giggles. I picked up Trixie and looked her square in the eyes. "You'd better hope it's not expensive."

She wagged her tail and licked my nose. And didn't look one bit concerned or remorseful.

We walked along the sidewalk to The Blue Boar. Suddenly, Zelda ran her fingers through her hair and fluffed it up. "There's Philip," she hissed. "Isn't he just perfect?"

He stood in front of The Blue Boar, blocking our path and staring toward the inn.

"Hi." It was simple, but let him know he was in our way.

He jerked in surprise and looked around at us. "Holly. Zelda." Scratching the side of his neck, just under the collar of his button-down shirt, he said, "You might have told me who you were."

"Me?" I asked.

"Yes, you! I had no idea you were a Wagtail Miller."

"She's Mrs. Miller's granddaughter," offered Zelda, clearly eager to jump into the conversation.

"So I hear. She was out slumming with the rest of us last night."

Slumming? I didn't know quite how to respond. What was he getting at? "I'd hardly call Hair of the Dog slumming."

"No? Maybe not. I just meant there are only a few big names in town, and your grandmother ranks right up there."

"She's lived here for a long time. People will probably say the same sort of thing about you in a few years," said Zelda.

He raised his eyebrows but appeared pleased by the thought.

"Holly!" Ben waved at me from across the plaza.

"Who's that?" asked Philip.

"Her boyfriend." Zelda had turned quite chatty.

Philip shot me an inquisitive look. "Must be serious if he followed you here."

I didn't go into details. What was I going to say? He's not here because of me?

Ben panted like a worn-out hunting dog. He grabbed my arm. "I can't find her anywhere."

Under other circumstances, I probably would have pitched in to help him. But honestly, with everything that was going on, Kim's successful maneuver of ditching Ben didn't worry me in the least. "Is her car still at the cabin?"

He nodded.

"Then she hasn't left town. I'm sure she's shopping or having her hair done or something. Want to come with me to buy a collar?"

Ben smirked. "Like that's more important than finding Kim?"

It was to me.

Zelda tilted her head coyly at Philip even though she addressed Ben. "You could get a latte and sit outside. Maybe you'll see her walk by."

Zelda, Trixie, and I walked away, leaving Ben and Philip together.

Zelda spoke in a hushed voice. "I have such a crush on that guy. Maybe it's because my ex was such a slug. Philip is everything he wasn't—successful and industrious, and, well, neat. I have this fantasy that he picks up after himself and does dishes. He doesn't lounge around on the sofa watching TV all day. He's making something of himself. I've heard he's interested in the old Wagtail Springs Inn at the end of town. He wants to expand and be successful. But I don't think I'm his type. Not everyone can accept that I'm a psychic."

"I wouldn't be so sure about that. Last night it sounded like he's convinced there are such things as ghosts. Maybe he's open to the concept of psychics."

"You think? I could ask him over to dinner some night. Hey, would you mind giving me a hand for a minute? I'm not far from here."

"Sure."

We turned and walked almost two blocks. "This is me," said Zelda.

If I had walked past the house by myself, I would have guessed Zelda belonged there. Instead of a white picket fence, a rough two-foot high, stacked stone fence meandered along the edge of the front yard. The bottom half of the house had to date back a hundred years or more. Built of stone, it supported a wood-clad second story with a steep roof. Dormer windows jutted out of the roof. The diamond-shaped panes in the glass added to the charm but imparted a slight witchy-gingerbread-house touch. Ivy climbed the walls of the house. Tall pines and overgrown shrubs provided privacy from the neighbors. A lantern hung from a wood post by the front walk, along with a hand-painted sign that stated *Animal Psychic, by Appointment* along with a telephone number. But a huge box blocked the red front door at the end of the stone walk.

"Isn't this awful? I ordered a new chair and got a great deal on it, but it turns out that when they say curbside delivery, that's as far as they take it. I managed to shove the box this far, but I can't carry it inside by myself."

"No problem. I'll lift this side, you get the other one. And you," I said to Trixie, "please don't get underfoot."

With that, Zelda swung the door open wide.

Twenty-six

✿ ✿ ✿ ✿

Six cats waited on the other side. Trixie yelped at them, then pulled at the leash, her feet scrambling like a cartoon character.

The cats scattered, except for a big gray one with yellow eyes, who stared Trixie down.

"You don't lock your doors?" I asked.

Zelda snorted. "This is Wagtail. Nothing horrible ever happens here. Well, not until recently."

We lifted the box and carried it inside the house. The front room served as foyer and living room. Ancient hardwood floors moaned as we walked on them.

Zelda had already made room for the new chair and did a little dance of delight when it was out of the box and in place. She curled up on her big new chair and a half by the fireplace. A long-haired cat with tufts on its ears leaped onto her lap. "All I need now is hot apple cider and a book. Maybe a little snow."

"This is quite a house."

"I don't know what's going to happen now that Jerry is dead. It belongs to him. I'm just renting it." She raised her eyebrows and frowned, tilting her head to the side. "Jerry gave me a really great deal on the house because I solved a problem for Chief. He had an obsessive digging problem. When I talked to Chief, he told me he wasn't getting enough exercise. Jerry took him places, but never gave him time to play or just sniff around—which is very important to hounds. Once Jerry made time for Chief to be a dog, he was much better behaved. That, and clicker training. Jerry had tried using a choke collar to train Chief, but he responded better to clicker training."

She pointed at Trixie. "She will, too. They're both food motivated. Anyway, Jerry was so happy that he rented me this house for a steal. I'd love to buy it, but there's no way after what my ex did to our credit. I love it here, though." She clutched the cat to her tightly. "I don't want to leave!"

"Wouldn't his mother have inherited his rental properties?"

"I don't know. I haven't asked yet because it's too soon to broach that with her. It would be insensitive."

That was true. It would have been thoughtless of her to ask Ellie right away. "I guess you'll find out soon."

Trixie watched the cat with way too much interest. I tightened my grip on the leash.

"Zelda, this morning I ran into the weirdest guy in the woods. Tall with glasses—"

Her eyes went wide. "The Runemaster! You really saw him?"

"Runemaster?"

"That's what we call him. He's a recluse. Hardly ever comes into town. Just turns up in the woods when people least expect it, like he's spying on people. He's very scary."

I was glad I hadn't known that. "He did show up suddenly and then he disappeared, but he wasn't that scary."

She shivered. "No, thanks. He creeps me out."

She walked me to the door, thanking me profusely for my help.

"Anytime."

By my calculations, we were one block over from the street where Sven had been mowed down. For no good reason, when I left Zelda's, I crossed the street, ambled down a block, and wound up in front of Ellie's house again.

Trixie sniffed the sidewalk. "I wish you could tell me who opened that gate."

She inspected the base of the gate eagerly. Not that it would mean anything. Half the town had gone through the gate to convey their condolences since Jerry died. We strolled toward the shopping area, but an angry voice caught my attention. Trixie pulled at the leash again, her ears perked up.

Rose stood inside the doorway of her quaint cottage, speaking in an elevated voice. Not yelling, it was tempered, but as angry as I'd ever heard Rose.

"Lord a'mercy! I've a mind to call your mother about this. She would be plumb ashamed of you. Imagine coming over here and insinuating I've been running around killing people. Now you get on out of my house and don't you come back until you're ready to mind your manners. You used to be such a nice boy!"

Dave exited, murmuring something I couldn't hear. Apologies, perhaps?

I timed my walking speed to accidentally intersect with him at her gate. "Dave!" I lowered my voice. "What was that all about?"

Rose shook her finger at him. "And don't you go mixing Holly or Holmes into this mess. Do you understand me, young man?"

His cheeks and ears blazed plum red. He shook his head and fell in step with me. "How am I supposed to investigate a murder if everyone treats me like a fourteen-year-old Boy Scout? Your grandmother won't tell me anything, and Rose is offended that I dare ask her questions."

"Maybe one of the cops from Snowball should take over the investigation."

He gasped. "No! This is the biggest break I've ever had." He clapped a hand to his forehead. "Will you listen to me? That's not what I meant. Not at all. You must think I'm a terrible person."

"I know what you mean. After years of returning lost purses and giving directions, there's finally a big case in Wagtail."

"That's it exactly. This is my town. These are my people. It's my jurisdiction, and by George, I'm going to get to the bottom of this. Thanks for understanding, Holly. I didn't intend to sound happy about the deaths of two terrific people. Did you get anything out of your grandmother?"

"Nothing helpful. Unless you think . . ." I stopped midsentence. I couldn't offend Prissy Clodfelter again if he was interested in her.

He stopped walking. "What? What did she say?"

"It's just that stupid old animosity between the Clodfelters and the Millers. But Oma said it's been going on so long she hardly thinks they'd have waited this long to do something rash."

"What's the deal there? Why don't the Clodfelters like your family?"

"I honestly don't know. Must have happened ages ago. I'm sorry I said something awful about Prissy yesterday. I didn't know you two were an item."

"That's nice of you to say. I appreciate it, Holly."

"Hey, I've been wondering—did you track down the source of the phone call to the inn that night? Wouldn't that lead us straight to the killer?"

"You'd think so, wouldn't you?" He clammed up. His mouth pulled into a taut line, and he looked me straight in the eyes, assessing me. "It came from the public phone at Hair of the Dog."

Surprised that he'd shared confidential information, I said, "Thanks."

"Don't go thinking I'm telling you anything secret. I've been asking questions about who was there around that time. Half the town was watching when that phone was fingerprinted."

"Was Jerry there?" I held my breath.

"You're not the first person to suggest that Jerry drove the car that hit Sven."

"Dave, do you think Oma was the intended victim that night?"

Dave shuffled his feet, then scratched the side of his face, clearly uncomfortable. "You figured that out, huh?" He sucked in a deep breath of air. "I can't imagine Jerry killing Liesel. I always thought they managed their opposing views well and that they shared a mutual respect. But maybe something pushed him over the edge. Only Liesel could tell us that, but she takes great pride in keeping her secrets. To answer your question, nobody has mentioned seeing Jerry at Hair of the Dog that day."

"So it's possible that Jerry killed Sven but meant to murder Oma. If that's the case, he certainly was a cool customer the next day at breakfast."

Dave rubbed his ear. "I'm not supposed to be talking to you about this."

He needed all the help he could get, but I understood his concern. "Okay. I don't want to get you in trouble."

"You're the only person in town who's being nice to me. Everybody else expects me to spill everything I know. If you ask me, there are too many secrets in this town. A lot of people are hiding something."

Twenty-seven

I watched Dave hurry away, winding through the crowds in the shopping area. He was right about Oma having secrets. When I was nine, I'd accidentally caught a guest, Mr. Winestock, exiting the room of another guest, a Mrs. Garland, at six in the morning. They'd engaged in a lingering kiss at her door, and Mr. Winestock had carried his trousers over his arm.

The thought of his expression when he turned and saw me still made me giggle. Poor man. He'd called Oma immediately, not to apologize but to demand that I keep my little mouth shut around his wife, who would be arriving in a few hours and, naturally, was not Mrs. Garland.

Oma had sat me down and explained that innkeepers owed a special duty to their guests not to divulge their secrets. That it wasn't really any of our business if they didn't sleep in their own beds or eat their vegetables.

I laughed aloud at the memory of torturing Oma all that summer about the intersection of lying, being a tattletale, and keeping the secrets of guests. She must have been glad to see me leave that fall!

We arrived at Puppy Love and were immediately greeted

by a shih tzu and a woman with generous curves who wore her thick gray hair cropped close to her head. She threw her hands in the air, clapped them together, and trilled, "You must be little Trixie!"

Trixie waggled all over, and when the woman crouched, Trixie had the nerve to stick her nose into the woman's pocket.

"I'm so sorry!" I tugged at Trixie.

"It's okay. She's darling. She knows I keep goodies in my pocket for sweet little doggies, don't you, baby?" She pulled out thin treats the size of half my pinkie fingernail and fed them to Trixie and the shih tzu. "I've been waiting for you."

"Are you psychic, too?"

She guffawed. "Goodness, no. Zelda called me and said you were coming. I picked out some of our prettiest collars." She bent and showed them to Trixie. "With your white fur, you can wear anything. Do you like black Halloween collars with ghosts or candy corn? Or this one with colorful autumn leaves? That would be nice for Gingersnap. Or a pretty girly pink?"

Since Zelda wasn't there to tell me Trixie's preference, I took it upon myself to choose. "We'll take the candy corn for Trixie, and the autumn-leaf collar as a gift for Gingersnap. Do you have a candy-corn collar for a kitten?"

While Trixie played with the shih tzu, I spent the next few minutes punching information into a machine for tags. Given the unreliable nature of cell phones in Wagtail, I decided to use both my cell phone number and the phone number of the inn on the tags.

Trixie tugged at her leash, pulling away from me. "Just a minute, I'm almost done."

"I know you! You're that little pest that was chasing my foals."

Trixie backed away, pulling against her collar as hard as she could. I rushed to pick her up and turned to find a wizened little man staring at Trixie. White hair fluffed around a face that bore deep leathery creases from long hours in the sun, but the blue eyes sparkled with mischief.

His exquisite tweed jacket hadn't been in style during my lifetime, nor the jaunty tweed ivy-style cap, or plaid bow tie. He peered at me from under bushy eyebrows, his eyes wide.

"Good night, Nelly! You must be a Miller."

"Mr. Wiggins?" I jostled Trixie to extend a hand. "I'm Holly Miller. I used to play with your daughter." He had always seemed old to me. I guessed he was only in his seventies now.

"Prissy is not my daughter!" He trembled and spoke with vehemence.

"I meant Clementine."

"Well, that's all right then." He squinted at me and took my hand. "You're the spittin' image of your grandmother, child. Does that little troublemaker belong to you?"

"I'm afraid she does. She's really very sweet." I scowled at him. "You haven't been shooting at her, have you?"

His mouth twitched sideways. "I chased her, and did some shouting to scare her." He waggled a finger at her. "You stay away from my foals from now on."

A loud bay issued from the beagle on the floor next to him.

"Hah! Baby agrees with me."

Trixie wriggled. It was getting hard to hold her. I backed up a step and set her on the floor, which prompted Baby to bay again.

"She remembers seeing your dog run through our farm with that rat in her mouth."

"Rat?" *Ugh.*

"Might not have been a rat. Some little furry beast. You staying with your grandmother?"

"I am. How's Clementine?"

"Bossing me around is how she is. I'm surrounded by women, and they all boss me like I'm some kind of weak-minded idiot."

The store clerk bustled over. "I'll never do that, Mr. Wiggins." She handed him a plain brown paper grocery bag. "I think Babylicious will enjoy this."

"Babylicious?" It slipped out.

Mr. Wiggins stood a little straighter when he proudly said, "Fireside's Babylicious Boogie. She's the best beagle to ever come out of Fireside Farms. A real winner, aren't you, Baby?"

I didn't know much about beagles, but she was pretty. A beautiful white blaze ran between her gentle eyes. I had a feeling this little beauty lived the good life.

Mr. Wiggins thanked the clerk and told me to give Oma his best.

The clerk chuckled as soon as he left. "Did you see that? He hates Peaches and Prissy so much he won't even patronize their store."

"I thought he was married to Peaches."

She winked at me. "He is! I always give him a plain brown bag so they won't know what he's carrying if they see him."

"Won't they know once they see what he bought?"

She hooked the dog tag to Trixie's new collar. "Word is that he kicked Peaches out of his mansion. She and Prissy are back at their old house here in town. About a year ago, he quit subsidizing their store, and Prissy had to get a part-time job over at the police department in Snowball. Heaven knows, no one around here would hire her."

"Their store isn't doing well?"

She snickered. "Let's just say no one shops there twice. You got to be nice to people. I swear Prissy and Peaches think they can just stand around all dressed up with their fancy jewelry and beauty-salon manicures, and the store will run itself. We've been expecting to see a *Going Out of Business* sign any day. There you go!" She handed me the collar.

I fastened the candy-corn collar around Trixie's neck. "You're mighty lucky Mr. Wiggins didn't pick you off, Trixie. He's a hunter."

"Aww, he's an old softy. He'd never shoot a dog. How long will you be in town? I can have a leash embroidered with Trixie's name for you by tomorrow."

"Given all the leashes around, that might not be a bad idea."

She bagged the other collars in a cute red and brown tote bag bearing the store's name, *Puppy Love*.

No sooner had I thanked her than I heard, "There you are! I've been all over looking for you."

I knew Holmes's sultry voice, masculine yet warm and friendly.

"You have?" We walked out the door together. "What's up?"

"I met Ben. He's kind of a nervous guy. Um, did you know he's looking for some girl named Kim?"

"So I've heard." I gazed into his concerned eyes. Did I

detect a hint of amusement? "Something's up, Holmes. I can't quite figure it out, but it all ties in with Sven's death."

"How about I buy you a cup of coffee, and you tell me about it? Maybe I can help."

"I'd love that, but I should get back to Oma to keep an eye on her."

He tilted his head. "Since when does she need watching? Besides, I just left Grandma Rose there. I got the feeling they wanted me to leave so they could speak privately. How about an ice cream cone? We can find a bench with a good view of the inn."

I agreed, and Holmes led the way to Moo La La, a tiny corner place with only a takeout window. A black and white cow with long lashes held a chalkboard out front showing off the store's latte and ice cream specialties.

Armed with salted caramel-chocolate cones, we settled at a bench on the plaza outside the inn. I was nervous about not checking on Oma first, but I soon spotted her on the porch with Rose. Their heads bent toward each other, they appeared to be deep in a discussion.

I elbowed Holmes. "Check it out. Wonder what they're up to now?"

"I'm afraid to imagine. On the other hand, I hope we're as spunky when we're their age. So what's going on?"

Trixie jumped up on the bench between us and snuggled under my arm.

"What has Rose told you about the night Sven died?"

"Rose and my parents keep telling me to be careful what I say. That this isn't Chicago. The tiniest rumor can swell into a big problem if I'm not careful."

"Surely you're not really a suspect?"

"Surely, I am—in Jerry's death." He licked his ice cream. "Someone says he saw me running away from Jerry's house that morning." He grinned. "And you know what? That's absolutely true."

Twenty-eight

❖ ❖ ❖ ❖

"I went out for a run," said Holmes, "and jogged by Jerry's place so I'd know where I had to go to meet with him later on. Technically, I *was* there, and I *was* running."

I licked my creamy ice cream to buy some time. Holmes had motivation because of that land deal and could be placed at the scene of the crime. No wonder Dave still considered him a suspect. Had Holmes wanted me to walk over to Jerry's with him so I would be present when he found the body? When I had run into him after buying clothes and walked with him to Jerry's, it seemed like a coincidence.

Wait, what was I thinking? This was Holmes! He would never kill anyone. It wasn't possible.

I debated how much to tell Holmes. I had to trust someone. Oma had been her usual stubborn self. Ben had been appropriately appalled, but something fishy was going on with Kim. And he didn't know Wagtail and its residents like Holmes did.

I took a deep breath and told Holmes my theory about Sven being the wrong victim.

"Aw, man! I hate to think that anyone would want to murder Oma, but it makes so much sense. I knew Sven. He was popular, well liked by everyone. A guy's guy." He flicked a horrified gaze toward me. "Not that I'm saying Oma isn't wonderful. She's like a grandmother to me."

"Someone is out to get her, but I can't talk her into leaving town. She thinks we can help Dave catch Sven's killer. Meanwhile, everybody's treating Dave like a nosy little boy, instead of a cop. You know the people around here better than I do." I gulped hard before I asked, "Who would want Oma dead?"

Holmes ran a hand through his hair.

"What about the Clodfelters?" I asked. "Peaches and Oma have never gotten along."

"I don't really see Peaches hitting someone with a car. But Prissy might. She's totally unpredictable."

"Didn't you take her out once?"

He pretended to be annoyed. "You do a nice thing for a person once in your life and no one lets you forget it. She was taller than all the boys her age, and no one asked her to the dance. You remember when she was all gangly limbs like an awkward colt."

"I didn't recognize her when I saw her again. Who would have imagined she would turn into such a knockout? I hear Dave is chasing her. Think he'll consider her a suspect?"

"Doubtful. Where's the motivation?"

"Apparently Peaches made a huge scene at the inn when Mr. Wiggins was having lunch with Oma. Think there's something going on between them?"

"Not that I've ever heard of. He tossed Peaches and Prissy out of the mansion, but I think they'd be inclined to kill Clementine for that, not Oma. Unless . . ."

I scootched around to face him better. "Unless what?"

"Unless Peaches is already working on her next conquest. Everyone knows Thomas, from The Blue Boar, is sweet on our Oma. But maybe Peaches is eyeing him and wants Oma out of the way?"

Seemed kind of flimsy to me. "Who else?"

He snorted. "Jerry. Kind of ironic, eh?"

"I thought about him, too. In fact, I wondered if he was murdered because he tried to kill Oma."

Holmes pulled back and scrutinized me. "Why Holly Miller! I never realized that you were so sly."

"You would be, too, if . . ." I smacked my forehead and gasped so loud that Trixie barked. "How could I be so dense? It was right there in front of me the whole time." I leaned over and whispered, "Mr. Luciano."

"Who's that?"

"One of the guests. I don't know what's going on with him, but the night I arrived, he came in after I did. He was a mess and claimed that someone had beaten him up."

Holmes's forehead crinkled. "I'm not seeing the connection."

"Don't you get it? Nobody attacked him. That was a line he made up—because he's the one who pushed the car over the cliff! He probably fell in the process. Maybe it's harder than we'd think to shove a car over the side of a mountain."

My pulse quickened as my thoughts became clear. "And the next morning, I saw him running right along there." I pointed at the east side of the walking zone. "He could have been on his way to Jerry's, to lie in wait for him."

"Motive?" asked Holmes.

Air fizzled out of me. My brilliant idea deflated like a balloon. "Kind of falls apart right there. I don't know. I wonder what he's doing here. Oma met with him in her office earlier today."

"Maybe he wants to buy the inn."

Few things could have sent as big a shudder through me. "No! Do you think so?"

"You okay? You're pale."

"I never thought about Oma selling the inn. That would be like losing a family member. It would . . ."

"Oh, Holly! Don't cry."

I blinked back the moisture in my eyes. "I'm not crying. It just never occurred to me that the inn would be out of the family."

"You could still come back and visit."

"It wouldn't be the same, and you know it. They would change things."

"You'll get used to the idea."

"Do you know something? Tell me!"

"I don't know beans. But Oma isn't getting any younger. Most people her age have retired and are cruising with drinks in hand instead of waiting on people."

I slumped back against the bench. "Now I'm depressed."

"You have to be kidding me. What did you think would happen? You know your dad and his sister aren't interested in the inn. They fled Wagtail as soon as they could. And Josh, I don't know about him. If he was ever going to quit globe-trotting and settle down, you'd think he would have done it already."

I nodded. My cousin, Josh, had itchy feet. I couldn't imagine him taking over the inn.

Holmes shot a sideways glance at me. "*You* don't have a job."

"I'm a fund-raiser. My life is in Washington. Ben is there, my house, my friends." Trixie whined softly and licked my chin. "Don't worry, you'll go with me. I can't just uproot myself."

"Oma's right." He grinned at me. "You're dry as toast."

"Am not. You just called me sly."

"That just proves there's hope for you."

"I don't see *you* moving back to Wagtail, Mister I-have-to-visit-every-other-weekend-but-I-live-in-Chicago."

"Touché." Holmes gazed at the inn. "I'd try to finagle a way to buy it in a heartbeat. But it's a big place, Holly. With the inn and the grounds and the new additions, we're talking megabucks. It's not like Joe Schmoe can come along and buy it. Besides, my fiancé would never agree to live here." His sigh reflected my feelings.

I knew what he meant. We had other obligations. We had built lives where we lived. I tried to push the ugly thoughts about losing the inn away. "Back to where we were, do you think Luciano would have tried to kill her so he could buy the inn?"

"Let's walk through this. He steals the car—"

"The car was stolen weeks ago."

"Okay. So he stole the car and hid it somewhere. Then he parked it on Oak Street?"

"Right. He opened the gate to let Dolce out, walked over

to Hair of the Dog, called the inn and reported that Dolce was loose, then returned to the car, and wham—he hit Sven instead of Oma."

"Then why did he kill Jerry?" asked Holmes.

"I don't know. In fact, nobody seems to know where Jerry was that night."

"Are you suggesting that Jerry murdered Sven and Luciano killed Jerry?"

I grabbed his arm. "Maybe! Luciano couldn't have made the phone call. Chloe said she was busy giving him directions when the call came in." I handed Trixie the empty butt of my ice cream cone. "Okay, here's what we'll do. You ask around town to see what you can find out, especially where Jerry went that night. In the meantime, I'll find out what I can about Luciano."

"Deal. Uh-oh. Here comes trouble."

Ben ambled toward us. "I can't find her. Not anywhere. Wagtail isn't that big! What am I going to tell Kim's father?"

"You're looking for a little girl?" Holmes sat up in alarm. "I thought we were talking about an adult!"

"Relax, Holmes. Kim is an adult. And she intentionally ditched Ben."

And just like that, she reappeared, carrying a shopping bag from Prissy Clodfelter's store.

"Where have you been?" demanded Ben. "I've been looking for you for hours."

"Don't be put out, schnookums." Kim held her head down and raised her eyes in a manner calculated to be flirtatious.

That raised Holmes's eyebrows.

"They used to date," I explained.

"I just stopped to do a little shopping." She leaned over to Trixie. "Look what I bought you!" Kim reached into the bag and withdrew a cat-shaped cookie.

Trixie almost lost her balance in her eagerness to reach it. Her tail wagged, and she extended her neck as far as she dared trying to reach the bag. Her little black nose twitched. There must have been more in the bag.

"Thanks, Kim. I'm going to have to put her on a diet. People have been offering Trixie treats all day long."

"Trixie!" Kim crooked her neck. "That's so cute. "Well, you'd better enjoy these treats, Trixie, because I'm not shopping there again. The woman in that store was so rude. Cute place with a terrific window display, but she was such a snoot."

Trixie wore an expectant expression and wiggled her behind. No doubt hoping for another treat.

"Aww. I want a dog," Kim whined.

"Want that one?" asked Ben.

I pulled Trixie closer. "Very funny."

"They don't allow dogs in my building," Ben reminded me.

"I don't live in your building."

"What are you going to do with her when you come over? Leave her in the car? Hey! Speaking of cars, where is mine?"

"Parked in the inn lot." I dreaded the moment he would see it. Might as well get it over with.

"I'll drive the golf cart back to the house and change for dinner," chirped Kim.

Ben seized her arm without looking at her. "Not so fast. *You* come with me. I'm checking out of the inn and sleeping at your cabin tonight."

Twenty-nine

❀ ❀ ❀ ❀ ❀

"I can't trust you not to say or do something that might get you into trouble," said Ben, scowling at Kim. "I'm not losing you for hours again. I could use a leash for you."

That was a fine excuse! Painfully aware that Holmes watched me, I tried to play it cool. "Do you need a chaperone?"

Kim's eyes flickered over Holmes, head to toe. "Depends on who it is."

"Down, Kim. He's engaged." I apologized for not introducing them.

Kim swayed a little, cocked her head again in her obnoxiously provocative way, and made eye contact with Holmes. "Engagements were made to be broken."

Ben huffed.

"Well, hurry up! I don't want to miss all of Yappy Hour." Kim glanced at her wrist as though she'd forgotten she wasn't wearing a watch. "Let's all have dinner together. Won't that be fun?"

I couldn't think of many things that would be less fun.

But Holmes was game. "In an hour and a half at Hair of the Dog?"

Kim pouted. "Oh, not there." She wrinkled her nose. "Can't we go someplace more interesting? Let's see, I feel like . . . barbecue!"

"Hot Hog, then." Holmes stood up and stretched. "I'll meet you there."

At nine o'clock that night, Holmes walked Trixie and me back to the inn. During dinner, Kim had flirted with everyone except me. She knew no bounds. Ben, Holmes, the waiter—everyone seemed to love her.

"Not that it's any of my business," said Holmes, "but I don't think I'd trust Kim alone with Ben."

"She's quite an operator. But I trust Ben. He's too . . ." I stopped myself. I almost said he was too *boring* to have an affair! That was terrible on so many levels that it boggled my mind. "He's too decent to have an affair."

We walked up the front steps, and Twinkletoes greeted us at the front door, mewing and twisting around our ankles. She even touched noses with Trixie.

Holmes gazed at the guests milling around in the Dogwood Room. "Where do you suppose the dotty grandmothers are?"

Twinkletoes scampered through a dog door in the wall just past the dining tables.

The second I removed Trixie's leash, she followed Twinkletoes.

"Kitchen." We said it simultaneously.

I opened the door that bore the words *Staff Only*, and found that Oma's private kitchen looked almost like I remembered it. Oma, Rose, and Gingersnap lounged comfortably before a blazing fire.

"I'm so glad you left the kitchen intact!" I gushed. "I always loved this room."

In the glow of the fire, Oma seemed healthy and relaxed. "Me, too, liebchen. It has always been my private refuge."

Ancient beams ran across the ceiling. A fireplace with a raised hearth occupied a spot in a stone wall. The huge center island was still a blue that verged on farmhouse turquoise.

Although it was dark outside, I knew the big windows over

the kitchen sink on the far end of the kitchen overlooked the mountains and the lake. The door to the left led outside to a small herb garden and Oma's private patio.

But, sadly, the back staircase had been a victim of the remodeling. In the rear right corner, where the stairs should have been, a bookcase lined the wall.

Holmes fetched two wine glasses. I poured Pomeranian Pomegranate wine into the glasses.

"It's research," said Oma. "I wouldn't want to offer our guests something I hadn't tried first."

I perched on the hearth, warming up by the fire. Candles flickered gently. Oma had switched on only the lights under the rustic pine cabinets. Their cozy glow bathed the room in golden light.

Holmes snagged another comfortable chair and relaxed, his long legs outstretched so that his shoes nearly touched mine.

Classical music that I couldn't quite identify played very softly in the background. If I hadn't known about Oma's troubles, I would have thought it the most wonderfully warm and comforting moment. The way life should be. Good wine with good friends and beloved family. Twinkletoes kneaded in my lap while Trixie looked on. She fixated on my eyes, sending a very clear message—*That should be me on your lap!*

I reached out to stroke her fur. Apparently, that wasn't enough. She curled up next to me, pushing against my thigh as tightly as she could.

Oma didn't make eye contact with me when she said, "I heard the Ben checked out. Did he go home?"

Holmes snorted. "Sorry, Holly. You're being too calm about this." He faced our grandmothers. "Ben is staying with Kim at her dad's cabin."

A smile twitched on Oma's lips. Why did I get the feeling that she and Rose would high-five if I wasn't present?

"There's nothing to worry about," I assured them. "Ben is a very responsible person. I'm sure that's why Kim's father insisted he accompany her. She pulled a fast one on Ben earlier today and disappeared for hours. She claimed she was shopping, but all she carried was one bag with dog treats in it. A flimsy attempt to back up her shopping story if you ask me."

"I hope you're right about Ben's character, because Kim is definitely a vamp," said Holmes.

Rose frowned at Holmes. "Does that still mean what it used to mean?"

"Sure does. Ben is probably fighting her off as we speak."

I had to come to Ben's defense. I might have been let down by his totally unromantic proposal, but poor Ben was a good guy. "I hardly think he would have proposed to me if he planned to fall into Kim's arms."

Oma bit her lip.

Rose snickered. "Are you talking about that e-mail he sent you? Honey," she shook her head sadly, "you marry him, and I swear I will be the one who jumps up and makes a fuss when the preacher asks if anyone objects to the marriage."

"That's because you don't know him. He's a nice man."

Trixie took that inopportune moment to yawn and let out a complaining wail.

Fortunately, we all laughed, and the subject changed to getting Trixie a vet appointment. In the chaos, I'd forgotten all about that.

"So Oma," I said, "what's the deal with Peaches and Prissy Clodfelter? Why do they despise us so?"

Rose spewed wine. She sat up straight and dabbed at her blouse. "I hope this doesn't stain. Liesel! You never told Holly?"

"Told me what?"

My grandmother sucked in a deep breath and gazed at the ceiling. "I suppose you're old enough to know now. Peaches is what my generation called a gold digger."

Rose chuckled. "She's a devil in a skirt."

"She wanted to marry your father."

"*My* father?" I shuddered at the thought. "When was this?"

"About the time your parents decided to divorce. Peaches came around claiming your father had gotten her pregnant."

"With Prissy?" My hair stood on end. "Please tell me Prissy isn't my sister!"

"Have you seen the size of that girl?" Oma asked. "There's never been a Miller that tall. No, Prissy's father was someone else, but Peaches thought she could con your dad into marriage."

"Wait a minute," said Holmes. "I'm the tallest in my family. It happens."

Rose leaned toward Holmes and me. "The reason Peaches hates Liesel so much is because Liesel had the baby tested."

"Oma!" I exclaimed.

"I am many things. But I am not a fool. I was not going to allow that woman to destroy your father. If the baby had been his, that would have been one thing. But I knew it wasn't."

My head reeled from the revelation. "Why didn't you tell me this before?"

"It is no longer important," said Oma. "Old stuff that no one cares about anymore."

"Peaches still cares about it," I said.

"If she resents me, then it is her problem. She is the one who lied. I did what I had to do and have no regrets about it."

An hour later, Holmes walked Rose home, and Oma trundled off to bed with Gingersnap. I pretended to go up to my quarters, but I simply left my purse on the coffee table and promptly returned to the second floor. I located the housekeeping closet, where we kept the cleaning supplies and linens, and rummaged around. Trixie waited outside the door. I found two blankets and a pillow. That should do the trick.

I tiptoed down the hallway to the balcony overlooking the reception area. Murmuring voices stopped, and I could hear footsteps on the stairs. Probably Oma! There wasn't any place to hide.

I hurried back to the housekeeping closet and called Trixie. The silly girl wouldn't come. Would—not—come. Evidently, she had a fear of small spaces—the elevator, the bathroom, and now the housekeeping closet, which was the size of a walk-in closet. Glancing toward the staircase, I lunged at her, scooped her into my arms, smuggled the writhing dog inside, and closed the door.

She fought me with all her strength. "Quit that! No one is going to hurt you." Thank goodness she didn't bark.

I counted *one Mississippi, two Mississippi* until I thought Oma must have passed the point where she could see me.

The hallway lay still when we emerged. I set Trixie down and grabbed my blankets and pillow. Trixie didn't quite understand the stealthy nature of our operation, but I did my best to walk very quietly.

My timing couldn't have been better. I peeked around the corner just in time to see Gingersnap's tail vanish inside Oma's apartment. The lock clicked behind them.

Perfect! I tiptoed to her door, spread out one of the blankets on the floor, and propped the pillow up against her door. If I fell asleep, I would surely wake if it opened for any reason.

Twinkletoes showed up and demonstrated how she'd acquired her name. She walked along the banister of the balcony as unconcerned as if she were walking on the floor. I knew cats were supposed to right themselves when they fell, but it scared the wits out of me anyway. Moving slowly, so I wouldn't alarm her, I approached her and gently gathered her into my arms, away from that dangerous railing.

Beneath us, Casey worked at the desk. I could only assume that he hadn't heard us yet. I hoped to keep it that way.

I snuggled, as much as anyone could, on the hard floor. I had covered it with one blanket and thrown the other one over me. My trousers cut into my waist, and I wished I had taken the time to brush my teeth. I didn't dare leave, though. I unfastened the top of my trousers and felt more comfortable. Trixie must have forgiven me for wresting her into the tiny housekeeping room because she curled up next to me, her body pressing against the blanket by my hips.

Twinkletoes roamed the balcony. Sconces lighted the area where I lay. Through the ornate wrought iron of the railing, I could see the lights on the antler chandelier that hung in the reception area below.

Easing back against the pillow, I closed my eyes but couldn't help thinking about Ben and Holmes. Just between me and myself, I knew deep in my heart that if I thought I had even a remote chance with Holmes, I would drop Ben. The thought crushed me. I'd been so sure Ben was the one for me. In spite of Oma and Rose's assessment, I knew he was a warm and caring man. Okay, given his two terrible proposals, I could scratch *warm*. The second one hadn't really been a proposal of marriage at all. He was smart, even if Kim had managed to elude him today. He was genuine—that was important. He didn't pretend to be something he wasn't. He was serious. So he didn't make me laugh much. What was more important? Laughter or taking life seriously?

I squiggled down into a more comfortable position, landing on my cell phone. Probably not a good thing.

The phone at the reception desk rang softly beneath me.

I yanked my phone out from under the blanket and realized with horror that I'd managed to dial the inn when I sat on it. "Uh, sorry, Casey," I whispered. "My mistake."

I set the phone on the floor, on the other side of Trixie, where I couldn't accidentally roll over on it in my sleep.

I settled down and closed my eyes. The truth was that my love for Holmes was just a remnant of a schoolgirl infatuation. Honestly! What had happened to me? I came to the land of dogs and cats, where people spoke of ghosts like they were real, and I'd lost all good sense. Holmes wasn't available, and even if I woke up tomorrow morning and discovered that he had broken off his engagement, he probably wasn't the person I had manufactured in my mind as the perfect guy. So there. I had to get back to reality. Ben might be unimaginative, but he was a solid person.

I must have drifted off. The next thing I knew, Trixie barked. Like a periscope, Twinkletoes aimed her attention at the hallway. Trixie barked again. Scrambling to her feet, she kicked my phone over the balcony and took off running.

"Shh!" I loped after her. "Trixie?" I hissed.

Where could she have gone?

The door to *Heel* opened, and Mr. Luciano stepped out. "What's going on?"

I had to stop, however briefly. "My apologies for the noise, Mr. Luciano."

He tightened the belt of his black satin bathrobe. "Do you need help? Is there anything I can do?"

"No. Thank you." I said softly, hoping we weren't waking everyone. "Everything is fine."

Almost, anyway. I took off running as quietly as possible

along the hallway. At the main stairs, I listened. No barking. No pitter-patter of little paws. I ran up the stairs to my floor. No sign of Trixie.

I trotted downstairs to the main floor and looked in Oma's private kitchen. No dog. Breathing hard, half from fear and half from rushing around, I hurried through the library, the hallways of the cat wing, the sitting area, and back upstairs to my fancy quarters. My last hope was that she had returned to the balcony where we had slept. I stumbled down the stairs and back through the hallway on the second floor. No sign of Mr. Luciano this time. I held my breath as I rounded the corner. The blankets and pillow remained undisturbed.

Gingersnap barked inside Oma's apartment.

"Shh, Gingersnap! Everything is okay."

I kept saying that to pacify everyone else. Meanwhile, *my* nerves had stretched to their limit. "Shh."

It didn't help. Gingersnap barked like she'd seen a squirrel run through Oma's apartment.

As quietly and reassuringly as I could, I said, "It's all right, Gingersnap. No barking."

She still barked. *Woof, woof, woof. Woof, woof, woof.* Oma must be awake by now. I dashed down the stairs.

"Casey, could I have a key to Oma's apartment?"

His lips pulled tight, grim. "I'm not supposed to give them to anybody." But he handed me a ring of keys. "It's the pink one."

I staggered back up the stairs, anxious to halt Gingersnap's incessant barking. *Woof, woof, woof.*

I slid the key into the lock, twisted it, and opened the door to a dark apartment. Gingersnap butted her head into my thighs and refused to budge. At least she wasn't barking anymore. I stroked her head and gave her a big hug.

How could Oma have possibly slept through that? I managed to evade Gingersnap, who continued to demand my attention, and tiptoed over to Oma's bedroom. Could she have slept so deeply that she missed the commotion?

Gingersnap burst past me and leaped onto the bed. She wouldn't sleep through that!

"Oma, I'm so sorry."

She didn't respond.

"Oma?"

Nothing.

My heart sped up again, beating like it would fly out of my chest. I flicked on the light.

Thirty

❀ ❀ ❀

No Oma. Except for the wrinkles Gingersnap had probably caused, I didn't think her bed had been slept in.

I looked around in case she had fallen. Although I found no sign of Oma, there, on her dresser, in plain sight, lay cruise brochures. Hong Kong, Singapore, Japan. I flapped them down with irritation. Either she was planning a vacation or Holmes knew all along that Oma was ready to let the inn go. Rose had probably confided in him. Why hadn't Oma come right out and told me? It seemed so obvious to me now. She was ready to retire and sell the inn.

Where was she, though? I had seen her go into her apartment and heard her lock the door. There was no way she could have left, unless she escaped through a window and rappelled down the outside of the building.

I had to be losing my grip. First Trixie vanished, and now Oma. *Aha*. Of course. Oma must have departed while I was out looking for Trixie.

Releasing a huge sigh, I left, taking Gingersnap with me so she wouldn't start barking again. I locked Oma's door and returned the keys to Casey, suddenly feeling very, very tired.

"Do you know where my grandmother went?"

Casey's eyes rounded, wide with fright. "I haven't seen her."

"She must be here somewhere. Maybe she's making hot milk so she can sleep."

"Where's your dog?"

"I don't know. With Oma, maybe? I'm so tired. Just watch, I'll head over to the kitchen and will find the two of them having a grand old time eating a midnight snack."

"I saw the blankets. Why are you sleeping up there?"

"To keep an eye on her."

"That didn't turn out very well."

Little smarty-pants! "Thank you. Now I feel so much better," I said sarcastically.

He handed me my phone, which he must have rescued after Trixie kicked it over the balcony. "You're lucky the phone didn't break. But you're going to feel worse. I'm sorry. I read the message."

I flicked it on. *I hereby rescind all prior proposals of marriage.*

I laughed too loud and clapped a hand over my mouth, hoping I hadn't woken anyone.

"It's funny?" Casey repositioned his glasses.

My entire body shook with laughter. In fact, I couldn't stop laughing. It was too weird. I'd been offended by the original proposal, and now I had been electronically dumped!

Casey looked at me like I had lost my mind.

I was still laughing when I left him and returned to Oma's kitchen with Gingersnap. But in one second, nothing was funny anymore. No Oma, and no sign of Trixie.

Where had they gone? I wandered back to the grand staircase. The front door wasn't locked. What time did they lock it at night? I peeked out at the rocking chairs on the porch, and scanned the plaza in front of the inn—dead quiet. Not a soul moved.

I returned inside and locked the front door behind me.

"Didn't find her?"

A little squeal escaped me. I whirled around and found Mr. Luciano in the Dogwood Room. He still wore the black bathrobe, but now he held an old-fashioned glass that contained an amber liquid.

"Scotch?" he asked.

It wasn't my drink. "No, thanks. Have you seen my grand-mother?"

"Not since earlier this evening. She's a wonderful person, your grandmother. I hope you cherish her."

"I do." I smiled at him reassuringly.

He sat down and crossed his legs, displaying surprisingly elegant gold jacquard pajama pants. "My own grandmother came here from Italy. But not the Italy that everybody thinks of—Rome or Sicily. My family came from the mountains in northern Italy. Tyrol, they call it. Have you been there? It's beau-tiful. Very relaxing, like it is here." He stroked Gingersnap's head.

"It sounds lovely."

"It is. I love coming to the Sugar Maple Inn, too. But this has been a stressful trip for me."

A little shudder hammered through me. Was he about to confess to murder? What had he done with Oma? Had she left her suite right after me and run into him in the hallway while I raced around like an idiot looking for Trixie?

"Where is Oma?" My voice came out breathy and nervous. "Where is my dog?"

He didn't seem to notice my agitation. "You know, when you're born, your mother and father love you like no other person ever will. Not even your wife."

Was he delusional? I played along. "You're married?"

"Not anymore. She left me—" he waggled his head from side to side "—and now she's not with us." He sipped his Scotch. "But a dog . . . a dog will love you like your mama. Unconditional, they call it. No matter what you do, a dog will forgive you and defend you."

"What happened to your wife?" I whispered, almost afraid to hear his answer.

"Oddly, I find I do not care about her any longer. She is not worthy of my devotion or my interest."

My patience wore thin. Did he know where Oma was? "What about my grandmother? Is she worthy?"

"Oh my, yes. I'm grateful for her kindness and wisdom. She has been most considerate this week."

I couldn't help myself, my voice rose to a shrill pitch. "Then where is she?"

He stood up and faced me. "Are you saying she's missing?"

I blinked at him, unable to discern whether he was lying or being honest. "I can't find her—or Trixie."

"It's the middle of the night. They must be around here somewhere."

I dearly wanted to get a peek inside his room. The rational side of me hoped I was being melodramatic. Only on a TV show would a guest hide the innkeeper in his room. Still . . . what excuse could I use?

"You don't suppose Trixie dodged into your room while the door was open?"

"Let's go look!"

He must not be hiding Oma there or he wouldn't have been so eager. Nevertheless, I sidestepped to the house phone in the entrance and called Casey. "I'm going upstairs to *Heel* to see if Trixie sneaked into Mr. Luciano's room."

The moment of silence on the other end clued me in— Casey didn't understand why I was calling him. "Won't Mr. Luciano be upset if you wake him?"

"He's right here with me."

"Oh. Ohhhhh! Gotcha covered!"

Mr. Luciano made small talk about Oma, and we ventured up the stairs with Gingersnap leading the way. As we turned down the hallway, Casey peered around the corner and immediately flipped his back against the wall to hide.

I hoped Mr. Luciano hadn't seen him.

"That Casey is a funny fellow," he said.

Whoops. No question that he'd seen Casey.

He unlocked the door to *Heel*, left it open and called, "Trixie. Trixie, treat! Please—" he swept his arm to the side in a grand gesture "—feel free to look around."

I checked the bathroom and called out Trixie's name, hoping that if he'd tied up Oma in a closet, she would hear me and bang against the door. I observed Gingersnap, whose superior nose would surely know if Oma or Trixie was stashed away somewhere. She sniffed around, wagging her tail, evidently unconcerned.

Over the years, I had seen a lot of guest rooms. Mr. Luciano kept his tidy. The only thing that threw me for a loop was the luxurious faux fur bolster dog bed with the name *Gina* embroidered on it. I hadn't seen him with a dog. I was afraid to ask about her. He'd spoken with such sentimentality about the love of a dog that I feared he might have lost his Gina before I arrived.

"Thank you, Mr. Luciano. I'm sorry to have troubled you."

"You did the right thing calling Casey. You'll be a fine innkeeper one day. Just like your grandmother."

He closed the door behind Gingersnap and me, and I felt an idiot for having suspected him of anything sinister.

Casey waited for us where the hallway met the balcony. "You should start carrying a walkie-talkie with you."

"I didn't expect to be nosing around in a guest room. Where could they have gone?"

"Mrs. Miller has to be around here somewhere. I never saw her leave."

"She must have slipped out of her room when I shot down the hallway in search of Trixie. That's the only reasonable explanation."

"All I know is that she didn't leave through the reception door. I would have noticed that."

"The front door was unlocked. She must have gone out that way."

His eyes grew wide. "I forgot to lock it tonight!"

"Don't worry about it. She could have simply unlocked it and left."

The adrenaline that had pumped through me waned, and the exhaustion of the wee hour of the morning weighed on me. I needed to wake up and keep a clear head to find them. "I'm going to make coffee. Want some?"

"Sure. That would be great. I'm almost done with bills for the guests checking out in the morning."

I took my time walking back through the quiet inn. I paused and remembered Christmas in the Dogwood Room, with a towering tree full of Oma's old blown-glass Christmas ornaments from Germany. Did Oma still hold a big Thanksgiving dinner for family and friends in the dining area? Why had I missed out on all that fun? I knew the answer. The divorce. Each of my parents had remarried and started new families, and I had bounced around between them on holidays and vacations like a beach ball. They had made new lives for themselves elsewhere and hadn't been interested in returning to Wagtail, even for holidays. Even though they were my parents, I'd often felt like the occasional visitor, instead of family. I had spent my holidays trying to make everyone happy. Everyone except me.

Oma had done a wonderful job with the renovation. Now that I suspected she wanted to retire, I knew why she'd updated the inn. It was gorgeous. Mountain chic, as Oma would say. Rustic elegance. My eyes misted at the thought of losing it.

I wiped my eyes. When did I turn into a big softie? It was a business. That was all. Just stone and wood and . . . and—

Shrill yipping tore through the quiet.

Thirty-one

❀ ❀ ❀ ❀

Trixie? Where was she? The pitch of her barks was enough to wake the proverbial dead and most certainly the sleeping guests.

Ginger and I followed her excited yaps to the door. She waited on the front porch, yipping and jumping up to peer through the glass. When I opened the door, she dashed inside, her entire body wriggling with joy. She planted her front paws on my knees, and I bent over to hug her. Her tail whipped back and forth so fast I warned her that it might fly right off.

When I straightened up, she pranced around my feet, never taking those devoted eyes off of me. Mr. Luciano's words came back to me. *Unconditional love.*

I crouched to hug her again. She couldn't get enough affection. But my joy at her return quickly dampened and morphed into horror.

Her new Halloween collar and dog tags were gone. The Sugar Maple Inn collar with GPS was also missing. She wore a simple brown collar attached to a yellow leash.

Someone had taken her.

Trixie might have been able to back out of her collars

somehow, but no matter how I tried to rationalize the situation, she could not possibly have put on the brown collar or the unfamiliar leash.

My hands shook when I removed them. Could they be fingerprinted? Even if they could, no one would bother with two murders to be solved. They'd think I was a nut if I asked.

But someone had taken my little Trixie on purpose. Why would anyone want her? "You're such a good girl to come back. Who took you, sweetie? Did you escape from that horrible person? C'mon."

She and Gingersnap launched ahead of me down the hallway to the reception area. She pranced with joy at seeing Casey, too.

I slammed the strange collar and leash on the reception desk. "Look at this! Someone took her."

He stroked her back and stared at her neck. "Where's the GPS collar?"

"Gone!" I spoke louder than I should have.

His eyebrows dived into a worried V, and he chewed on his upper lip.

A voice with a charming German accent accosted us from above. "What's going on? What are all these blankets doing here?"

I turned my gaze upward to Oma. Clad in flannel pajamas and a fuzzy white bathrobe, she peered down at us. Gingersnap raced up the stairs to her.

"Did you see her come in?" I whispered to Casey.

"Sure didn't. And I haven't left this general area for even a minute."

There were other doors, of course, and Oma had the keys to all of them. "I think we need to talk."

"Liebling, it's so late. Go to bed." She hastily returned to her room and closed the door.

"I just don't know what to think." I pulled out another inn collar with GPS, as well as a leash.

"Is there any reason your grandmother would have, um, taken Trixie?" asked Casey.

I wanted to scream *no!* But the same thought had crossed my mind. The timing was too coincidental. "Not that I know of. Now that she's back, I guess I'll skip the coffee and curl up outside her door. Is that okay with you?"

"Yeah. You might as well go up to bed, though. She managed to leave and come back without either one of us seeing her."

"To tell you the truth, I'm more worried about someone getting into her apartment."

Maybe he had a point. I was so exhausted that someone could probably step on me without waking me. I said good night, and with the leash firmly around my wrist, I collected the pillow and blankets. We walked along the hallway to the stairs. I thought I heard a cat cry. "Twinkletoes?"

Tired as I was, I headed downstairs again to be sure she was all right. We discovered her in the darkened library, on the window seat facing the plaza. She sat hunched, ready to pounce, peering out into the night, emitting an occasional complaining yowl.

We hopped up on the window seat with her. "What do you see?" I whispered. "A bunny? A raccoon?"

If she did, I didn't notice, because my attention went straight to the lone figure in the shadows just to the side of the plaza. I couldn't make out anything about him or her, but I knew that person was watching the inn.

I dropped the blankets and rushed to the phone in the entrance. I dialed Dave's home number. After I told him the situation, he said, "Holly, it's not illegal to stand on the plaza, even at this ungodly hour."

"Are you kidding me? With all that has happened, you're not going to check to see who it is?"

Silence. "Okay, yeah."

I hung up and returned to the window seat. The person had left.

I collected the blankets again, stopped by the phone to call Dave and tell him to go back to bed, and then headed straight back to Oma's apartment, where I slept by her door until she opened it and said, "Ja, what is this?"

My sleep-deprived brain convinced me to imagine Oma would be fine. Shelley and the cook had arrived. Early-bird guests were stirring, and Casey was awake. I dragged upstairs, with poor Trixie on a leash so she couldn't make any mad dashes. Twinkletoes scurried along in front of us. When we reached the top, Trixie sniffed the floor and turned to the left. "Wrong way, cutie!"

She faced me, wagging her tail but not budging, as though she expected me to let her into the storage area.

"This way, silly!" I was too tired to think clearly. I'd look in there later, after some sleep.

We fell into bed. I remembered to take off Trixie's GPS collar since we were safely inside, and the three of us slept in.

I woke at eleven, mainly because Twinkletoes was sitting on my chest, touching my face with a soft paw. Either she wanted food or she was trying to figure out if I was still alive. The former, I decided. When I rose and staggered into the kitchen to serve her shredded chicken in gravy with minced egg for cats, Trixie stayed behind in bed, upside down with all four paws in the air.

After showering, I realized that the only garments that didn't need washing were the dresses. I chose the least dressy one. Made of cotton, it had a white background printed with occasional peach, pink, and yellow flowers that increased over the length of the dress until they ended in a colorful pile at the hemline. Sort of like fall leaves, only for summer. I liked the square neckline, but it might be getting too late in the year for sleeveless garments.

Starved, I roused Trixie and put the GPS collar back on her. The second I opened the door, she ran to the storage area door. She pawed and tried to wedge her nose underneath it.

"What do you want in there?" Twinkletoes and I started down the main stairs. "Come on, Trixie." She gave up on the storage room and raced ahead of me with the kind of energy I wished I had.

Oma happened to see us and came to the bottom of the stairs. She held out her arms and hugged me. "Casey told me what happened last night." She placed one hand on my shoulder. "I cannot believe that you would sleep on the floor to protect your Oma."

"I'm worried about you."

She held my hand between both of hers. "We will make it through this together. You and me, Holly. Now, go have some brunch. You're going to freeze in that dress."

She bustled off, and I turned to the dining area. And who had the nerve to wave me over to his table? Ben. Mister I-hereby-rescind.

Thirty-two

✻ ✻ ✻ ✻

Oh, joy. What could I do? I searched around, desperate for a reason to sit at another table. The place was packed.

"Holly!" Ben nearly jumped up. He acted like the kid in school who was always absurdly eager to have the teacher call on him.

I squared my shoulders. There was no reason we couldn't be friends. "Come on, Trixie."

I sat down. "Good morning. Where's your girlfriend?" Okay, so maybe that wasn't the nicest way to start, but it was how I felt.

"She's sleeping in. Dave knows he's not allowed to speak to her unless I'm present. I have the golf cart, and I really don't see her walking all the way down here. So, to my way of thinking, I've got all my bases covered. Man, I slept better last night than I have in years. Must be the fresh mountain air."

He grinned at me brightly, but I suspected his perfect night's sleep was the result of a certain romantic interlude, and I thought it downright rude to rub my nose in it.

Shelley poured me a cup of tea, winked at me, and left the pot on the table. "What can I get you this morning?"

Swell. Casey had already blabbed to everyone about the rescinded proposal.

"I'll have what Holly had yesterday, with the home fries and the toast and the works!" Ben beamed.

I'd never seen him so happy. Why did I want to blow a raspberry at him?

"What's the special today?" I asked.

"Eggs Benedict. Your choice of smoked salmon or Canadian bacon."

"Does that come with the home fries?" asked Ben.

"If you want it to."

"I'll change to that, please, with the salmon."

"I'll have the same, with fruit salad instead of the home fries."

"Same for you, Trixie?" asked Shelley.

"Salmon for dogs?" asked Ben.

"They love it! But we use baked salmon for the dogs, not smoked, because it's so salty." Shelley rested her hand over top of mine briefly. "How you doin', hon?"

I did my best to seem on top of the world. "Great!"

But I caught her tilting her head and grinning at someone. When I turned to look, Holmes ambled up to our table. Easygoing with that natural smile of his, he slid into one of the chairs at our table. "Mornin' all."

Without having to ask, Shelley poured coffee into his mug. "Eggs Benedict?"

"My favorite!"

She tittered like he'd flirted with her and scooted away to another table.

"Heard you had a rough night here," said Holmes.

When I was about ten, Holmes, my cousin Josh, and I had gone through a stage where we formed a fist with a knuckle sticking out, and punched one another in the upper arm. I reached over and pretended to punch him.

"What's that for?"

"For being so annoyingly right. Rose told you about the cruise, didn't she? You knew all along."

He held up his palms. "I swear she never said a word about it. So Oma confirmed it?"

"No. I found brochures in her room last night."

"What's wrong with her taking a cruise?" asked Ben. "Sounds like a good idea."

I flashed a warning at Holmes that I hoped he understood. I didn't want to talk about the inn being sold where guests might hear. "Nothing. She could use a vacation."

Ben's gaze flickered between Holmes and me. He knew something was up. He played along, though. "So what happened last night?"

Again, I skipped the part about Oma. There was no point in guests overhearing and thinking she was out wandering through town in the middle of the night. "Someone stole Trixie."

She perked up at the sound of her name.

I told them the whole story, ending with the curious change of collars. Shelley served tables near us, but she listened in as I talked.

"Why would anyone *want* her?" asked Ben.

I forgave him for the callous way it sounded. I knew what he meant. I shrugged.

Shelley placed a platter on the table in front of me. A beautiful yellow sauce covered an egg. Bright orange salmon peeked out from underneath it.

Trixie danced on her hind legs.

"Yours is comin', darlin'." Shelley served Ben and Holmes, then bent down to place Trixie's dish on the floor. Trixie's nose was in it so fast I barely caught a glimpse of egg and salmon.

"Not that it's any of my business," said Shelley, "but you could track the GPS on the collar. Now, if the dog thief has any sense at all, he would have tossed that collar out in the woods somewhere so it wouldn't be connected to him. But it's worth a try."

Another patron signaled her, and she rushed off.

"That's brilliant!" I exclaimed. "Why didn't I think of that? Those collars must be expensive, so at the very least, we ought to recover it."

"I think we'd better come with you," said Holmes. "You don't know where it might take you."

"Yeah!" Ben speared a home fry. "What if it's in somebody's house? You don't want to come face-to-face with the dog burglar." Gazing at his plate, he added, "These are so good they don't need catsup."

The rich hollandaise sauce complemented the flavor of the salty salmon. We finished our delicious, if indulgent, breakfast quickly. I reminded myself that it wouldn't be long before I was back in my own home, eating dry toast or boiled eggs for breakfast. I might as well enjoy the inn while I could. If Oma sold it, this might be the last time I would come here, a thought that depressed me to the core of my being.

We hurried over our second mugs of coffee and, in my case, tea.

Unfortunately, now that Trixie knew the drill, she kept pulling at the leash, wanting to eat other dogs' food. We were going to have to learn some table manners.

I carried her out of the dining room, far easier than tugging her away from the dog dining bowls on the floor. She scampered along happily, though, to the registration desk. Oma gave us a questioning look when we trooped in.

"How do you track a GPS collar?" I asked.

"Aha. Very clever of you."

I gave Shelley due credit for the idea.

Oma went to the computer and looked up the number of the collar, which made me feel very guilty because I had simply grabbed another one last night without logging it in. We corrected that immediately.

She handed us a small black box similar in size to a TV remote control. A screen filled one side, and a tiny antenna stood on the end. "This will show you the direction of the collar. This number shows how far away it is."

As we watched, the number flickered and reduced by one, then by two.

"It's moving," said Holmes.

"Maybe the thief is carrying it," I suggested. "Or put it on his own dog."

"It's toward the front of the inn," said Oma.

Trixie leading the way, Holmes, Ben, and I rushed to the front porch.

"This is like a treasure hunt," said Ben.

If I hadn't been so upset about the theft of Trixie, I would have thought it fun, too.

I held the transmitter in my outstretched hand so they could see it. "It's still moving, but toward our left a little." Like a unified military unit, we all changed our position.

I looked out over the plaza in front of the inn. It could be anyone. Brewster, wearing a Hair of the Dog T-shirt, walked toward us with his Irish setter, Murphy. Philip, the B and B owner, juggled a couple of bakery boxes not too far behind him. To their left, Peaches Clodfelter argued with Tiny.

Jerry's mother, Ellie, trained Dolce, trying to get him to sit and ignore everyone around him. Dolce didn't show any interest in the other dogs, but Ellie struggled to keep him focused when Philip passed by them. Dolce refused to sit and tried to follow him.

My dreaded Aunt Birdie marched toward us. Even Mr. Luciano paced on the plaza, checking his watch every few seconds.

Oma hobbled up behind us and peered at the receiver in my hand. "That collar is coming back on its own. It's only twenty-five feet away."

I held my breath, waiting for the little signal on the gizmo to turn away. Instead the number of feet continued to decrease.

Thirty-three

A lone figure broke out of the crowd and headed straight for us. A loosely-knit sweater hung on her frail frame. The woman who had pocketed the ballet slippers at the shoe store walked up the steps. "Mrs. Miller?"

"Hazel Mae!" exclaimed Oma. "Did you walk all the way down here?"

"I'm used to it." She held out her hands, offering Oma the GPS collar. "My kids found this collar in the woods near our house this morning. It says *Sugar Maple Inn* on it. I figure it belongs to you."

Oma took the collar. "My goodness! What was it doing all the way up there? Thank you, Hazel Mae. Could I offer you some apple cider or a cup of tea?"

"Oh, no thanks! That's not necessary."

"Well, let me give you something for your trouble." Oma pulled some bills from her pocket and pressed them into Hazel Mae's hand. "Now, don't you fight me on this. It would have cost much more to replace that collar. Take it and buy a little treat for your children."

I thought Hazel Mae might cry. "Thank you, Mrs. Miller."

Her voice cracked with emotion when she spoke. She turned and walked away, her head high.

"I'll reimburse you," I whispered.

"Nonsense. I would have found a way to get some money into her hands. This provided an excellent excuse."

Before we could scatter, Aunt Birdie was upon us. "Well, well. Wouldn't you think a niece would bring her fiancé by and introduce him to her only aunt?"

Birdie wasn't my only aunt, and she knew it. Seemed futile to point that out to her. Was it a slight to offend Oma by pretending her daughter wasn't my aunt as well? I thought it better to overlook it. "Aunt Birdie, I'd like you to meet Ben Hathaway. Ben, this is my aunt, Birdie Dupuy."

They shook hands. Birdie had the nerve to look him up and down like he was livestock for sale.

I felt obligated to clarify our relationship, especially in light of his recent I-hereby-rescind text, so I continued, "We were never engaged, Aunt Birdie. And actually, we're now just friends."

Holmes's head swiveled so fast that it sent a jolt of hopefulness through me. Wrinkles creased his forehead. I wanted to think he was conveying a silent question. Maybe. But Ben shot me a curious glance, too.

"Hmmpf. Well, I'm glad to hear that—given that he's shacking up with Mortie's daughter."

Ben's face flushed. Even practicing law hadn't prepared him for the taunts of someone like my Aunt Birdie.

"It's not what you think!" he sputtered.

The joys of small town life! So little got by the residents. Rumors flew fast and thick. Yet no one had information about who murdered Sven and Jerry? Impossible. Someone knew something regarding the murders. But why wouldn't that person step forward and tell Dave what he knew?

Aunt Birdie pinched my arm. "Aren't you going to invite me in? Have you no manners, Holly? Do you expect me to stand out here on the porch all day?"

I was doomed. "Would you like to have a seat out here? Maybe some hot cider?"

"Still on the porch? What does a person have to do to be invited inside?"

There was no salvaging the situation.

Oma surprised me by stating in a no-nonsense voice, "This isn't a good time for a visit, Birdie. I'm letting the entire staff go to Sven's memorial service in about an hour. Holly is the only one who didn't know him, so I'm counting on her to stay behind and take care of the guests while we're over in Snowball."

Sad as I was about Sven, I had to bite my upper lip to suppress a grin. Oma came up with a humdinger. No one, especially Aunt Birdie, who set so much stock in manners and social niceties, could argue with a memorial service.

It worried me that her expression changed from a storm cloud to pleasant, almost gleeful.

"How thoughtless of me. I understand completely." She took in Oma's black pantsuit, accessorized with a geometric black and white silk scarf. "If you only have an hour, I'd best be on my way so you can dress appropriately."

Birdie walked down the stairs like a beauty queen, head high, back erect, as though she floated effortlessly.

The four of us released a collective sigh of relief. We turned and hustled inside, where everyone spoke at once.

"Great excuse, Oma!" I said. "Thanks for getting me off the hook."

"Are you really related to that . . . that awful woman?" asked Ben.

Holmes shook his head. "Birdie never changes. What did your dad call her? The wicked witch of Wagtail?"

"How dare she suggest I change clothes?" Oma grumbled. "What's wrong with this outfit?"

We assured her that she looked fine.

"Holly, I'm afraid it's not just an excuse. I do need you to look after things while we're gone."

"Shouldn't I go with you?"

"Now, don't start that again. I won't have you sleeping by my door or pretending to be a bodyguard. Besides, Holmes is driving Rose and me."

At her reminder, Holmes said good-bye and sprinted down the stairs, heading for his parent's house to change clothes.

"Could I have a second with you, Holly?" asked Ben.

Oma left us alone, saying to meet her in the office so she could explain a few things.

Ben, Trixie, and I edged over to a quiet corner of the front porch.

"What's this about just being friends?" he asked. "I know we have issues—like the dog. But I thought we were on track for you to move in with me eventually. Maybe soon if you don't find a job."

I gave him my very best you-have-to-be-kidding look.

"I know you're not excited about moving into my place, but I didn't think we were over."

"How can you say that?" How could he not understand what he had done? Although he approached our relationship like a business transaction, and ineptly at that, even a businessman would have been stunned by the retraction. The funny thing was that I didn't feel heartbroken. A little bit out of sorts, perhaps, because it heralded a major change in my life, in my plans, in my future, but not heartbroken. Maybe Rose had been correct. Maybe Ben wasn't the right guy for me after all. "'I hereby rescind' is pretty final, don't you think?"

In a rare speechless moment, Ben studied me. "Okay, I don't know what you're talking about."

"Oh, please! Your text. I believe it said, so eloquently and full of emotion and love, 'I hereby rescind all offers of marriage,' or something to that effect."

"I never texted you that."

"You're going to deny it? I can show you the text!"

He rubbed his fingertips against each other beneath his chin. "What time was it sent?"

"I don't know exactly. During the night." And just like that I knew what he was thinking. "Kim."

"That's my guess. Holly, I'm very sorry. That must have been devastating to you, especially after all my offers to have you move in."

The trouble was that it hadn't been particularly hurtful. "Ben, I'm not moving in with you. I thought I was fairly pragmatic about love. Realistic and not prone to hearts and lace and romance. Apparently I was wrong. I suppose things could change between us, and I might feel differently in the future, but I do know that I will never marry someone who texts a proposal."

"I thought that was hip."

I sighed. He seemed so sincere. "Not hip, not cool, not even amusing."

"If it's Kim—"

"Kim has nothing to do with this. I think I need to feel more special to my husband. I don't want to be with someone just because he pities me."

Ben nodded and walked away, his head bowed. He looked back at me once, but I hurried inside and down to Oma's office with Trixie.

She showed me where things were and what to do if someone checked in or out, and ended by saying, "Shelley and Zelda and the whole crew are going, so we've set up a light buffet with coffee, tea, and hot cider in urns. Just make sure everything is replenished. Okay?"

"No problem."

The guests kept the inn lively, milling around the buffet and helping themselves. Trixie roamed inside off her leash, even though she didn't have any tags. She behaved surprisingly well, sticking close to me.

But not a half hour after Oma and the staff departed, Aunt Birdie flounced through the front door.

What did she want now?

"Holly, darling! How nice. A little afternoon tea." She sniffed and drew her lips back, gazing around at the floor. "*With dogs.*"

"Please feel free to help yourself, Aunt Birdie."

She studied me. "I like the dress. It's too summery for the season, of course, but it will do. Go upstairs and put on some powder and lipstick."

"Aunt Birdie, I'm working." I dashed into the kitchen for another pot of coffee.

When I returned, she was tapping a blood-red fingernail on the buffet table.

"Don't you ever do what you're told?"

I poured fresh coffee into the urn. "I'm not eight."

"I have never understood why you have to be so ornery. Very well, it's out of my hands if you ruin this for yourself."

"What are you talking about?"

"I have found you a suitable mate."

I nearly dropped the coffee pot. Surely I hadn't heard correctly. "I beg your pardon?"

"Now, Holly, don't be cranky, I'm doing you a favor. If you play your cards right, and you're quite old enough to know what I mean—don't go giving away the milk or he won't buy the cow—then you could have a very fine husband."

Who was she kidding? "Excuse me. This is America. We don't arrange marriages here."

"You can be *so* taxing. I'm doing you a huge favor. He's a fine man, good-looking, and he has a successful business. Now that you don't have a job, you need to consider those things. You're not getting any younger. One of these days, you'll develop the Miller jowls, those perky little breasts will droop, and strange hairs will sprout from your chin."

"I may not have a job this minute, but I'll get another one. I'm fully capable of supporting myself. Besides," I pulled my ace out of the hole, "you're not married. What makes you think I have to be?"

"Holly. My dear girl. I have my reasons, and they are not pertinent to this conversation. However, since you were sufficiently insensitive to bring it up, I admit, as I approach sixty, I recognize that there are certain benefits to marriage." She clenched her teeth, and her nostrils flared. "You're all I have. I don't want you to be in that position." She embraced me, not quite as stiffly as usual. "I'm so glad you came home to me."

Oh dear heaven! What could I say? Of course, she had my mother. I wasn't her only living relative. But mom lived all the way across the country and wasn't close with Birdie—for good reason.

"Aunt Birdie, I'm sorry you feel so alone. Maybe you're the one who should be looking for a husband."

"Don't you talk back to me! I expect you to be on your very best behavior."

Behind her, Philip strode into the front lobby carrying a giant bouquet of red roses and dog cookies in the shapes of bones, mounted on sticks, and iced in white with red frosting piped around the edges.

Aunt Birdie glanced over her shoulder. She turned back to me and hissed, "Now be nice!"

At that very moment, I wanted nothing more than for the floor to open up and swallow me. I couldn't run screaming from the room. I couldn't pitch a fit in front of the guests. There was just no option but to be gracious and privately explain to Philip that my Aunt Birdie was an obnoxious busybody and a deranged loon.

I accepted the flowers and thanked him. A bit louder than normal, so Aunt Birdie would hear, I said, "I'm so sorry. This isn't a good time for me. Maybe we can have a cup of coffee later?"

"No problem," he said, "I'm happy to pitch in."

"That's really not necessary. I have everything under control." But he walked up to the cider urn and opened it to check the contents. I tried to be polite. "Why don't you and Aunt Birdie help yourselves to some of these goodies?"

"Aunt Birdie won't mind."

She didn't appear to. She gathered a sampling of sandwiches, scones, and pastries on a plate and sat down at a table. "Philip, would you be a love and bring me some coffee, light?"

I didn't like this setup. Not one bit. Philip held a coffee cup in his hand. I grasped his wrist. "I can't let you do this. Really." I took hold of the coffee cup, but it was a bad move on my part.

He ran his hand over mine. "I was so pleased when Aunt Birdie stopped by to tell me that you and Ben had broken up."

Why did he keep calling her Aunt Birdie? As far as I knew, we weren't related, and if we were, then—*ewww.* I forced a smile. "Won't you please keep Aunt Birdie company? I know I hate to eat alone in public. She probably feels very awkward."

He looked into my eyes for a long, excruciatingly uncomfortable moment. "That's very thoughtful of you. At least let me bring her coffee over to her."

I nodded and rushed to the kitchen for a moment alone. A huge sigh shuddered out of my mouth. I shook my arms and hands, put off by him. Why did Aunt Birdie have to be so irritating? If she was a stranger, I could just ignore her and make a point of not socializing with her. But she was a relative.

I leaned against the cold, stainless steel prep counter and counted to ten.

The door swung open. Philip poked his head in and waved at me. "We need more scones and lemon curd, sweetie." The door swung shut behind him.

I looked down at my clenched hands. If I didn't get out there, he would take over. I grabbed a platter of scones and more of the lemon curd and took a deep breath before I returned.

As he had promised, he joined Aunt Birdie, and the two of them had a grand old time, while I did everything I could to keep busy so they wouldn't call me over to their table.

I bussed other tables, and replenished everything, even when it wasn't necessary.

Until a scream rattled down the stairwell.

Thirty-four

❀ ❀ ❀

I scrambled up the stairs and stopped on the first landing with Philip on my heels. I peered down the hallways on each side but didn't see or hear anything amiss.

Trixie and Twinkletoes knew where the trouble was. I should have just followed them. They scampered up to the third floor, where I was staying. Philip and I rushed up behind them.

My door stood ajar, and the cleaning cart blocked the entrance. Philip shoved it to the left, and we ran inside.

The housekeeper with the dark ponytail and expressive eyes stood on top of a dining room chair, holding a floor duster with a long handle.

"What's wrong?" I asked, breathing hard. Everything looked okay to me.

She pointed at the buffet. With a tinge of a British accent, she said, "I hope you have a big hamster. Because if you don't, there's a rat hiding under the sideboard."

Philip dropped to his knees immediately. "Something is down there, for sure. Hand me that duster."

As much as I didn't relish the thought of a rat in the inn,

mere inches from me, I was not going to let him take over and rescue me like I was some kind of damsel in distress.

I held my hand out for the floor duster and took it from the housekeeper. Summoning courage, I knelt on the floor and peered under the buffet. I flinched at the sight of the furry beast.

"Watch out, Philip," I warned. I tapped it gently with the floor duster but it didn't budge. Probably scared.

Trixie sniffed and wedged her nose as far under the buffet as she could. I imagined she wasn't helping the situation. Even a rat knew when to be terrified and stay where it was safe.

I gave it a gentle push. It moved away from the duster but still didn't come out. "Sorry about this," I said to the rat, and whacked it in Philip's direction.

It flew out of the other end.

Trixie vaulted over Philip and launched herself at it, catching it the second it left the protection of the buffet. She seized it and shot out like a white torpedo. We scrambled to our feet and chased after her. By the time we reached the doorway, we could see a blitz of white blazing down the stairs. We hurried behind her. Why hadn't I had the presence of mind to close the door? I cringed at what Oma would think about a dog running through her beautiful lobby with a rat in its mouth.

Oh dear heaven! How could this be happening? We weren't fast enough to catch her before she reached the main floor.

But we were fast enough to witness Mr. Luciano opening the door for her.

"Noooooo," I screamed.

Seconds later, I stood on the inn porch, and Trixie was nowhere to be seen.

Philip slung an arm around me. Maybe it was a nice gesture, but I was too upset to appreciate it.

Aunt Birdie ambled out. "That was quite a commotion. I hope that's not a regular event around here. Rats in the inn. How disgusting. Holly, the creamer needs refilling."

At that moment, I wanted to pour the cream right over Aunt Birdie's head. Instead, I stared ahead, searching for any sign of Trixie. I weighed my options. Get the receiver for the GPS collar she wore and find her before she got too far away or refill the creamer.

My responsibility to Oma came first. I returned, washed my hands, brought more cream to the buffet, and smiled at everyone as though nothing had happened.

Philip and Aunt Birdie, already back at their table, chuckled about something. I checked everything on the buffet, intending to take a brief break to fetch the GPS receiver. When I passed the front door, high-pitched barking stopped me. Once again, Trixie stood on her hind legs, straining to see through the front door sidelights.

I opened the door for her, and she trotted in like she owned the place, pleased as punch with herself for having rid the inn of a rat. Laughing with relief that she wasn't missing again, I told her what a wonderful dog she was. The guests in the dining area even broke into applause when we returned.

Somehow, that little nightmare reset my mood. Trixie clearly thought she lived at the inn. As long as no one stole her and locked her up, she appeared to be inclined to come home. That took a heavy weight off of me. It didn't erase the fact that someone had taken her the night before, but she knew we were a team.

I decided I should be grateful for having an aunt who cared about me, even if she went about it all wrong.

Philip might be a little too eager for my taste. Perhaps *I'd* been too quick to resent his jumping in to help, but wasn't that actually a good trait in a person? It would have been far worse if he'd expected to be waited on hand and foot.

I returned to the third floor briefly to check on the housekeeper. She insisted she was fine. It turned out that she hadn't known Sven, since Oma had only hired her recently.

Filled with my new feeling of generosity toward all, even Aunt Birdie, I returned to the dining area, where I poured myself a mug of hot cider, filled a plate with a cucumber sandwich, an egg-salad sandwich, a piece of cherry strudel, and a twice-baked crunchy dog cookie for Trixie, and joined Aunt Birdie and Philip for tea.

Philip gushed about my beautiful suite until Aunt Birdie insisted they have a tour. I indulged them because it was gorgeous. Oma deserved enormous credit for it.

When we came downstairs, it seemed like an opportune time to thank them for coming. Philip probably had entirely the wrong idea, but I would cure him of that as soon as I could out of Aunt Birdie's range of hearing.

Philip handed me another business card. "I jotted my new phone number on here."

Aunt Birdie raised an eyebrow. "You haven't shared it with me, yet, Philip."

"Just got it, Aunt Birdie. I must have dropped my other phone somewhere. Maybe it was fate. They offered me this new easy to remember number for the bed-and-breakfasts—1864Bed. How cool is that?"

He took Aunt Birdie's arm and walked her down the stairs. She departed, pleased as punch with herself. I knew she'd complain nonstop once I made it clear that I had no interest in Philip.

Oma and Rose returned soon thereafter. I listened politely to how guilty Oma felt about Sven's death. I understood completely. It never should have happened.

I confessed the story about the rat, telling it as humorously as I possibly could.

Oma did *not* find it remotely funny. "We have no rats in the Sugar Maple Inn. We never have. Is impossible."

Okay. Maybe it would be a good time to buy a replacement collar for the one that mysteriously went missing the night before. I mentioned that I needed to do that.

"Holly," said Oma, placing her hand on my shoulder. "Do not run back here in a rush. I am fine. No one here will hurt me. Yes?" She chucked me under the chin and winked, like I was a two-year-old.

I hooked the unfamiliar leash onto the strange brown collar and headed out. Trixie pranced along, stopping now and then to sniff some invisible scent on the ground. I didn't mind. The afternoon sun shone on us with unusual warmth for the time of year. I window-shopped as we strolled, admiring fancy dog beds with canopies. A shop called For the Birds carried everything a bird lover could possibly want, from bird-themed jewelry for people to amazing cages. An African gray parrot climbed a ladder in the store window. She stopped to look at us and shrieked at Trixie, who nearly bolted. Thankfully, I had a good grip on the leash.

For the first time this visit, I walked all the way to the other end of the shopping area. The old Wagtail Springs Hotel still stood, though clearly empty. Porches ran across the front of the two-story building on both floors. It had been creepy when I was a kid. We used to dare each other to run inside, and it was even more sinister now.

"Have you ever seen a ghost in the window?"

I looked around. Mr. Luciano studied the building. His hands rested on the handle of an odd stroller. But the child appeared to be encased behind mesh.

I peered at it.

Trixie sniffed and tentatively wagged her tail.

"This is my Gina." He walked to the front and opened the mesh so we could see her. A darling white bulldog with a brown spot over one eye looked back at us.

"She can't walk?" I asked, wondering where she'd come from.

"Not yet. I brought her here for surgery. She had an elongated soft palate, which made it difficult for her to breathe. They let her come home to the inn today. She's not supposed to run around yet, but it's such a lovely day that I thought she would enjoy getting out a little."

"She's a beautiful dog."

"Thank you. Gina is my joy. They say she will be fine."

"I'm sure she will. And she has that fabulous fur bed to lounge on in your room."

"A most thoughtful gift from your grandmother." He gazed up at the empty, lifeless windows of the building again. "A lot of people in Wagtail think this place is haunted. No one wants to buy it and renovate it."

"That's silly. Ghosts don't exist. Besides, I heard Philip might be interested in acquiring it."

"How can you be so sure ghosts aren't real?"

I flipped it around on him. "Do you believe in ghosts?"

"I know they make for good TV shows."

I laughed. "I'll agree with that. I like a good scary show as much as the next person, even though I know it's only fantasy."

"We'll find out soon enough. I'm bringing a team of ghost

hunters to town to check out this old place. They're going to film a show here. Did you know that several murders took place in this building?"

"Jerry was murdered in his house. Do you think he's haunting it?" I asked.

Mr. Luciano pulled a snazzy phone from his pocket and made a note. "That's an excellent point. I have to see if I can get into Jerry's house. Thanks for mentioning it." He zipped Gina's stroller shut. "I'd better get her back for some rest."

"See you later!" I hugged Trixie. "I have to get you over to the vet for a once-over. Have you had your shots?"

She licked my chin.

"Let's go get that collar."

The woman who helped us the day before greeted us warmly. "Trixie! Your leash is ready . . ." She tucked her chin in, aghast. "What's this? You went to Prissy's store?"

I explained about the strange middle-of-the-night dognapping and the new collar and leash.

"Sweetie, are you okay?" She patted Trixie, making cooing sounds. "That's terrifying! A dognapper in Wagtail? Maybe that's what happened the night Sven died. Maybe someone was trying to steal Dolce! He has dog royalty in his genes." One eye squinted a little as she looked Trixie over. "Honey bunch, you're as cute as can be, but somehow you don't strike me as a show dog." Speaking to me, she said confidentially, "They're always a little haughty. Like they know they're stars."

She checked out the leash closely. "This is definitely Prissy's cheap, excuse me, *inexpensive* line. No one else in town carries this brand."

Maybe Dave could find out to whom she sold it. I certainly wasn't taking Trixie into her store again.

"Shall I set you up with another collar?"

"Yes, and I think I'll take a little halter, too. Just to be on the safe side. That might take a dognapper longer to remove."

Half an hour later, Trixie pranced out in her new halter, collar, tags, and leash. I supposed I could have used the brown collar, but it seemed tainted to me. *Oh no!* I was beginning to be superstitious like Oma!

"From now on," I said to Trixie, "if someone tries to remove your collar, you have my permission to bite him. If I have to buy a new collar and leash every day, we're going to go through my savings much faster than I expected."

She stood on her hind legs to smell the shopping bag, which contained some sample treats for her and Twinkletoes to try.

I broke one in half and gave her a piece.

In the grassy middle of the shopping area, I spotted Zelda with a Great Dane and a basset hound, undoubtedly Dolce and Chief. "Zelda!" I waved at her.

She turned her back and released the dogs in a fenced play zone. There was no way she hadn't heard me.

Thirty-five

❀ ❀ ❀

I crossed over to Zelda. "Zelda, hi!"

She turned her back to me again. A definite snub.

I tried again. "Zelda, is something wrong?"

She didn't rotate away from me this time but kept her eyes on the dogs, who were racing in wild circles. "I thought we could be friends, but I clearly misjudged you. I work for your grandmother and that's all, okay?"

"I don't understand."

She closed her eyes briefly, as though pained, and pointedly averted her gaze when she said, "A friend doesn't go stealing the guy her girlfriend has a crush on."

Duh. It finally dawned on me. "Philip!"

"Philip!" she mimicked. "Yes, Philip."

"How could you possibly have heard about that already? You went to the memorial service over in Snowball, and you can't have been back for more than an hour."

"Wagtail is a small place, Holly. Sneeze and half the town will catch your cold."

Trixie yelped at me. I opened the gate to the play area and released her. She took off running behind Dolce. Silly me. If

Zelda had Dolce, she must have seen Ellie. "How did Ellie know?"

She scowled. "Your Aunt Birdie stopped by Ellie's place to crow about having made the perfect match. I hear you're moving to Wagtail, and the wedding will be in the spring, if not in the snow over the holidays."

I couldn't help laughing. "I'm not seeing Philip. He's nice enough, but I wouldn't go behind your back like that. I was stuck at the inn when Aunt Birdie brought him over. What could I do? I tried to be polite, and the next time I see him when Aunt Birdie isn't around, I'll make it very clear to him that I'm not interested."

She cocked her head like a puppy. "Really?"

At that exact moment, Dolce trotted over, joyfully lifted his paws, and whapped them on my shoulders. The two of us tumbled, my purse and the little shopping bag flew through the air, and I landed on my back.

"I'm so sorry!" Zelda extended her hands to help me up. "Are you all right? Dolce knows he's not supposed to do that, but he has the zoomies."

"I'm fine." I stood and brushed myself off. I wasn't sure whether the grass stains would come out of my dress, but otherwise I felt fine.

Trixie already had her nose in the shopping bag, snarfing the free treats. "Trixie!" The paper bag clung to her head when she bolted. The sight of her running with a bag on her head excited the other dogs. Chief howled and tried to catch the inexpensive leash, which was falling out of the bag.

I ran to rescue Trixie. She wriggled, trying to get away from me. When I removed the bag from her head, she shook as though she were wet.

Zelda worked at gathering the contents of my handbag. "I hope you didn't lose anything. I found lipstick, lip balm, a couple of pens, and your wallet. I don't see your cell phone."

"I left it at the inn. Thanks for picking everything up for me."

She blinked hard. "I should apologize for ignoring you. I just thought . . ."

"No worries about that. Besides, I'm not moving here, and there's no wedding planned, with Philip or anyone else."

"Not even Ben?"

I threw my hand up in mock surprise. "You knew about Philip, but you didn't hear that Ben sent me a break up text?"

"That's horrible! A text? Who does that?"

I couldn't bring myself to tell her about the red roses in my room. If she could snag Philip, she'd know soon enough that he was a romantic. I tucked the cheap leash into the crumpled and beat-up bag. Zelda chattered, but I didn't hear what she was saying. Something nagged at me. A bag from Prissy's shop. I'd seen one recently. *Kim!*

Kim, who had no dog that I knew of, had purchased something there the day before and offered Trixie a treat. I called Trixie. "Excuse me, Zelda, I think I have to pay Kim and Ben a little visit."

I snapped the leash onto Trixie's collar, and we hurried back to the inn. I found Oma in her office and asked for directions to Kim's father's cabin. She frowned at me but marked it on a map. Borrowing one of Oma's golf carts, I loaded my purse in the compartment in front of the seats and hustled away from Wagtail on a country road, Trixie riding by my side like she'd done it all her life.

Tall pines lined the road, with an occasional driveway or gravel drive leading away and disappearing into the trees. A few cabins had been built close to the road, inviting A-frames with large windows and wraparound balconies.

Children played outside of a battered old farmhouse. Hazel Mae's place, perhaps?

Not much farther along the road, I found a paved driveway to Mortie's cabin, marked by a post with a painted fish on it. I could just imagine what his wife had said about that!

The one-story log cabin was small but adorable. A cute roughly hewn wood railing wrapped around it from the driveway to a porch overlooking the lake. A green golf cart sat in the driveway next to the house, along with a red Miata.

Trixie and I hopped out of our golf cart and walked up to the door. I knocked on it and waited. And waited. I knocked again and could hear muffled voices. Ben opened the door, his shirt hanging outside of his pants. I'd never seen him that way before. "Holly! What are you doing here?"

"Who's that, honey?" Kim's voice came from inside. She made a point of peering at me, even though she wore nothing but a sheet wrapped around her like a toga. Kim squealed, and her eyes opened wide at the sight of Trixie.

"Kim, put on some clothes already." Ben pinched the bridge of his nose. "It's not like it looks, Holly."

I didn't really care. Well, maybe a little. "It looks like you've been busy."

"Just relaxing, that's all." He tucked his shirt in.

I really hadn't expected Ben to be seduced by Kim so fast. How stupid of me. After all, they had dated once. Being thrown together in a cozy little cabin in the woods had proven too tempting.

I got to the point. "I'd like to know why Kim kidnapped Trixie last night."

She tucked the sheet around her legs. "I did no such thing. I don't know what you're talking about."

"Give it up, Kim. I know it was you." I didn't know that, but I had a strong suspicion.

"I was here with Ben all night. You can ask him."

"You're barking up the wrong tree," Ben agreed. "I slept on the sofa. I would have noticed if Kim left the bedroom. What's with you, Holly? I told you Kim must have sent the text rescinding all proposals."

"I did not!" Kim lied without flinching.

He retrieved his phone from the kitchen counter and flicked it on. I looked over his arm and saw the offending text.

The muscles in Ben's jaw twitched. He marched over to Kim and held it in front of her. "I did not write this."

Kim focused on Trixie and ignored Ben.

"Kim! I know it had to be you who sent the text. Will you please tell Holly?" Ben asked.

"Don't be silly."

"I was already asleep when this was sent. I'm sorry, Holly."

Kim tossed back her hair, placed her free hand on her hip, and said, "I just seem to be a very convenient scapegoat for the two of you. Ben, I can't help it if you changed your mind after you sent that text, and I swear I had nothing to do with your dog."

I swept Trixie into my arms. "Then stay away from her from now on." Carrying Trixie, I marched past Ben. "She's your problem, pal."

I admit that I quivered a little bit once we sat safely in our golf cart. Kim didn't scare me, but something smelled wrong. Maybe she *had* hijacked Ben's phone. But why had she come here anyway? If her father's car was stolen, then why did she make an appearance? Couldn't that be confirmed by phone? Why hadn't Mortie come instead?

I pulled my purse out and applied lip balm. Was it remotely possible that she was telling the truth and someone else had snatched Trixie?

Leaving my purse on the seat, I walked over to her dad's golf cart. There were precious few places to hide anything. I stuck my hand into the pocket in front of the seat and felt something crinkle. Aha. The bag from Prissy's store. Although that might not be evidence of anything, it raised my suspicions even more.

The basket in the back was empty. My gaze ran down to the black vinyl where golf bags were usually stashed. A bit of orange and yellow clung to it. The missing collar. Complete with tags that clearly identified them as Trixie's. I could only imagine that she tossed the collars into the basket, they slipped through the gaps, the GPS one fell off, and the other went unnoticed.

I returned to Oma's golf cart, turned it around, and we chugged back the way we had come. Trixie raised her nose in the air, sniffing.

Why would Kim want her? What could possibly prompt her to snatch Trixie? It wouldn't win her points with Ben. She could probably talk her daddy into buying her just about any dog she wanted. Was it just to hurt me? She hadn't struck me as being particularly vindictive.

I knew one thing—tonight I would be waiting for her. If she made a little trip out after Ben had dozed off, I would be ready.

Thirty-six

※ ❀ ※ ❀ ※

On my return to the inn, I did laundry and asked Oma if I could borrow some things to wear.

As I expected, she was very accommodating, and even seemed happy about it. She thought I needed sweaters and jackets, and I didn't correct that impression. It was almost right. I needed black clothes that wouldn't be readily seen in the dark.

I pawed through her closet. In the very back, I discovered a casual black fleece jacket that would do the trick. Looking down at Trixie, I said, "If we only had a dark coat for you."

Acting casual, I checked out a GPS collar and receiver. A delivery guy arrived with a package. I signed for it and checked the guest's name so I could take it to the correct room.

Oh no! The rich brown box from Pawsitively Decadent, wrapped beautifully with a white ribbon embossed with gold paw prints, bore *my* name. My heart sinking, I pulled out the little white envelope and opened it. *Truffles for my sweet. Philip.*

I grunted aloud. "Huh. Didn't expect that." I had to make it clear to him that we weren't an item.

That evening, I enjoyed a leisurely dinner with Oma, just the two of us, at Chowhound. For two hours, I pushed thoughts of murder and dognapping away and reminisced with my delightful grandmother. Gingersnap and Trixie accompanied us. No amount of money would have been enough to convince me to leave Trixie at the inn. She was staying safely by my side.

We split an appetizer of earthy portobello mushrooms, stuffed with salty cheese and heavenly bacon. Oma ordered grilled salmon over quinoa with mixed berry sauce and a wilted spinach salad.

I was delighted with my pork tenderloin medallions topped with cider-braised onions, so soft I could cut them with a fork.

Gingersnap and Trixie appeared to be equally happy with their pork medallions, served with the same creamy mashed potatoes and red Swiss chard I was enjoying.

"Oma," I said, trying to sound nonchalant. "What's with all the meetings with Mr. Luciano?"

She appeared to be surprised. "Just work, liebling."

"Really? Since when does Rose attend your business meetings?"

Oma laughed so hard that her eyes watered. "Apparently you're more observant than I thought. Naturally, I comped his room and have been catering to him because he was attacked. It is the least I can do. He is bringing a television crew and ghost hunters to the inn next month. They will almost fill the entire inn. That kind of guest gets special treatment. Rose is chairwoman of special Halloween festivities in Wagtail and is acting as his liaison to the community."

"That sounds like fun!" If I didn't have a job, maybe I could return for it.

It was over a dessert of sweet apple tart with vanilla ice cream and caramel sauce that I dared broach the topic of selling the inn.

"I saw your cruise brochures."

"It would be wonderful, no? Rose and I have talked about it for a long time."

"When are you going?"

"Maybe never." She shrugged.

"Because you have to sell the inn first?"

"*Ach du lieber Gott!*"

I recognized the phrase from my childhood. The German equivalent of "Dear lord!"

"No! I will never sell the inn. It is my home. Where would I go?" She swallowed a bite of ice cream and caramel sauce. "Whatever gave you such a strange idea?"

I couldn't exactly say she was getting old. "I thought you might want to retire."

She didn't miss a beat. "It would be nice to semiretire."

"Because of your health?" I held my breath.

"Oh, Holly. You worry too much."

"Do I? When Rose called me, she sounded so desperate that I thought you were dying."

"I apologize for that. She shouldn't have made you worry so. As you can see, I will survive this twisted ankle."

Holding my spoon between my thumb and forefinger, I flipped it back and forth. "What I don't quite understand," I said, trying to make it sound as innocent as possible, "is why Rose sounded so urgent when she called me. Don't get me wrong, I'm glad that she called, but somehow, she gave me the impression that you had something far more serious than a twisted ankle. Maybe she thought you would have trouble dealing with Sven's murder?"

Oma froze. Toying with the ice cream, she finally said, "We had to get you to come here."

"But, why?"

Oma heaved a great sigh. "We had to time it when Holmes would be here." She finally met my eyes. "Liebling, please understand. I couldn't see you spend your life with the Ben. He's so *dull*. He has sucked the joy out of you." She reached across the table to me. "You used to be fun, but somewhere along the way, you became parched like a desert. You need to find laughter again and the merriment that I know you have inside you."

"You terrible woman! You and Rose played matchmaker? You thought if you threw Holmes and me together that we would fall in love?" I snorted. "Well, that didn't work."

"A pity."

"So you're not sick? You never were?"

"No. Please don't be angry with us. We did this from the love in our hearts for you and Holmes."

"Does Holmes know?"

"I doubt it. He's not as pushy as you are."

Nothing like a grandmother to tell you that you're dry as the desert and pushy. *Way to boost my self-esteem, Oma.* I should have been angry—furious, really. They deceived me and worried me to death. What had Holmes called them? Dotty. They were crazy as loons.

"Rose doesn't like Holmes's fiancé?"

"Not in the slightest. He's not happy in the big city. Did you know that I hired Holmes to design the renovation of the inn?"

"He never said a word."

"He loved doing it. It wasn't fancy architecture, of course, but I could see the change in him. He needs to come back here."

"How soon do you think you could book that cruise?"

She perked up. "I don't know. Are you saying . . ."

"I don't have a job at the moment. If you trust me to take care of things, Trixie and I would be happy to fill in for you."

It felt great to clear the air. Silly woman, she should have just told me from the beginning. I imagined it hadn't been easy for her, though. How can you tell someone that you took desperate measures to matchmake? Still, it was a relief that she wasn't ill. Plus, if she went on that cruise soon, she'd be out of town and away from the possible harm of the killer. As far as I was concerned, she should leave as soon as possible.

Just before ten o'clock that night, I donned my clean jeans, a dark green turtleneck, and the black jacket I had borrowed from Oma. I dressed Trixie in her halter. She would give me away with her white fur, but I could cover her with the jacket if need be. That would help conceal her a little bit. I filled my pockets with my cell phone, a little cash in case of an emergency, and the GPS collar and receiver.

When we stepped out into the stairwell, voices drifted up to me. I didn't dare leave the building by way of the reception area. Casey would see us for sure and pelt me with questions. We hurried down the stairs and out the front door. Pretending we were simply going for a late doggy stroll, we walked over to the Blue Boar and cut down the sidewalk that intersected with the inn parking lot.

Minutes later, we were back in the golf cart, retracing the route we took earlier in the day. I parked on the side of the road and tiptoed to Kim's cabin in the dark. They didn't have a dog, but I worried about triggering motion detectors that might shine a spotlight on us.

We made it to their golf cart under the cover of darkness. I tucked the GPS collar in the recesses of the dark vinyl bag in front of the seats and crossed my fingers that it would work. We ran back to our own golf cart, Trixie eagerly leading the way.

Near Hazel Mae's house, I pulled off the road, angled the golf cart so it was facing town but was partly hidden by trees, and turned off the engine. "If Kim comes by, we'll follow her. Okay?"

Trixie hopped out and sniffed the ground. She could go fairly far, thanks to the leash. I had a bad feeling that if she hadn't been tethered, she'd be off running through the woods.

I turned on the GPS remote receiver. It worked! It showed the GPS collar located behind us. I turned it off to save the battery. If Kim came by on the golf cart, we'd probably notice it.

I relaxed and strolled around the golf cart so Trixie could investigate scents. The chilly night air held the promise of winter. Stars sparkled in the dark sky. They never seemed so close or vivid at home.

I couldn't remember the last time I saw the Milky Way so clearly. We returned to the golf cart. Trixie sat up, alert, her haunches pressed against me. My arm around her, I stroked her chest.

Time ticked by slower than molasses. I flicked on my phone. No bars. Not a mile away, at Kim's cabin, they could get a signal, but not here. Weird.

I began to wonder if I had misjudged her. Maybe she wouldn't be sneaking around again tonight. It just made no sense whatsoever that she would want Trixie. I clutched Trixie even closer at the thought.

Kim had to wait until Ben fell asleep, which I suspected would be around midnight. Of course, if they'd rented a movie to watch, it could be later than that.

I toyed with the notion of looking for a spot where I could get a cell-phone connection. What could I text him that would get her attention? Assuming she went through his phone messages again. What a rat. Being nosy by nature, I understood the desire to peek, but I had enough respect for other people not to pry. Good grief, it was like steaming someone's mail open. Wasn't that a felony?

What if I was wrong about Kim? I couldn't be totally off because I'd found Trixie's collar on her golf cart. It would be hard to explain that as a coincidence. If it had been some kind of joke or trick, wouldn't she have admitted it?

Trixie turned her head toward the road, concentrating. Very briefly, I switched on the GPS remote. Indeed, the collar moved toward us. I covered Trixie with Oma's black jacket in case Kim happened to look our way.

It would have been easy to miss the golf cart rolling along without any lights because the engine was virtually noiseless. I sat perfectly still until she had passed, switched on the GPS, and waited until I thought she was far enough ahead before I pulled out behind her, my lights off, too, which I was fairly sure was illegal.

As I expected, she headed to town. The GPS allowed me to stay far behind her. Without it, I would have missed her turn onto Oak Street. But then the collar stopped moving.

I parked in front of Ellie's house in a rush. Grabbing the dark jacket and Trixie's leash, I ran along the middle of the street. Too bad Kim wasn't wearing the GPS collar. We might lose her.

A few lights remained on in windows, but most were dark. A dog in a yard barked as we sped by. Trixie yapped a couple of times, excited to be on the run.

"Hush!" I could only hope that barking dogs wouldn't draw Kim's attention. After all, dogs and cats ruled in Wagtail. Barking was the norm.

We discovered her golf cart parked at the very end of the road, where it intersected with the pedestrian zone. She had left it in front of Philip's 1864 bed-and-breakfast. I paused to collect the GPS collar from the golf cart.

We ran again. The cold night air burned in my lungs. When we hit the shopping area, we came to a stop. Which way had she gone?

To my surprise, a few people walked dogs, even at that late hour. I tried to be methodical about scanning the area. Fortunately, I spotted her—mostly because she was running.

We cut across the green in the middle and followed her to—good heavens! Was she going to Jerry's house? Didn't they say the killer returns to the scene of the crime?

She walked past it and vanished along the side of the house next door to it.

Thirty-seven

❧ ❧ ❧ ❧

We casually walked by the house. Lights shone upstairs. Another light turned on and seconds later, the downstairs windows glowed, too.

I peered at the green mailbox with shamrocks on it, hoping to see a name. No such luck.

We doubled back and quietly slipped into Jerry's yard. At least we wouldn't disturb anyone there.

Trixie tugged at the leash, sniffing the ground and trying to pull me where she wanted to go. We sneaked along the side of Jerry's house. From the backyard, I could see inside a brightly lighted window in the back of the neighboring home.

Tall cabinets mounted on the wall indicated it was the kitchen. I coaxed Trixie deeper into Jerry's backyard. Bingo! Another window and a much better angle. I could see Kim's blond hair shining under the lights. She gestured. A plea? I wished she were yelling. I might be able to hear what she was saying.

A tall man with fluffy reddish hair styled in high waves came into view. Brewster!

Trixie dug in a flower bed, tossing dirt. "Stop that," I hissed, using my shoe to push the dirt back into place.

But when I looked up, a movement in the window upstairs caught my eye. Someone else was in Brewster's house. She leaned over to close the window. There was no doubt about it. Prissy Clodfelter wore a scant nightie in the middle of the night upstairs in Brewster's house. *Well, well, well.* I wouldn't have expected that matchup. Poor Dave! Did he know about Brewster and Prissy? Probably not.

I shifted my focus back to Brewster. He seemed calm. He even laughed. Was Kim pulling some kind of stunt on Ben? I might have suspected hanky-panky if I hadn't spotted Prissy upstairs.

I watched their expressions, trying to read them. Kim did not appear happy. Was she fearful? More like worried, I decided.

She left the house, and the door banged shut behind her. I grabbed Trixie and covered her with the black jacket. We huddled in the back corner of the yard, my main concern that Trixie might bark. My heart pounded. And then she yelped, high and shrill.

I cringed and glanced at the window.

Brewster peered out, his neck craned. He switched off the light, but the dim glow coming from another room allowed me to see him press his face against the window, his hands cupped around his temples.

I turned my head so he wouldn't see my face, and covered Trixie with my body. When I looked back, the downstairs lights had been doused.

I wasn't taking any chances. We scurried across the back of Jerry's yard and around the other side to the street. I hurried Trixie along the sidewalk away from Brewster's house, just in case he looked out a front window.

When we reached the shopping area, a bright streetlight revealed that Trixie carried something in her mouth. "Ugh." I grabbed it from her. A dirty little bag. It had some heft to it. At least it wasn't a rat this time.

That had been a strange encounter. Aside from the surprising relationship between Prissy and Brewster, which I didn't think Dave knew about, two things stood out in my mind.

First, Kim felt the need to keep her visit to Brewster secret. She could have simply phoned him or paid him a visit at Hair of the Dog during the day. That meant they didn't want anyone to know they had a connection, especially Ben. Or they didn't want anyone to overhear their conversation.

Second, the only obvious connection between Kim and the murders was her father's car. It was remotely possible that her midnight visit to Brewster arose out of some other reason, but it seemed more likely that it involved the car. What was it about that car that was so important?

Trixie raised her head, and her ears pricked. She backed up quickly when two intoxicated men stumbled by, laughing and talking far too loud. We cut across the green and passed the stores on the other side. Just in case Kim was still around, we cut down the next street and walked by Aunt Birdie's house—a typical white Victorian with a turret and a front porch. I could tell it was immaculate, even in the dark of night. A porch light illuminated wicker chairs and a table that evoked thoughts of lazy summer days. Never at Birdie's, though. I doubted that anyone had ever dared sit in one of her chairs. Her house was for show-and-tell. My mother had always hurried me out lest I touch a wall or one of the dolls Aunt Birdie collected.

Sparkling lights next door caused me to stop on the sidewalk in awe. The tree house that caused Birdie such pain was a fanciful masterpiece. Why on earth did she complain about it? Fairy lights outlined windows and doors with eyebrow arches. An electric candle glowed in one small round window. Sparse fairy lights wound in and out of a railing. The broad pickets had been laboriously cut to resemble the silhouette of a cat. Enchanted, I itched to be invited inside. Tiny's house, on the other hand, lay dark in the night. Not a single light glimmered anywhere.

We walked on. In spite of the recent murders, the sleepy streets of Wagtail embraced us with their charm. We arrived at the golf cart all too soon.

Back at the inn, I didn't hesitate to enter through the reception area. Now that we were back, mission accomplished, it didn't matter whether Casey saw us.

"Where have *you* been?" he demanded.

"Out for a walk. I saw Tiny's tree house. It's amazing."

"He built it with stuff they threw out when they were building Hobbitville. It's all cast-off stuff."

"Then it's even more incredible. I hope his kids appreciate it." I gazed up at Oma's apartment. "Everything okay here?"

"Very quiet tonight."

"Want me to stick around?"

"Gosh, no!" He puffed out his chest. "I've got everything under control."

Trixie and I walked past the dark gift shop to the lobby. I double-checked to be sure Casey had remembered to lock the front door. He had.

Dog-tired, I schlepped up the stairs. Off her leash, Trixie darted around, smelling the floor and, undoubtedly the lingering scents of the other dogs who had walked there during the day. She raced up to the third floor ahead of me.

When I reached the third floor landing, I found it peculiar that once again, Trixie had turned the wrong way. She snuffled at the base of the door to the storage area and pawed at it.

Oh no! It finally dawned on me why she was showing so much interest. The rat must have siblings. *Ugh*.

I couldn't do anything about it at the late hour without waking half the guests. My stomach turned at the thought, but we would have to relocate the rat family the next day. Oma must have traps somewhere.

Hoping none of them would make an appearance that night, I unlocked the door to my quarters and discovered Twinkletoes inside, watching TV in the sitting room. At my very quiet urging, Trixie gave the storage room door one last wistful glance and finally joined me.

I spread paper towels over the kitchen counter. The bag Trixie had carried turned out to be a sock. When I unknotted it and poured out the contents, two gold necklaces and a gold coin tumbled out.

"Did you dig this up in Jerry's yard?" I asked.

Trixie ignored me and watched TV with Twinkletoes.

The day Jerry died, he'd shown us something similar. Had that been a ruse? Could Jerry have been involved in the thefts at Snowball Mountain? But why would this have been buried in his flower bed?

I stashed the sock and the contents inside an empty cachepot for the night.

I turned off the TV, and the three of us went to bed.

Morning came too early for those who had been out sleuthing in the night. Twinkletoes woke me. She sat behind my head and tapped my forehead with her paw.

I didn't need Zelda to translate. *Hello? Is anyone in there?*

I dragged myself to the kitchen. In the future, I had to remember to leave her a nighttime snack so she wouldn't be so eager to wake me in the morning. Twinkletoes waited patiently while I spooned tuna mousse into her bowl.

Trixie still lounged in bed, where I wanted to be. A shower went a long way in waking me. Unfortunately, I remembered the rat issue. I pulled on the jeans I'd worn the night before in anticipation of going into the musty storage room. The deep-pink top brightened up the informal jeans. If I stayed much longer, I'd be tempted to buy some warmer clothes.

I called Dave and left a somewhat cryptic message about finding something of interest. How was I going to explain that I had been sneaking around Jerry's yard? Nevertheless, I had to turn it in. I wrapped the sock in paper towels and jammed it in my pocket.

The nightmare of being unemployed weighed heavily on me. I hadn't done a thing in the last few days to find a new job. I would have to start that ball rolling soon. Otherwise, I'd find myself in a big bind before I knew it.

"Come on, Trixie," I called, heading for the door. "Twinkletoes!"

Trixie came running. We waited for Twinkletoes. I called her name again and again. Where had that silly girl gone? I ran a quick check through the rooms. No sign of Twinkletoes. She must have curled up somewhere to sleep after her breakfast. I would check back before the great rat eradication.

Trixie zoomed into the hallway and straight to the door of

the storage room. Ugh. Breakfast first. No one should ever tackle a rat problem on an empty stomach.

Trixie had already figured out our routine. She beat me to the dining area. By the time I arrived, she was going from table to table begging for food. *No! No, no, no! Why had I left the leash upstairs?*

I snagged my little cutie and carried her into Oma's private kitchen, hoping I might find a string or some twine to use as a temporary leash.

Instead, I found Twinkletoes, comfortably curled up in one of the cushy chairs by the fireplace.

"How did you do that?" She hadn't slipped by me when I opened the door to my room.

Twinkletoes didn't seem to care. She lifted her head and regarded us with disinterest. She yawned, displaying pink gums, itty bitty white teeth, and a rosy tongue, then curled up tight for a nap.

Someone else must have had leash issues, because I found a little stash of Sugar Maple leashes in a closet. I snapped one onto Trixie's collar and returned to the dining area, keeping the leash very short so she would be forced to walk close to me and wouldn't be able to lunge at the breakfasts of other dogs.

We joined Oma, who ate oatmeal for breakfast. "The temperature is dropping," she said. "See the mist rising from the water? Won't be long until the trees turn glorious colors."

I pulled the wrapped sock out of my pocket. "Remember the gold coins that Jerry showed us? Trixie found this in his yard last night."

Oma studied the necklaces and the coin. Her forehead furrowed, she dabbed the corners of her mouth with her napkin. "He must have been involved with the thieves in Snowball."

"That's what I thought."

"Or someone put it there to make it appear that way."

Dave rushed in. He perched on the edge of a chair. "I don't have a lot of time. What's up?"

I shoved the sock and contents his way.

Dave stared at them. "Where did you find this?"

I had to tell him the truth, even if put me in a bad light. "Trixie dug it up in Jerry's flower bed."

"You should have left it there, untouched."

"I didn't realize she found it."

Dave closed his eyes for a second too long. "And what were you doing there? Snooping?"

"Spying, if you must know."

Oma coughed. "That's my girl!"

Dave stared at me with tired eyes. "On whom?"

"On Ben's girlfriend, Kim."

"And why was Kim there?"

"To see Brewster."

"About what?"

"That's what I'd like to know. She stole Trixie in the middle of the night. I have no idea why."

Dave's shoulders sagged forward. "Two murders and you're worried about a spat over a dog? Or is the dog just a pawn in an argument over Ben?" He stood up, pulled a plastic bag from his pocket, and turned it over his hand, inside out. He grabbed the items, slid the bag over his fingers and sealed the gold inside. "This, however, could be helpful. Thank you."

He turned to go.

"No breakfast?" asked Oma.

"Not today, thanks." He loped out.

That off my mind, I turned to my other immediate problem. I had to bring up the rat issue carefully. A waitress I didn't recognize came to take our order.

"Could I interest you in caramel banana oatmeal?"

Caramel put a decidedly unhealthy but ever so yummy spin on oatmeal. Who could resist? I ordered one for me and a doggy version for Trixie.

Instead of upsetting Oma by suggesting there could be a rat, or more than one, in the storage room, I told her about Trixie's behavior.

Oma finished her coffee. "Most peculiar. Do you mind having a look around?" She handed me her key ring. "I'm sure it's nothing."

I would have to show her a rat nest before she would believe it. I shuddered at the thought.

The waitress delivered our breakfast and scuttled off to other tables.

"Where's Shelley?" I asked.

"You like Shelley, too, I see. It's her day off. I worry about her. She has a lot on her plate taking care of her little boy while her husband is overseas on military duty."

"You worry too much."

"Me?" She laughed. "At least Zelda dumped that no-goodnik who was mooching off her. We have to find her someone better."

"Oma!" I scolded. "Look, I think I was pretty nice about that stunt that you and Rose pulled to throw Holmes and me together. But you have to stop doing things like that. I know you mean well, but you have to butt out of other people's love lives."

"Yes. You are quite right, my Holly. I will keep this in mind." She rose. "You will excuse me, yes? And don't forget to tell me what you find upstairs."

She could bet on that.

Caramel turned out to be just about the best thing ever on oatmeal. I savored every bite of the sweet, slightly gooey caramel, which clung to the oatmeal and fresh slices of banana. I noticed that Trixie had no problem polishing off her bowl of oatmeal, sans caramel, either.

I lingered over a second cup of tea to put off the rat excursion as long as possible. It was a bad call.

Thirty-eight

❧ ❧ ❧

If I had only stopped at one cup of tea and gone off to hunt rats, I wouldn't have been there when Philip waltzed in.

I was trapped. Even if I made a beeline for Oma's private kitchen, it would be too late. He would have seen me. It was time to straighten him out.

He had the nerve to peck me on the cheek. Pulling a chair too close to me, he held onto the back of my chair, like he was staking a claim.

"Thank you for the chocolates."

"My pleasure. I can't stay long. I just had to stop by to say good morning."

"Look, Philip. I'm sure you're a wonderful guy, but I just . . ." *Aha!* I could tell him the truth, sort of, without hurting him. "Well, something happened, and now I'm not sure that Ben and I are over after all. You understand."

His face fell. "Aunt Birdie won't like this."

Who cared what Aunt Birdie thought? I tried another tack. "Maybe you don't realize that Zelda is crazy about you. I would never want to hurt her."

"Zelda? The psychic? She *is* crazy! No, Holly. We're meant to be together. It's our destiny. We belong together."

"Philip," I said gently, "we hardly know each other."

"There's chemistry between us."

I was beginning to feel chemistry all right—noxious chemistry. It was time to make my exit. Dire circumstances called for extreme measures. "I'm sorry, Philip. You're going way too fast here. It's not public knowledge yet, but Ben and I have set the date. We're getting married." Okay, that was a big, fat honking lie, but this guy needed to back off! I rose, clutching Trixie's leash and hauled out of there as fast as I could without attracting more attention. We climbed the stairs quickly, and in case he followed us, I headed straight to the storage room, preferring to deal with the rodents.

I unlocked the door and let it swing open.

Trixie strained at the leash. I shuddered to think what she smelled. My puny human nose didn't register anything—it wasn't even very musty. What did rats smell like?

Fearing Philip might follow us, I quickly closed the door behind us. Not that I particularly wanted to be trapped there with a rodent.

Dormer windows on both sides were cracked open, allowing a breeze to blow through. That explained the lack of odor. The space was huge, much bigger than I remembered, and not as scary as I had expected. Desks, dressers, and chairs filled the middle. Headboards leaned against walls. A few armoires blocked my view. Extra dining tables, Christmas decorations—a rat paradise. They could hide anywhere.

Reluctantly, I unsnapped Trixie's leash. She would find the pesky little creatures faster than me.

Her nails clicked across the wood floor as she raced through the room, her nose leading her. She yipped a couple of times. *Ugh*. Did that mean she found them?

Weighing Philip versus a furry rat, I cracked the door, so I could make a hasty exit if necessary. I peeked out, relieved that he wasn't hanging around outside the door to my quarters.

I followed Trixie slowly, stepping cautiously and hoping a rat wouldn't run across my thong sandals. The mere thought sent shivers through me. Clearly not the best footwear for this kind of work.

Consoling myself with the notion that maybe one lonely rat hid from us, scared out of its mind, I peered ahead but couldn't see much for all the bulky furniture. Maybe the rat Trixie dispatched left behind a nest of tiny babies that could be easily removed?

I made my way to the far corner, where Trixie wriggled upside-down on a bed. Someone had put together an entire bed. Footboard, headboard, and all. On top of the mattress lay a pink sleeping bag with fluffy white kittens and silver crowns printed on it. A nearby table held a flashlight, an empty soda can, two peanut butter and chocolate candy bars, and a set of keys. The keys drew me closer. They hung on an open ring with a golf ball on one end and a golf club on the other. Sterling silver if I had to guess.

A flurry of fur zoomed by me. I shrieked and scooted back. Twinkletoes landed on the bed briefly. Uninterested, she sprang to the table and swatted the keys onto the floor. They jingled as they fell. In an instant she pounced on them and played kitty hockey with them, sending them flying across the floor.

I let out a great breath of air. No rats. At least it didn't look like it. Someone had fixed a little nest up here, but it appeared to be a larger, human rat. I had to tell Oma.

Leaving the door open for Twinkletoes, I headed for the elevator. Trixie followed me until she saw I planned to step into the scary little room that moved. She balked. I called to her from inside the elevator. She ran forward, then backed up again. I picked her up and carried her into the elevator.

"You'll be happy to know that there are no elevators in my house. Of course, no one will cook meals for you, either. You'll have to eat kibble like other dogs."

She didn't seem too worried about that. I exited the elevator and set her down. She raced along to Oma's office as though she knew where we were going.

I arrived just in time to see her collect a treat from Zelda and zoom into Oma's office to beg for another one. Good thing the dog cookies were tiny!

Easing into a chair, I said, "We have a little problem. Some-one is sleeping in the storage room."

Oma's hands flew up in shock. "Who?"

"I don't know. A bed is set up with a sleeping bag and a few personal items."

Oma's forehead wrinkled. "Ja? Who would do such a thing?"

I sighed. It would probably be better if she figured out the worst part of it herself. "Oma, I had to unlock the door to get in."

She blinked at me. "You are saying it must be an employee. One who has access to house keys."

"Seems that way, doesn't it?"

"This makes no sense. Zelda, Shelley, Tiny, Casey, the new housekeeper—all my employees have homes."

"Maybe someone had to move out and had nowhere to go? Although, honestly, I didn't see clothes or dishes or much personal stuff."

She rose and accompanied me to the elevator. I scooped Trixie up before she could do her dance of fear.

Minutes later, Oma and I searched the storage room for clues to the identity of the mysterious, as she called it, "attic guest."

We were stumped. Barring fingerprints or DNA tests of some sort, the person hadn't left anything special behind, except for the keys. After crawling around on my knees, I finally spotted them under a dresser and fished them out with a broom.

Oma shook her head upon seeing them. "I do not know these keys."

"You probably don't ever see the keys of your employees."

"This is true," she conceded.

"What now?"

Oma held the keys in her hand. Her head didn't move, but she looked me in the eyes, her lips pursed with displeasure. "Golf? Sounds more like a guest than an employee."

"I'd think it might be Prissy or Peaches, but I can't imagine how they could have gotten in here."

"Come, my dear. We have work to do."

I collected Twinkletoes, and Trixie followed us out.

Oma locked the door and tested the knob. "Tonight we will wait to see who comes. Yes?"

"You're such a sneak."

She laughed. "I love a good mystery, and this certainly qualifies."

I stopped her before she stepped into the elevator. "Maybe we should tell Dave."

"No. If it is an employee with problems, I would rather be of help, not cause legal difficulties, too."

"Someone tried to kill you. Under the circumstances . . ."

She massaged her forehead. "Perhaps you are correct. Could you track down Dave and let him know?"

"Absolutely." I hurried back to my suite and placed a call to Dave. He didn't answer his home phone or his cell phone. I left messages for him, telling him we'd discovered that someone with a golf club key ring was camping out in the attic of the inn. Given the circumstances, we thought he should be with us when we confronted the unofficial guest.

Not an hour later, I browsed through Pawsitively Decadent in search of turtles. *Jackpot!* Exactly what I wanted. Pecan turtles made fresh on the premises with bourbon and dipped in chocolate. I bought a box, which the saleswoman very kindly gussied up with the store ribbon of gold paw prints on a white satin background.

Too bad I couldn't teach Trixie to carry it, since the gift really came from both of us. I had a sneaking suspicion she would rip it open and eat the contents given half a chance.

She accompanied me to HEAL!, where I sought out Eric, the pharmacist, and presented the turtles to him. "We wanted to thank you for helping us. I can't tell you how grateful I am that you called when you saw Trixie."

He knelt and ruffled her fur. "It's reward enough that she's home safe and sound. We've had too much trouble in Wagtail this week. I'm glad there was good news, too."

He must hear a lot of gossip. "Any word on whether they're making progress on identifying the killer?"

"Everyone has a theory. The only thing we know for sure is that Mortie's car was stolen from Northern Virginia. Not from Wagtail. So that means either the thief went up there to get it, or someone stole it from the thief."

"How do you know that?"

"Police reports and gossip. The Snowball newspaper runs the police reports every week. It wasn't reported stolen up here. I believe in coincidences, but I have trouble imagining that Mortie's stolen car just happened to turn up here, you know?"

So did I. No wonder Mortie sent Ben to Wagtail. Someone from Wagtail had gone to a lot of trouble to steal Mortie's car. I had to wonder if that person had known all along that he would use it to commit a murder. "Have they established that Mortie's car is the one that hit Sven?"

"Everyone is assuming that's the case."

"Why Mortie's car? Why not use another car that was more readily available?"

"Precisely. And then his daughter shows up with a lawyer in tow?"

"They were with me hours away from here when Sven was killed. There's no way Kim or Mortie could be involved."

"Ever hear of murder for hire?"

"Mortie paid someone to steal his car and commit murder?" It boggled my mind to even contemplate that scenario.

"Yeah, well, that's where the whole thing falls apart, isn't it?"

The door to the pharmacy slammed open, and I recognized Casey's shock of dark hair, but he didn't even bother stepping inside. "Eric! They're arresting Holmes!"

Thirty-nine

❖ ❖ ❖ ❖ ❖

I ran out of the store, Trixie bounding along, sensing excitement. We trailed Casey by fifteen feet. He headed for Oak Street.

A police car was parked in front of Rose's house. It seemed like the whole town had gathered to see what was going on. Tiny, Brewster, Shelley, Philip, Prissy. I knew many of the faces.

The door to Rose's house hung open. Holmes walked out, raised his arm and waved, more like an athlete who'd scored than someone in trouble with the law.

I dodged everyone to get to him. "Holmes! What's going on?"

"Stand back, Holly." Dave sounded tired.

I walked along to the car with them.

Holmes squeezed my shoulder. "Not to worry. I haven't done anything."

He wasn't in handcuffs. Maybe that was a good sign. "Then why are they arresting you?"

"I'm not under arrest. I'm going to Snowball voluntarily just to talk."

"No! Don't say anything. Don't you watch TV shows about crime? Don't say a word."

"Holl, I have nothing to hide. I didn't do anything."

He bent to wedge into the backseat of the police car.

I whipped around and faced Dave. "I felt sorry for you. But this isn't right. You've got the wrong man."

Quietly, almost apologetically, Dave said, "Motive, means, and we have an eyewitness who can place him at the scene and running away."

"He was jogging!" My voice rose, not nearly as calm and controlled as Dave's.

"How do you know that?" Dave slid into the car and shut the door.

Even though he couldn't hear me, I whispered, "Because he told me so." It wasn't enough. Even I knew that.

Compelled to watch the police car leave, I stayed until it disappeared from sight, as though I thought it would help Holmes in some way.

The crowd dispersed, and Philip approached me.

"I apologize for coming on so strong, Holly. The prospect of a relationship with someone like you was . . . intoxicating. I think I was a little bit giddy. I hope Ben appreciates you as much as I would." He touched my shoulder gently. "I'm here for you if it doesn't work out."

I thanked him. At least he had backed off. At the moment, I couldn't have cared less about Philip or a relationship with Ben. Holmes was in trouble. I dragged home, numb with despair.

Zelda hugged me when I returned to the inn. "Your grandmother said to tell you that you're in charge. She drove Rose over to Snowball because Rose is too upset to drive. They're going to find Holmes a lawyer."

A lawyer! I knew a lawyer. "Thanks, Zelda." I removed Trixie's leash and ran to Oma's office to look up the phone number for Mortie's cabin. When I called, Kim didn't want to put Ben on the phone. I held my temper in check when I insisted, but my nerves had been stretched to the point of fraying.

I explained the situation to Ben. "Can you go over there and bail him out?"

"There's no bail yet if he's not under arrest."

"Can't you do something to help him?"

"Actually, I can't. There could be a conflict of interest."

"Is that another way of saying that you expect Mortie to be charged with murder?"

"No!"

"Then where's the conflict? Why does Mortie need representation anyway?"

"I can't discuss that with you."

Steaming mad, I said good-bye and hung up the phone.

Zelda leaned against the doorframe. "Holmes didn't do it."

"I know. Why would someone steal Mortie's car to use in a homicide?"

"Because he didn't want to use his own car." She let out a little screech and her eyes opened wide. "Because he wanted to frame Mortie!"

"That," I pointed at her, "is the first plausible explanation I have heard."

Zelda beamed. "But it wouldn't work unless Mortie was actually here when the murder happened."

"Good point. And the car was reported stolen, so that would let Mortie off the hook in any case. Then why would he send Ben up here? Unless . . . unless the car wasn't actually stolen."

"Yes!" Zelda shouted. But her enthusiasm waned quickly. "How exactly would that work?"

"I don't know. We should be concentrating on Jerry's murder anyway. That's the one they think Holmes committed."

Zelda paced to the French doors. "If Brewster hadn't seen him running away from Jerry's house that morning—"

"Brewster?" I sat up straight. Now there was a coincidence. "Brewster is the one who saw Holmes there?"

Zelda turned around. "Sure. Brewster is Jerry's neighbor. Makes perfect sense."

"And Brewster brought Dolce back to Ellie," I mused.

"He loves dogs, especially his Irish setter, Murphy. I'm not surprised that he brought Dolce home. He would have known who Dolce was." She squinted at me. "Do you find that odd for some reason?"

I debated telling her about Kim's nocturnal visit to Brewster but decided against it. As much as I liked Zelda, she would repeat it to the others in the circle of inn employees immediately. I fudged a little. "I think it's terrific that he was thoughtful enough to bring her home to Ellie. It worried me sick when Trixie was missing." I smiled at the sight of her sleeping, upside down on the loveseat, all four little legs sticking up in the air.

No matter what I said to Zelda, Kim's contact with Brewster last night put him in a different light as far as I was concerned. Maybe he had returned Dolce out of kindness. Or maybe he had let him out of his own yard to begin with. But Kim and Brewster were involved in this mess somehow . . .

Why didn't anything fit together? Brewster must have something to do with the car. If he had stolen it, Kim wouldn't have paid him a midnight visit. I tried to recall their expressions. He hadn't seemed in the least bit upset. But he'd peered out the window. I would have, too, if my neighbor had been killed in cold blood.

Zelda watched me, perched on the chair in front of Oma's desk. "What are you thinking?"

I scrambled to find something to say. "Do you know anyone with a golf club key ring?"

"Not me! It sounds cute, though. That oaf I married took every nice thing I owned when he absconded. I never should have told him to get out and then left for work."

"I'm so sorry, Zelda."

She shrugged. "Onward, right? I can't dwell on what might have been. Golf club, huh? Sounds like something Mr. Luciano might have. Did you find one or something?"

"Yes. I don't know to whom it belongs."

"I'm sure the owner will be looking for it. I'll let you know." She jumped up to help someone at the front desk.

For the next few hours, I followed up on inn matters, making sure guest rooms were ready for new guests, taking calls from vendors and a couple of nervous dog owners who couldn't believe we didn't have weight restrictions on dog guests.

Zelda and I were considering eating lunch in Oma's office together when Dave burst through the doors. Flushed and tense, he demanded, "Where's the key ring?"

"Upstairs. We left it where we found it," I said.

"Did you touch it?"

"Yes. Twinkletoes knocked it on the floor. I picked it up."

He sagged. Zeroing in on Zelda, he said, "Not a word about

this. Do you understand? If you breathe even a hint, you'll mess up my best opportunity to nab Sven's killer."

"What?" Zelda appeared confused.

"Show me!" Dave demanded.

I nabbed the key ring off Oma's desk.

Acting a lot like Jerry had, Dave shook a finger at Zelda as we headed for the elevator. "Not a word!"

I scooped up Trixie and stepped inside. "So Holmes is off the hook, then? You let him go?"

"No."

"Dave! You can't have it both ways."

"I've got two murders. Doesn't mean it's the same killer."

I shut up. We stepped off the elevator, and I unlocked the door. Trixie bounded in and jumped on the bed again.

Dave didn't touch a thing. "Get the dog out."

I picked her up off the bed and held her.

Dave studied the items next to the bed, licked his lips, and locked his lower lip over the top one. He scanned the room, taking everything in, then focused on the key ring again. After a moment, he said, "It's him."

Forty

❀ ❀ ❀

"The killer?" I whispered. "How can you tell?"

"These are Mortie's keys," said Dave. "They match the description given when he reported the car stolen. The odds of them being someone else's on this kind of circular golf club key ring are crazy slim. Possible, but unlikely."

"Think I ruined fingerprints when I picked them up?"

"Probably. But it would take longer to get the prints back than to wait for this creep to return tonight."

I could hardly breathe. The killer had been right under our noses, sleeping in the inn!

Dave swallowed hard. "You and Liesel have to act completely normal. You understand? You cannot let on that anything is different, or you'll tip this person off. No talking to anyone about it. Not that boyfriend of yours or employees or guests or anyone. And especially not Holmes or anyone in his family. Got it?"

"Absolutely. Neither Oma nor I would sleep a wink if we knew a murderer lurked here among us. But, you said *person*. You don't think it's a man?"

"It would take a pretty macho guy to use a sleeping bag with kittens on it."

Oma and I shared a quiet dinner with Rose and Holmes in the private kitchen that night. The fire crackled, and candles flickered on the table. Gingersnap, Twinkletoes, and Trixie roamed underfoot. It would have been a wonderful evening but for the nightmare that hung over us all.

The garlic fettuccine smelled divine but Rose barely touched her food.

Holmes appeared none the worse for his interrogation that afternoon. He chowed down on the pasta laden with red peppers, caramelized onions, and shrimp. "They asked me if they could take a sample of my hair." He swept a hand over the side of his head twice.

"They must think they have a sample of the killer's hair." I twisted my fork in the fettuccine.

"I certainly hope you refused!" Rose clutched the base of her throat.

"Not a chance. I know I didn't kill anybody. I wish they'd eliminate me so they could concentrate on other suspects. The hair must have been longer than mine. They kept trying to get me to admit that I had it cut recently—like yesterday!"

"I hope you gave them the name of your barber in Chicago," murmured Rose.

"You bet I did!"

"You might have to switch barbers. Can you imagine what they'll think?" I said it in jest, hoping to lighten the mood.

Oma and Rose didn't seem to be amused in the slightest.

"I wouldn't mind wearing it a little longer again."

"So, uh, just how long did they want your hair to be?" I asked.

"They didn't say."

I studied his hair. More than half an inch, I decided. An inch long, maybe? That included a lot of people.

"Can they determine gender from a hair?" I asked.

"If there's DNA on it," said Oma.

"Then they might already know whether it was a man or a woman."

Rose spoke in a dull tone. "It was a man."

"How do you know that?" asked Oma.

"Oh, please. You're the one addicted to *Murder, She Wrote*, Liesel Fletcher." Rose toyed with her fork. "Jerry was neither large nor particularly strong. Whoever dropped that choke collar over his head must have overpowered him."

"Or Jerry fell down, and the killer slid it over his head. Don't forget that the murderer bashed him in the head, too," said Holmes. "Maybe he stumbled and that gave the killer the opportunity to slip the collar over his head."

"Do we know what killed him?" I asked.

Holmes winced. "Given the questions they asked, I gather they think someone had a leash connected to the choke collar. I imagine it cut off his air when he fell on the stairs. Remember that outstretched hand?"

I would never forget it.

A knock on the door stilled us, but Trixie barked like a squirrel waited on the other side.

I rose and opened it, only to find Dave. My little barker wagged her tail and waited to be petted. For the first time during my visit, Dave wasn't wearing his uniform. I knew why he'd donned black jeans and a black sweatshirt.

Dave froze at the sight of Holmes.

Holmes sprang up from his seat. "Dave! Want some fettuccine? There's plenty."

Dave sucked in a big breath. "Thanks, I've eaten."

"Aw, come on." Holmes slung an arm around Dave's shoulders. "We've known each other forever. I don't hold a grudge against you. You're just doing your job."

"Well, I'm madder than I've ever been at anybody." Rose's voice soared to a shrill pitch. "What the devil do you think you're doing? Leave Holmes alone! Don't you tell me you came to arrest him!"

Dave didn't rise to her bait. Low and level, he said, "That's not why I'm here. I apologize for interrupting your dinner. Holly, could I have a word with you?"

"Sure." I stepped into the empty dining area. Trixie followed, and I closed the door behind us. "You're early."

"Don't want to miss him."

We walked up the stairs. I spoke in a loud voice in case anyone was listening. "You'll be amazed by the third-floor suite. I think it would be just the place for your cousin's honeymoon."

A smile twitched on his lips. "She's very picky."

"She'll love it! We can take some pictures to send her if you like."

We reached the third level, and he muttered, "It disturbs me that you're good at this."

"Did Holmes's hair match the ones you collected at the crime scene?"

Dave stopped dead. He exhaled and chuckled. "Holmes is no dummy. No, they didn't match."

"What does the hair look like?"

He paused and assessed me as though weighing how much to tell me. "Weird hair. Most of it has been sent to Richmond for analysis."

"Weird? What does that mean? Dog fur or something?"

"Or something. Maybe a toy. It's a mixture of human hair and some kind of synthetic hair."

I gasped. "Jerry's extended arm—he must have been holding something the killer wanted. So maybe it was a burglary! But who would kill over a toy?"

Dave didn't say another word.

I pulled a duplicate key to the storage room out of my pocket. "Are you all by yourself? Shouldn't you have backup?"

"I've got a backup in the parking lot, one on the front porch, and another in the lobby."

He strode over to the bed. "No one has been here. Nothing has been moved. Okay, Holl. Thanks."

I'd been dismissed. I handed him the duplicate key to the room. "Just in case you need it." I called to Trixie and locked Dave inside.

Forty-one

* * * * *

When I returned to her kitchen, Oma was rinsing the dishes.

"Holmes and Rose left?" I asked.

"Poor Rose. We told her to take a sleeping pill so she could get some rest. Holmes is everything to her." Oma smiled tearfully. "Like you are to me. I don't know what I'd do in her shoes."

"I do. You'd try to figure out who really killed Jerry."

"It's not as easy as it is on TV shows."

"Oma, what's the deal with Mortie?"

She rinsed a dish and slid it into the dishwasher. "What do you mean?"

"You seem to know him fairly well . . ."

"Oh, that. Wagtail is such a small place. I had met him a few times. He put up extra guests here occasionally. Then when Kim was fourteen, she ran away from home with a seventeen-year-old boy. Mortie called and asked me to keep a lookout for her. I found them at Mortie's cabin, sent the boy packing, and kept Kim here for a few hours until her father arrived to pick her up. It wouldn't have been a big deal, except they discovered later that the boy was a drug dealer. Very bad news."

That explained a lot. No wonder Mortie continued to be grateful to Oma even after all these years. "Why did he send Ben to watch over her? She's an adult now. Mortie still doesn't trust Kim?"

Oma turned to me and winced. "I might have had a hand in that. Mortie called to see how I was doing."

"Uh-huh." I waited, certain that wasn't all.

"The subject of the Ben might have come up." She averted her eyes and busied herself sweeping imaginary crumbs off the island. "Mortie and his wife wouldn't mind seeing him back together with Kim. He's a stabilizing influence on her."

"So you suggested they throw them together?"

She held up a cautionary forefinger. "That was not my idea. Kim insisted on coming here, and Mortie was worried about her."

"As well he should have been. She's been sneaking out at night. She's the one who tried to steal Trixie."

Oma plopped her fists on her hips. "What a terrible thing to do! I knew she was devious, but not cruel."

I couldn't help being a little bit resentful. The whole thing was a setup. Ben hadn't come because of me at all.

"Butterscotch hot cider?" she asked.

"Butterscotch?"

"I add butterscotch schnapps. It's very popular with guests."

"Okay. Not much schnapps, though. We want to be alert tonight."

I pulled out a pot and poured in cider to heat up. Oma finished tidying and handed me two glass mugs with butterscotch schnapps in the bottoms. I poured the steaming liquid over the top, and the scent of crisp apples wafted up.

When we sat comfortably before the fire, the dogs lay at our feet, but Twinkletoes had vanished. I told Oma about Kim visiting Brewster in the middle of the night.

"I hope it's not Brewster who will show up for the keys. He's a big man. He could overpower Dave."

I assured her Dave had backups all over the inn. "And he seems to think it might be a woman. It would be nice to have radio contact with him so we would know what was happening."

Oma nodded. "Unfortunately, when something does happen, I fear everyone in the inn will be awakened."

"Oma, I don't mean to pry, but where did you go the other night? And how did you get out without Casey or me seeing you?"

She laughed so hard that she slapped her knee. "Now, now, Holly. Even a grandmother gets to have a few secrets."

"Please?"

"Once a week, Thomas—"

"The owner of The Blue Boar?"

"The very same. He and I gather our leftovers and take them up to Hazel Mae's house."

"In the middle of the night? You just leave them there?"

She smiled. "Sneaky of us, isn't it?"

"Don't they spoil during the night?"

"She has a refrigerator on the back porch. We put everything in there."

"And no one hears you?"

"With all those children? One has to assume that someone has heard us."

"So they know it's you."

"Probably. But it permits them to save face. They're too proud to take charity."

I sat up. "Hazel Mae isn't too proud to steal." I told Oma about seeing her take the ballet shoes.

"Most of the merchants like to help them out."

"Isn't that setting them up for trouble? Maybe someone should give them jobs."

Oma clucked. "Hazel Mae takes in laundry, and Del mows lawns in the summer and shovels walks in the winter, but it's not enough to support their big family. Besides, Hazel Mae will find a way to reimburse the shop owner for those shoes. She does her best to pay everyone back with some act of kindness. Perhaps it seems odd to you, but Hazel Mae and Del are part of the marvelous diversity that weaves into the Wagtail fabric. We take care of our own here."

At ten o'clock, we turned in. I knew I wouldn't sleep, especially across the hall from the action—if there was any. No wonder Dave had been adamant about keeping quiet. It would be easy to tip off the killer and inadvertently cause him to stay away.

Since my arrival, I'd done little in my lovely suite except shower and sleep. Restless, I puttered around, incredulous that Holmes had managed to carve the wonderful space out of the attic. Trixie followed me through the rooms until a little, mostly white tornado tore through. Trixie yelped and chased her.

Where had Twinkletoes come from? I followed them but they had vanished. I felt like an idiot standing in front of the fireplace and looking around. They had to be in the suite somewhere.

In less than two minutes, they raced through the suite again, Twinkletoes in the lead. This time I was ready. I watched to see where they were going. But Twinkletoes jumped up on the hearth.

Trixie focused on her, ready to play.

Thinking I had missed my opportunity, I flicked on the fire and settled in one of the cozy chairs with my feet up. I strained to hear any indication of activity across the hall. Nothing.

Twinkletoes sprang off the hearth. Dancing sideways like a Halloween cat, with her back arched, she whapped Trixie on the nose with one of her paws and took off again.

Trixie's claws rustled against the wood floor as she scrambled after Twinkletoes. I jumped up and chased them, just in time to see Trixie disappear through the bookcase in the dining room.

What on earth? I knelt down and peered at the bottom shelf. They had gone through a round pet-sized hole in the back. I stood and stepped back. In the dark cherry wood, it was almost invisible. No wonder I had missed it.

I grasped a shelf. A little pressure caused that section of the bookcase to swing open to a stair landing. A light switch to my right turned on overhead lights. I trotted down the stairs, laughing at how stupid I'd been. These had to be the old back stairs to the kitchen. Indeed, a landing on the second floor provided an exit, undoubtedly hidden on the other side. I continued down another flight of stairs. At the bottom, I pushed against a wood panel with a pet door in it and found myself in Oma's private kitchen with Twinkletoes and Trixie.

Oma must have built a similar hidden staircase between her suite and her office when she put on the new addition. That

would explain how she managed to leave without being seen
by Casey or me.

That tricky woman! I couldn't stop smiling. My dear old
Oma was one of a kind. I should have known she would use
the renovation as an excuse to build hidden passages. She loved
things like that.

I carried Twinkletoes up to my suite. Trixie raced ahead of
us. I located some heavy books and blocked off their escape
hatch. That way I wouldn't have to worry about Trixie being
stolen from the kitchen.

I settled back in the big cushy chair with my feet on the
ottoman, waiting for something to happen. Trixie jumped up
on the chair, and twisted and turned until she wedged herself
in beside me. I felt my eyelids grow heavy.

Trixie's yelp woke me at one in the morning. She
sat up at attention, listening. One more yelp and she ran to the
door of the suite and barked like crazy.

Forty-two

❀ ❀ ❀ ❀

I peered through the peephole in the door. Someone was out there. More than one someone. I couldn't tell who they were. I heard murmuring and thought I saw Dave.

Holding Trixie back so she wouldn't run out, I cracked the door. Dave escorted Tiny to the elevator.

Leaving Trixie and Twinkletoes cooped up in my suite, I stepped out. "Tiny?"

Handcuffed, his eyes wide with fright, he said, "They're not my keys. I swear! Somebody mailed them to me. I didn't murder anybody. Specially not Sven."

Dave didn't say a word. He pressed the button for the elevator.

"Are you the one who's been sleeping up here?"

"I didn't mean to upset nobody."

"Why? Why were you sleeping in the storage room?"

Tiny lowered his voice and hung his head. "I'm next. He's gonna kill me next. Them keys were a warning. I been hiding there."

"Then you know who the killer is."

His head lifted, and his eyes conveyed fresh alarm. "I didn't say that. I don't know. For sure I don't know who was driving that car, and that's the God's honest truth."

"Tiny!"

"Look, Holly, Dave. I'm ashamed of myself, I am. I done something real bad. I'll fess up to it 'cause I know it was wrong. The night you drove up here, Holly, that was me you saw out on the highway. I . . ." He appeared to be thinking fast. "I was afraid the driver, you—" he pointed at me "—would recognize me, so I followed you to the inn. I looked in the glove box in your car and saw Ben's name on the registration. When Mr. Luciano come around the corner in the fog, I thought it was Ben, and I clobbered him." He hung his head when he said, "I meant to kill him. But I couldn't." He met my eyes.

"You were going to kill the person who saw you on the highway?"

"I don't have it in me to kill nobody. I don't. I'm right sorry about Mr. Luciano. But I didn't kill nobody. I swear. I didn't want nobody to know I threw the car off the mountain. That's why I told people there was a ghost out on the highway, and he must have done it."

"Why did you throw the car over the side of the road?"

Tiny closed his eyes like he'd realized his mistake in telling us so much. "Oh, man! I done it now."

The elevator doors opened. They stepped into the elevator and turned around to face me.

"You gotta believe me," said Tiny. "I didn't kill nobody. I didn't! I swear."

Dave grunted with disbelief, and the elevator doors slid shut.

I didn't know what to make of Tiny's arrest. I returned to the suite, changed into my T-shirt, and wrapped the Sugar Maple Inn robe around me. Too agitated to sleep, I poured a glass of wine and walked out on the bedroom balcony to look out over Wagtail. Trixie and Twinkletoes came along. Their noses twitched as they caught scents on the night air.

White lights twinkled in trees along the pedestrian zone. Streetlights helped illuminate the walkways. Shop windows glowed in the night. It was enchanting.

But my thoughts kept returning to Tiny. I hadn't anticipated

that he would be the one arrested tonight. His pleas of innocence still rang in my ears. And the look on his face—he knew
more than he'd said. I wished I could be in the car with them.
I bet he was spilling his guts at that very moment.

I tried to piece together what I knew. If Tiny was telling
the truth, then he must have done something terrible to feel he
had to kill the person who saw him on the highway. That didn't
exactly bolster his protests of innocence. Surely stealing a car
didn't rise to that level.

Something else was bothering me. Something was wrong
with that picture. Why would the car thief have Mortie's keys?
No one had said it was a carjacking. That meant someone had
swiped Mortie's keys to steal the car. I knew of only one person
who had easy access to those keys. *Kim.*

Surely she hadn't stolen her own father's car! Had she
handed the keys over to someone else? I intended to find out.

In the morning I rose early, hoping to catch a
minute with Zelda before she was too busy to talk. She knew
Tiny far better that I did.

A quick step onto the balcony confirmed it was a gorgeous
day, but fall had arrived and brought colder temperatures with
it. My sandals would have to be replaced with something
warmer soon. I unblocked the pet door to Oma's kitchen so
Twinkletoes could come and go as she pleased. Dressed in the
khakis and the sleeveless white turtleneck, I took Oma's black
jacket with me to walk Trixie.

Trixie and Twinkletoes scampered down the grand staircase ahead of me, stopping to sniff various spots. Even so,
they beat me to the bottom. Trixie turned right and dashed
into the dining area.

I could hear her barking and rushed after her. She followed
Shelley's replacement, yelping at her for food.

Swooping down on Trixie, I attached her leash and coaxed
her away. "We don't bark for food like that. As soon as we get
home, you're going to doggie school."

Slipping on Oma's jacket as we went, I led her out the front
door. Even in the cold at that early hour, some guests sat on

the porch, bundled up with steaming coffee in their hands and dogs in warm coats at their feet or on their laps.

I hurried Trixie past The Blue Boar and along the sidewalk to the inn's doggy-duty zone. Oh no. I bet Tiny usually maintained it. Fortunately, it appeared that most people were pretty good about cleaning up.

Trixie led the way back to the reception desk, clearly used to the doors that opened automatically. I kept her on her leash, though, so she wouldn't run straight to the dining area again.

Zelda had just arrived and still wore a blue fleece jacket. Casey hadn't left yet.

"I guess you heard about Tiny?" I asked.

Casey puffed up his chest. "I was here last night with the backup guy. Tiny went with them peacefully, though. It was pretty anticlimactic."

"Zelda?" I prompted.

Her brow wrinkled. "Something stinks to high heaven. Tiny would never have hurt your grandmother. Quite the opposite— I think he would have protected her. It doesn't add up for me."

Casey's eyes opened wide behind his glasses. "I never thought of that. You're right! But why did he have the keys to the car?"

Exactly what I had suspected. Oma's employees seemed to adore her. They were like a big extended family. Something wasn't right. But I knew who held the missing link. *Kim.* Her only connection to the murders was the car. Somehow, Kim and Brewster had to be involved.

I skipped the inn breakfast, which I hated to do since I'd become spoiled by it, and headed to the Sweet Dog Barkery on the theory that one ought not go empty-handed to beat information out of someone. I bought three large lattes and a selection of croissants and muffins as well as two miniature peanut butter cookies for Trixie.

Borrowing Oma's golf cart, we tootled out to Mortie's cabin for a confrontation with Kim.

Picturesque against the pines, the cabin lay in stillness, interrupted only by the occasional chirp of a bird. The sun glinted off the water like sparkles undulating with the current.

I knocked on the door and waited.

Ben answered, rubbing his eyes. "What are you doing here?"

Kim shuffled out of a room. "It's the middle of the night! What's going on?"

I barged past Ben, who wore only a pair of jeans. "Good morning. I brought caffeine and goodies."

Ben yawned. "I'll just put on a shirt."

He stumbled toward a different door. I wanted to think that detail wasn't of interest to me, but I took note. Someone had been sleeping on the sofa.

Kim had wrapped herself in a sheet again. She reached out for a muffin. "These look good! Is that cinnamon I smell?"

"I think those are cinnamon pumpkin."

Trixie barked. She wagged hopefully and tried to reach the box.

I didn't like the way Kim looked at Trixie. Was she thinking of stealing her?

I held up the peanut butter cookie. "Sit."

Trixie barked again.

"Sit." I pressed down on her rear delicately and put her in a sitting position. "Good girl." I broke off half of the cookie for her.

Kim bit into a cinnamon pumpkin muffin. "Mmm. Delish!" She popped the top off a latte. "To what do we owe this surprise visit?"

Maybe it was best if I hurried and got her to talk while Ben was out of the room and couldn't stop her from blabbing. I thought fast. What would produce a response from her? "I know about you and Brewster."

She spewed latte all over the sheet she wore. "Please don't rat me out. Oh, please, Holly! I'll break up with Ben if that's what you want."

From the looks of the sofa, I wasn't sure there was anything to break up. But that was beside the point. I had to get her to tell me what was going on. I kept my question open-ended. "Why did you do it?"

She dabbed at the mess with a corner of the sheet. "I had to. I didn't know what else to do. Brewster insisted on collateral, but I had already sold almost everything. He was my last resort. I rue the day I went to him for money."

I heard Ben's electric razor whirring. I had a few more minutes. I took a guess. "Day trading?"

Kim collapsed on the sofa and held her forehead with one hand. "I lost so much money. You can't even imagine. I borrowed from everyone I knew, even Ben! When Brewster offered me a loan, I jumped at it. But he wanted collateral, so I borrowed Dad's car and gave it to him." She sat up. "You have to believe me, Holly. I never thought anything like this would happen. I thought I'd make a few trades, pay off Brewster, the car would be returned, and everything would be fine."

"You stole your father's car?"

She winced. "Borrowed, really. Who knew my dad would go and file a police report?"

What had she expected? Wouldn't most people report a stolen car? "Then why did Tiny have your dad's keys?"

She emitted a little shriek and sat up straight. "Tiny? He must be the one who stole the car from Brewster."

Forty-three

❀ ❀ ❀ ❀

"You can't be serious," I said. "A stolen car was stolen again? More likely Brewster made that up to save his own hide."

Kim looked like she might be sick. "Brewster was fuming when he found out it had been reported stolen by my dad. But then it was stolen from him, and that person hit Sven and killed him. It must have been Tiny!"

"I thought Brewster and Tiny were friends. Why would Tiny steal from Brewster?"

"I wouldn't know." She rubbed her wrist. "Now Brewster has my gold watch and is pressuring me for more. I should have left it at home."

"If you'll pardon my saying so, your parents are loaded. Why didn't you just go to them?"

"Oh no! You don't know my parents. They gave me some of their money to invest—and it's gone, gone, gone. Everything is gone. I'm so deep in the hole I can't see daylight anymore. I don't know how I'll ever crawl out."

"And now you have the issue of stealing a car to deal with, too."

"I didn't steal it. I borrowed it. And I never dreamed something like this would happen. Imagine that stupid car turning up in a hit-and-run. Seriously, what are the odds of that? I'm cursed."

Ben strolled in, shaved and dressed. "What's going on?"

I eyed Kim.

"He knows. I confessed the whole thing to him last night."

Ben's mouth fell open. "Kim, you didn't! What part of 'don't breathe a word about this to anyone' wasn't clear to you?"

"She already knew. Quit yelling at me. I'm miserable enough as it is."

I'd never seen Ben so confused. My mission was accomplished, though. I took my latte and a muffin, along with Trixie's remaining cookie. After all, we hadn't had breakfast. But it dawned on me that it might be a good time to add more bad news. "I'm really sorry about your car, Ben. I'll pay to replace the carpeting."

"What?!"

I could hear the two of them squabbling as Trixie and I left.

Trixie couldn't take her eyes off the remaining peanut butter cookie. She ran in front of me and danced on her hind legs, nearly tripping me up.

Once we were back in the golf cart, I fed her a piece and drank some of my latte. Trixie alternately yelped like a nut and nudged my hand until all the food, hers and mine, had been consumed.

I wasn't sure that I understood anything more about Sven's murder. My mind raced as I tried to sort out the facts. But I did know that I had to find a way to let Trixie run off some energy. I had a feeling that she'd been fairly good in the beginning because everything was new to her, and she wasn't sure of herself. Now all that good behavior had built up, and she was ready to run.

I drove back to the inn, pondering the new information. So Brewster had been in possession of the car. That explained why Mortie's keys had turned up. But it didn't explain why Tiny had them.

There weren't too many possibilities. Tiny stole the car from Brewster. Or Brewster gave or lent Tiny the keys to the car. Or, as Tiny claimed, Brewster mailed the keys to him as a threat. If Tiny was telling the truth about that, it meant that Brewster or someone else had dumped the car. Otherwise, how would that person have the keys to send to Tiny?

None of it made sense. Unless . . . unless they were in cahoots and had turned against each other?

I parked, and we hopped out of the golf cart and returned to the reception area, where Zelda worked at the desk.

"How do people let their dogs run and get exercise around here?" I asked, removing the leash from Trixie's collar. "The little play areas in the green?"

"You can also book one of the private runs."

"What are those?"

"They're trails that are entirely fenced in. Quite discreetly, of course. You can't see the fence unless you wander off the trail." She typed on her computer keyboard. "They're all booked for today, though."

"She did pretty well on the back side of the inn the other day. Maybe I'll try that again."

With a cat-that-caught-the-canary grin, Zelda leaned toward me and whispered, "Look what I found." She held up a cell phone. "I think it's the one Philip lost. It was over near the play area where I take Dolce. I'm charging it to see if it's his."

I shot her a scolding look. "And to see who's calling him?" Shades of Kim! "Don't you dare send people messages from him!"

She straightened up. "I would never do that. Maybe. It's an interesting idea, though, now that you mention it."

I was sorry I'd put the notion in her head. "I'll be out back, letting Trixie run."

Trixie bounded out the door and zoomed to the tree where she had seen a squirrel before. She raced in a zigzag, her nose to the ground, while I walked down to the dock. She barked twice gratuitously at another dog, who walked by on a leash. She lifted her head and gazed around. Had she lost me?

"Trixie!"

She flew to me, her feet barely touching the ground. She stopped abruptly, put her nose down again and followed a scent down to the lake.

Wagging her tail with pure joy, she trotted over to me on

the dock and sniffed the water. I dipped my hand in it but withdrew it quickly. The lake that had been refreshing had turned far too cold for comfort.

I would have to locate some dog parks at home. She obviously needed time and room to run. I looked up at the sprawling inn, the patios on multiple levels, the huge windows overlooking the lake and the mountains, the steep roofs and quirky slopes. It dawned on me that the inn was more of a home to me than anyplace I had ever lived. I breathed in the clear, cold air, relieved that Oma had no intention of selling it.

Trixie raced across the grass, chasing a bunny. But she was almost out of view. I hurried up the steps to the inn in search of her.

I spied her digging furiously in Oma's herb garden just outside the door to the private kitchen.

"No! Trixie, no! Get out of there!"

She paid me no mind at all. Her little rump stuck up in the air while she churned through the soil with fierce determination. Dirt flew under her and to the sides, landing on basil plants.

I ran toward her. She glanced at me, grabbed something, and sped around the side of the inn. That little scamp! I rushed after her, hoping she wouldn't run along the green in the middle of town. She would be too fast for me.

Happily, I saw guests making way for her as she tore up the front porch stairs. A couple of guests laughed as I lumbered along behind her.

"Looking for a dog with a rat in its mouth?" They pointed inside.

It wasn't too hard to follow her after that. Tiny flakes of dirt led me to Oma's private kitchen. Trixie had gone home to our suite.

I took a minute to clean the lobby floor. We didn't need everyone tracking the soil everywhere. They'd said she was carrying a rat. Ugh. Had she dug up the dead rat?

Forty-four

I trudged upstairs and unlocked the door. Trixie watched me from the hearth with guilty eyes and filthy front paws.

Where had she put the nasty thing? The tip of her tail flapped up hopefully. Once, twice.

I burst into laughter. I had almost called her a bad dog. Maybe Zelda really was a psychic and the poor thing thought her name was Bad Dog. It was a good bet that she'd heard it a lot wherever she came from.

She had returned through the cat door in the dining room. With any luck, she'd left a trail of dirt to follow. I had to remove the decaying rat before it started to stink, which would be almost immediately.

She must have left most of the dirt in the lobby. I didn't see a speck in the dining room. I knelt to see if she hid it under the buffet again. Yup. There it was. A shudder wriggled through me.

I needed a stick, something long and relatively thin. And gloves. I certainly didn't plan to touch it. At least I knew it was dead. It wasn't going anywhere. A visit to the housekeeping closet on the second floor yielded a broom, a trash can with a liner in which to deposit it, and cleaning gloves.

Armed for rat patrol, I sucked up my courage and knelt on the floor by the buffet. Trixie scurried to my side.

"Oh no, you don't. This time we're getting rid of that disgusting thing. No more burying it in Oma's garden."

Using the straw end of the broom, I scooted it close. Trixie wedged her nose under the buffet as far as it could go, but I beat her to it. I grabbed the awful thing, and flung it into the trash can.

The two of us peered at it. That was no rat. I picked it up gingerly. It was hollow, like a fake pelt. One side was furry, but the other held the fur together with a fine mesh.

Trixie barked and tried to grab it.

"You're not getting this back. It's filthy." She continued to yap at me, and I felt terrible. I hadn't bought her any toys. Not one!

It didn't really look like a toy. There weren't any eyes or other features. It seemed more like a fur hat. A hairpiece! "This is a rug! Where did you get this?"

I might not have Zelda's psychic powers, but everything clicked into place. Jerry's outstretched arm, the police asking Holmes for a hair sample. Dave saying the hair was weird.

Dear heaven! Jerry had torn off his assailant's hairpiece. Trixie must have been there and grabbed it from Jerry's hand when he fell. That might explain why someone had been tracking Trixie.

I looked at her. "Were you at the scene of Jerry's murder?" It was possible. It must have happened about the time she was lost. Had she picked up Chief's scent and tracked him to his house? But how did she get in? "Does Chief have a doggy door?" I asked her. Hadn't Ellie said something about that?

The killer must have seen Trixie nab the toupee and was afraid she would turn up with it. And now she had. I looked down at my little dog with the earnest eyes. The killer had been shooting at her! She had carried that thing around with her like a beloved toy.

I dropped the hairpiece and hugged her to me.

Even worse, it put Kim's entire story in doubt. She had stolen Trixie.

Scooping it up and holding it over the trash can, I flicked the hair lightly with my hand to shake off some of the dirt. No wonder the police hadn't been happy with Holmes's hair sample. This was much longer and reddish in tone.

Brewster. There wasn't a doubt in my mind.

I phoned Dave and told him what had happened.

Half an hour later, Dave arrived very quietly to collect the hairpiece.

We spoke softly in the inn library.

"Huh. Never knew Brewster wore a rug. He's usually at the bar where the lighting is dim. And to tell the truth, they make these things pretty well these days. You can't always tell when a guy is wearing a hairpiece anymore. Can't imagine who else this color would suit, though." Dave mashed his lips together and examined the toupee. "Brewster. Who'd have thought that? He's a pillar of the community. Makes sense in a way. Living next door, he would have been able to sneak in and out of Jerry's house to murder him without the whole town knowing about it."

"So Brewster murdered Jerry? But why?"

"Don't jump to conclusions yet, Holly. We'll know pretty soon. If this rug matches the fibers from Jerry's hand, it'll be solid evidence. But first I need to find out if Brewster wears a hairpiece, and if he does, we need to prove this is his." Dave tsked and shook his head. "Maybe Jerry pushed him too hard on moving Hair of the Dog out to the highway."

"By the way, I have some issues with the theory that Tiny probably killed Sven."

Dave gaped at me. "Detective Miller, I presume?"

I ignored his sarcasm. "Somebody went to lengths to be sure Oma turned up on Oak Street at exactly the right time. I just have trouble imagining that Tiny wanted to kill her. What was his motive?"

"You think Brewster had a motive to kill your grandmother?"

"Not that I know of."

"I don't mean to sound unappreciative to you or your dog for digging up this potential evidence, but it's my job to figure that out. It looks like we have our guys. It will probably all fall into place now. Thanks, Holly."

Dave turned to leave but stopped at the doorway. "Not a word to anyone about this. I don't want Brewster to take off or go into hiding."

Dave departed. That hairpiece could nail Brewster for Jerry's murder.

I'd have to check with Kim, but I'd bet he talked her into nabbing Trixie in exchange for payment of her debt. He must have seen Trixie seize the toupee from Jerry at the scene of the crime.

Still, something about Tiny's side of the equation still bothered me.

I helped Oma around the inn for the next few hours. Right up until Ellie called her in hysterics about the police searching Brewster's house.

Oma, Trixie, and I rushed over to Ellie's home.

She met us on her porch, sobbing. "Brewster wouldn't have killed Jerry. He brought Dolce back when he was lost. He—" she sniffled and gulped air "—came to express his condolences. I don't understand."

I left Oma to console her friend and hurried over to Brewster's house, along with most of Wagtail's residents.

Holmes was there with Rose. Mr. Wiggins stood by watching, and far away from him, Peaches and Prissy observed the goings-on. Pale and nervous, Prissy looked like she might lose her lunch. The sun glinted off her sparkling rings as she nibbled at her manicured fingernails like a frantic mouse.

I squinted at her. Did anyone else know that she and Brewster were an item? No one else in the crowd appeared to be quite as nervous. Why had they kept their relationship a secret? Maybe they thought Peaches wouldn't approve.

Trixie and I wound our way through the crowd. Murphy, Brewster's Irish setter, must have remembered me from the pub. He trotted over to me, carrying a sock to play tug.

I grabbed the sock, dirty from being buried, and pretended to want it. Murphy had fun, but Trixie didn't seem to like that game and growled at him.

Murphy persisted, and I grabbed the other end of the sock. It felt unusually heavy. I wanted to think it was some kind of training toy, but I'd held something just like it all too recently.

"There he is!"

The crowd fell quiet as two officers escorted a handcuffed Brewster to the police car parked in front of his house. Dave followed behind them.

The formerly amiable face of the pub owner revealed his true colors. Angry eyes flashed. His ruddy skin flushed crimson. "I didn't kill anyone. They have the wrong person. Jerry probably killed Sven. Let me tell you though, Jerry was a thief," he spat. "He stole from me, little by little, thinking I wouldn't notice. But I saw him. Like a weaselly troll, coveting my wealth. He had no right to take it from me."

My gaze fell to the sock Murphy tugged on. I bent and asked Murphy if I could have it. I untied the knot in the end of the sock and poured the contents into my hand. Two gold coins and a watch, probably Kim's, shimmered under the sun.

Undeterred, Murphy ran to a bush in his own front yard, dug up another sock, and returned to play tug. It too had a heavy toe. And I had a heavy heart. Had Brewster murdered Jerry for something his own dog was stealing and burying around the yard?

I took the other sock from Murphy and handed them to Dave. "I think you might have your Snowball thief."

Dave nodded. In a hushed voice he said, "We found a bunch of socks containing gold items in a basket with laundry on top of them. I guess Brewster believed in hiding things in plain sight. It's a good bet he's connected to the thefts on Snowball Mountain. I don't think he worked alone, though. I hope Brewster talks."

"An accomplice, you mean?" I glanced toward Prissy, who'd been so snarky about my call to 911. "How about a police insider? Someone who heard about the sting and could warn him?"

Dave's eyes snapped up to meet mine. "What do you know?"

"Remember the night I spied on Kim and she visited Brewster? I saw Prissy upstairs in Brewster's house wearing a skimpy negligee.

Dave's brow furrowed. "You don't have to like Prissy but that's really low. What a nasty accusation."

"I'm sorry, Dave. I'm just telling you what I saw. Maybe I'm the one jumping to conclusions. Maybe she's not involved with the thefts at all." I had told him where my suspicions fell. Planted the seed, so to speak. "You're in charge. I'm sure you know best. I guess the hairs of the toupee that Trixie carried around matched the ones in Jerry's hand?"

"Perfectly. And Brewster has a couple of identical extras in the house. It's a lucky thing Trixie grabbed the hairpiece from Jerry and ran with it."

Holmes ambled over and slung an arm around me. We watched as the police car pulled away and the remaining cops began poking around the yard. Dave shook his head as they turned up more of the socks.

Holmes took a deep breath. "It tears me up that they arrested Tiny for murdering Sven. I've known him forever. I thought he was a good guy. But that means I'm free to go. I've got a flight out tomorrow morning. How about dinner tonight with Oma and Grandma Rose?"

It sounded like just the ticket to me.

My cell phone buzzed with a text. I pulled it out, surprised to hear anyone texting me. It had to be Ben.

I read the message and howled with glee. "I've got my job back! Even better, not my job, but my boss's job. They canned him and want me to take his position. Yippee!"

Trixie danced on her hind legs. Holmes hugged me, but Rose's face fell.

"You won't be staying in Wagtail?" she asked.

The cruise! I'd forgotten all about it. "You and Oma book your cruise, and I'll wangle vacation time to come take care of the inn while you're gone. I promise."

"Grandma," said Holmes, "you can't expect Holly to pack in her life and move here just to make you and Oma happy."

She nodded, but I knew I'd broken her heart. "Dinner tonight, though. Right?"

They promised to set it up with Oma and walked away with Murphy to find him a temporary home.

There was one person in whose nose I wanted to rub my good news. Ben. Ben who said I was persona non grata. Ben who said they wouldn't want to hire a troublemaker. Hah! I would show him.

I called the landline at Mortie's cabin. Busy. I tried Ben's phone. It rolled over to voice mail. "I think this is worth a trip up there, don't you, Trixie?"

We walked back to the inn. I shared my good news with Zelda, probably a little bit too gleeful about rubbing Ben's nose in it. Nevertheless, I checked out the golf cart, and headed straight to Mortie's cabin. I felt a little bit guilty for wanting to prove to Ben that he was wrong. But not guilty enough to turn around.

I thought about Brewster and Tiny as I drove. Brewster had clearly been the one who killed Jerry. The hairs on Jerry's hand that matched Brewster's toupee would be hard evidence to overcome.

Had Brewster also been the one who drove the car and hit Sven? Why he would have mailed the keys to Tiny was beyond me. Maybe Tiny knew what Brewster had done? That was the only thing that made sense. But why would Brewster want to kill Oma?

He had no business with her as far as I knew. His pub was far enough away that the noise didn't disturb the inn guests. Had Oma even mentioned him? I didn't think so. Oma didn't have gold coins or expensive items hanging around. What would Brewster gain by knocking her off? Unless he wanted the inn.

But the only person who seemed interested in the inn— chills ran through me, and I hit the brake—was Philip.

No, I was being silly. There wasn't a shred of anything tying Philip to the car or the murders. Still, it would explain his behavior and his interest in me. He'd swept into the inn as though he was taking over.

No, no, no. That was absurd. Days of stress trying to figure out who wanted to kill Oma had taken a toll on me. I suspected everyone.

Before we reached Mortie's cabin, Trixie sat up and barked incessantly, like she had the night we saw the man in the road. I shushed her and held her close but half expected someone to leap out of the woods. She stopped barking but whimpered softly.

I turned the golf cart into the driveway.

Not too far away, in the cabin's backyard, I could see Philip striding toward the lake with his back to me. In front of him, Kim and Ben walked slowly into the cold water. Kim was sobbing and pleading for her life. Philip had to have a weapon to make them do something so stupid. The water must have been frigid.

Doing my best to keep Trixie from barking, I dismissed the idea of calling 911. It would take them too long to arrive. Philip would turn and see me soon—and then there would be three of us walking into the water.

Praying that we wouldn't hit anything noisy on the drive-way, I drove the golf cart downhill toward them. Every snap under the tires as they rolled over pebbles and twigs sounded amplified to me. But Philip must have been concentrating on Ben and Kim, because he hadn't heard us creeping closer behind him. Kim's wailing probably helped drown out the sounds we made, as well. At the end of the pavement, a mere twenty feet from Philip, I accelerated, fearing that Philip would finally notice us any second. The golf cart sped up, much faster than I'd anticipated, and catapulted downhill with alarming speed.

Kim, glanced back toward Philip, saw me, and screamed even more loudly. Now in waist-deep water, Ben turned around, grabbed Kim's arm, and struggled to move out of the path of the golf cart.

Philip looked over his shoulder and finally saw me hurtling toward him. His eyes widened in shock. But it was too late.

I grabbed Trixie and leaped off just as the cart hit him full force. Philip rolled over the front and fell backward into the passenger seat.

Forty-five

·❀·❀·❀·

I rolled on the ground, clutching Trixie underneath me to protect her. Philip's gun flew through the air in a big arc. Happily, it didn't fire when it landed.

I darted over and picked it up.

The golf cart had plummeted into the chilly lake.

"Help!" cried Philip. "I can't move. I can't feel my legs. I'll drown."

Kim screamed, "I hope you do!" She fled the water as fast as she could and ran for the cabin.

The golf cart sank at a worrisome speed.

"Ben! Maybe we should get him out of there," I yelled.

"Not a chance." He signaled me with a thumbs-up.

Huh? I called 911 but heard a siren before anyone answered. I turned around to see Dave pull into the driveway.

I inched closer to the golf cart. No wonder Ben wasn't worried. The wheels in the back had hit bottom. It wouldn't sink further.

"He's injured," yelled Ben to Dave. "I don't think he can get out."

"You'd better go inside to warm up and change into dry clothes," I said to Ben.

Now that Dave had arrived, I wasn't afraid. Okay, I was shaking. It wasn't every day that I ran a golf cart into someone.

Dave radioed for an ambulance, and I handed him the gun.

"How did you know we were here?" I asked.

"Thank Zelda. She stuck a GPS collar into this golf cart because she was so worried about you. Then, when she charged Philip's phone, she heard a rather interesting message."

Philip groaned.

"You wanted the inn," I baited him. "*You* drove the car that hit Sven. It wasn't Tiny after all. *You're* the one who let Dolce out and called the inn hoping Oma would come so you could plow her down."

His jaw tightened.

"Oh my gosh." I rambled on, speculating. "But then you decided that you didn't have to kill Oma because you thought you would weasel your way into ownership of the inn through me!"

Dave tsked. "Lucky for your grandmother that Philip determined it would be cheaper and easier to inherit an inn than to buy it after her death."

Ugh! He probably would have killed Oma and me eventually. I felt like the blood had drained out of me. "It was so easy for you because you live on the same street as Ellie. But why did you steal the car from Brewster?"

Philip grunted.

"And why would you be up here trying to murder Kim and Ben? They had nothing to do with . . ." Suddenly I felt like pushing him farther into the water. "You thought Ben stood in your way of conning me into a relationship." I held the top of my head between my hands. I'd been so stupid using Ben as an excuse not to date Philip. I'd caused this nightmare by telling Philip that Ben and I were engaged. "I hope you and Brewster end up in the same place. You're two of a kind."

"I've got more guts than Brewster."

Dave poked Philip's leg, but he didn't respond.

A spinal injury?

"Philip," said Dave, "I'm going to wait for the med techs to move you."

"I don't get it," I said. "If Philip killed Sven, then why did Tiny throw the car over the cliff?"

"He confessed once we brought up Brewster's name," said Dave. "As near as I can make out, Brewster hired Tiny to kill Jerry by hitting him with Mortie's car. But this schlub, Philip, got wind of their plan, and thought he would change the victim so he could get rid of your grandmother. Pretty sneaky, actually. If Philip's plan had worked, Tiny would have unwittingly killed Oma, and no one would be the wiser about Philip's involvement."

"It was Philip who sent Jerry in search of downed electric wires and called Oma to come search for Dolce?"

"Looks like it," said Dave. "He knew she would come running to Ellie's house if Dolce was lost."

"So why did Tiny have the car?"

"Tiny was supposed to drive the car. He parked it at the end of the street in front of Philip's house, left the keys inside, and took a walk to think about it. He needed the money Brewster promised him, but he didn't want to kill anybody. Tiny didn't know how to get out of that mess without angering Brewster. That's when Philip stepped in. He stole the car, intending to hit your grandmother, but killed Sven by accident. Then he parked it near Hair of the Dog and took the keys." Dave snorted. "Pretty obnoxious. Meanwhile, Brewster thought Tiny had killed Sven and was steaming mad. Tiny was afraid to tell Brewster he didn't know who had driven the car. So he took credit for it but told Brewster he lost the keys. It really was Tiny you saw coming back from pushing the car over the cliff. Brewster had made a spare key. Brewster didn't go out to the highway. Tiny walked back through the woods, where Brewster picked him up in a golf cart. According to Tiny, Brewster pressured him to kill the driver who saw him out on the highway. Brewster's no dummy. He knew that if the driver identified Tiny, everything would lead back to Brewster."

I gasped. "So Philip mailed the original car keys to Tiny."

"Apparently so. Tiny mistakenly thought Brewster mailed him the keys as a threat. That's why he was spending nights in his daughter's sleeping bag up in your storage room. He was afraid to go home."

Dave stared at Philip with a scowl. "The frightening thing is that Philip could have gotten away with it. We had enough against Tiny and Brewster to convict them and nothing tying Philip to any of this. Not until Zelda found his cell phone." Dave crossed his arms. "Should have worn waders, this water is freezing. Hey, Philip, how'd you lose your cell phone?"

Philip didn't say a word.

"I'm thinking you lost it running back and forth to Hair of the Dog to make phone calls the night you killed Sven," said Dave.

"I'm going to have hypothermia. I can't feel my legs. I'll tell you if you get me out of here."

"Okay," said Dave. "You first."

"It was that stupid dog, Dolce. He was crazy wild when I let him out. In the middle of the green, he jumped up and put his paws on my shoulders, knocking me down. My phone must have fallen out of my pocket. Now get me out of this water!"

It wasn't going to happen. We couldn't move him without the danger of making his injury far worse, and the golf cart weighed way too much for us to pull it out of the lake by hand.

The ambulance arrived minutes later. The medical technicians didn't hesitate to splash into the water to stabilize Philip. They immobilized his head and strapped him onto a stretcher.

Trixie and I were the only ones who weren't wet.

Forty-six

* * * * *

Oma and I invited everyone to dinner that night, including inn employees, interested guests, and even Aunt Birdie. Zelda, Shelley, and I shoved the tables in the dining area into a big circle and arranged side tables for a buffet. Thomas catered it.

Only Aunt Birdie, Dave, and Ellie declined. Not surprising under the circumstances. Mr. Luciano showed up, with Gina on a leash, looking healthy and happy. Holmes and Rose arrived together. Even Ben and Kim came to celebrate. Our guests mingled before dinner with Appletinis and ginger pear Getaway cocktails in their hands.

To my surprise, Dave showed up after all. I hurried over to him. "I thought you weren't coming. Let me get you a drink."

"Thanks, I can't. I have a lot of work to do tonight." He studied the floor for a moment. "You were right about Prissy."

"Oh, Dave. I'm so sorry."

"I didn't want to believe you. I thought Prissy had a thing for me but it was just an act to get on my good side. She took the job as police dispatcher to help Brewster." Dave snorted. "He had a pattern of hiring people to do his dirty work for him. Prissy kept him apprised about the situation in Snowball and fed him information about where the police would be patrolling. We've arrested a couple of young guys over on Snowball who stole the goods from homes and hotel rooms for Brewster. Apparently, he feared they would turn on him and raid his house, so he hid everything in socks in a laundry basket where he thought no one would look. Periodically, he sent it off to be smelted."

"Do you think Jerry was onto him?"

"I doubt we'll ever know for sure. Brewster knew the socks were disappearing. Apparently, he saw Murphy dig up a couple of socks in Jerry's back yard. Brewster jumped to the erroneous conclusion that Jerry had buried them there to hide them. After Jerry ate breakfast with us, he returned home where Brewster confronted him. According to Brewster, they got into a fight upstairs, and Jerry managed to snatch Brewster's toupee. Brewster slammed a golf club on Jerry's head, causing Jerry to fall, which gave Brewster the opportunity to slide the choke collar and leash on him. Jerry tried to get away but fell again when he was running down the stairs, and the collar choked him."

"I don't get it," I said. "Hair of the Dog seems like a thriving business. Why would he throw all that away and get involved with a ring of thieves?"

Dave met my eyes. "Greed. Plain old greed."

"What a twisted mind! It was okay for him to steal from other people, but he killed Jerry for stealing those same ill-gotten gains from him. And the saddest thing of all is that it wasn't Jerry who took them—it was Murphy, Brewster's own dog, who was taking his treasures."

Ben shook his head. "I can't believe that Kim went to a scumbag like Brewster for money. She's lucky he didn't try to kill her, too."

"Hey," said Dave, "even I thought he was a nice guy! I went to Hair of the Dog all the time."

I whispered to Ben, "What's going to happen to Kim?"

"Grand larceny carries a penalty up to twenty years." Ben sighed. "All I can say is she'll have the best legal representation possible. It's her first offense, but it's a whopper, even if she does claim she meant to return the car eventually."

"Can't Mortie drop the charges?" I asked.

Ben's lips puckered. "If the state brings charges, only the prosecutor can drop them or reduce them. Who knows? Maybe Kim will get lucky this time."

I looked at Dave for his opinion. He held up his hands. "That's in another jurisdiction, up where the car was stolen. I have to get going." He leaned forward to hug me. "Thanks for your help. I hope I wasn't too hard on you."

"You were just doing your job."

Dave waved to us, and left at a fast clip.

"Did you know Kim had stolen the car?" I asked Ben.

"Nope. Mortie didn't know a thing about it, either. Remember how Kim slipped away from me that first day? She was off having a little meeting with Brewster. He threatened to expose her as the car thief if she didn't do what he asked. Kim didn't tell me until yesterday morning that she had taken her father's car and handed it over to Brewster."

Kim ambled over with an Appletini in her hand.

"Did Brewster offer to expunge your debt if you brought him Trixie?" I asked.

"Close. He wanted me to kill her. I didn't know why, of course."

I stared at her in horror.

"Oh, don't look like that. I could never hurt a dog. I love dogs." She reached down to pet Trixie. "I planned to drive her out in the country, far enough away that she wouldn't find her way back."

"That's horrible!"

"Hey! I was under a lot of pressure," she whined. "Besides, Trixie got away from me, and everything turned out fine."

"Holly!" called Zelda.

Good timing. I was ready to let Kim have it.

I joined Zelda, who stood in the center of a cluster of people.

"I had to hand Philip's phone over to Dave," said Zelda, "but in anticipation of that, your grandmother and I taped this from Philip's voice mail." She hit a button on a small device.

It wasn't very loud. We all craned our necks to listen as Brewster instructed Tiny on the details of the hit-and-run murder plot.

"On Friday night, you'll be sitting in the SUV at the end of the street with the lights off. Wear gloves so you don't leave fingerprints anywhere. Got it? Jerry arrives at his mother's house for dinner at 7:15 sharp. They're calling for rain, so that will give you extra cover. You hit Jerry. Take him out. Then drive to the highway and hide the car in the trees. Go back around midnight or one in the morning when there's no traffic and nobody there to see you, and roll it over the cliff. You understand? Don't mess up."

"When do I get my money?" Tiny spoke softly. I felt as though I could hear the doubt in his voice.

It clicked off. The recording ran for less than a minute, very short, but certainly enough to land Brewster in the slammer for a long time.

Mr. Luciano scowled. "Why would this be on Philip's phone?"

"We wondered about that," said Zelda. "It's on Philip's voice mail. We think it was an accidental pocket dial. You know—when the buttons on your phone are accidentally pushed, and you can hear a conversation going on but they don't hear you. Except Philip's voice mail answered the call and taped it."

Philip was as devious as Kim. He'd heard that conversation and then made arrangements for Jerry to be called away about a phony emergency. Ironically, Philip had saved Jerry's life that night. He knew a murder was going down, and instead of reporting it, he'd used that knowledge to further his own desires by substituting Oma as the victim, instead of Jerry.

When everyone had helped themselves to the buffet, Oma dimmed the lights slightly, and we sat down to eat. Through the huge window wall, a harvest moon shone in the sky like a beacon. A golden path sparkled across the lake reflecting the light. Inside, a fire crackled in the rustic stone fireplace. Candles and bouquets of sunflowers and chrysanthemums adorned the tables. Even though we weren't all relatives, the horrible events of recent days bonded us like one big family.

Oma clinked a fork against her glass. "Thank you all for coming. It has been a terrible time for us in Wagtail. We mourn the loss of two of our beloved residents, Sven and Jerry. We are grateful, though, that the perpetrators have been apprehended, and we thank everyone who played a role in that effort, especially Zelda, Trixie, and my wonderful granddaughter, Holly. Enjoy your dinner!"

I caught a glimpse of Kim. She turned away quickly, no doubt ashamed of herself for her involvement

We dined on savory spinach and bison lasagna and blackberry-wine venison stew that I could have eaten by the vat. Miniature versions without onions or wine were available for the dogs. Assorted salads, grilled zucchini with fresh herbs, and spicy sweet potatoes rounded out the meal.

Over after-dinner coffee and chocolate-glazed profiteroles filled with rich vanilla ice cream, Ben said, "I'm heading home tomorrow, and I'd like to take my car. Can you be downstairs prepared to go by nine?"

I wasn't quite ready to leave Wagtail. But, like a vacation, my visit had to come to an end. I had to get back to my job. They wouldn't hold it for me forever. "Guess I'd better head back with Ben," I said to Oma. "Assuming he'll allow Trixie and Twinkletoes in his car."

Oma couldn't hide her disappointment. "If this is what you want."

Around the room the chatter stopped in a wave, and everyone listened.

Even Trixie watched me with a glum, apprehensive look.

"We'll be back to take care of the inn when you go on your cruise."

Oma brightened a little bit. "You could stay a few more days if you drove my car home. I don't use it very often since we have the golf carts."

"That would be so complicated. I'd have to come back to return it."

"Exactly." Oma smiled. "Then I would know that I will see you again soon."

I felt terrible. Would another year, or five or ten, pass before I returned for a longer stay? I gazed around at their faces. Zelda, Shelley, and Casey, appeared disappointed. Even Gingersnap, who walked over and buried her face between my knees. They had been so good to me. What was my big rush to return to Washington? To a relationship that had ended. To a job where I would turn into a workaholic again. If I was going to work all the time anyway, shouldn't it be fun? In a place I loved?

"Oma, if you were to semiretire, wouldn't you need a manager of sorts?"

"I was thinking more along the lines of a partner."

A partner? That thought had never crossed my mind. "Really, Oma?"

"This has been my dream for a very long time."

It was a huge decision—a major life change for me. But there was no place in the world I would rather be. Running the inn and meeting new people was fun, and different every day. I stood up and hugged Oma. "I accept!"

A cheer went up. Gingersnap, Trixie, and even Mr. Luciano's Gina barked and danced in crazy circles. Twinkletoes leaped to the safety of a tabletop, but she held out one paw, and Zelda seized the moment to high-five with her.

Only Ben looked on in shock.

Oma hugged me again. "Welcome home, liebling."

Wagtail might not be as sophisticated as Washington. There weren't any high-rises or big chain stores, and it was miles and miles away from everything. But the Sugar Maple Inn was where I wanted to be, with Trixie, Twinkletoes, Gingersnap, and especially Oma.

Author's Note

One of my dogs suffered from severe food allergies that did not allow him to eat commercial dog food. Consequently, I learned to cook for my dogs and have done so for many years. Consult your veterinarian if you want to switch your dog over to home-cooked food. It's not as difficult as one might think. Keep in mind that, like children, dogs need a balanced diet, not just a hamburger. Any changes to your dog's diet should be made gradually so your dog's stomach can adjust.

Chocolate, alcohol, caffeine, fatty foods, grapes, raisins, macadamia nuts, onions and garlic, salt, xylitol, and unbaked dough can be toxic to dogs. For more information about foods your dog should not eat, consult the Pet Poison Helpline, at petpoisonhelpline.com/pet-owners/.

Recipes

❧ ❧ ❧ ❧

Sugar Maple Inn Caramel Banana Oatmeal

For people. Makes 2–3 portions or 4 small portions.

Caramel

¼ cup heavy cream
¼ cup sugar
¼ cup dark brown sugar
2 tablespoons butter
dash of salt

Place ingredients in a microwave-safe bowl. (I use a Pyrex 2-cup measure.) Microwave in short bursts from 20–50 seconds, stirring each time until it bubbles up and is hot. Set aside to thicken and cool slightly.

Cook oatmeal in your preferred method. Or fill each individual bowl with oatmeal and add enough water to barely cover it. Microwave for 1 to 2 minutes.

Slice one banana for each serving, and cover the cooked oatmeal with the slices. Drizzle with caramel.

Oma's Hungarian Goulash

For people. Contains onions—*do not* feed to dogs.

¼ cup vegetable oil
2 pounds cubed stew beef or pork (do not use lean
    meat, like a tenderloin)
2 cups chopped onions
2 teaspoons marjoram
2 cloves garlic
1 tablespoon sweet paprika
1 cup water or stock
4 carrots, peeled and sliced
4 medium potatoes, cubed (optional)

Heat the oil in a deep pot. Brown the meat and remove. Sauté the onions in the same pot. Add the marjoram, garlic, paprika, water, carrots, and meat. Cover and simmer 1 ½ hours over low heat until the meat is tender.

If you wish to add potatoes, you may cook them in the goulash for the last ½ hour. Or, so they won't soak up the sauce, you can cook them in another pot and add them to the goulash for the last five minutes.

Sugar Maple Inn Cherry Strudel

For people.

10 sheets 12 x 17 filo dough
2 cups pitted and halved fresh cherries
¼ cup sugar (I use sweet black cherries, you may
need more if you use sour cherries)
⅓ cup graham cracker crumbs
½ of a lemon
1 teaspoon vanilla or brandy (optional)
6 tablespoons butter
powdered sugar

Mix the cherries, sugar, lemon and vanilla or brandy in a bowl. (If you're very lazy, you can skip this step. Watch for the ** later.)

Melt the butter and brush a little bit on a baking sheet. Preheat the oven to 350.

On an ungreased baking sheet, spread the first sheet of filo dough. Brush with butter. Lay another sheet of the filo dough on top of it and brush with butter. Repeat until you have ten sheets of filo dough.

Spoon the cherries onto the filo about an inch from the edge in a line along the long side of the filo. Sprinkle with the graham cracker crumbs. (** If you're not using vanilla or brandy, you can just lay the cherries in a line, sprinkle with sugar, sprinkle with graham cracker crumbs and squeeze the lemon over top of it all.)

Roll the cherry end slowly, brushing the top of the filo as you go. Lay it seam side down on the buttered baking sheet and add one more buttery swipe to the top. Cut small diagonal vents along the top. Bake 25 minutes, brush with butter and return to oven for another 20 minutes. Sift powdered sugar over the top to dress it up—and serve. It's good warm and cold!

Sweet Dog Barkery
Cinnamon-Pumpkin Muffins

For people. Makes 12 muffins.

1 ½ cups flour
1 teaspoon baking powder
1 teaspoon baking soda
½ teaspoon salt
1 teaspoon cinnamon
2 eggs
½ cup vegetable oil
½ cup dark brown sugar, packed
¼ cup regular sugar
¾ cup canned pumpkin

Swirl

½ cup dark brown sugar, packed
2 teaspoons cinnamon

Preheat oven to 350. Fill cupcake pan with liners.

Mix the flour, baking powder, baking soda, salt, and 1 teaspoon cinnamon in a bowl and stir with a fork to mix. Set aside.

Whisk the eggs, and add the vegetable oil, ½ cup dark brown sugar, the regular sugar, and the pumpkin. Blend well. Dump in the flour mixture and mix with a spoon until just blended. Do not overmix.

In a separate bowl, combine the ½ cup dark brown sugar with the 2 teaspoons of cinnamon.

Fill the liners almost full. Add 1 teaspoon or so of the cinnamon-sugar swirl mixture to the top of each muffin. Using a cake tester or bamboo skewer, sweep through the muffin to mix the cinnamon into them.

Bake at 350 for 15 minutes or until a cake tester comes out clean.

Peanut Butter Cookies

For dogs.

¾ cup flour
½ teaspoon baking powder
pinch salt
1 egg
¼ cup olive oil
1 tablespoon milk
⅔ cup peanut butter

Preheat oven to 350. Line a cookie sheet with parchment paper. Mix flour and baking powder and set aside. In a mixer, beat the egg with olive oil and milk. Add peanut butter and mix well. Add flour and mix. The dough will be thick. Roll into ½ inch diameter balls for large dogs, and ¼ inch balls for small dogs. If you prefer crisper cookies, flatten them with the heel of your hand or a fork. Bake 15 minutes.

The Blue Boar Pumpkin Dessert

For dogs.

3 tablespoons canned pumpkin (not pumpkin-pie mix)
3 tablespoons no-fat or low-fat Greek yogurt

Swirl together so there are pretty pumpkin and white swirls. Serve.

Sugar Maple Inn Seafarer Supper

For dogs. Makes 2–3 Gingersnap-size servings
or 5–6 Trixie-size servings.

*1 average wild-caught cod filet (about
½ – ¾ pound raw)
3 cups cooked barley
2 cups steamed green beans*

Preheat oven to 400. Place the cod in a glass baking dish,
and cook 20–25 minutes or until the fish flakes apart easily. Flake the fish and combine with barley and green
beans. Serve slightly warm.

Sugar Maple Inn
Travel-Tummy Dinner

For dogs. Makes 2–3 Gingersnap-size servings
and 5–6 Trixie-size servings.

*1–2 tablespoons olive oil
1 pound 4 percent fat ground beef
3–4 cups cooked white rice
1 cup cooked spinach, chopped*

Heat the olive oil in a 3 to 4-inch-deep pan. Make rough
burger shapes out of the ground beef, and cook on each
side 3–4 minutes until the middle is red but not raw. Use
a metal spatula to roughly chop the meat into pieces. (For
picky eaters, chop the meat into tiny bits.) Add the rice
and spinach. Mix thoroughly. Serve slightly warm.

Turn the page for a preview of Krista Davis's
next Domestic Diva Mystery . . .

The Diva Wraps It Up

Coming soon from Berkley Prime Crime!

Dear Natasha,

My son-in-law is quite a cook. I would love to give him a set of professional quality knives for Christmas. Can you recommend some good brands?

Hungry Mom in Turkey, Arkansas

Dear Hungry Mom,

Never give knives as a gift. The gift of a knife is believed to sever the friendship. In this case, it might even sever the relationship between your daughter and her husband! Unless, of course, that's what you had in mind, in which case any old knives would do.

Natasha

Horace Scroggins poured hot chocolate into a mug. "It's my own special blend." He glanced out the door of his office as though he thought employees might be eavesdropping to hear his secret ingredients. "I add vanilla! Learned it from my true love."

He was too cute. I accepted the mug and made a fuss like I thought vanilla in hot chocolate was very special indeed.

Horace had always reminded me of Santa Claus. A petite man with rosy round cheeks and a belly that jiggled, 364 days of the year he wore a bow tie and suspenders, and at Christmastime they were inevitably red. On the day of the Scottish Christmas Walk, he donned a kilt and proudly paraded through the streets of Old Town.

I had never heard Horace utter a bad word about anyone. In his early sixties, he had a head of fluffy hair as white as snow. He always smiled, amazing in itself since he was married to Edith Scroggins, the most odious and unfriendly woman imaginable.

As an event planner, I didn't typically handle small company gatherings, but for the past few years, Horace had talked me into arranging his real estate company's Christmas party. It kicked off the Christmas season in Old Town. Horace had bought a magnificent historical town house for his real estate business many long years ago. His staff delighted in decorating it with a towering balsam fir in the two-story foyer. Scottish tartan ribbons curled through wreaths in the most tasteful and elegant manner, and groups of ruby red poinsettias graced antique tables and mantels. The muted colonial green walls provided a perfect backdrop for the tartan ribbons and bold reds.

It was Horace's habit to invite people to whom his company had sold homes in Old Town, Alexandria, which included half my neighbors.

He sat down in his desk chair. The weathered leather gave, soft and cushy under his weight. He drank from his mug like he was thirsty and smiled at me. "Always settles my stomach. There's nothing like hot chocolate to cure whatever ails you." He held an orange box out to me. "Peanut brittle?"

"No, thanks. Queasy tummy?" I asked. "The party is going very well. You needn't worry."

"You did a lovely job, Sophie. Just getting older, I guess. Can't eat everything I used to."

Luis Simon, a prominent psychiatrist who had bought a home on my street through Scroggins Realty, popped his head in the doorway. With prominent cheekbones and sultry bedroom eyes, Luis was worthy of posing for the cover of a romance novel. He carried a cup of English Bishop, a flaming holiday punch loaded with rum and oranges studded with cloves. "Horace! Where's the Scottish dirk you were telling me about?"

"Dirk?" I asked.

Horace jumped up. He steadied himself briefly, his fingertips on his desk. "A traditional Scottish dagger, my dear." He turned to the bookcase behind his desk, took a tiny key from a book, and unlocked a desk drawer. He removed the knife gingerly and proudly presented it in his open palms as though it were a prized possession.

"An antique. The sheath bears sterling silver thistles."

Probably hand carved, the sheath appeared to be ebony. I didn't have to be an antiques expert to see that it bore the hallmarks of age.

He grasped the handle. A silver crown on the top held a large amber stone. Horace withdrew the handle to reveal a gleaming knife. "I like to imagine that it was really used, and not just worn for ceremonies."

Luis whistled his admiration and took the knife from Horace. "It's sharp! And heavier than I expected. You could do some damage with this thing." He danced backward and extended his arm as though it were a sword.

"They made things to last in the old days, didn't they?" Horace beamed. "Let's find Babineaux. He wanted to see it, too." He locked the drawer again and tucked the key back into the book.

They scuttled out of Horace's office with the enthusiasm of little boys who had found a shiny object. I followed them out, and moseyed toward the buffet to check on the food. Guests couldn't seem to get enough of the oysters on the half shell and rolls of salmon on pumpernickel with pink peppercorns and crème fraîche. The baked Brie with toasted pecans and fig glaze was always a hit. I couldn't resist a taste of the melting cheese with a hint of salt and a smidge of sweet fig. Heavenly! And I had to try the seared foie gras with caramelized pears. The caterer had outdone himself.

Everyone appeared to be having fun. I checked my watch, grabbed my pashmina, and slipped out the front door in search of the carolers I'd hired, shivering at the chill. Mother Nature had cooperated beautifully, sending us sparkling snowflakes. Not enough to have to shovel, but the right amount for perfect ambiance. I had worn a red velvet dress in the spirit of the season, but it lacked sleeves. No matter. The pashmina would cover my bare arms. Besides, I didn't plan to be outdoors long.

The carolers hurried along the street toward me. Dressed in traditional Victorian garb, with white faux fur trim on their clothes, they fit in perfectly on Old Town's colonial streets.

They gathered in front of the door, and at the signal, I opened the door and stepped aside on the sidewalk to watch them.

They began with "Deck the Halls." The doors to the upstairs balcony opened, and Horace led a small group out to watch. From below I couldn't help but notice the blanched color of his normally rosy face. He still smiled, though, and listened to the voices blend.

But then I saw him grasp the railing with both hands and appear to sway. None of the people behind him seemed to realize that he wasn't well.

He leaned forward, his upper body draped against the railing, and they finally clustered around him in concern. With an enormous snap, the railing split, and Horace plunged headlong onto the sidewalk.